D1355477

PRAISE FOR
TARA J

BREAKING LOOSE

"Janzen adds a potential woo-woo twist to her latest high-stakes SDF adventure, in which everyone is after an ancient Egyptian statue that may hold the key to immortality. Besides doing her usual excellent combo of fast-paced action and passionate sizzle, Janzen also throws in a major series twist. Fans will be elated!" —*Romantic Times*

"Reading a Tara Janzen novel is like eating an ice-cream sundae. Each spoonful delivers a sensuous treat while uncovering another tantalizing experience. *Breaking Loose* is an enthralling story.... Fantastic story, memorable characters and an ending that leaves you breathless, Tara Janzen delivers a top-notch read." —Night Owl Romance

LOOSE AND EASY

"Hot, fast, and sexy."

—Cindy Gerard, *New York Times* bestselling author

"Sexual tension crackles and snaps.... Crossing and double-crossing is on most of the characters' agendas, which keeps the pace fast and the action sharp.... Janzen's place in the romantic suspense pantheon is assured." —*Romantic Times*

CUTTING LOOSE

"Bad boys are hot, and they don't come any hotter than the Steele Street gang. This high-octane chase drama accelerates out of the starting gate and doesn't look back.... This novel is smoking in the extreme!" —*Romantic Times*

"*Cutting Loose*...is a wonderful, fast-paced, and exciting read." —Fresh Fiction

"Tara Janzen once again takes readers on a non-stop thrill ride...an exciting and engaging story. Don't miss *Cutting Loose*!"
—Romance Reviews Today

ON THE LOOSE

"[A] wildly romantic thriller." —*Booklist*

"Nonstop action, a mysterious mission and a rekindled romance make *On the Loose* a winner."
—Romance Reviews Today

CRAZY HOT

"A cast of memorable characters in a tale of fast-paced action and eroticism." —*Publishers Weekly*

"Edgy, sexy, and fast. Leaves you breathless!"
—Jayne Ann Krentz, *New York Times* bestselling author

CRAZY COOL

"Wild nonstop action, an interesting subplot, a tormented-but-honorable and brilliant bad boy and a tough girl, and great sex scenes make Janzen's . . . romance irresistible." —*Booklist*

CRAZY WILD

"While keeping the tension and thrills high, Janzen excels at building rich characters whose lives readers are deeply vested in. Let's hope she keeps 'em coming!" —*Romantic Times*

CRAZY KISSES

"The high-action plot, the savage-but-tender hero, and the wonderfully sensuous sex scenes, Janzen's trademarks, make this as much fun as the prior Crazy titles." —*Booklist*

CRAZY LOVE

"Readers [will] instantly bond with [Janzen's] characters. Driving action and adventure laced with hot passion add up to big-time fun."

—*Romantic Times*

CRAZY SWEET

"Exciting and adventurous suspense with nonstop action that will keep readers riveted. I highly recommend it, and can't wait to read more."

—Romance Reviews Today

BY TARA JANZEN

Loose Ends
Breaking Loose
Loose and Easy
Cutting Loose
On the Loose
Crazy Sweet
Crazy Love
Crazy Kisses
Crazy Wild
Crazy Cool
Crazy Hot

Books published by The Random House Publishing Group are available at quantity discounts on bulk purchases for premium, educational, fund-raising, and special sales use. For details, please call 1-800-733-3000.

LOOSE ENDS

A STEELE STREET NOVEL

Tara Janzen

DELL
NEW YORK

Sale of this book without a front cover may be unauthorized. If this book is coverless, it may have been reported to the publisher as "unsold or destroyed" and neither the author nor the publisher may have received payment for it.

Loose Ends is a work of fiction. Names, characters, places, and incidents are the products of the author's imagination or are used fictitiously. Any resemblance to actual events, locales, or persons, living or dead, is entirely coincidental.

A Dell Mass Market Original

Copyright © 2011 by Glenna McReynolds

All rights reserved.

Published in the United States by Dell, an imprint of The Random House Publishing Group, a division of Random House, Inc., New York.

DELL is a registered trademark of Random House, Inc., and the colophon is a trademark of Random House, Inc.

ISBN 978-0-440-24610-7

Cover photograph: © age fotostock / SuperStock

Printed in the United States of America

www.bantamdell.com

9 8 7 6 5 4 3 2 1

For all the readers who made the Crazy/Loose series such a great and awesome ride. Thank you from the bottom of my heart.

TJ
xxoo

CHAPTER ONE

Lost boys.

Dylan Hart sat in the deepening gloom of his thirteenth-floor penthouse at 738 Steele Street, his gaze fixed on the large, dark painting hanging high up in the pipes and rafters criss-crossing the vaulted space of his ceiling.

He'd hung it there years ago, all twelve by eight feet of it, so he would never forget the price some men paid. The price they'd all paid. Now he had to wonder for what: freedom? justice?

Maybe.

A few times over the last fourteen years he'd believed in justice, maybe a few more times in freedom, but overall, he'd never been that naïve, not even in the beginning of his military career, when Special Defense Force, SDF, had first been created. The world revolved on power and the ties that bound men together, and Dylan was bound to the man in the painting: J. T. Chronopolous, *The Guardian*, wielding a broadsword in his hands, dressed in black jeans and a black T-shirt with his dark wings spread out on either side of his body, the feathers dragging the ground, an angel god of retribution without mercy.

Merciless—God knew the world was that and worse... far worse.

A heavy sigh escaped him, and he slid deeper into one of the overstuffed leather chairs in his living room, slid deeper into the ocean of guilt waiting to drown him.

Jesus, sweet Jesus, what have I done?

His throat was tight.

To die was one thing. Everyone in Special Defense Force, a black ops team run out of the underbelly of the United States Department of Defense, *his* team, knew their life was on the line for the job, and they'd all signed on willingly. Hell, they'd signed on eagerly, then trained their guts out, through blood and sweat and the crucible of their own experience to keep death at bay. They won their fights. They'd always won—except once.

He lifted his hand to his face and covered his eyes, let his palm rest there, a shield against the hard truth scrolling down the screen of his computer, the results of an eight-month investigation.

"This is ugly, Dylan, and it's only going to get uglier," said the woman who'd spent the day decrypting the files he'd brought with him from Washington, D.C. She was sitting across from him, blond and beautiful, dressed in a pair of bad-girl high heels and a simple, incredibly expensive gray dress that fit her like a glove. "Randolph Lancaster needs to have an accident, a very bad accident. Gillian and I can get on a plane to Washington tonight. No one else ever needs to know. We can survive this."

Assassination of a top-level U.S. government official, that's what she was proposing; that she and Gillian Pentycote, an SDF operator known as Red Dog, go to Washington, D.C., and rig Randolph Lancaster's car to fail, or arrange for him to go swimming one night in his pool stone-cold drunk, with too much precisely administered alcohol in his blood, and drown. Or maybe one of the girls would take him out on his sailboat and drop him over the side, while the other shadowed them in a getaway speedboat.

Either of those plans was a better death than Lancaster deserved.

Through his own auspices at State, and through his "foreign policy adjustments" using a legion of pawns put at his disposal by the various intelligence agencies of the U.S. government, most notably the CIA, Randolph Lancaster had accumulated millions of dollars selling American soldiers through a company called LeedTech.

Lost boys—and none more lost than J.T., because of a LeedTech contract with a Southeast Asian company called Atlas Exports.

Two hundred and fifty thousand dollars, a quarter of a million, the price of a man's life—the computer had over a hundred invoices for the sale and delivery of over a hundred extremely skilled, superlatively fit soldiers to Atlas for "enhancement and experimental use," each invoice tagged with a coded Department of Defense Special Operations Forces (SOF) identification number.

Dylan's team in Denver, Colorado, comprised eleven elite SOF soldiers, and six years ago one team member's coded ID number had been duly printed on an Atlas Exports invoice—J.T.'s number. He'd been sold by Lancaster as military chattel, set up to disappear during a sanctioned mission in Colombia and be sent to Southeast Asia.

He'd been sold out while under Dylan's command—and then everything had gone even more horrendously, sickeningly wrong.

Dylan slid his hand down to cover his mouth for a moment and lifted his gaze to the woman across from him. She was right. Lancaster needed to be brought down.

Geezus. The depth of the betrayal was numbing.

Randolph Lancaster had been a friend.

Enhancement and experimental use—he knew exactly what the words meant. On the computer screen, on an

Atlas Exports invoice dated three years ago, he'd seen his own coded SOF ID number typed across the top of a page.

Sometimes, at night, the bite of the needle would come to him again, waking him with a scream lodged in his throat, his body drenched in sweat. More pain than what he'd been subjected to was literally beyond his imagination. Yet he knew J.T. had suffered much more, torture beyond bearing, transformation beyond reversal. J.T. had been changed into someone else, something else, a half-man/half-genetically altered beast going by the name Conroy Farrel, and that creature was on the loose, out there somewhere in the world and closing in on Denver. Dylan knew it down to his bones. He'd been the one to bait the trap, and "the bait" was showing all the signs of impending escape—heightened alertness, hours spent either pacing or standing stock-still, looking out toward the windows, refusing to speak. Somehow, somewhere, even with her locked deep inside Steele Street, incarcerated on the tenth floor, Conroy Farrel had communicated with Scout Leesom. The message would have been simple: "I'm coming to get you."

"We need to bring J.T. in first, secure him," he said to the blonde. "Then we'll go after Lancaster."

"No." She was adamant, her arms crossing over her chest, her chin firming up, her gaze meeting his with mutinous intensity. Her name was Skeeter Bang-Hart, and out of all the bad girls in the world, she was his. "We go after Lancaster now, take this party to him, give him something to worry about besides trying to kill J.T., and you, and probably the rest of us while he's at it. He needs to go *down*, Dylan. He needs to go down as hard and as fast as we can make it happen, and SDF can make it happen pretty damn hard and fast."

She wanted blood. She'd wanted it since she'd found the invoices deep-sixed in the no-access files he'd hijacked off an ultra-secure computer in Washington, D.C., but Dylan wasn't going to let her have it, not yet.

He shook his head. "This party started eight weeks ago in Paraguay, in Conroy Farrel's compound on the Tambo River, and it's going to end here, at Steele Street, when we have him back. Then we'll take Lancaster out."

She crossed her legs, tightened her arms, and looked at him long and hard. "You lost him in Paraguay, Dylan, you and Hawkins and Creed and Zach, all four of you, even after Creed hit him with a tranquilizer dart damn near big enough to drop an elephant. The girl was a secondary target at best, and if he doesn't want her back, we've got nothing."

Count on Skeeter to lay the failure of their last mission on the line, but she was wrong about the girl.

"He wants her." Guaranteed. "You saw her. She's not worried. She hasn't been worried from the beginning. Angry, yes, but not scared. She knows he's coming for her, and she doesn't think we have a chance in hell of stopping him. That he might fail hasn't crossed her mind, and four days ago, she started actively looking for him, actively preparing for her escape. He's here now, Skeet, and I need you here, too, you and Gillian. This isn't the time to be splitting the team up. We need everybody on board, everybody in place. How's Cherie doing with the changes on the security system?" Cherie Hacker, a world-class computer nerd and electronic security expert for Steele Street, had been fine-tuning the building ever since they'd brought Scout Leesom to Denver.

J.T. was going to be thinking about how to get inside, and Dylan had decided to make damn sure he could, almost at will. When he hadn't shown up in the first four weeks after the botched mission in Paraguay, Dylan had decided to loosen the security here and there and tighten it in other places, hoping to lure him into making his move. In effect, Dylan had left half the building unlocked. There was risk in the plan, but if he'd thought it would bring J.T. in, he'd have laid a trail of bread crumbs from Ciudad del Este, Paraguay, straight to Steele Street's front door.

"She's got all the outside doors wired into one set of controls, including most of the garage doors, and she's almost finished wiring the elevators," Skeeter said. "We should get down to the office. Cherie's got another shakedown planned in an hour."

He checked his watch. "What about her Quick Mart runs—how are those going?"

"Right on schedule, every day," Skeeter assured him.

The Quick Mart runs were a long shot, sending Cherie out for coffee, making it look like the building was wide open for people to just come and go as they pleased. It was more bait, a low-percentage shot compared to the high-priced piece on the tenth floor, but Dylan was putting everything he had into play. If he didn't get to J.T. first, Lancaster would, and that was a possibility he wasn't willing to accept.

"Who's on the street with her today?"

"Zach," she said.

"Good."

Zachary Prade was one of the original chop shop boys. An ex-CIA agent, he'd been so deeply undercover in the drug trade at one point that Dylan had lost track of him for years. Zach had "been there, done that" in dozens of hellholes around the world. He could more than handle Cherie's coffee run.

Dylan stood up and offered Skeeter his hand, and after a moment of meeting his gaze, she took it and let him pull her to her feet.

He held her there for a moment, then cupped the side of her face with his palm and leaned down to take her mouth with his. The bad girl was all his, and she proved it with her kiss, melting into his arms, holding him close as he slid his hand down her neck and over her breasts, before letting it come to rest low on her belly. Yes, this girl was his, for now and forever.

Deep down, he knew she was scared for all of them, for what their investigation had uncovered and what it could mean for their future, but she would obey. He didn't have a doubt. There'd be no takedown of Randolph Lancaster until he gave the order, and he would when the time was right. Chances were, the team would survive Lancaster's betrayal despite the damage he'd done.

Conroy Farrel was a different matter. The chances of all of them surviving a live capture of the beastly creature J.T. had become were far, far slimmer. He was a warrior at heart and a monster by design—and there wasn't an operator at Steele Street who didn't know it.

CHAPTER TWO

Ketamine hydrochloride. Special K. Monkey Morphine delivered in an automatic syringe shot out of a .22-caliber rimfire rifle. He knew the drill.

Yeah.

Conroy Farrel rubbed the side of his neck where he'd been darted two months ago in Paraguay. With all the cutting-edge psychopharmaceuticals pumping through his bloodstream, he would have thought he could handle a few cc's of the date-rape drug.

Think again, Con, old boy.

The ketamine, a hallucinogenic animal tranquilizer, had damn near twisted him up and tranquilized him into the fifth dimension for weeks, and the guys who had doped him lived across the street from where he was standing in a Denver, Colorado, alley. Worse, far worse than the doping, they'd stolen his girl.

He'd come six thousand miles to get her back.

Con let his gaze slide up the length of the wildest, most contraption-like freight elevator he'd ever seen. It crawled up the side of the building at 738 Steele Street, all iron and steel, looking like a gothic suspension bridge set on end and, somehow, oddly, familiar—damned familiar. Shrouded in the shadows cast by the setting sun, all he could think was that the elevator reminded him of the bridge that spanned the Kwai River just outside

Kanchanaburi in western Thailand—not that he liked to think about Thailand too often. Bangkok had been nothing short of brutal on him, half a breath away from the deep sleep. Or maybe less than half a breath. Resurrection, he was sure, was the only thing standing between him and eternity.

And the only thing standing between him and his girl was the building across the street. If she was in there, he was going to get her, and if she wasn't in there, he was going to get whoever was and ask them once where they'd taken her—only once. Scout was tough, as tough as she'd needed to be to survive alone in Southeast Asia, before he'd finally tracked her down on the streets of Bangkok. They'd celebrated her eighteenth birthday in Rangoon, her nineteenth in Vientiane, her twentieth in Phnom Penh, her twenty-first in Da Nang, and her twenty-second in Amsterdam—a promise he'd made her father, Garrett Leesom, a soldier like him, one of the world's warriors whose last breath had been wrung out of him in the same hellhole that had all but killed Con.

Yeah, Scout was tough, like her father. These thugs on Steele Street wouldn't have what it took to break her. But he had what it took to break them, and it would all come to bear on every single one of them, starting with a guy named Dylan Hart, until he had Garrett's daughter back.

He reached into his pocket, felt the business card there, but didn't pull it out. He didn't need to pull it out. The words on the card had been burned into his memory the instant he'd seen them: DYLAN HART, UPTOWN AUTOS, WE ONLY SELL THE BEST, 738 STEELE STREET, DENVER, COLORADO. He'd found the card on his kitchen table in Paraguay the day they'd taken Scout.

These boys knew he was coming. Hell, they'd left him an engraved invitation—and they weren't car salesmen. He didn't give a damn what the card said.

No. They were operators of the highest order. They'd done what no one else had come close to accomplishing in six years: They'd gotten the drop on him. He hoped they'd enjoyed their momentary success. He hoped it had gone straight to their heads.

He shifted his attention to the roof of the building opposite the alley to 738 Steele Street, the Bruso-Campbell Building. The Bruso was a story taller than 738, a good vantage point.

Con couldn't see him, but he knew Jack Traeger was up there on top of the Bruso, manning the listening post they'd set up, a laser mike sighted on one of the banks of windows fronting 738. No one could see Jack, and no one would, not until it was too late.

Con checked his watch—6:30 p.m.—then glanced back to the building. Right on cue, a classic piece of Sublime Green American muscle from 1971, a Dodge Challenger R/T, rolled out of the seventh floor onto the sleekly modern freight elevator on the opposite side of the building from the gothic contraption. Actually, rolled wasn't quite the word. Lurched was more like it. He and Jack had been watching 738 for four days, and the list of rare iron they'd accumulated was nothing short of amazing. These Steele Street assholes knew their cars. He had to give them that.

What he didn't know was why anyone with a car like the Challenger would let some ditzy-looking redhead abuse it every day at 6:30 p.m. She was pretty in a skinny sort of way, but she couldn't drive worth beans. Fortunately, she never went more than three blocks to the closest convenience store, where she parked in a small lot next door and went inside to buy a pack of cigarettes, a couple of candy bars, and a machine-brewed double-shot latte. Then she'd get back in the Challenger and lurch her way out of the parking lot and back three blocks to 738 Steele Street.

Her name was Cherie.

He'd followed her into the Quick Mart once and had Jack follow her in once. The clerk and she were on a first-name basis, and from their chatter, he and Jack had figured out that she was some kind of computer tech.

She was also predictable.

Dangerously predictable.

The weak link in the Steele Street chain.

Every day she'd exited the building at 6:30 p.m. and returned within half an hour. Con needed her to do it only one more time.

While the Challenger made its descent to the street, he turned and started walking toward the convenience store, turning south on Wazee Street and making his way through all the folks leaving work late and hitting the bars early. This section of the city was called LoDo, for lower downtown. It had remnants of industry and a bit of ghetto to the north and enough restored old buildings to the south to qualify as a historical district, all of them renovated into restaurants, boutiques, bars, bookstores, cafés, art galleries, and architectural antique shops. On a late-spring evening, it was crowded with cars and people, office people, city people . . . beautiful people.

He slowed his steps for a second, and then another, his gaze locking on a woman a block away—*very beautiful people.*

He'd always had a soft spot for slinky brunettes, and this one moved like a cat, her long, straight hair tossed over her shoulder, lifting in the light breeze, her strides supple and easy.

Always had a soft spot for slinky women, from way back when.

Yeah, always. That was a definite skip in his cylinders. A man with no more than six years' worth of memories to fill out his scorecard had a damn sketchy concept of *always.*

Sketchy or not, though, she fit the bill, all legs and silky dark hair, slender curves wrapped in a short, golden sheath of a dress, very short. A leopard-print belt cinched the dress in at her waist, and she had jungle bangles on her left wrist, three of them: zebra print, tiger striped, and ebony. Wild girl. All the way. A short-cropped black leather jacket, very sleek, very stylish, topped the outfit, and each of her strides was taken in a pair of ankle-high, high-heeled, black suede boots. Large, black designer sunglasses covered half her face, and she had a big, slouchy, zebra-striped purse slung over her shoulder.

She looked like a model and walked like she owned the street, and there wasn't a doubt in his mind that she did, especially this one.

As she crossed 19th, the clouds broke behind her and a shaft of sunlight caught the gold hoops in her ears, throwing glinting sparks of light into the shadows behind the lenses of her glasses. For a tenth of a second, he could see her eyes—not the color but the shape, the slight tilt of the outside edges and the thick sweep of her lashes.

No one else could have seen so much with so little, but his senses were ramped up, awareness hard-wired into his every cell the same way the muscles in his body were ramped up and hard-wired for speed and strength and reaction times that could be measured in hundredths of a second.

He didn't take any personal credit for being so ripped. That was the way they'd made him, to be damn near indestructible, and he was. Dr. Souk had been the mechanic, but the orders for the torture he and Garrett had suffered in the name of demented science and the never-ending search for the perfect warrior had come down from a man in Washington, D.C., the spymaster. He was the brains behind some of the blackest operations ever to come out of the CIA and the Department of Defense, Con's nemesis, a man who pulled strings across half a dozen of the United States' most clandestine agencies. He had a lot of names, but his given name was Randolph Lancaster, and getting it had cost more than one man his life.

Con had no regrets. Everyone in the game was playing on the same field, and everyone knew his life was at stake. Politics and war were just different names for power, and the price of power was predictably high and could be precisely measured—in dollars, yen, euros, rubles, riyals, and blood.

Keeping his pace steady, he allowed himself the luxury of letting his gaze travel over the jungle girl—urban jungle. She was "city" from the top of her head to the discreet black leather straps wrapped around the ankles of her boots. If beauty had an edge, she was it, the gloss of sophistication highlighting her attitude and the toughness he saw in the way she carried herself, in her awareness of her space. The sidewalk was crowded, but she had a way of not letting anybody get too close. He knew it wasn't an accident, the way she kept herself apart, because he had the same skill, the same instinct. It was survival learned the hard way.

Thirty yards and closing, twenty yards, ten yards and he caught her scent, picking it out of the thousands in the air, exotic, sensual, female, and, yes, feral—a kindred spirit. He couldn't take his eyes off her, and the smallest smile curved a corner of his mouth.

Wild Thing.

Five yards and something shifted in her stride, a hesitation. Her next step came slower, and then she stopped, her mouth opening on a soft gasp. She was looking straight at him. He could feel her gaze, felt her awareness of him spike and redline. He was scarred—on his face, on his arms, his hands, his chest—hell, everywhere—but it wasn't horror reaching out to him from her. It was something . . . something . . . something else.

Something he hadn't felt in a long time.

She reached up, lowered her sunglasses, and took a step closer as he started to pass, nearly brushing against him, her other hand lifting ever so slightly, as if she might touch him, but all he felt was the intensity of her pale green-eyed gaze, the heat of it holding him captive for the brief moment of their encounter.

He kept moving, kept heading toward the Quick Mart. But for the space of a breath, the street disappeared, the people, the buildings, the cars, and all he could see was her face, the angles and curves, the slight dusting of freckles and the small white scar across the bridge of her nose, another scar across her left cheekbone, the sheer wild beauty of golden skin with the wind blowing her dark hair across it like a veil. She was mystery and enthrallment. She was unexpected.

She was trouble, but easily avoidable. All he had to do was keep walking, and he did.

His pulse was racing, though—not a good sign. He never lacked for women, but there had never been anyone like this urban jungle girl, not on any street in the world, a chance encounter that set off a dangerous mix of lust and warning bells. She'd broken his concentration, and he hadn't thought that was possible. His concentration had not faltered in six years, not since the day he'd woken up, and always it was focused on the mission.

Always.

He glanced back, and she was still standing in the middle of the sidewalk, watching him.

Trouble—that's what she was, and he didn't need it. He was in Denver to get Scout, not to get laid.

Forcing his attention away from her, he continued south on Wazee Street and ignored the siren call he felt running through his veins—that maybe, just maybe, with the right timing, the right circumstances, the city girl could be his.

But probably not. If all went as he and Jack had planned, they'd be out of Denver by midnight, but he wouldn't forget her scent. It had melted into him, a gift to be treasured.

After pulling a ball cap out of his coat pocket, he snugged it down on his head, slipped a pair of sunglasses on his face, and lengthened his strides, focusing back on the mission. He'd timed the route to the convenience store and knew exactly how many minutes he had—plenty to do what needed to be done.

Half a block from the Quick Mart, he could see the Challenger in the small parking lot crammed between the store and an old, rundown hotel, which meant weak-link Cherie was still inside buying candy and cigarettes. She used the street lot every day, but Con's favorite downtown parking was the high-rise garage catty-corner from the store. He liked it so much, he'd spent an hour in it last night, rigging a smoke bomb at the entrance and putting it on a radio signal controller.

The setup wasn't overly dramatic, just enough to get people's attention, especially the attention of whatever guy was sitting at a certain outside table at the restaurant opposite the garage. A man had been there every day when Cherie pulled up, a different guy each day, and twenty minutes after she headed back to Steele Street, each one of those guys had gotten up and left.

They were surveillance, and when Con spotted today's observer, he conceded that the man was just as good, just as subtle as every other guy who'd been keeping the same schedule at that table, but they were all watchers, and what they were watching was Cherie and the Challenger. From the outside table where they'd all sat, they had a perfect line of sight to the store and the car, but today's guy was going to have to turn his head to see what was happening at the parking garage.

And he would turn his head. The smoke, with the added distraction of the scent Con had packaged with the "bomb," guaranteed it. A couple of seconds, that's all he needed.

Coming up on the parking lot, he saw Cherie walk out of the store, and he timed his approach to be just ahead of hers. He had his hands in his pockets and the radio signal controller in one of his hands. At a precisely calculated moment, he flipped the switch and turned toward the Challenger parked three cars in from the sidewalk. He heard the small ripple of commotion when people saw the billow of smoke come out of the garage entrance, felt a spike of fear run through the crowd, and knew a fair percentage of them had flashed on 9/11 and the World Trade Center. He saw Cherie look back over her shoulder to see what was happening, and he didn't hesitate. Stepping up to the rear of the Challenger, a lockpick in his hand, he popped the trunk. Up ahead on the sidewalk, a couple people quickly complained with an "ohmigod, can you smell that" while they were all trying to figure out just how frightened they needed to be. By the time they'd finished grousing, he'd climbed inside the trunk and pulled the lid closed on top of himself. The whole operation took less than five seconds. By then, the smoke and the smell were gone, and the crowd was curious but starting to feel relieved. It was a nonevent—except that people had noticed, and the man at the restaurant would have noticed. Guys like him were trained to see the forest *and* the trees. He would have looked.

Inside the Challenger, the trunk space was a little on the shy side, but not unpleasantly so. Con had been in worse places, smaller spaces, all of them in the Bangkok prison laboratory of the long-dead, never-missed, demented Dr. Souk. He didn't remember much of anything before awakening in one of Souk's cells, but he did know he hadn't been in many places that smelled like baby powder.

Baby powder—what the hell? he wondered. He knew from the car's badges and the sound that the Challenger had header extensions and a 426 cid Hemi under the hood, a power plant with the well-earned nickname of King Kong, the biggest production engine ever to come off a line in Detroit. Nothing about the 1971 Mopar street machine said "baby powder," but that was exactly what it smelled like in the trunk.

He sniffed the air again, then reached toward the front right corner and found a diaper bag. He'd never actually seen a diaper bag, but he'd heard about them, and he knew this soft, padded cotton satchel he'd found was one, because it had diapers in it, and baby powder, and lotion, and wipes.

That set him back a bit.

The Challenger, one of the toughest, meanest, most unbeatable pieces of Mopar muscle to ever hit the streets, was a family car.

He didn't see much of that in his line of work, families. He and Scout had cobbled together a family of sorts, but he never fooled himself into thinking he could ever take the place of her real father. He'd kept her safe, and kept her out of trouble as best he could, and so far, in a battle he knew he was bound to lose, he'd kept her out of Jack Traeger's bed. The pirate had come far more than six thousand miles to get her back, though, and this time Con figured Jack had come to take her for good.

He'd barely set the bag back in the corner when, just like clockwork, the car door was opened and Cherie the computer tech got back inside. He felt the slight shift of her weight and knew she was lighting a cigarette before she started the engine. When she turned the key, the

Challenger came to life, and it was a beast, just like him, all rumble and roar with that badass 426 Hemi under the hood. The chassis rocked with the power she was feeding it through the gas pedal, and then, with a lurch, she pulled out of the lot and into traffic and they were heading back to Steele Street.

Game time.

CHAPTER THREE

Jane Linden walked quickly toward 738 Steele Street, breaking into a run every few steps, her zebra bag clutched close to her chest, her prize inside.

Good God Almighty. Her heart was pounding. *J.T., J.T., J.T.,* the name ran through her mind. *Here. In Denver... alive. My God.*

Or maybe she was wrong—but that man on the street, *my God.*

She knew J. T. Chronopolous. She knew the clean, lean lines of his face, the deep-set eyes, the thick, straight eyebrows, the hint of dimples when he grinned. She knew he'd been one of the original chop shop boys, a juvenile car thief of superlative skills and intensely delinquent tendencies back in the day. She knew he'd gone on to become a Recon Marine and that he'd come back to Denver to work with his friends out of the old garage on Steele Street.

And she knew he'd caught her red-handed one night, trying to steal his buddy's wallet.

She could count on one finger the number of times she'd missed a score, and he'd been it, snatching her up by the scruff of her neck and hoodie in the middle of her lift and handing her off to the guy whose pocket she'd just picked.

A wild thing, that's what he'd called her that night in

front of the Blue Iguana Lounge, while he'd pried Christian Hawkins's wallet out of her fist, as in: *"Here's your wallet back, Superman. I think this wild thing is all yours. Better run her by Doc Blake before you throw her back on the street. She looks a little worse for wear."*

She had been worse for wear that night, hungry and roughed up, her body aching from a run-in with a junkie over on Blake Street. Still, she'd squirmed and twisted and tried to break his hold—and all the while she'd been wondering what in the hell had made her think these guys would make good marks. They'd both looked like some kind of superhero. J.T. had been especially incredibly beautiful, a real traffic-stopper, clean cut, tall, and superbly fit, his shoulders broad, his arms strong, with a bone-deep confidence radiating out of every pore that had set her heart aflutter—and that's what she'd been thinking, how hot he was, instead of paying attention to the lift.

Then he'd really short-circuited her brain, looking down at her after he'd handed her off, still grinning. She'd been struck straight through the heart. Their eyes had met, his smile had faded, and she'd never been the same, not ever, not even now. He'd changed her, even though a guy like him wouldn't have looked twice at a street rat like her, not back when she'd been picking pockets. Unless, she'd found out weeks later, if a night got so wild that even the good guys started crossing the lines.

He'd crossed the line with her.

Much to her everlasting mortification, she did know that much about him. But the most important thing she knew about J. T. Chronopolous, the hard thing, the worst thing, was that he'd died. They'd buried him six years ago on a summer afternoon in a cemetery in Denver. She'd been one of the hangers-on that day, just a street kid in the background, not really part of the mourning that had gone on. But she'd felt the grief, hard and heavy and aching, right along with his friends.

God, she'd cried for him, for things that had never had a chance in hell of really beginning, let alone lasting.

She stopped at the corner and looked back, but he was gone—*J.T., John Thomas Chronopolous, Kid Chaos's older brother, the best of them all.*

He'd told her once how much he'd loved being a Marine, but he'd loved his friends more, and when they'd asked him to come home, he'd left Recon behind. He'd told her a lot of things during the long, hot summer of their unexpected friendship. The city had been scorching that year, the temperatures soaring close to a hundred for days on end, the nights little better. So she'd taken to the rooftops, and one night, so had he...

What a score!

Jane ran down the street for another half block, legs pumping, before turning into an alley off Wazee, a plastic bag full of Chinese takeout swinging from her fist. The food was still hot and had barely been paid for when some hapless old dude with a limp had set it down to unlock his car.

Fool. She'd slid by him and scored an amazing dinner. She could still hear him back there yelling for the cops, but she was long gone—and so was his meal.

She slowed to an easy alley-eating lope, and her mouth curved into a wide grin.

Gourmet Chinese, from the coolest new restaurant in LoDo, a place called the Lucky Moon. If she'd had a cellphone, she would have called her friend Sandman to come and share.

Partway down the alley, she took a right turn into the parking lot of Sprechts Apartments, one of lower downtown's pricier addresses. Every apartment had a balcony, and the people who lived at Sprechts were the kind who grew gardens on them and had lots of plants, even trees. Sometimes the Sprechts people would sit around on their balconies and drink wine. More than once, she'd scored a half-empty bottle in the wee hours when the city was asleep. But the nicest thing about Sprechts was the roof—specifically, its location.

She came to the fire escape and started up, moving quickly and silently, her steps as light as her fingers were fast. It was five floors to the roof, but she would have climbed twice as high to get the view she wanted—the alley at 738 Steele Street and the undying long-shot hope that the hot guy who'd busted her boost two weeks ago would show up tonight.

It was a little silly, and fun, and kind of comforting to have such a crazy crush on a guy. In this one way, at least, she was like all the other teenage girls in the city, the normal ones. None of them could have cruised the dark alleys of Denver or stolen their dinner off the street, and she doubted if very many of them had ever been on the rooftops. But they had crushes on hot guys, and so did she—the hottest guy ever.

Her smile returned.

At the top of the fire escape, she made a small leap onto a balcony rail and quick-stepped across, balancing herself with her arms outstretched, her small backpack in one hand, the Chinese food in the other. When she reached the end of the balcony, she threw her backpack up on the roof, gripped the plastic bag of food in her teeth, and swung herself up. She had her place all picked out and settled in with her dinner for the long haul, sitting in the prime place for watching the alley backing 738 Steele Street. A lot of buff guys went in and out of the building, but she was only interested in one—her crush.

Cripes, she'd had a day. Taking her jacket out of the backpack, she spread it out in front of her on the roof and unloaded her take: five wallets; a small clutch purse; four DVDs she'd copped out of the drugstore, all new releases; a couple of candy bars; a silk shirt with the tags still on it; and a Batman action figure. She thought Batman was pretty cool, but the action figure was for one of the new kids on the crew, a squirrelly little towhead named Jeffy. She should have gotten him a Batman shirt. His looked like it had been handed down about forty times. But she'd snagged the action figure instead so the kid could have some fun.

Not bad, she thought, looking the stash over and reaching into the bag of food. The first thing she pulled out was a box of wontons, and after taking a big bite out of one, she started her nightly sort. Cash went in one pile, credit cards in another, identification cards in another. Sometimes, if a wallet had a lot of good stuff, she'd keep the whole thing intact for an ID sale, squeeze a few extra bucks out of it to feed her crew.

A few minutes later, she'd counted up two hundred and seventy-seven dollars in cash, eight credit cards, four driver's licenses, and one learner's permit, whatever that was worth. She didn't have a clue, but it never failed to amaze her what some people wanted to buy.

Reaching back into the bag, she took another wonton and decided that what she needed was a DVD player, and every now and then, maybe she'd keep a movie. The kids would love it.

During the sort, she'd kept her eye out for people coming and going in the alley below, but so far, the night had been a bust.

Disappointed but still hopeful, she scooped up the day's cash and cards and stowed them into her pack before settling in to wait, and watch, and eat. She was into her fourth wonton when her luck changed.

"Chinese?" a deep voice asked.

Cripes. Her heart took a jump, and she jerked her head around but didn't see anybody.

"You're going through those wontons pretty fast." The guy spoke again, and she quickly turned her head in the opposite direction.

There, in the deep shadows cast by the moon, he was standing with his back against the air-conditioning unit.

"Go find your own roof," she said around a mouthful of wonton, the rest of the bag clutched close to her chest. "This one's already taken."

"I'll leave as soon as I find the thief who stole my boss's dinner. He ordered takeout from the Lucky Moon, that new restaurant up on Blake. Have you heard about it?" the guy asked, and oh, so help her, she suddenly recognized him.

The wonton turned to instant sawdust in her mouth.

Oh, God. Nobody's luck could run this bad.

"General Grant, my boss," he continued, "picked up his food about half an hour ago, but before he could get it home, the bag got snatched by someone he described as a coltish brunette."

Coltish? That didn't sound good.

Her eyes narrowed. "What did he mean by coltish?"

"Long legs, a little on the skinny side, and fast as hell."

That was her, all right.

"He probably left the bag lying on the street," she said, while simultaneously determining the quickest escape route, and all the while hating that her wonderful summer crush was over. It was darn hard to stay infatuated with someone who thought you were a thief, even if you were. "Anybody could have come along and picked it up."

"No," he said. "Not anyone. General Grant isn't a patsy. It took someone good to get his dinner away from him."

A backhanded compliment, but beggars—and thieves—couldn't be picky.

"That's a great story," she said, casually slipping her arm through the handles on the plastic bag and then wrapping her hand around the strap on her pack. "But these are my wontons." Deny. Deny. Deny. Those were the first three rules of stealing on the street.

"Maybe." The guy seemed to be giving her the benefit of the doubt. "But he sent me to track down the thief, and here I am, and there you are with a bag of Chinese food."

Impossible, and she told him so.

"Nobody can track me on the streets." Hell, she'd been chased by the cops dozens of times, and she'd never been caught. Never.

A small laugh escaped him, and she could see him shaking his head. "Oh, yeah, babe. I can track you, and I did."

He sounded damned sure of himself, but she wasn't buying it, even with that sweet little "babe" business. "No," she said, shaking her own head. "Nobody's that good."

"Actually, Ms. Linden, I'm better than that," he said, his voice coolly serious. "Way better."

He knew her name, her real name.

The shock froze her in place for all of a nanosecond before she bolted.

But damn, he was fast—faster than her, and when she would have cleared the southernmost corner of the building and made her jump for the balcony, he was two steps ahead of her.

She skidded to a stop, and before she could change directions, he reached out and took her pack and the bag of food, just snatched them right out of her hands.

The loss stopped her cold.

Dammit. She couldn't go home without her backpack.

She wouldn't go home without it. Delivering the goods was how she kept her standing with her crew. It wasn't just her livelihood at risk here tonight. It was how she kept the whole sorry pack of them safe—by being better, by never getting caught, by having the cash to feed them.

"I need that," she said, using her firmest voice, letting him know he'd gone too far. "You can have the Chinese food. I'll even pay you for the wontons, but I need the pack."

He stood there in front of her, bigger than life, so calm and sure of himself, still the most beautiful guy she'd ever seen. Five minutes ago, he'd been everything she'd wanted. Now she just wanted away—one more dream down the tubes.

"Ten minutes," he said with a lift of his eyebrows. "Stay and talk with me for ten minutes, and I'll give you your pack back. I promise."

She thought his offer over for all of two seconds.

"With everything in it?"

"Everything," he promised.

Ten minutes of talk to claim two hundred seventy-seven dollars and eight credit cards? That would be the best deal she'd made all day.

And she believed him, for whatever reason, believed that if she talked to him for ten minutes, he would return her pack, and she'd be on her way—wiser and sadder and wondering what, if anything, would come into her life to replace the thrill of hoping to see him.

But that was over now. It really was, no matter how good he looked standing there.

"How do you know my name?" she asked. She hadn't given her name to his friend or to the doc who'd looked her over two weeks ago, not her street name, Robin Rulz, and sure as heck not her real name, Jane Linden. She never gave anyone her real name.

"When I was younger, I used to own these streets. So

I asked around to see if anybody knew a green-eyed girl picking pockets in LoDo who had long dark hair and a face... yeah, well, an unusual face."

Unusual face? Coltish?

Well, this was damned embarrassing, but she needed that damn backpack back.

"You're beautiful," he said straight out of the blue, then glanced down and let out a soft laugh. "You probably hear that all the time."

No, she didn't, and standing there in a pair of cast-off tennis shoes with holes in her jeans and an old Rocket Girl T-shirt, she wondered if he was talking to somebody else.

A quick glance around killed that idea. There was just the two of them up there on the Sprechts roof.

"Stunning, really." He looked back to her, meeting her gaze with a half smile teasing his mouth. "I've never seen anyone like you, not ever, and I've been from one side of this planet to the other."

Okay, well, ten minutes of this wasn't going to be so hard to take, even with a blush warming her cheeks.

"I've never seen anybody like you, either," she admitted. "But I've mostly just been from one side of Denver to the other."

He laughed at that and dragged his hand back through his hair, and looked like he was feeling a little shy.

Geez. She must be having a darn good hair day.

"So what's your name?" she asked.

"J. T. Chronopolous," he said. "Ask around, you'll hear about me and my friends, Christian Hawkins and Creed, maybe a few of the others. We used to run a pretty tight crew around here."

Good. Great. It never hurt to have a few names to throw around.

"Does your friend Creed have a last name?"

He laughed again, a rich, deep sound that warmed her heart. "Just Creed. Come on, have a seat. We can finish the general's takeout. I'm sure the guys have gotten him a whole new dinner by now."

Chinese food, her backpack, and ten minutes of conversation with J. T. Chronopolous, her ex–hot crush. She'd sure had worse offers and, truthfully, seldom, if ever, had a better one.

She sat where she stood, a few feet away from him, and he grinned but didn't press the point, sitting down where he'd been standing and leaning over to hand her the small white carton with the rest of the wontons.

"A general," she said, taking a bite without taking her eyes off him. "So are you with the Army or something?"

"Something like the Army," he said, opening another of the cartons and bringing it to his nose. "Sesame chicken, mmmm."

She loved sesame chicken, and when he cracked open a pair of chopsticks and offered her the carton, she didn't hesitate.

"So how old are you?" he asked.

"Twenty-two," she said without hesitation. Twenty-one always sounded like you'd made it up, but twenty-two was solid.

"Twenty-two?" he repeated, sounding damned doubtful.

She gave a quick nod and kept eating, sticking with her story. That was always best—to keep it simple and to keep it straight.

"How did you get the scar on your cheek?"

"The same way I got the one on my nose." Her gaze down, she kept eating.

"Which was how?" he persisted.

"You're damn nosy." She snagged another piece of chicken and popped it in her mouth.

"I'm interested in you," he said. "And because of my

work, I don't always have a lot of time, so if I want to know something, I ask."

"Your Army work." She liked that he was a soldier. It fit him perfectly and had a solidness to it.

"Yeah, my Army work."

She ate another two full bites of sesame chicken, watching him the whole time, before deciding to answer his question. In her work, being able to size up people and risk was second nature, and anyone who couldn't do it in a split second wouldn't last a day on the streets, let alone a night.

J. T. Chronopolous checked out.

"Before I went independent, I used to work for this guy, and he was always knocking us around. Not just me, but the whole crew, and we were so damn little, we just kind of took it. Then Sandman and I went out on our own—so there's been no more knocking around."

"Does this guy have a name?" The question came out immediately, not like he had to think about it, which she found interesting. Cops were like that, quick with the right questions.

"He used to," she said. "Now he's got a number down at the prison in Cañon City."

He definitely thought that bit of news over.

"I checked with the cops, asked them about you, too," he finally said, and she almost choked on her chicken. "They told me you and Sandman are headed for a fall. That you've had a good run, and they like that you're trying to take care of all those homeless kids, but that you'd be better off shifting the whole kit and caboodle over to Social Services and giving yourself a break, before they give it to you, and they're talking jail time, Jane. They want you off their streets. No more Robin Rulz."

"You talked to the cops about me?" Unbelievable. And he knew about Sandman and the kids? Good God,

he was no crush. He was a disaster. "Why in the hell would you do that?"

"You're in a tough spot. I've been there. We've all been there. I thought if I knew what was going on with you, I could help. I just didn't think I'd be getting the chance to talk with you about it tonight."

Damn him. Mr. Superhero talking to the cops.

"I don't need your charity." She dropped the chopsticks and reached for her pack. Before she could take it, he put his hand on top of hers.

"It's not charity."

"Then what is it?"

His answer, when it finally came, proved even more unnerving than him talking to the cops. "I don't know. Probably the same thing that's been bringing you up to this rooftop almost every night for the last two weeks."

He'd known she was watching for him?

Now she was really embarrassed.

"Right." To hell with the backpack. She'd make it up tomorrow.

She started to her feet, but he grabbed her wrist.

"Please," he said, and carefully, slowly released her. "Don't go, not yet."

"It's late," she said—and she felt like a fool.

"Can I buy you breakfast, lunch, dinner tomorrow?"

He wanted to see her again?

"Which one?" she asked, skeptical as hell. Maybe he was working for the cops on the side. She knew the Denver Police wanted to clean out her crew. This one cop, Lieutenant Loretta, really had it out for her and Sandman. Social Services was that woman's answer for everything.

"All three," he said. "I'm headed out of town at the end of the week, the Army thing, and I don't know exactly how long I might be gone. I'd like to spend some time with you."

She didn't know. Somehow it seemed damned risky, and yet...

"How about just breakfast?" he asked.

Sure. She could agree to breakfast.

"All right," she said, and then had to fight the stupid grin she felt coming on. She was going to see him again, talk with him. For the first time in a long time, she felt light inside, like all those things that weighed on her every day were lifting a bit.

"Great," he said, a broad smile spreading across his face. He rose to his feet and reached his hand down to pull her up. "Do you know Duffy's?"

"The bar on the corner," she said, accepting his hand and standing up.

"Yeah. They serve breakfast. Can you meet me there at seven tomorrow morning?"

He was still holding on to her hand, and as much as she loved it, she was also unnerved. In her line of work, it was hard to make a living if a person was holding your hand.

"Duffy's at seven. Sure." She pulled her hand free and swung her pack over her shoulder.

Good God, she had a date at one of the classiest breakfast joints in Denver. So what in the world was she going to wear?"

A skirt, she remembered. That's what she'd come up with, a gauzy little ivory-colored summer skirt with black bows at the waist, a pair of pink-and-white striped leggings, and a black tank top, everything scored at a secondhand shop on her way home, a secondhand shop with a broken basement window.

She'd shopped there a lot back in the bad old days.

Still looking down the street, a pained sigh escaped her, echoing the ache in her chest. Why hadn't she moved faster to stop him?

Shock had held her where she stood, but she should have moved faster. Instinct alone had guided her hand. She'd seen an opportunity, and she'd taken it, but, damn, she wished she'd said something to him.

J. T. Chronopolous—he hadn't been scarred back then, except for three straight lines he'd had on his upper left arm.

The man on the street had been scarred everywhere, on his hands, his neck, his face—but so help her God, she knew that face.

Looking down, she reached into her zebra purse and flipped open the wallet she'd just lifted off him. It was made out of olive green canvas, heavy-duty, with double-stitched seams, and she'd had to work like light-fingered lightning to slip it out of his back pocket. She was good—for all the good it had done her.

Hell.

Conroy Farrel, that's what his driver's license said, the whole of it in Spanish, issued in Paraguay.

Farrel, not Chronopolous.

Her heart sank just a little bit, and she looked back down the street. Every sense she had was telling her she'd just seen J. T. Chronopolous, not some man named Conroy Farrel. It had been in his eyes. "Forever eyes" she'd called them, back when she'd been ridiculously infatuated with him, like she'd seen all the way to forever whenever she'd looked into them, like they'd opened onto the cosmos, a window not into his soul but out to the far, depthless reaches of the universe. What a romantic sap she'd been back then, and yet, as a woman, she would still call them compelling, intensely so, and the eyes that had held hers for that brief second of contact had been exactly the same as those she remembered from so long ago—J.T.'s.

The light changed at 20th and Wazee, and after checking both ways first, she crossed and kept heading north.

She had been heading home, but she needed to get to 738 Steele Street to see Christian Hawkins.

Superman had saved her half a dozen times over the years. She owed him her life.

She sure as hell owed him the wallet she'd just lifted off the man heading south on Wazee Street.

From where he was settled into his hide on the roof of the Bruso-Campbell Building, Jack Traeger checked his watch, then looked through his binoculars one last time. Four days of recon on 738 Steele Street had finally given him what he wanted—a lock on Scout's location.

Tenth floor. West side.

He hadn't seen her, but he knew Morse code, and he sure as hell knew what *dit-dit-dit* meant, and he'd seen it flashed from the tenth floor two hours ago; then an hour ago, he'd gotten *dah-dah-dah*. Three dots, the letter *S*, the first letter in the international distress signal, SOS. The three dashes were the letter O.

Close enough.

Four days of chatter, with him switching from floor to floor with the laser mike and a laptop, and they'd only been teased with the sound of her voice a few times, each time from a different floor. She sounded good, but he wouldn't be happy until he saw her for himself, and now he had a lock on her location—so they were going in.

The gods of war were with them.

He keyed his radio.

"Alpha Two, my money is still on the tenth floor," he said, talking while he stowed his binoculars with the rest of his gear. Every move he made was practiced, smooth, timed. "Did you catch Cherie at the Quick Mart?"

"Roger," Con replied. "Alpha One heading in. Give me fifteen minutes."

"Roger." Fifteen minutes to create utter chaos. Fifteen

minutes to get inside 738 Steele Street and turn the place inside out. Fifteen minutes for Jack to get to the tenth floor and rescue Scout.

That was his job, his only job. Con had all but beaten it into him: *Get Scout, and get her out.*

Nothing else. No sidebar heroics, no coming back into the building for any reason. Get her and get her out of Denver, out of Colorado, out of the country. That was the mission, and Jack was all for it. If he'd been in Paraguay doing his job, instead of in Eastern Europe picking up work on the side, she wouldn't have been captured in the first place, and he'd felt the heavy weight of that mistake ever since Con had contacted him. By then she'd already been gone for over six weeks.

He didn't blame Con for the delay. The guy had been fighting for his life. But they'd finally gotten here, and Jack had to save her, whatever it took. God forbid, if she'd been hurt in any way, these bastards would go down in fucking flames.

She wouldn't be glad to see him, not after the last time she'd seen him, in Key Largo. He knew that much. He wasn't an idiot. The Florida situation had been a disaster, but she was smart enough to put their personal situation aside to get the job done—he hoped.

Personal situation—*cripes.* It was never supposed to have gotten to a "personal situation" between them. God knew he'd done his best to keep their relationship strictly on the up-and-up, purely professional, no entanglements.

He should have known better. They were tangled, all right. They'd been tangled from the minute he'd first laid eyes on her four years ago in Rangoon, a gorgeous mulatto girl, with Con the protector at her side. She'd been eighteen, and he'd known better—then. Now he didn't know anything when it came to Scout, except that he was getting damn tired of keeping to the high ground.

Okay, the middle to the low ground, if a person included the blonde he'd shacked up with in Key Largo for a few weeks last winter. She'd been a great girl, a Key-easy cocktail waitress, short, round, sweet, and unlikely to kick his ass—the exact opposite of everything that was Scout.

Scout kicked him. She kicked him hard, especially in the small, unguarded part of his heart that he hadn't even known he'd had until he'd seen her.

It was ridiculous, the height of stupidity, and had been for four years, ever since Con had found her. He didn't need it. Scout was trouble. He and Con made a good team. For a price, they provided the best personal security on the planet. For a price, they guaranteed delivery of anything anywhere, from cargo, to cash, to ransom, to the unknown. For a helluva price, they did hostage rescue and facilitated negotiations between a hundred varieties of despots and governments, most of which were barely discernible from each other on any given day of the week. Today's warlord was often tomorrow's prime minister in the places where his and Con's reputations ensured the highest remuneration for their services. They lived well. Jack had cash stashed in banks from the Caymans to Switzerland, and he wasn't about to screw it all up wanting what he couldn't, or shouldn't, have—namely Scout.

Good. He was glad he had that all straightened out in his head—again.

Besides, Con had told him she had a boyfriend now, some Dutch asshole she'd met in London named Karl. He just hoped old Karl had enough brains to stay out of Jack's reach, or Scout would be looking for a new boy.

Yeah, right. So glad he had everything all straightened out in his head. Con had made a damn point of telling him how great the guy was, how good he was for Scout, some kind of college professor idiot.

How in the hell Scout could take up with a professor was beyond Jack. Hell. The only degree Jack had was his Ranger tab.

He closed the last compartment on his backpack and slipped the straps over his shoulders, then bandoliered a length of climbing rope with a grappling hook across his chest. He'd rigged a zip line from the Bruso-Campbell to 738 Steele Street last night, running it behind the old freight elevator. With him accessing the building in daylight, he was counting on Con to provide the appropriate distraction with a few flash bangs or whatever the hell it took to get the job done. Once they got Scout out, he didn't care if the building crumbled to the ground, not that the explosive devices he and Con had rigged were likely to do that much damage—but they sure as hell would get everyone's attention.

Leaning over the roof, he used a carabiner to clip a handgrip onto the pulley on the zip line, and then he checked his watch again and settled in to wait—twelve minutes.

Karl, a damned Dutch professor.

What was up with that? She'd never had a boyfriend before.

He'd ask her. That's what he'd do, ask her about her jerk boyfriend, clear the air between them, and then he really needed to move on.

Great. He had a plan. He was moving on.

He checked his watch.

Eleven minutes.

CHAPTER FOUR

"Fill me in," Dylan said, coming out of the Steele Street elevator with Skeeter.

His second in command, Christian Hawkins, glanced up from where he was listening on the phone, signaled him to hold on just a second, then went back to the call. Skeeter headed straight to the security camera console and checked the monitors. A wall of windows in the office overlooked the seventh-floor garage.

Hawkins keyed a sequence into his computer and glanced up again after hanging up the phone.

"That was Jane Linden," he said, his face grim. "She swears she just saw J.T. down on Wazee, heading south."

"South?" Dylan asked calmly, controlling a sudden rush of excitement. The Quick Mart was south. "Have we heard from Zach?"

Hawkins nodded. "He checked in just before Jane called."

"And?" Dylan asked.

"There was a distraction at the Quick Mart, a small amount of smoke and a rank smell coming out of the parking garage across from the store."

"Diversion?" he asked.

Hawkins shrugged. "No sound, no visual noise, and the smoke and smell dissipated in seconds—pretty damn subtle for a diversion. Could have been anything, a blown engine, a diesel belching out junk."

"Or it could have been J.T.," Dylan said, turning toward his wife. "Skeeter, are all the cameras on the seventh-floor garage up and running?"

"I'm going through them now." She keyed in the security cameras and started checking monitor screens.

"Where's Zach?" he asked, turning back to Hawkins.

"On Cherie's tail," Hawkins said. "He broke for the Quick Mart as soon as the smoke hit."

"Go ahead and have him follow her in."

J.T. was here. Now. He knew it in his heart.

The game was on.

And Dylan would win—absolutely, unequivocally. The only thing he didn't know was what the final price might be. There were very few things he wasn't willing to risk to save J.T.

"Jane got his wallet," Hawkins said, dropping the bomb with the barest hint of a grin curving his mouth.

Geezus. One of Dylan's eyebrows went up.

"No shit," Hawkins said, his grin widening. "When she passed him on the street, she made the lift. She thought we might like to take a look at it."

"Good girl." He was impressed. Jane Linden was a street rat from way back. She managed Katya Hawkins's upper-end art gallery, Toussi, in LoDo now, but he was damn glad to know she hadn't lost any of her old-school skills. Lifting a wallet off J.T. had to have been some kind of trick. "Where is she?"

"Almost to our front door. I just sent the elevator to bring her up to the office."

"Good. Where's everybody else?"

"Creed, Quinn, and Travis are doing rounds," Hawkins said. "I'll have them head toward seven. Red Dog and Kid took guard duty on the girl. They're up on ten with her now."

Dylan nodded. "Get a shooter on the south side of the seventh floor, whoever is closest." To put J.T. down chemically was their plan, their best bet, even after the failure of the ketamine, even with the risks involved. Half of Dylan's team was carrying .22 rimfire rifles loaded with drug darts, but they'd changed tranquilizers to Halo-Xazine, also known as Halox, if you were buying top-of-the-line brand-name stuff, and Shlox, if you were selling it on street corners to day-trippers. "Tell everybody we may be having company."

Inside the Challenger's trunk, Con felt the freight elevator come to a stop and heard the door open. By gunning the engine a few more times, Cherie the computer geek got the car to lurch into the building and across the floor until it shuddered to a stop.

Geezus. Her driving had just about made him seasick.

He waited until she got out and he heard her footsteps recede, and then he waited some more, searching the silence. One by one, she went up a flight of stairs, and when he heard a door open and close, he popped the trunk just enough to peer out.

"Alpha One, ready," he said softly into his radio.

"Copy, Alpha One." Jack's voice came back at him over the dedicated channel.

The building was cool. The lights were low. A long, slow look around revealed a couple dozen other cars, a lot of them classic American muscle, and a lot of those were Camaros. On the north end of the garage, he saw the stairs Cherie had gone up. The door at the top of the stairs was flanked by a set of large windows overlooking the cars. All of the windows were shuttered from the inside, making it impossible to see what was going on in the room behind.

After slipping out of the trunk, he kept low to the floor and moved into the shadows close to the wall. The plan was simple: Head to the tenth floor, create a diversion along the way to draw these boys down on top of him, give them all a run for their money, and when Jack had Scout out of the building, get the hell out of Steele Street and the hell out of Denver.

No one else could have done it, not the way he could do it—fast and clean and damn near risk-free. The only reason these guys had gotten to him last time was because he'd been distracted with other business, mostly the banshee bitch who had been tearing his house up with a .50-caliber rifle mounted on a gunboat and the twenty or so armed troops she'd had with her, all of them bent on destroying him. He wasn't distracted this time. The Steele Street boys had his undivided attention, and he knew where they were and what they wanted: him. Scout was just bait, a very poor choice on their part. Four days of recon had given him precise knowledge of the outside of the building and the surrounding area and a damn good idea of the layout of the inside of the building—very few windows, the freight elevators, and the cars coming and going meant work areas and warehousing on the lower floors; big windows and lots of lights on the upper floors after dark suggested living areas. He could find his way around without too many problems. As a matter of fact, he could find his way around with damn few problems.

Continuing his observation from close to the wall, he looked across the garage full of cars again. His senses were extremely acute, but he wasn't prescient, or omniscient, or any such thing, and yet . . . and yet he knew where the door under the staircase went—to a couple of storerooms and an out-of-the-way corner room with a table, a few chairs, and a refrigerator full of beer.

Looking the door over from top to bottom, he tried to place the sense of knowing, then decided it was only logical, he supposed, to have a fridge full of beer somewhere close to a garage, where guys might be working all day, someplace to go and sort through business and any personal junk that was getting in the way, a place where the gloves came off, a place to tell the truth, to put your guts on the line, to tell the guys what you really thought about the shit hitting the fan on your last mission.

Mission.

Yeah, these guys had missions, not car sales, and they had a bullpen behind the door under the staircase. It only made sense; that was all.

Holding steady up against the wall, he let his gaze track more slowly across the garage, going from Camaro to Camaro, to a badass 1970 Chevelle SS 454, cherry red with double black stripes. Another funny feeling went up his spine. He knew that car. He knew it had a 780-cfm Holley four-barrel carburetor under the hood, and he didn't care how much sense a Holley four-barrel made on a 454, he shouldn't know that. No way in hell.

He shifted his attention to the next car, and the funny feeling going up his spine got sharper, even more intense. Sleek, deep blue, so blue it was almost black, a 1967 Pontiac GTO glimmered in the low light, beckoning.

Corinna, Corinna...the words of a golden oldies song drifted across his mind. *Corinna, Corinna*...

Sweat beaded on his upper lip, and he wiped the back of his hand across his mouth.

Corinna—it was the car's name. He knew it deep down where it counted, and it unnerved the hell out of him. Who named their cars, he wondered, then instantly knew the answer.

These guys named their cars. He looked back to the Challenger, *Roxanne,* then returned his gaze to the Chevelle—*Angelina.* Next to Angelina was Charlotte the Harlot, a 1968 Shelby Mustang Cobra. He knew them all, but how?

When in the hell had he been here before?

And if he knew all these damn cars, why didn't he know the answer to that question?

He wiped the back of his hand across his mouth again, felt his pulse racing, and moved forward, out from the wall and toward the GTO. She was a beast, tough, and she gleamed with dual exhaust and red-line tires. Her windows were rolled down, and coming up on the driver's side, he leaned on the doorframe and looked around the interior of the car.

"I've got movement coming up on Corinna," Skeeter said at the same time as Dylan heard Creed in his earpiece.

"I have a shot."

"Can you positively identify the target?" he asked, speaking into his mike while walking over to his computer.

"John Thomas," Skeeter said.

"J.T.," Creed confirmed.

"Copy. Stand by."

There was a slight pause.

"Boss? I repeat. I have a shot."

Dylan heard the hesitation in Creed's voice, the hint of confusion, but he gave the same order.

"Stand by. Hold red." There were risks. The team had debated, considered, and calculated them, but the choice came down to Dylan. This early in the game, he hoped there might be another way, what Dr. Brandt at Walter Reed Medical Center had called the possibility of "memory cognition." If being in a home environment triggered any kind of memory response in J.T., and if Dylan could talk to him, explain to him that he wasn't in danger, they might be able to avoid a confrontation.

That would sure beat the hell out of the Halox. The

tests Dr. Brandt had been running on the drug had been inconclusive at best. Brandt thought the Halox would work on J.T., sedate him without doing even more harm, but he didn't *know*. He had not been able to give Dylan any assurances of how bad it might get if the drug proved toxic to someone whose body chemistry had been altered as severely as J.T.'s.

"Stand by?" Skeeter asked, her confusion more blatantly expressed in the eyeball-to-eyeball look she was giving him.

"Get Brandt on the horn. Now," he ordered. "I want him available, if we do this thing."

She immediately punched a number into the closest secure land line. "What's up?"

"Eight weeks," Dylan said. "What in the hell took J.T. eight weeks to get his ass to Denver to get the girl back? Hell, he knew exactly where we'd taken her."

"We came up with three explanations," she said without missing a beat. "A miscalculation on our part of the girl's importance to him—"

"Which we now know we got right," he interrupted her. "He's here. He wants her back."

"That he would elevate planning over expediency," she continued. "That he'd take his time to consider contingencies and recruit a team."

"Still possible."

"Or the ketamine put him down hard."

He could tell from the look on her face that she remembered just exactly how hard he had been put down by the chemical soup Souk brewed up for his Thai syringes.

"The Halo-Xazine might be a real bad deal," she continued. "We considered that, Dylan, and chose to go ahead with drugging him."

Of them all, only Red Dog had a physiology even close

to J.T.'s, and that girl couldn't take an aspirin without paying the price. So she didn't. Not ever.

"Brandt didn't think it would kill him," Skeeter reminded him.

"But it might make him wish he was dead," Dylan said, remembering all too clearly what Souk's drugs had done to him, and how to a slightly lesser extent than Red Dog it made his reactions to other drugs unpredictable. Gillian only took meds given to her by Dr. Brandt, and over the years, those meticulously researched drugs and dosages had made it easier for her to manage her physical condition.

Dr. William Francis Brandt, the doctor who'd first seen Gillian the night she'd been tortured, had made a new career for himself out of researching her and Dylan, all in hopes of being able to help them and of reproducing the drugs they'd both been given. His lab, equipment, salary, and assistants were all funded by the Department of Defense, who were banking on him to replicate Dr. Souk's ultimate warrior research while simultaneously overcoming the negative side effects, like memory loss. Dylan hadn't lost his memory, but neither had he physically become the ultimate warrior in the way that Gillian had become Red Dog.

Over the years, the good doctor and his associates had restored about ninety percent of Gillian's memory, but they'd only had nominal success in re-creating Souk's drugs, which was fine with Dylan. The last thing SDF needed was to be going up against a bunch of chemically altered superwarriors.

Like J.T., the realization came to him.

Hell. Nothing was ever easy.

The smell hit Con first, vinyl and gun oil, pizza, a trace of cola, and a chocolate bar or two. Or half a dozen, he decided, seeing the pizza box and a bunch of candy wrappers on the back floor alongside a few empty sports drink bottles and soda cans. Looking forward again, he noticed a small dent in the dash, and an unbidden grin curved his lips. That was where Danielle Roxbury had all but buried the spike heel of her size-six, silver sandal the night they'd been parked out at the...

His face suddenly felt hot. In his mind, he could see where they'd been, the midnight blue GTO pulled up next to a mile-long strip of asphalt that came from nowhere and went nowhere, a stretch of street laid down on the eastern plains, past the city limits and the suburbs, a place to race cars. And there had been cars, dozens of them from all over the Denver area, jacked-up, souped-up, ready to blast down the strip and test their drivers' mettle, racing for pink slips, cold cash, and glory.

He saw too much—the color of Danielle's blouse, silky yellow, the tightness of the skirt pushed up around her waist, the headlights of the cars racing at the other end of the dead-end street. She'd been kissing his face, kissing his mouth, and calling him by name...

For a fleeting second, her voice was so soft and wondrous, the memory painfully stark and clear—but he couldn't hear the name. He could nearly see the shape of it on her mouth, but he couldn't hear it.

Fuck. Memories were such goddamn unreliable things, dangerous things. At least his were. There'd been a few times in the last six years when he'd thought he remembered something, but none of it ever tied together. None of it had ever given him anything except a frickin' holocaust of a headache, which he could sure as hell feel coming on. He started to push away from the GTO, when a piece of paper clipped to the driver's-side visor caught his eye. He reached in and flipped the visor down, and his heart caught in his throat, hard and sudden, holding him stock-still where he stood.

The paper was a picture of three men and a car, the

photograph creased and faded where the clip held it to the visor. Corinna was the car, and a man with long blond hair, a rough-looking golden boy with a surfer's easy smile and a wicked-looking sheath knife on his belt, was leaning back against her hood—the man who'd come after Con in Paraguay. Standing next to him was a younger guy, a good-looking kid with a jarhead's haircut and a shit-eating grin. And next to the kid was a guy Con recognized without a doubt in his mind. The man was strongly built, ripped, and lean through the waist in a stark white T-shirt. His hair was dark and longer than the kid's, but not by much. Like the younger guy, he had straight, dark eyebrows and deep-set eyes. Both were broad-shouldered and tall, the same height. Both had dimples when they smiled, especially the younger one.

Both had been cut from the same cloth. And somewhere, at some time between when the photograph had been taken and now, the older one had been cut in a hundred different places and had a scar to mark every wound. Con knew who he was looking at. There was no mistaking what he was seeing, and it made his gut churn.

A brother and my life before... before he'd been butchered and put back together by Dr. Souk.

The heat in his face spread, running down his neck and onto his shoulders, sliding like water down his chest to his stomach and down his legs to his feet—but doing nothing to thaw the block of ice his heart had become. It was beating hard and slow, feeling like a half-ton weight.

This wasn't a memory. This was real, the evidence staring him in the face. He had a brother, and they'd been together in this place, standing next to the GTO, along with the guy with the blond hair and the big knife.

He pulled the photo off the visor and stared down at it in his hand, and the longer he looked at it, the tighter the knot in his stomach grew. A brother. *Geezus*. He needed to wrap his mind around that, but not now, later. He was already edging too close to his own personal disaster.

Way too damn close.

He dug in his pocket and pulled out a fistful of pills, feeling a sick twist of pain eddying into life at the base of his skull—the headache from hell. Green, blue, red, yellow, purple, orange, every color was a path to salvation. All he had to do was choose the right ones, and nobody did that better than he. Skull cracking open was best dosed with two of the red gelcaps, the gut-churning symptom of impending doom needed a yellow.

And over and over and over again, from one month to the next, from one week to the next, and especially since the ketamine, from one day to the next he needed more and more pills just to maintain the status quo.

It wasn't a good sign, and he knew it.

He picked the brightly colored red and yellow gelcaps out of his palm and tossed them in his mouth before shoving the rest back in his pocket. *Geezus*. He was so fucked. These guys knew more about him than he did, and he couldn't think of a better way to get himself killed tonight, because he would not be taken alive. Not ever, not by anyone. Been there, done that for endless eons of pain under Souk's tender care. Capture was not an option, and yet he was here, in their lair. The fools. Whatever he'd been before, he wasn't that now, not even close, and this game was played only one way: for keeps. They had Scout, and he'd come to get her back.

The tiny twist of pain in his medulla oblongata curled tighter, squeezed harder, and he closed his eyes.

Yeah, right, focus on the mission—if you can make it through the next couple of breaths. He lowered his chin toward his chest and tried to ease the pain tightening and twisting and exploding in increasingly larger bursts where his spine met his brain. Streaks of light flashed across the darkness behind his eyelids—not a good sign, but not the worst.

Then he got the worst—or damn close to it.

An elevator door opened somewhere off to his right, and he heard the sound of footsteps, of someone entering the garage.

CHAPTER FIVE

Well, hell, Jane thought, coming to a stop and looking around at all the cars parked everywhere. As far as she knew, the elevator from the main entrance only went to one floor, and this wasn't it. She was supposed to be at the main office, not in the garage, but she was definitely in the garage.

Letting her gaze slide over all the automotive muscle on display, she was impressed as hell, as usual. This was where the big bad boys kept all their biggest baddest toys.

She'd been working at the Toussi Gallery for Superman's wife for about six years or so, managing it for the last two, but other than her first unexpected visit, she'd only been inside 738 Steele Street a dozen or so times.

The place was very cool, a whole huge floor full of old Chevys, and Dodges, and Fords—*oh my*—and under any other circumstances, she'd be looking around. But she was here on a mission, and she needed to get up to the office.

Walking over toward a Mustang named Babycakes, she took her phone out of her purse to give Superman another call, let him know she'd ended up in the wrong place, when something caught her eye—movement.

Next to Corinna.

A guy—tall, dark, probably handsome, and probably

Christian Hawkins. She started toward him, reaching back in her purse and taking Conroy Farrel's wallet out, curious as hell to see what Hawkins made of it, especially when he saw the guy's photo on the Paraguayan driver's license.

"Do we have Brandt on the phone yet?" Dylan asked, making a point of not pacing.

"No, but I've got movement in the northeast quadrant of the seventh floor," Skeeter said from her console of security camera monitors. "I'm putting it up on your screen."

Dylan watched the picture appear on his computer and swore under his breath.

"Jane Linden." Skeeter identified the woman walking toward Babycakes at the same time as he did.

"Hacker!" Dylan called out to the red-haired woman huddled over a computer and a double-shot latte at the far end of the office.

Hawkins was already coming around his desk and heading for the door. "I'll go get her."

Cherie Hacker looked up over her computer with the slightly glassy-eyed gaze she got when she was deep in the guts of a program.

"Yes, boss?" she said.

"Did you shut down my elevator?" It was a rhetorical question, and he didn't wait for an answer. "Get it back up and running—now. Creed, status?" he said, keying his mike.

"I see her, Dylan." The Jungle Boy's voice was calm in his ear, smoothly steady. "She's entering the garage at two o'clock."

"Do you still have a shot?"

"Affirmative."

"Superman is coming out to get her. If J.T. moves on her..." He paused, thinking, running through his options at light speed and not coming up with anything he liked, which only left the option he didn't like.

"Say again, Dylan. I didn't copy." He heard Creed in his ear.

Geezus.

"If he moves on her...take him down."

"Affirmative."

Hell. He didn't look over at Skeeter. She knew as well as he did that the risk had to be taken.

"Status all," Dylan said, speaking to the rest of the team.

"Quinn, second floor clear, coming up to seven in the east stairwell."

"Travis, third floor clear, coming up to seven in the south stairwell." The Angel Boy gave his status and location.

"Zach here. I'm still on Wazee, and I think we've got company from the Company out here, cruising our neighborhood."

By "Company," Zach meant CIA, and that was the last damn thing they needed, but if anybody could have spotted his former employers, it was Zachary Prade.

"We have an enemy at the gate?" Dylan asked.

"Copy, Dylan, a black Mercedes."

Hell.

"Stay with them. Everyone else, stand by." He looked over at Skeeter, who was looking at him.

"What enemy at the gate?" she asked.

"CIA," he said.

"Lancaster," she countered, and Dylan knew the odds were stacked way in her favor for being right. "What do you want to do?"

It was his call. Bottom line, it was always his call, and this one, like all the others, was about percentages and odds. Dylan didn't know what the Halox might do to J.T., but he knew J.T. didn't have a chance if Lancaster got hold of him. None. Randolph Lancaster had shown his hand, and it was death and destruction. Atlas Exports proved his treason beyond a shadow of a doubt.

But he also knew Conroy Farrel, and Farrel had been outrunning and outgunning Lancaster for six years. Odds were, he could do it again today, unless they screwed him up with the Halox and it still didn't drop him hard enough for them to capture him—like what had happened with the ketamine.

"Creed," he said into his mike. "Stand by. Unless J.T. poses an imminent threat to Jane or Superman, I want you to hold red. We're going to have to bring him in the hard way."

There was another pause.

"Copy. I tried the hard way in Paraguay and got my clock cleaned."

Yeah, Dylan remembered, but in this game, nothing was ever easy.

CHAPTER SIX

Footsteps, one after the other, drawing nearer.

Female—the gender given away by the light *snap snap snap* of small, sharp heels.

Gritting his teeth, Con covered his face with his hand and leaned against the doorframe of the GTO, everything inside him resisting the disaster building in his head—the trail of pain widening and deepening and plowing a path through his skull, heading toward the soft tissue of his brain. He *would not* succumb to annihilation—*never . . . never . . . never.* Through that door lay madness.

Been there, done that, not going back.

He drew in a long breath, fighting the pain, waiting for the pills to kick in, and he listened.

She was headed straight for him.

He took another breath, and her scent hit him like a freight train, sensual, female, and feral—*wild thing,* the woman from the street, the long-haired brunette with the slinky curves and the catlike grace.

His head came up, and he opened his eyes a bare slit. White light streaked across his vision, but he could see her coming toward him—phone held to her ear, her attention on him, a half smile of recognition curving her mouth. She knew him, or thought she did, and for a single, perfectly clear moment, he had only one thought: that he wanted to know her, too. Whoever she was, he wanted the memory of her to come back to him.

And if that wasn't the kind of crap that could get a guy killed, thinking about a woman when you were in the enemy camp, Con didn't know what would.

The sound of another door opening, from above and behind the woman, had him lifting his gaze higher, away from her to a man standing at the top of the stairs leading to the offices.

"Jane!" the man called out, and with the one word, Con felt everything inside him shift. The hard, cold thing that was his heart froze solid, and he could barely breathe.

He *knew* that voice, the quality and the timbre of it. One word, four letters, *Jane*, and he was transported to a long-ago place, *this* place. The smell of oil and grease and tires, of gasoline and exhaust, the heat of summer nights and hot cars running fast, stolen cars with the thrill of the boost still jumping him up.

It wasn't just a memory, a fleeting possibility. He *knew* he'd stolen those cars, and he'd stolen them with the man at the top of the stairs and brought them here, to this place.

The woman hesitated, still looking at him, her brow furrowing in confusion before she started to turn toward the man who'd called her name.

No, Con decided, breaking into a run and pulling a concussion grenade from the inside pocket of his dark gray jacket. *Divide and conquer, confuse and overcome.*

That was the mission. That's what he'd come to Denver for—to prevail at any cost, to free Scout.

And then he was hit, a sharp, piercing pain stabbing into his arm, through his coat.

Geezus. It knocked the breath out of him, but he reacted instantly, reaching up and pulling the dart out.

Oh, shit. He glanced at the syringe barrel before tossing it away from him. Halox was written on the side, *fucking Shlox.* Another damn tranquilizer that had made a lightning-fast transition into a street drug. He didn't know what effect Halo-Xazine would have on him, but he knew it probably wouldn't be doing him any good.

Move, he told himself, *and keep moving until you drop. You can worry about the damn Halox later, if you make it out of here alive.*

He slid the pin out of the grenade and, without hesitation, lobbed it behind him to keep whoever had shot him from doing it twice. The concussion grenade landed with a blinding flash of light and an explosion of sound. He kept moving, rounding the front of the GTO, picking up speed and pulling another flash bang from his pocket and tossing it to the far end of the garage, past the woman, to land at the bottom of the stairs. His aim was impeccable, and all hell broke loose on impact with more blinding light and explosions, but no shrapnel. He wasn't going to detonate anything too damn dangerous until he knew exactly where Scout was being held or until he knew Jack had her out of the building.

Then these boys were on their own.

But not the woman.

He shot a quick glance in her direction.

No. Not the wild thing.

In all the mayhem of exploding light and deafening noise, she'd dropped to the floor and was trying to scramble back to her feet, her hands over her ears, her face stark with fear and shock.

Right. He was such a great guy—and she looked like a deer in the headlights, like she didn't know which direction to go next.

He did.

In two steps, he was by her side, lifting her off the floor, and in another two, he was back at the GTO, shoving her inside. Flash bangs wouldn't kill her, but they'd been specifically designed to disorientate and scare the hell out of people. In her case, they were doing their job, but the guy at the top of the stairs didn't look too damn fazed, and the other guy, the one coming out of the office, the one slipping a rifle sling over his shoulder, didn't look too damn scared or disorientated, either. The first guy had drawn his pistol, and both of them were moving quickly down the stairs to the garage's main floor, their faces hard set, their intentions clear.

They were looking for him, but he was already on his way out, up a staircase on the east end of the building to the tenth floor, to get Scout.

Time to rock and roll, Jack thought, hearing the explosions and raising his AR-15 carbine. He put one shot into each of the two security cameras on the near side of 738 Steele Street's roof, then, with an easy, smooth grace, slipped over the side of the Bruso-Campbell Building on the zip line. Seconds after Con's first flash bang went off, he'd crossed the alley and swung himself over the low wall on Steele Street's roof.

Con's diversion and his own speed were his two greatest assets, and Jack didn't waste time. He ran across the roof, passing an odd seating arrangement made up of a couple of old lawn chairs and a wooden crate bolted to a ragged square of Astroturf, making sure to trigger the proximity alarm before he reached the metal door that led down into the building—a very secure door.

He had his charge ready, packed it on the lock, inserted the detonator, and headed back over the side of the roof, using the collapsible grappling hook to secure his rappelling line. The building had thirteen floors, and he dropped two floors before stopping his descent just shy of the tenth-floor balcony.

"Alpha Two, ready," he said into his radio.

"Alpha One, on your count."

He could hear Con running, the sound of his boots on metal stairs, and knew the boss was heading in his direction, right on time.

"Roger," he said. With the security cameras out, once he blew the door, the Steele Street boys were going to have to come looking if they wanted to know what was happening on the roof. And while they were hunting him there, he was going to be three floors down, rescuing the one woman on the face of the earth who was guaranteed to give him hell, a long-legged, slim-hipped, mixed-race beauty with the face of an angel, a right hook to match her righteous roundhouse kick, and a jerk boyfriend from Holland named Karl.

CHAPTER SEVEN

Scout heard the first explosion from somewhere down below and knew exactly what was happening: Con.

She'd known he would come. She'd known nothing on earth would keep him from coming for her, and for eight long, grueling weeks that knowledge had been both her hope and her despair.

The second explosion came fast on the heels of the first and speeded up her already racing heart, but she didn't move from the chair where she sat at the kitchen table with her hands in her lap, her shoulders squared.

Con, dear God. She would have spared him, if she could. But he was here, and she wanted out of this place, away from the hard, awful truths she'd been forced to face.

A third explosion rocked the night, the noise and vibration coming up through the floor, but she still didn't budge, not an inch. He was somewhere in the labyrinth of car-filled garages below her. She didn't know how many floors down, but he was here—and he had no idea what he was up against.

She did.

She'd known since her capture in Paraguay, and it still left her heartbroken half the time and confused all the time.

Yeah, she knew what he was up against. She was looking right at it, and so help her God, it was looking straight back at her, standing not ten feet away, talking on a radio with a subgun slung across his chest and a .45 strapped to his thigh. His name was Peter Chronopolous, Kid Chaos, and everything Con used to be was molded in the curves and angles of the younger man's face. It was written in the sudden determination tightening his mouth, in the breadth of his shoulders and the squareness of his jaw, in the way he moved.

The similarities were inescapable, and they proved everything everyone in this damn place had been telling her, that Con was a man named John Thomas Chronopolous, J.T., Kid Chaos's older brother, and that he belonged to them.

Not to her.

Never to her.

She'd been hearing it nonstop, every day and every night in a hundred different ways from half a dozen hard men and two hard women, a blonde she might be able to take on her very best day, if the girl was in a slump, and an auburn-haired shooter she didn't think anybody except Con could take.

She shifted her attention from Kid Chronopolous to the beautiful, extremely tough woman sitting across the table from her. She was dressed in olive drab BDU pants and a black T-shirt, looking like she was ready to rumble. Her hair was short and wild, a deep chestnut-auburn with blond highlights—gorgeous, like her face.

Red Dog was her name, and she scared the hell out of Scout, not because of anything she'd done. Red Dog, also known as Gillian, had been nothing but professional, but the woman wasn't like anyone else Scout had ever known, except Con, and therein lay the second hard truth, the hardest truth of all.

"That's him, isn't it?" the female shooter said, listening, as they all were, to the explosions echoing up from below. The loft on the tenth floor was a wide-open expanse of hardwood floors over a hundred feet long and thirty feet wide. It had floor-to-ceiling windows on the north and the west sides and a gallery's worth of art adorning the inner walls.

Red Dog, Scout thought. What a name for someone with the warmest brown eyes she'd ever seen. They were amber colored, filled with compassion, full of concern, but more than once over the last two months, Scout had seen them freeze over to an unforgiving shade of cold, rusted iron. The woman was fierce, her body chiseled, and her husband was the single most beautiful man Scout had ever seen. Red Dog called him Angel, but everyone else called him Travis.

"We've been over this, Scout," the woman continued, her voice firm, with a thread of steel running through it. "The time is here, right now, today. This is your chance to help Con. Maybe the only chance you'll get."

Help him? Or betray him? That was the question that kept her up at night, and no matter how much information this crew of operators pumped into her, she still didn't know the answer.

"I know what he's been through, Scout," Red Dog said. "If you help us bring him in, I can help him. I'm a walking pharmacy for the kind of drugs that can keep him alive and help restore his memory, help him with the trauma of what the drugs he was given do to him. I've been where he is."

No, she hadn't.

No matter what Gillian/Red Dog had been through, she wasn't scarred like Con. She hadn't been tortured like Con.

"It's a miracle he's lasted this long, Scout. He's got to be on meds," the woman continued. "You must have seen him take something. What was it? What kind of drugs is he taking to keep himself alive?"

Pills, she could have told the woman, colored gelcaps, and sometimes a Syrette for pain. Scout could have given her that information eight weeks ago, the first time she'd asked, but this time, like all the others before, Scout wasn't telling her anything.

But the questions tore her up.

Con, the only person in the world she trusted, had been lying to her all these years. He'd said he needed vitamins and supplements to keep in shape, and sometimes the pain meds if his old wounds started aching and acting up. He'd never said he needed to pop up to twelve pills a day just to stay alive, to keep his blood flowing and his synapses firing. This woman said he did, that there was no other way for people like Con, not six years into his resurrection—and Scout believed her.

Resurrection. The hard truth twisted inside her. The word explained too much—not just the pills, but how he'd survived the butchery that had left him so terribly scarred. She wasn't an idiot. She'd known the pills were more important than he'd let on, but she hadn't known the truth. Con was the biggest, baddest, toughest, strongest man she'd ever met, ever known—and, according to Red Dog, his life was hanging by a thread. He couldn't last much longer, not without help.

Yes, Scout could have told the woman. He does get bad headaches, visual migraines. Sometimes his gut knots up on him. Sometimes pain takes hold of him, indescribable pain, like fire under his skin, and through it all, he pops the pills like candy, always maintaining, always self-assured, never like a man whose life could end at virtually any moment of any day.

The truth made her sweat, literally made her skin hot with flashes of anxiety.

"Are you going to help us?" the woman asked with a definite finality in her voice, reaching across the table and wrapping her hand around Scout's wrist. Her palm was callused, her fingertips rough, and she was strong—and Scout still didn't move, not a twitch, not a blink. She knew Red Dog could crush her bones in an instant if the older woman wished, but Scout was biding her time.

Con was coming, and when he breached the door, she needed to be ready. She would move then, Red Dog or no Red Dog, but until that moment, she was deliberately as passive as she could manage, trying to keep her muscles soft and her mind clear.

She needed to talk with Con. She needed the truth from him. So she sat, and waited, carefully keeping both of her guards in sight, who were returning the favor one hundred percent. She hadn't been out of at least one SDF operator's sight since her capture.

When she failed to answer the question, Red Dog turned to Kid. "What's the situation?"

"Two flash bangs in the seventh-floor garage," the tall, dark-haired man said, the radio still to his ear. Like the woman, he was dressed in BDU pants, camouflage, but his T-shirt was olive drab. "One in the office, and Skeeter's got a tripped proximity alarm on the roof. Unknown Tangos headed our way. No one got a positive ID on the guy in the garage, and the cameras are out on the roof."

"It's him," Red Dog said, the barest hint of satisfaction shading her voice.

Scout knew the woman thought she was ready for whatever happened next—more than ready. She knew the whole Steele Street crew thought they had the situation under control, that they'd covered all their bases, but no matter how much they knew about J. T. Chronopolous, they didn't know Conroy Farrel. They were expecting a man. They weren't expecting Con.

And she hadn't been expecting damn Jack Traeger, but the other unknown Tango couldn't be anybody else, which just made her wish . . . *oh, hell.*

This was going down right now.

A shadow of movement down the outside edge of one of the loft's huge windows caught her eye: Jack, half hidden by the adjacent brick wall, descending toward the loft's balcony. He was hanging from a climbing harness, his red hair sticking half on end, as wild as he was, his face and the grace of his movements as familiar to her as the breadth of his shoulders and the quickness of his mind. He had a pack on his back, a carbine slung across his chest, and a small device in one hand.

Oh, hell. She held her breath for a heartbeat, recognizing an electronic detonator when she saw one. Red Dog's hand instantly tightened on her wrist, her attention coming back full on her.

"What is it?" the woman demanded.

Scout dropped her gaze to the table, trying to keep from giving Jack away.

"You're never going to get out of here, Scout, not until we have him." Red Dog's hand tightened even more.

It was as close to a threat as the woman had gotten in eight weeks. Then she got a little closer, tightening her grip again, applying another few pounds of pressure per square inch, enough to let Scout know this was serious, that she needed to make the right decision.

Scout's gaze flashed back to the woman, ready to protest the painful grip or do something about it, if she could, and in that moment, Jack made his move. An explosion from up on the roof shook the rafters and the walls. Plaster and dust and bits of building material rained down inside the loft, and before any of it could hit the floor, Red Dog had released her and leapt for the .22-caliber rimfire rifle she'd positioned on the kitchen counter—a tranquilizer gun.

Oh, God. Oh, God. The woman was so freaking fast. She had the weapon slung up and was signaling Kid Chronopolous almost before he'd broken for the door, and he reacted damn near instantly. It all happened in a flash, the two of them moving like clockwork. When Kid disappeared through the door, Red Dog moved back toward her.

Oh, hell, no, Scout thought. No way was she letting the tough woman get hold of her again.

She whirled out of her chair, grabbing it with one hand on the back, keeping Red Dog's attention on her, not giving her even a second's chance to turn around and look out the loft window—but Jack had disappeared. He'd dropped to the balcony and moved behind the door leading into the loft.

He was going to blow it. She knew it. Jack loved blowing up stuff. She hoped like hell that he used something a wee bit smaller than what had just gone off on the roof.

Still moving, her grip tight, she brought the chair around with her, letting it pivot and rise as she got her feet under her. Kid Chaos was long gone into the hallway and no doubt flying up three flights of stairs. He'd find Jack's rappelling line quick enough. God, everybody else in the building had to be heading this way, chasing Con.

Using her momentum, she swung the chair sideways with all her strength, then released it at the apex of its arc, aiming it right at Red Dog, keeping the woman focused on her attack, on defending herself. When Jack blew the balcony door, Scout needed to get to it fast, like a bolt of lightning.

She wanted out, yes, the quicker the better, but she also couldn't let Red Dog get a shot off and knock out Jack Traeger. Oh, no. That pleasure was going to be all hers, someday soon, she swore it, if the two of them made it out of there alive. Except she'd be doing it with a right hook instead of a dope dart.

But first, he was coming in.

The explosion on the roof was still sending plaster down from the ceiling when the balcony door blew and her rescue ranger burst through, materializing out of a cloud of smoke and debris with his carbine leveled at Red Dog, a typical damn grand Traeger entrance. Scout dashed past the woman, who'd easily blocked the chair but now suddenly seemed to be frozen to the floor. Red Dog didn't make a move to stop her, and Scout didn't ask why. The tenth-floor balcony door was less than ten yards away. Escape.

Jack signaled to her that they were going over the side on his rappelling line, then pulled a flash bang off his tac vest and lofted it past her into the room.

It all made perfect sense to her—ten floors on a rope. They'd pulled the move before. They'd pulled a lot of moves and maneuvers together over the years, before they'd gotten all sixes and sevens with each other. Still running full-out, Scout gauged her timing, and she and Jack came together in a fluid slide of bodies melding into one entity bent on escape, arms coming around each other, legs leaping in rhythm for the balcony railing.

Headed over the side, she looked back, one fleeting glimpse before the grenade landed, and saw what had riveted Red Dog's attention and her rifle: Con, standing in the front doorway, his gun drawn, his gaze and the muzzle of his .45 locked on the auburn-haired shooter.

CHAPTER EIGHT

Stay down! That's what Christian Hawkins had yelled at Jane on his way out of the garage, and, sure, she could do that. As a matter of fact, her legs were too damn wobbly to do little else. And she'd scraped one of her knees raw when she'd landed on the garage floor. Her ears were ringing. Her breath was shallow, her senses reeling.

My God! It had been Conroy Farrel standing next to Corinna, not Hawkins, and that only meant one thing to her: Conroy Farrel was John Thomas Chronopolous.

J.T.—back from the dead. Her heart was pounding, and aching, and the building seemed to be coming down around her ears. The last explosion from somewhere above on the higher floors had sent a tremor racing down through the walls of the garage. Corinna had trembled, and scrunched down in the passenger seat, her hands over her ears, Jane had trembled with her.

J.T., my God. Hawkins had been in full-out kick-ass mode, his gun drawn, his war face on, and Dylan had been right behind him, a rifle to his shoulder and held at the ready.

She had to warn them. This was so awful. If one of them accidentally killed J.T., it would be too horrifying. He was alive, and she didn't understand any of it, how it could be possible. They'd buried him, but so help her

God, she'd seen him, and she'd seen the photo on the driver's license, and it was J.T. Somehow, someway, those bones in Sheffield cemetery were not J.T.'s. He was here, in Denver, trying to blow up Steele Street with hand grenades—and she didn't understand any of that, either.

Stay down, Hawkins had told her, but she needed to pull herself together and go find them, tell them who they were chasing, before disaster happened.

Still shaking, she reached for the door handle, and *hell,* another explosion sounded from up above, rocking her world one more time, and she buried herself back in the seat. *My God.* There was no getting into the middle of this business, not without making it all worse. Hawkins and Dylan wouldn't shoot J.T., she told herself, not once they saw who they were after.

But what if J.T. really is bent on destroying the building and everyone in it? The thought flashed across her mind. She'd seen him throw those grenades, and he'd looked like he knew exactly what he was doing, and if he did, then he needed to be stopped—and she didn't even want to think about that. The scars on his body hadn't come without a price, and some of the prices people paid changed them forever.

Forever and ever—and just the thought hurt. That J.T. could have come back as an enemy of the chop shop boys. She knew they'd all run wild as teenagers, stealing cars and getting into nothing but trouble, and she admitted that on some level she'd liked knowing he'd been a street kid just like her. It had made their unexpected friendship and affinity for each other more real, made what had happened that one crazy night between them less embarrassing and more of something to believe in.

She'd been wrong, and maybe she was wrong now. Maybe Conroy Farrel was a man who had been changed with plastic surgery to look like J.T. and he really was an enemy of the Steele Street crew.

Oh, God, that opened up a whole new realm of danger...and yet he'd picked her up off the garage floor and put her in the car, and in the seconds when she'd been cradled in his arms, she would swear that for the briefest moment, he'd pulled her even closer against his chest and pressed his face into her hair.

She didn't know what to think, except that she needed to get out of the damn car and do *something* to keep the situation from turning into everybody's worst nightmare. She reached for the door handle again and another damn explosion rocked the night, sending her back into the seat with a whole new game plan: *Catch my breath, stop shaking, and figure out how to get the* hell *out of 738 Steele Street.*

And now that she thought about it, wasn't she sitting in one of the fastest pieces of iron to ever come out of Detroit?

She looked and there wasn't a key—no such luck. But there were plenty of wires under the steering column.

Moving quickly, she opened her zebra bag and started looking for the knife she always carried: a pearl-handled, four-inch frame lock with a partially serrated blade.

Con entered the tenth-floor loft and locked in on the woman standing in the middle of the room: *Five feet five inches. One hundred and fifteen pounds of female curves and hard muscle. Auburn hair, blond streaks. Glacial, calculating stare, and a .22-caliber rimfire rifle perfect for delivering tranquilizer darts.*

Dangerous.

And staring down the muzzle of his Wilson Combat .45, she had to be thinking the same thing about him.

He saw no reason to kill her. Scout and Jack were clean away, with the concussion part of Jack's flash bang still echoing in the air. The woman hadn't flinched during the explosion, which took more than nerves of steel. It had taken a lightning-fast process of sequential logic: She would have already been informed of the flash bang explosions in the garage and figured out that a team working together to rescue Scout Leesom would be using more of the same, not throwing fragmentation grenades at each other.

So she'd held her ground, and in the same heartbeat that it had taken for him to assimilate all the information, he stepped back out the door and started down the hallway.

Her first tranquilizer dart sailed past less than an inch from his arm. She was fast, but not fast enough, not against him. He could hear the two men following him round the landing between the ninth and tenth floors, and judging from their speed, he had half a minute to come up with an alternate route.

He chose the door across the hall. It wasn't locked, and as soon as he was inside, he understood why. There wasn't anything inside the room, not even a whole floor, and where there wasn't any floor, there were trees growing up from the level below, tropical trees.

He didn't hesitate.

He knew where he was going, and that was *down.* He swung himself through the hole in the floor, with the trunk of one of the trees at his back. He felt a tug at his ear, knew he'd lost his radio earpiece and mike, and dropped into a jungle—plants everywhere, the loamy scent of soil, the soft heaviness of humidity, and somewhere, the sound of a waterfall, the rush of noise, the splashes, the swirling eddies, and the lapping of the water up against the tile edges of the pool.

Yeah, he knew the rock-faced water feature, remembered welding the frame, the heat of the molten metal, the brightness of the sparks through his welding mask, the craziness of the idea from the get-go, a waterfall on the ninth floor of their old building—but he wasn't taking delivery on any more goddamn memories. His bucket was full, and if he wanted to get out of this place, he needed to stop remembering and keep moving.

He was out the door and heading down the hall to the stairwell when he heard the woman shout at the two men to go back down. Then Con heard her drop into the jungle behind him.

Tough girl. He almost grinned. Most men thought twice about taking him on. But this girl was fast and unafraid to use her advantage, even if it meant going up against him alone. Those two guys who'd followed him up the stairs were seconds behind her. He could break her in half before they caught up.

He hit the stairs and vaulted over the rail to make the landing below, and he kept going. When he reached the seventh floor, he heard the sound of someone coming softly and quickly up from below. So he bailed on seven, leaving the stairwell and entering the garage where he'd first come in, keeping close to the wall, all his senses on high alert, searching for threats, and suddenly there were plenty.

He saw a rifle leveled at him from one of the office windows, another damn dart gun, the shooter concealed behind the wall. The auburn-haired woman chasing him had stopped at the entrance to the garage. Behind her, the first two guys were almost to the seventh floor, and from the other direction, the other person coming up the stairs. Five shooters and looters—and then two more, sliding through the shadows on the far side of the garage.

And suddenly that was a few shooters too many, with more than half of them armed with tranquilizer guns.

Oh, hell, he knew what they wanted—to put him down with another dart of dope—and he couldn't let it happen, not while he had a breath left in him. Ketamine or Halox, he had a feeling it didn't matter which one they hit him up with. The damn Monkey Morphine had almost killed him last time, and Shlox was bound to do the same.

He hadn't stopped running since he'd seen Jack and Scout go over the balcony up on ten, and he didn't stop now—and he never once pulled the trigger on his .45. With an eight-round magazine, he could have had them all, but probably not without taking return fire.

And besides, the two guys on the edge of the shadows looked startlingly familiar, startlingly alike—tall, lean, and mean, with longish blond hair and the same pale-colored eyes, the same shape to their faces. One of them had been in Paraguay. Con had fought with the guy, and in a split second of comparison, he knew which one—the man on the left, the one with the rougher looks, the harder edges, and the bitching long knife sheathed on his belt. The man pictured in the photograph he'd taken out of the GTO. It was the same face, but with some years added on.

Yeah. That guy was a fighter, fierce, and so were the other six operators with him in the garage. They had Con covered on three sides, which only left him one way out: the way he'd come in, through the freight elevator door.

From one tenth of a second to the next, he changed direction, running down through the line of cars, and then an engine fired up, a rich, deep, rumbling roar of horsepower and headers. The sound filled the garage, and it was easy to see which beast was shaking.

Corinna, Corinna.

Con didn't hesitate. He took the fastest available escape, rounding the rear end of the GTO and reaching for the door. He jerked it open and instantly saw the woman leaning over from the passenger seat, under the steering column.

"Move over," he commanded, because it was faster

than ordering her to get out and waiting for her actually to manage the deed.

She jerked up at the sound of his voice, which got her out from under the steering column, and he slid into the driver's seat. Her hair was wild, her eyes wide, her face stark with shock and more than a trace of fear.

Just like the last time she'd seen him, he thought with a fleeting weariness. She had a knife in her hand, and after throwing the car into first gear, he disarmed her and closed the blade. It was all one motion, and it was over before she had a chance to realize that he was hijacking her ride.

Just as well.

She'd done her job, and done it damn well, hot-wiring the Pontiac. The rest was up to him.

He shoved the knife in his pants pocket, working the pedals and the gear shift, and spun the car's steering wheel. The tires squealed and smoked. The freight elevator door was dead ahead, and in a flash, he got a memory he could use: The elevator worked off a pressure plate twenty feet from the door. Drive over it, the door opened. The old contraption on the other side of the building was all levers and cables, but the new one they'd installed was high-tech.

They. Them. The other guys. Us.

Perfect.

He'd been stretched pretty thin of late, and this place was crashing down around him from the inside out, starting with the city of Denver and ending here on Steele Street.

He heard shots, and when he checked the rearview, he saw the auburn-haired woman and one of the blond men break for a gold GTO, another 1967 like Corinna. The dark-haired guy from the stairs, the one who'd yelled "Jane," was running for the Sublime Green Challenger Con had ridden in on, and the other blond guy from the shadows was making his break for a red 1970 Chevelle with black racing stripes and that big 454 under the hood.

So this was going to be a race—but not much of one. He had the fast elevator to the street all locked up, which left everybody else either to wait in line or use the gothic contraption.

Corinna rode over the pressure plate. The door slid open, and Con hit the clutch and worked the brakes, letting the beauty roll into place. The elevator controls were easily reached through the open driver's-side window. Con punched GROUND FLOOR, checked the rearview mirror, and time stopped.

It stopped like the cut of a knife—suddenly wounding, brutally deep. It took his breath, and for a split second, it lifted the veil between *Then* and *Now.*

Peter—running into the garage and stopping to stare at the escaping car, his chest heaving, his breath coming hard.

Kid Chaos—the name Con had given the boy, something to toughen him up. *Geezus,* he'd been such a little nerd. But like all the others, the whole Steele Street crew, he'd been worth saving time and again... *and again... and again.* Forever and always.

Con's heart wasn't cold now. It was on fire, burning with an ache he didn't know how to control, his gaze meeting his brother's and the instant connection revealing all that used to be.

Yes. The word and the feeling welled up inside him, filling him with a painful longing.

Yes.

Then, with a *whoosh* of sound, the solid metal door fell back into place, closing him off from the garage and taking the younger man from his view. Immediately, the elevator started its rapid descent. The loss twisted inside him, bringing his hand up to his chest, but with each floor they dropped, the memory grew softer, the pain lessened.

Out of sight, almost out of mind, he thought, like so many of his memory jolts, and when the elevator stopped with a small shudder and the door opened on the ground floor, he was out of 738 Steele Street.

Hand back on the wheel, Con gunned the engine, and Corinna rolled onto the street, sliding into a break in the traffic.

Working the car up through her gears, he shot a glance across the interior of the car to the woman still perched sideways in the passenger seat—Jane, a plain, homespun name for a very exotic creature. Her mouth was slightly parted, as if she'd been taken by surprise, which he could guarantee she had been. Hell, *he'd* been taken by surprise. Her eyes were still wide and stark with shock, and he didn't blame her for that, either. She didn't look like she'd caught her breath yet, let alone figured out her current situation.

He could have saved her the effort. He was the guy in charge. He'd tell her what her situation was in just a second, maybe two, just as soon as he finished easing through his own latest shock.

Peter. His kid brother, Kid Chaos.

Geezus, he couldn't go back in the building. He'd just gotten out. The rescue had gone exactly as planned, and now he and Jack and Scout had a plane to catch. This whole trip down memory lane could be dealt with later, like in Paraguay, or maybe he should pull rank and reroute the endgame to Bangkok. Denver had turned out to be far more complicated than he could have predicted, and Thailand was a lot farther away than Paraguay. He didn't want anyone to be able to "reach out and touch" Scout ever again. Once she was out of the country and safe, the plan was for him and Jack to come back, a forty-eight-hour turnaround max, to get right back on the trail and follow these SDF dogs back to their master. Like all the hunters who had come after him before, he didn't have a doubt in his mind that SDF was taking orders from Randolph Lancaster, whether they knew it or not.

Yeah, the rescue mission had gone exactly as planned—except for the wild thing.

Get rid of her—that was the only answer. The Quick Mart would do, or he could get a little distance between him and Steele Street. Drive for a few miles, get into the suburbs somewhere and hit the eject button on the GTO: a quick slam on the brakes and an order to get out. Given her day so far, his biggest problem was making sure she didn't hurt herself scrambling out of the car and away from him.

Hell. Since when had kicking beautiful women out of his life become his modus operandi?

Too long ago to remember was the sad truth.

He gave her another quick glance and caught her watching him with an unnerving intensity, her still-startled gaze unabashedly holding his, her pale green eyes locking onto his own, as if she couldn't believe what she was seeing.

He didn't blame her. He was a mess. He knew it and had made a point of not spending too much time trying to imagine what had happened to him before he'd woken up in Souk's prison laboratory.

Jungle girl Jane had to be imagining plenty.

Looking back out the windshield, he tightened his hands on the wheel and shifted down into second gear to make a turn southwest on Blake. Forget getting a few miles between him and Steele Street. He was taking her straight to the Quick Mart.

"Don't worry," he said, putting the car back up into third after rounding the turn. "I'm dropping you off at the next block."

“I-I’m not worried.” Her voice came from the other side of the car, a little shaky but clear.

Right. Not worried. Just scared half senseless. Well, it wasn’t going to last much longer. He could see the Quick Mart up ahead on the right. There was traffic filling all three lanes of Blake, but none of the cars he’d seen at Steele Street were on his ass yet, and that was good. It wouldn’t take them long, though. The drop needed to happen fast, and he needed to get the hell on his way to the Star Motel, a dump up on the north end of Denver, his and Jack’s rally point.

With a smooth turn of the steering wheel, he sidled Corinna up to the curb in front of the convenience store.

“Get out” was the order—clean, simple, direct, with absolutely no room for misunderstanding.

“No” was her answer.

Which set him back a bit.

No?

What the hell did that mean?

“Get out of the car,” he said, elaborating a little, in case in all the confusion of the last few minutes, she was still struggling with shock.

“No,” she repeated, her voice even clearer than before.

His hands inadvertently tightened on the wheel. He didn’t have time for this. He really didn’t. He flicked his gaze up to the rearview mirror and, when it came back to her, found himself staring down the barrel of a Bersa Thunder .380.

“Turn off the car,” she said. “W-we’re staying here. W-we’re going to wait for Hawkins.”

Good girl. She had a plan, and a gun to back it up. He was impressed, but not with the plan and not with the .380. To his way of thinking, when it came to pistols, even hothouse-gorgeous, long-legged, slinky brunettes wearing a minidress should be carrying a .45, just because that's the way things ought to be. But she'd drawn down on him, and done it damn fast, which pretty much put *her* in the driver's seat for the next couple of nanoseconds, no matter where his butt was sitting, and he was impressed as hell.

He liked tough girls, even if she wasn't tough enough to take him on.

In a move so smooth she couldn't have seen it coming, even if he'd told her what he was going to do, he took her gun the same way he'd taken her knife. A lot of guys could have done it, but not a lot of guys could have done it without hurting her.

He didn't want to hurt her.

But he did want her out of his car. He checked the gun's safety, put it in his jacket pocket, and then looked up into the rearview mirror again.

"You're running out of—" *Oh, hell.* The green Challenger had just turned the corner, two blocks back.

He spun the wheel and popped Corinna's clutch, getting back into traffic, and when he saw the gold GTO pulling up to the corner at Wynkoop and 15th ahead of him, he had only two words for Jane.

"Buckle up."

CHAPTER NINE

Jack had spent four long days and three even longer nights up on the roof of the Bruso-Campbell Building formulating his plan, testing it out in his mind, going over it and over it, until he'd had all the kinks worked out—all the kinks, except this one.

Geezus. He wouldn't have had the balls for this kink, even if he had dreamed it up. Or maybe fantasized was the more accurate word, because, baby, this was as close to his favorite forbidden fantasy as he'd ever gotten, the fantasy that made him glad Con couldn't read his mind, the one where he was plastered up against Scout, hip to groin, her long legs tangled with his, her bodacious breasts pressed against his chest, her beautiful, wondrous face so close he could have kissed her.

And in another world, some alternate reality in a galaxy far, far away, he might have kissed her, but not here, with the Denver skyline falling away above them and twilight descending, sending shadows streaking across her face. They were jammed into a corner of Steele Street's gothic freight cage with a red 1970 Chevelle with black racing stripes taking up most of the space and a good damn bit of the breathable air.

He still had his arm around Scout's waist from their drop over the side, and he was painfully aware of exactly how careful he was being to keep his touch impersonal, to keep from holding her the way he wanted to hold her, the way he *needed* to hold her.

A hundred feet—that's how much rappelling line he'd brought to the party, enough for them to drop six floors to the old freight elevator. There was no top to the cage, so he and Scout had landed right on the lift's platform, where he'd planned to spend a couple of seconds unhooking the rope from his harness before they climbed down to the street. But two seconds had proven to be a second and a half too long. They'd no sooner landed than the garage door into the building had opened up and the Chevelle had roared in and come to a sudden, screeching halt.

He and Scout had melted back into the shadows so fast, the guy in the car hadn't noticed. He knew this because the guy in the car hadn't gotten out and tried to shoot his ass. It was dark. They'd been on the near side of the lift, where none of the interior light reached, and they were now laminated together, squeezed behind a support beam in the corner off the car's rear bumper, both of them being as damned invisible as they could get.

They were good at it, with him mostly in black and gray and Scout about the same in a two-tone olive drab/charcoal gray T-shirt and a pair of gusseted dark cargo pants. Stillness, that was the key, and they'd both gone mannequin.

Except Scout's heart was racing, her breath coming fast and shallow, and she was shaking, a low-level trembling she couldn't seem to control—but man, she'd nailed the escape without missing a beat.

"*Jack,*" she whispered his name, and he gave a short nod, letting her know he'd heard her and was ready to receive whatever information she was ready to give.

"*Jack . . .*" A short sob escaped her, and every cell in his body went on instant alert. This wasn't about intel.

When she sobbed again and her hand tightened on his waist, he instantly went into caveman mode, protecting what was his, pulling her in close, lamination-level close, and holding her tight. Scout crying?

Fuck. What had those bastards done to her?

They would die for it. He knew that damn much.

"Scout? What happened?" He was thinking the worst, so help him God. "Whatever they did, baby, you're safe now," he whispered a promise he could keep. "I'm here. I've got you."

And she whacked him, a solid torso hit. "You're *never* here. That's the damn problem."

True, but *geezus*. He'd just blown up a building and thrown himself over the side of it for her.

She hit him again, but it was halfhearted at best, and then she crumpled against him, holding him like she wasn't ever going to let him go.

Which would be damn fine by him. He'd been ready for her for a long time.

Too ready.

"I'm sorry," he whispered. "Sorry I wasn't with you in Paraguay. You and Con needed me, and I was—"

"His name isn't Con," she broke in, her words harsh in his ear, her hands tightening on his waist.

The news set Jack back on his heels—not that he hadn't been expecting it for years. Hell, he'd been looking for the boss's real name since the day they'd met.

"What do you know?" he asked. If she had a name, everything changed.

"He has a brother, here, at Steele Street, and a whole family, a father, aunts, uncles, cousins," she said through her tears. "He has a past, Jack, and it's here, in Denver."

Okay, that was great, really great, if it was true. All over the world, no matter the job at hand, the three of them had always been looking for clues to Con's past, and maybe Scout had fallen into the mother lode. Maybe.

"He was a Marine, like my dad, Recon."

And that explained a lot.

"They told me his name is J. T. Chronopolous."

Geezus. For something they'd wanted for so long, the name was surprisingly hard to hear.

"Sounds like you had a helluva eight weeks."

She nodded, still trembling.

"Okay," he said, moving ahead with the plan. "Let's get out of here, and then we'll figure out what to do."

She nodded again and, to his everlasting disappointment, pulled away. He wasn't surprised. She got only about an inch of distance, but he felt every long millimeter of it.

Yard after rattling creaking yard, the elevator ground its way down to the alley with the car rumbling and shaking. In all the diversionary tactics he and Con had gone over, there hadn't been one that included a mass exodus of Steele Street's classic muscle cars, but he noticed when, besides the Chevelle in the cage with them, another big-block monster, a midnight blue GTO, tore down the street. Moments later, another automotive street machine streaked past—the green 1971 Challenger the redhead had driven to the Quick Mart.

So where was everybody going? he wondered. For reinforcements? Or was it total surrender, an out-and-out retreat?

A small eternity of her silent tears later, they slid by the third floor, and he stifled an exasperated groan. The lift was taking for-fricking-ever, and he'd just about reached his maximum Scout Leesom saturation point, had about all he could take of breathing her in, of feeling her sadness and not being allowed to help. She owned the word "tomboy," but she smelled like a girl, felt like a girl. Worst of all, when they were this close, even with that damn inch between them, she felt like *his* girl.

And his girl was wound tight, the tension rolling off

her in waves, and, more than likely, a boatload and a half of it was directed at him. There were a few things he didn't know about her, like how she looked in a dress. But he knew how she felt about him: angry, day in and day out. It wore at him. The last time they'd been in the same room had been the day she and Con had come down to the Florida Keys to drag him back into the fold—his last great failed escape.

What had that woman's name been, the blonde's? he wondered, watching a white 4 painted on the fourth-floor garage door slowly disappear above them.

Ah, Maggie, it came to him. That was right.

A big white numeral 3 slid into view, and the lift kept descending, and still neither of them moved.

Well, Maggie didn't know how close she'd come to finally getting him banished forever. Scout had been so tight-jawed furious with him. And all he'd been doing was trying to forget her.

It never worked. Never.

For a moment, no more, he closed his eyes and inhaled the scent of her hair, let it fill his senses, but he didn't move. He didn't spread his fingers wider across the small of her back. He didn't pull her back in closer to him.

Closer into love, closer into inevitable disaster.

There was no winning, not here, not between them.

He'd tried to forget her hundreds of times, thousands, sometimes with another woman, most times just with the sheer adrenaline rush of living as far out on the edge as he could get. So he took jobs even Con walked away from, and he took chances no sane man would hazard, and he did his damnedest not to cross her path.

But here he was again, crossed every which way he could get and as close as he'd ever been.

The freight cage rolled past the second-floor garage door with its big painted 2, and a heightened sense of readiness passed through Scout to him. He understood.

He was ready, too. He couldn't have her, but he could get her out of Steele Street and out of Denver.

The elevator finally came to a grinding halt in the alley, and the Chevelle took off like a bat out of hell, all smoke and tires and rumbling exhaust. Scout was only half a second behind the car, bolting for the cage door, when he grabbed her and held her back.

"Wait," he said softly, his attention caught by a black Mercedes sedan slowly turning the corner up 19th at Wynkoop. The car was crawling along, making the rest of the traffic go around it. The back window was about a quarter of the way rolled down.

He didn't know the car, but he knew the pale blue gaze and the leonine head of white hair of the man in the backseat. Scout would, too. The mission room in Con's flat in Bangkok was plastered with images of the man: Randolph Lancaster, the spymaster.

Geezus Kee-rist. He tightened his grip on Scout and saw her shift her attention to the street and pick up on the Mercedes—and he felt her moment of recognition.

The window rolled up, and the sedan pulled to the curb. A man got out, not Lancaster, but a real piece of work named Rick Karola. At least that was the name he went by now. Who knew what his name used to be? Not Con, and not Jack, but Jack would bet that Lancaster knew the guy's former name, rank, serial number, and to the dollar what he'd been worth when the spymaster had chosen him to headline an Atlas Exports invoice.

Things hadn't gone so well on that deal, and Karola had ended up as a short-term memory lab rat with a storage capacity of about two weeks' worth of current data, enough to get a job done. He was a big, blond, rawboned guy with a butch haircut wearing a light gray suit. His eyes always had a certain vacancy in them, but he was supremely tough, hard as nails, and Lancaster held his leash. Jack had gone up against him twice, but being as how the last time had been over a year ago, odds were that old Rick wouldn't remember him, the poor slob.

But there was no sense in pushing his luck.

"Come on," he said, moving Scout forward, his hand still around her arm. They needed to get out of the alley and away from Steele Street as quickly as possible. Even with all those cars leaving, there were still people in the building who would want Scout back and his head on a pike. The unexpected, unprecedented addition of Lancaster and his goons to the party made it even more imperative that he and Scout exfiltrate *inmediatamente.*

Geezus. Lancaster out in the open. Jack could see his and Con's original plan of getting on a plane to Paraguay going up in smoke. This was a rare and golden opportunity for some major mayhem, for final justice. Con's personal hit list of some of the worst scum on the planet had been whittled down over the last few years. Tony Royce, an ex-CIA spook Con remembered showing up at Dr. Souk's Bangkok lab and spending way too much time staring at him and Garrett Leesom like they were rats in a cage, was dead. Erich Warner, the obscenely wealthy, psycho German underworld drug dealer who'd bankrolled Dr. Souk's experiments, and his bitch-girl bodyguard, Shoko, were dead. The demented Dr. Souk was deader than a doornail, his brains blown out by someone in Washington, D.C., which left Randolph Lancaster as the last loose end. The whole twisted, evil enterprise named LeedTech would disintegrate without Lancaster at its head.

And then maybe Con could rest. He needed it, especially if Scout's intel turned out to be true. Everything would change then. Jack knew Scout had been on the boss's case to slow down, to back off the mission a bit, maybe even take on an extra operator. But she was wrong. An extra operator wasn't going to turn this trick, and Con wasn't about to slow down or back off while Randolph Lancaster was doing his dirty deeds. No matter what he needed, the boss knew what he had to do: Step up and move fast before everything unraveled.

Because, baby, things *were* unraveling, and nothing faster than Con. *Geezus.* Jack saw it, had been seeing it for a while, and maybe that was another reason he'd been on the run.

Maybe he didn't want to be there when the end came.

Maybe he didn't want to watch it happen and know there wasn't a damn thing he could do to stop it—no grand heroics, no last-minute coming to the rescue.

No way to watch Scout's heart break.

So he'd been steering clear, keeping busy, and staying as far away as he could get—until these Steele Street boys had taken her.

Hell. He was back in now, deeper than he'd ever been, because there was no walking away after seeing Lancaster on the street. Even with Dr. Souk dead, the bastard was still running his LeedTech enterprise, using a knockoff lab in Bangkok and, from what Jack and Con had been hearing these last few months, coming up with some pretty weird stuff, altered warriors who made Karola's life look like a cakewalk.

He needed to be stopped.

The minute he and Scout were out of the cage, she moved away from him, which was to be expected, but it still demoralized him, like he needed more of that. He turned away from Karola, keeping a steady walking pace—until a man stepped into the other end of the alley.

He and Scout both ambled to a stop, and he reached down and took a pack of cigarettes out of a cargo pocket on his pants. After knocking one a little ways out of the pack, he offered it to her and produced a lighter out of his other pocket.

"Sam Walls," she said, wiping the tears off her face before taking the cigarette and bending over his hand for a light.

She was right.

Sam Walls, lowest of the low, another lab reject Lancaster had taken into his personal stable of wetwork wonders. This guy had been around for a long time. Despite his muscular build, the man had a squirrelly look about him, his dark hair a little long, a little greasy, his nose too thin, his jaw too weak. Sam had a great memory and a bum leg he'd gotten during some reconstruction work in Bangkok that hadn't gone his way. It made him slow but not stupid, whereas Karola was stupid but not slow.

They made a helluva team.

So did he and Scout.

"Karola," she said, and even without the question being spoken, he agreed. Of the two assholes moving in on the alley, he'd rather take on Karola.

"You want to be my drunk girlfriend?" he asked softly.

Her answer was to stumble and lean into him.

"You som-va-va-bitch!" she yelled, and let fly with one of her fists.

He grabbed her close, and caught her fist before she could land a good blow.

"All right, all right," he said, annoyed as hell and making sure not to keep his voice down. "You wanna drink yourself sick and throw up all over yourself, *fine*. Do it. But not on my dime, babe."

"Not your babe!" She dropped her cigarette and swung at him again, and with all the visible disgust he could muster, he started hustling her back the other way, heading toward Rick Karola.

"The hell you're not," he said, lengthening his stride

and half lifting her off her feet to make sure she kept up. "I own you, *babe,* and you're going home."

"Not your babe!" She tried to pull away, and he jerked her in even closer.

There were people on both sides of the street ahead of them, filling the sidewalks, and plenty of traffic, and Jack didn't hesitate to call out.

"Tommy!" he hollered, lifting his free hand to wave, his gaze focused past Rick Karola, out of the alley, while still keeping the guy in sight. "Joe! Hey, guys! Wait up!"

Coming off the sidewalk and heading into the alley, Karola angled himself toward the opposite side of where Jack and Scout were walking out. Jack would have done exactly the same thing. The last thing a guy with a job to do needed was to get involved with a couple of drunks stumbling along having a domestic dispute, especially if they had friends, also possibly drunk, hanging in the wings. It wasn't an insurmountable mess, if one of the drunks was your target. If they weren't, it was just a mess.

Jack had a gray Buick Regal parked in a garage two blocks over, and the plan had been to head to the rally point, the Star Motel in one of the northern suburbs, where they'd meet up with Con and the three of them would wait out the night. The flight to Paraguay left at seven a.m.

Lancaster changed all that.

He and Scout needed to light somewhere long enough to contact Con and come up with a new plan and see what the boss wanted to do with her intel.

"Karola!" he heard Walls yell behind them, from the far end of the alley. "It's fucking Traeger and the girl! Stop them! Wake up, man!"

Too late.

Scout was already breaking into a run, and even with crowds of people in her way, she'd be impossible to catch. The girl was quick, and Jack was right behind her, guarding her six.

At the end of the block, they rounded the corner, and Jack tagged her on the shoulder. She understood and ducked into the next doorway, a coffee shop Jack knew had a helluva double-shot latte and a small courtyard out back with a gate opening onto a private parking lot for some high-end condos. The alley driveway into the lot emptied out onto Wynkoop Street.

Once inside the coffee shop, they started down the east wall, both of them checking the street through the shop's windows. They were almost to the door to the courtyard, when Jack came to a sudden stop. A smile instantly curved his mouth, and he reached for Scout, stopping her, too—*yes!* Con had jacked a Porsche, about an '88, flat black and good-looking. He was idling in the turn lane at the light... *except*...

Jack's smile faded, and an odd, disconcerting confusion took its place. He kept his hand on Scout's shoulder and his eyes on the man driving the Porsche.

It wasn't Con.

And the implications of who the younger man was crashed into Jack's brain in one crystal-clear moment of understanding.

Geezus. For another moment, and then two, it was hard to breathe. The man Jack was looking at changed everything.

Everything.

"His name is Peter Chronopolous," Scout said at his side. "They call him Kid Chaos."

Kid Chaos, geezus. Jack couldn't take his eyes off him. He looked so much like Con, except younger, not so abused, not wounded, but just as tough, if that was even possible.

"I've been staking out the building for four days and haven't seen this guy." And they both knew he was better than that. He and Con had fucking *observed* the building, and they'd taken note of everyone's comings and goings.

"He's been with me 24/7."

Not exactly what Jack had wanted to hear.

"He's the biggest selling point they've got for their plan," she continued.

"Which is?" He had a feeling he wasn't going to like this next bit of conversation either.

"They want him back, Jack, and they want me to deliver him."

He'd been right. He didn't like that idea, no way in hell.

"Chronopolous," he said. It was a Greek name, and, yeah, he guessed he could see some Greek in Con, Greek like Achilles, a warrior for the ages.

"John Thomas," she said. "That's what the J.T. stands for in Con's real name. He was born here, raised here, and, according to them, stole a helluva lot of cars here."

He brought his hand to his chest, and for another long moment, it was hard to breathe. John Thomas Chronopolous. This was it then, the end, one way or another.

"So you've been looking at this guy for two months."

"Yeah."

"And his story hangs together?"

"Yeah," she said, her voice so soft, he could barely hear her.

He understood. Eight weeks of being with Con's younger brother and having to accept that everything you knew about the man was different now would take the stuffing out of anybody.

It sure as hell was taking the stuffing out of him.

The light changed. The Porsche made a U-turn, heading back the way it had come, and Jack returned his gaze to the woman at his side.

She was so beautiful, her skin the creamiest, softest color, like café au lait, her eyes so green, a dark, rich color to match the lushness of her wild mane of chestnut brown hair.

Pure tomboy and all girl, that was his Scout.

What was going to happen to her?

She didn't want him. She'd made that much clear. Most of the time, she didn't even want him around, and she'd made that pretty damn clear, too.

So how was he going to be able to help her after Con was gone?

He didn't have a clue.

Finding this Kid Chaos guy wasn't going to change what was happening to the boss. Jack knew more about what had gone on in Dr. Souk's lab than he liked to remember or admit, and no one who'd been in the cages was going to see their birthright of days—no way, nohow. Souk's drugs were insidious, abominations, and they dealt an early death.

Shit. Knowing it all these years and having to face it were two different things, and having to face it hurt. Con had saved him, and there wasn't a way on God's green earth for him to return the favor.

A man shoving his way through the people on the sidewalk caught Jack's attention. It was Karola. Without a word, he gave Scout's shoulder a gentle squeeze, and they both slipped out the coffee shop's back door and into the falling darkness of the Denver night.

CHAPTER TEN

"So much for the Halox," Dylan said, then spoke into his radio mike. "Kid, are you back in the building yet? Zach, give me your status."

Yep, Skeeter thought. *So much for the fricking Halox.*

"I think J.T. might have actually liked the new drug," her husband continued. "Do you copy, Zach?"

Yep, she did, too.

She was standing in the middle of the seventh-floor garage, looking across rows and rows of great American muscle cars, her gaze fixed on the high-tech garage door where Corinna, Roxanne, and Coralie had just disappeared. Angelina had gone down in the old elevator, but Skeeter didn't have a doubt that Creed would catch up to the rest of them with the Chevelle. Kid had been the last one out in Nadine, his Porsche, but Dylan had turned right around and jerked that boy's chain hard, telling him to get his butt back to Steele Street. Somebody had to stay in the building, and Dylan wanted Kid close. If things went bad out there, she knew Dylan didn't want any showdown to be brother against brother. None of them did.

The garage smelled of burned rubber and exhaust—and frustration. A ton of frustration.

"Did we do anything right?" her beloved commander asked.

"No." She wasn't going to sugarcoat anything for him, ever.

His attention shifted away from her, and she could tell he was listening to his radio.

"Copy, Kid," he said. "Check the freight elevator. Red Dog thinks Scout and her partner used it for their escape."

Quinn was finishing a perimeter check of the seventh floor. Red Dog had reported another man on Con's rescue team, a younger guy, fast, skilled, and armed to the teeth. He'd gotten away with the girl, rappelling over the side of the building—which was one more failure to add to the day.

Hell.

"Copy, Zach." Dylan was still on his headset, and after another long moment, he signed off with an order for Prade to stay with the CIA's car. He caught Skeeter's gaze and swore once, very softly, very vehemently, then he put Zach's intel out on the air for the rest of SDF to hear. "A Company car, a black Mercedes, just dropped off one of their assets at our back door. We've identified him as Sam Walls, five eleven, strong build, dark hair, brown jacket, khaki pants. He has a limp. The vehicle is cruising around the block. Do not let it get anywhere near Corinna or our target. Until we can identify the occupants of the Mercedes, no undue force is authorized. For those of you who were not on the seventh floor five minutes ago, we now have a hostage situation. Jane Linden was in Corinna when the car left the building."

If there was going to be any worse news than that, Skeeter didn't want to hear it. Despite the way she looked, Jane was a tough girl, street tough, but J.T. was a complete unknown, his memory gone. She'd seen him, had him dead to rights in the sights of her .22, and hadn't taken the shot, something telling her that two shots of Shlox was one too many. She would rather he'd gotten away. She would just rather he'd gotten away without Jane. Lancaster was her target, and with SDF going after Lancaster, they could—

She suddenly grew very still, the lights seeming to dim as a veil of shadow slid along the edge of her consciousness, cold and malevolent, luring her attention away from the hustle of the garage and the sound of Dylan's voice.

She shivered but held steady, her senses instantly alert, her mind searching for what was out there.

Lancaster, she thought, not knowing what else it could be triggering her psyche, not knowing where greater evil could lie than with what he'd done to so many and, for her, especially what he'd done to J.T.

The instant passed, but her readiness held at a higher level. Extrasensory perception was a natural part of her awareness, sometimes proving useful, more often than not proving to be a scramble of meaning that didn't become clear until long after the fat lady had sung and everybody had gone home.

She'd see how it turned out this time. They'd just found out that Sam Walls was out there. She'd put money on Lancaster being in that Mercedes—and she was guessing it was their presence she'd felt so profoundly.

"Copy, Creed," Dylan said, still talking into the radio mike. "Everybody get that?"

"What?" she asked.

"Creed's picked up a tail," he repeated for her.

Cripes.

"We need to know how many players Lancaster has on his team," she said. Whether he was here in Denver or not, he'd have more than one guy working the mission.

"And we're going to find out. Quinn." Dylan raised his voice and gestured for SDF's all-American jet jockey.

"Take Kid and go get the gimpy spook off our street. Be careful with him. Zach remembers him from a couple of undercover ops with the drug cartels in Colombia."

From across the garage, Quinn stopped and picked something off the floor, looked it over, then took a couple more steps and picked up something else.

"Hey, boss," he said, jogging back over to where she and Dylan were standing. He handed them a wallet and a phone. "Looks like Christmas came early. See you in ten."

Dylan kept the phone and handed the wallet to her. "Tell me what J.T.'s been up to, Skeeter."

She flipped it open and quickly went through the contents. It didn't take long to catalog everything: Paraguayan driver's license, no credit cards, no business cards, no library cards, no grocery discount cards, no membership cards, no pictures, plenty of cash, and one mag stripe key card.

She turned it over.

"He's staying at the Star Motel," she said.

Dylan looked up from checking the phone. "And Jane's last call was to us. I need you to stake out the motel."

Dammit.

"That's the crap job, Dylan. I want to be in on the interrogation." She wanted to get face-to-face with Sam Walls and see what he was made of.

Dylan obviously had other ideas. He gave her a look that said she knew better than to second-guess a direct order, and she did. *Dammit.*

Denver.

He breathed the word in through his consciousness, let it swirl though his mind. It smelled cool, and clean, and fresh with the coming rain.

Denver.

Armageddon.

Ragnarok.

The end of the world.

The end of Conroy Farrel's world.

Monk stood at the corner of 16th and Market, in the darkness of night, in his sunglasses, in front of the bus station in LoDo. He was young, and strong, and healthy, big and muscular, with silvery hair and pale, nearly colorless eyes. MNK-1, Monk, he had no last name.

He'd come a long way and needed to stretch his legs and start getting the lay of the land. He'd studied the maps of the city and every file on Conroy Farrel/J. T. Chronopolous that he'd been able to find in the Bangkok lab of Dr. Greg Patterson, a superheated cauldron where Monk had been reborn using formulas pioneered by the legendary Dr. Souk and tweaked into the new millennium by Dr. Patterson.

Monk knew his lineage, and he knew Con Farrel. The files had been his training manual. Alone in the lab, he'd pored over them, gleaning out his purpose in life, the reason he'd been created, even as he'd lamented his abandonment. He knew what Lancaster expected of him, what he wanted—destruction, utter and absolute—and Monk was going to give it to him, a gift to his master.

At times it drove him crazy with a longing he scarcely could bear. All Monk needed was to be by Lancaster's side, to do his will, to bear his arms and demolish his enemies—brutally, totally. It was what he'd been born to do.

But Lancaster had been lost to him, and, for that, Dr. Patterson had died.

Conroy Farrel was his way back to Lancaster's side, and the key to finding Farrel was to track J. T. Chronopolous. Monk had the cunning to have come to understand the nature of the hunt that consumed

Lancaster. Farrel had never been to Denver, Colorado. Chronopolous had been born and raised here. Whatever was left of J.T. would have more play in this place than in any other. Monk had struggled with the same situation in San Diego, his point of reentry into the world and the United States. Anywhere within a forty-mile radius of Coronado Island, and he'd felt himself slipping toward the consciousness of another man: the man he used to be, before Lancaster had recruited him four months ago for a trip to Thailand and the adventure of a lifetime, a chance to be the best that he could be.

Things hadn't gone exactly as planned under the Bangkok medical team's regime, nor exactly as Lancaster had promised, but Monk had no regrets.

He knew Lancaster couldn't say the same—not yet. The old man was a visionary, and he'd gone too far, asked for too much, and gotten Monk instead of the indestructible superman he'd wanted.

And yet Monk *was* nearly indestructible, much more so than any of his predecessors. And he was unique, a thousand times more intelligent than any soldier before him. There would be no more like him. He'd guaranteed it.

Death.

He was the wielder of it, the master of it, and he'd dealt it hard and fast in Bangkok when they'd come for him with their black needles in their hands.

They'd made a warrior. What had they thought, that he'd let them kill him? Fools.

A bus went by, its lights unnaturally bright, and Monk turned away, pulling the hood of his jacket closer around his face. He could see clearly to the horizon in all directions in the dark, which was yet one more way Dr. Patterson had overdone him. Light bothered him. Flashing lights blinded him and gave him actual, piercing pain. Flashing lights of any duration were agonizing, like bullets to his brain. He'd found pills in the lab to help, silver gelcaps the color of his eyes, except his irises were even paler than silver, albino eyes. Before Bangkok his eyes had been dark gray and his hair sandy brown. Patterson's drugs had changed him.

Lancaster—the name ran through his blood, his master.

Monk had tracked him easily. There had been invoices by the dozens to a company named LeedTech and a connection of Lancaster to LeedTech in the lab's computer files. Men of vision and power were easy to track. Farrel, the mud-sucking worm, had been much harder. If Monk hadn't been following Lancaster so closely, watching his every move, monitoring his every call, using every piece of technology he could find and every ounce of his intelligence, he might not have ever found the man Lancaster needed destroyed.

The gift he was going to give.

He took a deep breath. The air was thin, a mile high and lacking in oxygen, not like the rich brew of the Thai lowlands, but it would suffice.

A lot of men had died trying to capture or kill Conroy Farrel. Monk knew he would not, for a very simple reason. There'd never been anyone like him.

Never.

CHAPTER ELEVEN

Buckle up.

That had been a great idea, and Jane was duly grateful for the advice.

Staying in the car when he'd offered to let her out at the Quick Mart?

Not such a great idea.

What in the world had she been thinking?

All the wrong things was the answer to that. *Cripes.*

And her knee hurt like hell, and she'd gotten blood on her dress. *Dammit.*

She jerked the seat belt across her lap tighter with one hand while hugging her zebra purse closer to her chest with the other. Corinna probably didn't have air bags, and the way they were careening around corners made Jane pretty damn sure she was going to need one. She felt like she was in the middle of a carnival ride in the middle of downtown Denver, like the whirling teacup ride, where there were lots of other teacups, all of them going round and round without ever getting any closer to each other.

Hawkins was in the green teacup, also known as the mighty Roxanne. Travis was at the wheel of the gold teacup, Coralie, with Gillian "Red Dog" Pentycote riding shotgun—and Jane meant that literally—and she and J.T. were in the midnight-blue teacup.

And the last thing the party needed was another teacup weighing in for the ride, but that's exactly what they got on the west side, at the corner of 30th and Vallejo: Creed and his Super Sport 454 Chevelle, Angelina.

Jane didn't know whether to be relieved or even more unnerved. One way or another, this chase was coming to an end, and with the addition of Creed, it was going to be sooner rather than later. She just prayed it wasn't going to be a bad end for any of them. They were being herded God only knew where by the Steele Street crew, who were obviously communicating with one another.

They'd tried communicating with J.T., as well, but apparently he was one of those guys who felt safer off the grid. When a small computer screen had soundlessly slid out of the GTO's tape deck showing their location on a map of Denver, he'd barely taken a look before calmly reaching over and ripping the unit out of the dashboard.

That had gotten her attention, the quickness of the decision, the ease of the execution, the strength of his hand, even with him missing half of his ring finger, and, God, she didn't want to think about how that had happened to him, the same way she could hardly bear to look at his scars and accept what had been done to him.

The crumpled GPS/computer unit was now sitting in the backseat, a crunched-up mess of broken plastic, bent metal, and a dangling circuit board.

Fair enough. There had been plenty of times in Jane's life when she hadn't wanted to be found.

This wasn't one of them.

She sure as heck hadn't wanted to be found the morning she'd met him at Duffy's in her pretty summer skirt. She'd been a princess that morning, Princess Jane with little black bows around the waistband of her skirt and those gorgeous pink-and-white striped leggings. That she'd worn the outfit with her old tennis shoes hadn't even mattered once she'd sat down...

Nervous, but trying not to show it, Jane sat perfectly still with her hands folded in her lap while J.T. ordered croissants, scrambled eggs and bacon, and fresh berries and cream, real cream, for their breakfast. For a minute, she wasn't sure what she was more excited about, the food or him. Her confusion didn't last long, not past the grin he gave her when he looked up from the menu.

"And a mocha latte?"

Geez, he was beautiful. The thrill of it went straight through her, right down her middle.

"Sure," she said. She loved mocha lattes, and she was damned afraid she was going to end up loving him. She needed someone strong in her life, someone she could count on, someone stable, and he was like a rock, solid from the get-go. But in her experience, what she needed and what she got were usually two different things.

Breakfast, though, she could count on, and the more she ate and the more lattes she drank, the more comfortable she got and the more she talked about this and that and the other.

He listened to it all, her whole sad little story. Light-fingered mother who'd gotten sent up, a sweet woman with a penchant for bad company who now lived in a small town in southern Wyoming, absent father, family somewhere, maybe Kansas, maybe not, her crew of eight kids she seemed to spend her life trying to feed and keep out of Lieutenant Loretta's clutches, and Sandman.

"Tell me about him," he asked. "About Sandman."

Sandman, hell. What could she say about a best friend she didn't seem to have much in common with anymore. They used to be inseparable, and lately she'd found herself avoiding him.

"He's tall, skinny, a good scrounger." One of the best, for what it was worth. Surprisingly, lately, that hadn't been as much as she'd always thought.

"Is he your boyfriend?"

"No." She shook her head. No way. "We've been through a lot of hard times together, that's all, a lot of years. Our moms were friends. He's got a girl. They talk about getting married."

"What about you?" He seemed genuinely curious, leaning a little closer over the table, holding her gaze. "Do you have someone you think about marrying?"

Oh, yeah—she felt a sigh building in her chest and squelched it.

"No." She shifted her attention from him to her plate. "No. I keep thinking..." Her voice trailed off.

"Thinking what?"

"Keep thinking there has to be something more." She picked up her croissant, then put it back down and met his gaze. "I'm not stupid, J.T. I can see what's going on around me, and I see people with real jobs, and bags of groceries, and cars that work. It's right there in front of me every day, like right here in Duffy's, the people at all these tables, but I can't seem to see how to get from where I'm at to where they are."

Sandman thought that was crazy talk. He had everything all figured out. They were the good guys, the Robin Hoods, the Robin Rulz, taking from the rich to give to the poor, which was mainly themselves.

But J. T. Chronopolous was no Sandman. Instead of dismissing her, he understood.

"I remember thinking the same thing once when I was stealing a BMW."

"A Beemer?" Hell, she'd never stolen anything as big as a car, let alone a BMW.

"Yeah." He hunkered in closer. "I was over by the Denver Country Club, trying to jack this guy's 535i in a blizzard, and I was thinking what in the hell was I doing freezing my butt off trying to steal some guy's car, when he was all cozy inside this big damn house I was looking

at. And I was thinking I'd rather be him than me right about then. I'd rather be paying for the Beemer and getting it stolen and collecting on the insurance than outside being the schmuck stealing it for pennies on the dollar."

She just sat there and stared at him dumbfounded.

He got it.

The whole thing, her whole problem.

"So what are you driving these days?" She was damned curious.

He grinned and settled back in his chair. "A midnight-blue 1967 Pontiac GTO. I named her Corinna."

And lo and behold, he was still driving the same damn midnight-blue 1967 Pontiac GTO.

Stick with him—that had been her plan, her only plan, but it was looking a little shortsighted now. Corinna had hit sixty miles an hour for a stretch there back on 15th, blowing through a couple of lights and redlining Jane's pulse. Sixty wasn't much on the highway, but in downtown traffic, it was a thrill ride plus.

"What's his name?" J.T. asked, nodding at the 454 Chevy idling at the curb, facing him off on the other side of Vallejo Street.

"Creed," she said, her spirits sinking even lower, knowing he meant the guy sitting like the badass messenger of "shit outta luck" behind the wheel of the black-cherry red Chevelle. "Cesar Raoul Eduardo Rivera, Creed for short."

This was awful. He didn't know Creed, and if he didn't know Creed, one of the best friends he'd ever had, then who the hell was he really? Even if he'd been J.T., was he still J.T.?

"Creed Rivera," he repeated, seeming to give her answer some thought. "Back at the Quick Mart, you said you wanted to wait for Hawkins. Who is Hawkins?"

Another terrible question. She tightened her grip on her zebra purse again, just because it was something to hold on to.

"Christian Hawkins," she said. "Sometimes, on the street, they call him Cristo, and all the time, they call him Superman."

That got her a subtle snort of disbelief. *Superman,* she could almost hear him thinking. *Yeah, right.*

But it was "yeah, right," all the time, and J.T. would know that.

"Is he in one of these cars?" he asked, lifting his hips partway off the seat and shoving a hand into his front jeans pocket.

"The green Challenger." This was all so wrong. Roxanne and Hawkins were like peanut butter and jelly, and J.T. would know that, too.

"So Hawkins is one of the guys from the garage." He pulled his hand back out, and when he opened it, she saw a dozen or so brightly colored gelcaps in his palm. "The guy who was on the stairs, right?" He picked out a couple of green ones, tossed them in his mouth, and shoved the rest back into his pocket. "I saw him make a run for the Challenger when we were leaving."

Yes, the guy on the stairs in the garage, she thought. The one you threw a grenade at—*cripes.*

And what were those pills all about? The colors were almost iridescent, but it didn't make them look pretty or fun. They looked dangerously serious, intense, even toxic, as if even a little bit might kill you—and he'd popped those two green ones like candy.

He shot her a brief glance, his eyes the same depthless hazel she remembered. He was J. T. Chronopolous, so help her God. He had to be.

"He called you Jane."

"Yes. That's my name," she said, then went for broke. "What's yours?"

It took him a few seconds to answer, and for a moment, she thought he might not.

"Con," he finally said.

Con. A long sigh escaped her, and she brought her hand up to cover her face.

Well, this was all so perfect. They'd gotten the introductions out of the way, sort of. She was Jane, and he didn't know who he was. She was only about half sure herself. No matter who he looked like, he didn't know Creed, and he didn't know Hawkins, and he didn't know his own name, and to top it all off, unbelievably, he'd taken her knife, and he'd taken her gun.

She was smarter than this, savvier than this. She'd been on the streets most of her life and knew how to take care of herself—except, she guessed, when people were throwing grenades and were superhero fast. She'd never seen anyone move like him.

Well, actually, now that she thought about it, she had seen one person who moved like him, with that much speed and grace: Red Dog, Gillian Pentycote. But Gillian had suffered a run-in with some real twisted people, and the whole experience had changed her from the inside out. She'd been tortured with drugs and lost her memory.

Oh.

She went very still over on her side of the car, then lifted her hand just enough to angle her gaze over to Con's side of the car. *Oh, no.*

She took him in, letting her gaze slide over his jawline and down the side of his neck, taking in the scars that had never been there before, down to his hand and the half-missing ring finger. *Dear God.* She didn't spend a lot of time hanging out with the people at Steele Street, nowhere near as much as they spent hanging out with each other. She mostly ran with Denver's art crowd, but she'd been around enough to know that Gillian had been without her memory for a few years, quite a few, before her life's history had started coming back to her, which had explained a whole lot about her coldly awkward personality. She was actually kind of sweet now... sometimes, and just a little bit nice, but not a lot. She could still kick major ass.

Ah, hell.

Jane had been in some pretty rough situations, but she couldn't begin to imagine what it was like to be tortured until you lost your memories, even of who you were.

And she was sitting in a car with a man who was ripped like Red Dog, and fast like Red Dog, and who took pretty pills and looked like he'd been tortured, and who seemed to have lost his memory.

This was a disaster, and she was in the middle of it.

So what was she going to do?

Lowering her hand, she looked away from him and out toward the street, and realized the question might be moot. Roxanne was sidling up to the curb on Vallejo at the intersection.

The man next to her reached down and shifted the GTO into a different gear, drawing her gaze back to his mutilated right hand.

"Was it an accident?" she asked, suddenly needing to know. "How you lost your finger?" Maybe she was wrong. Maybe he hadn't been tortured. Maybe he'd been in a crash, a car crash, a train crash, a plane crash, a bad one that had left him without his memory and cut him in a lot of places.

"Probably not," he said, his voice calm, matter-of-fact.

She flicked her gaze up to his face, meeting his eyes, and they were calm, too, and very clear. Whatever had happened to him, he either didn't know, or he'd accepted it and moved on.

"Any one of these guys will give you a ride," he continued. "So why don't you get out and go home, do us both a favor."

He was right—but she had plenty of reasons to do her damnedest not to get kicked out of his car, none of which had anything to do with her ancient-history teenage crush. She was all grown up now, and that whole pathetically besotted time of her life was long gone. All she could hope was that if he really had lost his memory, he'd lost the one of her lurking around Steele Street, hoping to catch a glimpse of him from the roof of Sprechts Apartments. She hazarded another quick glance in his direction.

No, she surmised, he didn't seem to be connecting her with any latent memories of schoolgirl idiocy—thank God.

And if he'd forgotten the idiocy, maybe he'd forgotten the last time she'd seen him, the night things had gotten completely out of hand and the damned next morning when he'd left and she'd cried.

Oh, yes, she could only hope he'd forgotten all of that.

Watching her from his side of the car, Con refrained from a weary sigh. She wasn't budging, which made no damn sense at all, and he didn't like things that didn't make sense.

"Is this personal between us?" he asked, going with his least likely theory first. It sure sounded good to him, but it also sounded like wishful thinking, despite the intense awareness they'd had of each other when he'd first seen her on the street. "Why are you sticking to me like superglue gone wrong? Why are you still in this car?"

That's what he needed to know before he got rid of her, why she hadn't gotten out at the Quick Mart. He wanted to know what her stake was in the day's events.

"Or am I a job?" That was theory number two, and it was a helluva lot more likely. He'd been a lot of guys' job over the last six years, a world full of spooks and door-kickers determined to bring him in for cash, or glory, or both. She'd be the first girl he'd come up against, though, and if somebody had sent her, well, he could only give them credit for being the first ones to get it right. She had a helluva lot better chance of bringing him down than any guy.

He waited for an answer, but whatever she was thinking, she was keeping it to herself.

"Do I know you?" he asked, trying a different tack—and, much to his surprise, scoring.

She blushed, a wash of pink rising under her skin as she turned away and looked out the passenger-side window.

Fascinating—it *was* personal, all right, whatever it was between them.

So just how well had he known her, he couldn't help but wonder, and if he'd known someone like her, how in the hell could he have forgotten her?

Stupid question. Souk's soup had taken so much of his life. But it hadn't taken him, what he was at his essence, at his core, because he was still that: a soldier, a warrior, a gunfighter to the marrow of his bones.

"The guys who are after me," he asked, giving Corinna's rearview mirror another quick glance. "Are you working with them? Are you one of the operators at Steele Street?" She'd been armed, and he could A-1 guarantee every one of these guys out on the street tonight was packing something.

"No." She shook her head, and he watched in wonder at the silky movement of her hair, the dark slide of it across her shoulders, the flow of it down across her breasts—and he believed her. She wasn't like the woman who'd been holding Scout on the tenth floor. The auburn-haired operator was serious business, and Jane was nothing but trouble.

Personal trouble.

Hell. Like he needed any more of that.

CHAPTER TWELVE

Steele Street's basement was an interesting place, its concrete walls faced with green and black granite, a low-lit lap pool shimmering down its middle. There had been a time when Dylan had used the pool almost every night, swimming laps when he couldn't sleep. Now he slept with Skeeter.

There were stacks of clean white towels on a rack next to the door, a water cooler, a few comfortable deck chairs and chaise lounges—and there was one simple metal chair, nothing fancy, no cushion on the seat, just an attached rope and pulley setup that Dylan wouldn't want to trust his life to, not on a bet. The chair had a high back, the better to duct-tape a man's upper body to, and two good, strong metal arms, the better to secure a man's wrists and elbows with more heavy-duty duct tape. The chair had four metal legs, and, currently, a man's legs were taped to two of them, one leg good and strong and the other a medical mess.

"So how's your day going, Sam?" Dylan asked.

"Fuck you," the man sitting in his boxers taped to the chair said. Sam Walls had six-pack abs, bulging biceps, one thigh the size of Vermont, and another deeply scarred and shriveled. Except for the glaring deformity, he was juiced, more than juiced. He was superjuiced, Souk juiced.

Frankly, Dylan was damned impressed that Quinn and Kid had been able to snatch him without resorting to a ballistic solution.

"I don't know who you think you are, asshole"—Walls ground the words out between clenched teeth—"but you made a big mistake dragging me in here."

Yeah, yeah, Dylan thought, he'd had a lifetime of making these kinds of mistakes and gotten paid damn well to do it.

"I'm the guy who owns you now." Motivation, he guessed. Kid and Quinn had been damned motivated, and his guys were not without a fair amount of skill. Jet jockeys weren't normally known for their hand-to-hand combat expertise, but Quinn was a street fighter from way back, and then there was that stretch Kid had done with the Marines in Recon. Yeah, that was usually enough to put a guy ahead of the pack—way ahead.

"Bullshit," the man sneered. "Assaulting a federal officer will get you life, boy."

Boy? That was new. Not many people called Dylan "boy."

"Federal officer of what?" he asked. "Who do you work for, Sam? What agency?"

The basement was warm, maybe even too warm, especially for an extended stay, which Dylan could see in Sam Walls's immediate future.

"One that can take this place apart at the seams, asshole."

Dylan nodded, even though that wasn't the answer he'd wanted.

He was standing at one end of the pool deck, in front of where the securely bound Walls was strapped into the metal chair placed directly under a bright light hanging from the ceiling. Quinn and Kid were both standing behind Sam, far enough away to be out of the light and yet close enough to make the man nervous—but probably not nearly as nervous as he should be.

"Who was in the Mercedes with you?" Dylan asked his next question.

"Fuck you."

"Randolph Lancaster?"

"Fuck you."

"How many men did Lancaster bring to Denver?"

The only answer he got was another sneer.

Fine. The guy could have it his way.

Dylan signaled Quinn and Kid, and his two operators stepped forward and picked up Sam and his chair. Without a word, they moved him to the deep end of the pool and set the back legs of the chair precisely on the edge of the deck so that the man was facing Dylan with the water behind him.

There were a lot of reasons to push a captive taped to a chair into six feet of water, none of them good.

Dylan reached up and angled the ceiling light to hit Sam squarely in the face, blinding him to the rest of the room.

"I don't think you're a federal officer, Sam," he said. "I think you're a traitor to your country, and I think you're here in Denver on a terrorist mission. What the hell happened to your leg?" The deep, gouged scar running the length of his thigh was a real butcher job. The shriveled mess of the rest of it, Dylan could only guess at, but it was a pretty damn good guess.

"Combat, sweetheart."

"Where were you born?"

"In a cross-fire hurricane."

Two brilliant answers in a row. One more brilliant answer would get the guy tipped bass-ackward into the pool.

With luck, Dylan would have him pulled back out, but deep down in his heart, where the truth mattered, he didn't really think this was one of Sam Walls's lucky days.

"How many missions have you been on for Lancaster?"

"Fuck you." Succinct, but not brilliant.

"How long can you hold your breath?"

"Longer than you think."

"Have you ever been to Coveñas, Colombia?"

"You don't know shit about where I've been."

Torture was an ugly word and even uglier in practice. Dylan knew. He'd been tortured. In some ways, it made him more sympathetic to Walls's situation, but in most ways, it didn't, especially when he needed real answers and not misplaced bravado and insults.

"You may turn out to be a lucky guy, after all, Sam," he said. "I'm going to give you one more chance before I get serious."

He reached into his pocket and pulled out a small stainless steel case. The sequence of impending events was very clear in his mind. Yes, he remembered exactly how Souk had tortured him: first by injecting the drugs, an agonizing procedure, and second by half drowning him. The combination had been specifically calibrated to intensify the primordial terror of the hallucinations associated with Souk's chemical concoctions. It was as close to death, or praying for death, as Dylan had ever been.

Sam Walls didn't look impressed with the small stainless steel case.

But Dylan hadn't opened it yet.

"After I show you what's in here, I'm going to ask my questions again, and if I don't get your best answers, your very best, Sam, I'm going to... well, you'll understand everything in a minute."

"You have no idea what you're dealing with," Walls said.

"Maybe not," Dylan agreed. "But then again, maybe I do."

He opened the case and showed Sam Walls the beautiful array of colorful Syrettes inside, each one safely nested in a square of foam rubber. He literally had a rainbow of the drugs, the whole spectrum compliments of Dr. William F. Brandt's research lab at Walter Reed Medical Center.

"Have you ever heard of a Thai syringe?" he asked.

And by the blood-draining look of horror on Sam's face, Dylan knew that he had.

Poor bastard.

CHAPTER THIRTEEN

"I really should stay with the car," Jane said, because "stay with the car" was a helluva lot easier for her to say than "stay with you."

He let his gaze drift over her, shaking his head, like he couldn't believe what she'd decided, then went back to watching the street.

She let out a short breath and tried to look like she knew what she was doing.

"Your name isn't Con," she said, because, by God, she did know that.

"That's not exactly a news flash, honey." He slanted her a long gaze from over on his side of the car.

"So you know you have amnesia?"

A short laugh escaped him. "Yeah, I figured it out pretty quick the day I woke up strapped to a gurney and couldn't remember my own name."

Oh, God, she'd been right about the amnesia, and that meant the odds were good she was right about the torture.

Oh, geezus. He'd woken up strapped to a gurney. *Oh, God.*

"We should . . . I mean, I need to . . . no. No, what you need to know is that these guys chasing us are your friends." That's what she meant to say. "The best friends you'll ever have. They can help you. We should go back to the garage right now. You'll be safe there."

"I'm safe now," he said, his voice so cool and steady.

Of course he was. What was she thinking?

"These boys are going to try to run me to ground," he continued. "And I'm not going to let them do that, whatever it takes. Do you understand?"

She nodded. "Whatever it takes." Whatever the hell that meant. "Maybe you should let me drive."

The grin he flashed her was brief and devastating, a crooked curve of boyish dimples and white teeth that erased the years and the scars and made him what he once had been.

He shrugged out of his jacket, and her gaze dropped lower, to his chest. He was wearing a black Jimi Hendrix T-shirt with the words "Voodoo Child" across the middle, below the drawing of Hendrix.

Voodoo child for sure, she thought, witchy and wild, popping his pills and Corinna's clutch, dark and dangerous and beautiful, and lost to himself. So lost.

"You got your seat belt cinched real tight?" He finished pulling off the jacket and laid it next to him on the console.

Yeah, tight. She gave the belt another tug and wondered if it was time to start with the Hail Marys: *Hail, Mary, full of grace...*

Oh, sweet Jesus—she glanced over at him.

Talk about tight. The Jimi Hendrix T-shirt defined the word, and the word defined everything about his arms from the breadth of his shoulders, to the hard, sculpted fullness of his biceps and the confluence of veins running under his skin down the inside of his forearms. He had no tattoos, only the fine, incised tracks of his scars.

With her gaze riveted to him, to the hard line of his jaw and the straight line of his nose, to the softness of his cotton T-shirt and the even softer worn denim of his jeans, she tightened her hold on her zebra purse.

Touching him was not a good idea. She'd remembered it too many times for her own good, what it was like to wrap her arms around him, to be held by him, how he'd tasted when they'd kissed, how he'd felt inside her, the aching loss of it all when he'd left—and then he'd up and died, and she'd been forced to put her childish dreams away.

But here they were, despite death and everything, sitting in a car.

If this was fate, she was buying.

Yes, she was starting to see the bright side to the day. Her ears had stopped ringing, her nerves had calmed, and two of the greatest guys in the world were ready to do God only knew what to them the instant they moved off this corner at 30th and Vallejo.

What were Creed and Hawkins thinking? she wondered.

Then she knew. The sound of another set of perfectly tuned headers rumbled into earshot before Coralie made her appearance at the intersection with the rest of them. Now the board was set, but for what?

"Okay, time to get out of here," J.T. said, looking over at her with his oh-so-calm gaze. "Last chance, Jane. You in or out?"

"In," she said without hesitation, whatever "in" turned out to be.

He stretched his hand out to grasp the back of her seat and shifted around so he could look over his shoulder, out the rear windshield.

"The, uh, next run is going to be in reverse?" Maybe she needed to rethink her decision.

"Only the first stretch. Then we're sliding off the map, and these guys can spend the rest of the night chasing each other."

He seemed awfully sure of himself for somebody who didn't know Denver was his hometown, and what the hell did "sliding off the map" mean? It sounded like something she should know about—like something she was going to find out about the hard way, unless she bailed on him, and she wasn't bailing. She couldn't bear the thought of watching him disappear and wondering if she'd ever see him again—because, baby, that seemed like a real damn long shot.

"Still in?" he asked, slanting his gaze back to her and gunning the motor.

Oh, geezus.

She gave a short, quick nod, and he pressed down hard on the gas. The engine roared. The tires smoked, and when he checked through the rear window and released the clutch, Corinna took off like a shot, wheels rolling, headers growling. It was all flash. It was shock and awe, a rocket launch backward, crossing lines of traffic. It was a neighborhood in reverse. Some people honked, most slammed on their brakes, snarling the traffic and turning it into a maze for the Steele Street crew to navigate—and through it all she held on.

He made his first turn while still in reverse, with an instant 180-degree pivot of the car's front end around the brake-locked rear wheels, swinging them into forward motion and pressing her back into her seat with pure heart-pounding g-forces. Then he started up through the gears. The second turn was into a frighteningly narrow alley. She gripped the armrest on the door, her knuckles growing whiter with each passing second.

They weren't sliding off anything. Oh, hell, no. They were flying, nearly airborne on the turns.

They whipped past trash cans, dumpsters, and through a section where lines full of clothes flapped and billowed in the breeze behind chain-link fences, where people were out in their backyards, watching in consternation and flashes of horror as Corinna flew down the small, rutted road.

This was a car crash waiting to happen. She knew it down to her belly.

The next turn had her pressed up against the door, a hard, chassis-rocking left back onto pavement. Fifty yards later, he downshifted, double-clutching into a hard right, and they tore down another alley just like the last one. He might not know who he was, but he sure as hell knew this part of town, and he sure as hell knew how to drive.

Up ahead, she could see the parking lot of an industrial site, a conglomeration of big, rattletrap-looking, multistory metal buildings all crammed together, and she knew, if they could just get to the parking lot without hitting a dumpster, or somebody's garbage can, or, heaven forbid, somebody, they'd be okay.

She was wrong.

Corinna caught some air launching off the slightly higher dirt alley onto the asphalt of the parking lot, and while Jane was literally absorbing that bit of automotive rock and roll, Con accelerated around the corner of the first abandoned building and cut a sharp left, then a sharp right into a U-shape recess. A dark, empty space in the far wall loomed up in front of them, and he headed straight for it, double-clutching his downshifts again, smoothly and quickly easing back on the speed, but not nearly enough.

Oh, no, not even close.

The building came rushing at them, the empty space in the wall looming closer. They roared past the words TATSUNAKA PRODUCE painted in large, fading letters above the loading docks. Ahead of them, on either side of the opening, large, metal sliding doors were hanging off their tracks, looking like the open maw of a car-crushing, street rat–eating shark monster.

Holy cripes. Holy, holy... She sucked in a breath and held it. *Holy, oh, hail, Mary, full of grace. Holy, oh, holy, holy...*

They passed through the door into darkness.

Mary, Mary, Mary, Mother of God, O Mary, pray for us sinners.

He finally hit the brakes, *really* hit the brakes, and Corinna's front end slanted down steep-steeper-steepest with Jane backpedaling like crazy, virtually crawling backward over the top of her seat, until a strong arm came across the interior of the car and held her in place.

"You're fine" were the last words she heard before she and the amnesiac and the rocket-hot GTO fell into an inky black abyss.

CHAPTER FOURTEEN

"Alpha One, come in," Jack said, trying to raise Con for about the tenth time, and failing again. *Hell.* "Alpha One, come in. We've got a bearcat on the loose."

This was no good. He and Scout were parked in a restaurant parking lot not too far from Coors Field, Denver's baseball stadium, and not too far from Steele Street, still in lower downtown.

When they'd reached the Buick Regal, Jack had pulled off his black watch cap and put on a Rockies baseball cap and a pair of clear glasses with silver frames. He'd handed Scout a blue bandanna, and she'd done one of those hippie-girl-cruising-through-Thailand-and-the-islands things, roping it through her hair and tying it all up on top of her head. He'd seen her do the same thing with a silk scarf, add a pair of dangly earrings, and look like she'd just walked off the cover of a fashion magazine.

But he'd never seen her in a dress—which was just one of those things that bugged him every now and then.

They'd been cruising the area, keeping a low profile in the nondescript gray Buick, on the lookout for Karola, Walls, and Lancaster—especially Lancaster, the bearcat—and trying to contact Con. He should have checked in as soon as he was clear and away.

But he hadn't, and the game had changed. Jack couldn't leave Con with Lancaster and his men this close.

"The people who took me, Special Defense Force, they aren't out to kill him," Scout said from her side of the car.

So what?

"They didn't want to kill him last time, and he barely survived." Killing him with kindness, darting him with damn ketamine, like he was an animal. Jack had been curious as hell about why these assholes had done what they'd done to Con. More often than not, in their business, when the going got tough, somebody usually got killed—and the going had been as tough as it could get in Paraguay. Con's whole house had been destroyed. Everything had been shot, the walls, the deck, the windows, the furniture, and quite a few people—everything except Con.

No, they'd darted him, and just about killed the boss that way.

After seeing the guy in the Porsche, Kid Chaos, at least now Jack knew why they'd done it, and he knew why they'd kidnapped Scout, and he was willing to give them the benefit of the doubt that they weren't working with Lancaster. But now the spymaster was here, the man who'd been hunting Con for six long years with only one goal: to kill him.

"They took you, Scout," he said, a small warm-up to the questions that had kept him stone-cold focused every day for the last two weeks. "Did they hurt you? In any way?"

It would change everything if they had, no matter whose brother was whose.

"No." She shook her head. "They only want one thing, that's all. They want to help him. Geez, Jack, they've got pictures of him as a kid, pictures of his family, of when he was in the Marines, pictures of all of them together, and a thousand stories to go with the photos. They know things about him that we've only been able to guess at, and they want him back. They say he's theirs, and he is; you saw Kid."

Yeah. Kid. There was always something about coming up against an operator his age, a young guy still kicking thirty in the back, that brought out the worst of Jack's knuckle-dragging tendencies, of which he had plenty—but not this time. Peter "Kid Chaos" Chronopolous simply blew him away. Drop a few years on him, and the guy could be Con's twin, except for the scars.

When Jack had seen Con for the first time, in Bangkok, he'd been a mess. Brutalized. With hundreds of stitches in him.

Everything in Bangkok had been crazy, and Jack had been a too-smart-for-his-own-good kid with more balls than brains coming off a hitch with the U.S. Army Rangers. He'd gone looking for adventure in Southeast Asia and found nothing but trouble of the worst kind.

Transportation services, courier services, protection services—after Jack cashed out of the Army, he'd set himself up to provide all three to foreign investors and businessmen working from Myanmar to Vietnam, China, and Taiwan. Things had gone great for a year, until he'd had problems with a package and been sent by a securities trader in Taipei to Bangkok to pick up a replacement.

"Tuberculosis sanitarium" was what he'd been told. Dr. Souk ran a convalescent hospital in Bangkok for people suffering from TB.

Bullshit.

"Overzealous Colombians," Souk murmured with obvious distaste, looking down at the injured, dark-haired man on the gurney with all those hundreds of stitches in him.

Jack didn't know what the fuck was up. He'd come for a package, not to go on rounds with some creepy doctor.

Souk adjusted Con's IV, then ordered a team of orderlies to take him below. The South Americans had all but ruined his patient, Souk complained, but he'd done his best to save the man.

"Every time I fix him, he gets better," Souk added, which begged the question.

"How many times have you fixed him?"

"Dozens," the thin, sallow-faced doctor said, looking up at Jack through a pair of thick, black-rimmed glasses. His lab coat was stained. His hair was chopped short and dirty. "It's what I do with the good men. Fix them, then fix them better, though usually only from the inside out."

Geezus, Jack thought, looking back at the guy, and this time noticing that the man was wearing dog tags just like his—which sure as hell gave his heart a start, seeing a U.S. soldier in a way-too-strange TB sanitarium in Thailand.

By the time the doctor finished showing Jack around, he'd seen over a hundred of the patients under Souk's care and noticed that a good portion of them were American, but Con was the one Jack had remembered, him and a black Marine officer who'd looked to be dying.

"They want me to help them," Scout said, bringing him back to the problem at hand.

He turned and looked at her.

"Help them capture Con?"

She nodded, and he looked back out the windshield, swearing under his breath.

After a second, he turned and looked at her again.

"Betray Con?" he asked. "Set him up so these operators can what: Lock him down somewhere and 'rehabilitate' him?" He shook his head, growing angrier by the second, then shifted back into his seat and looked out the windshield again. "You know he's never going to willingly give himself up to these guys, no matter who they are."

It was too damn late for rehab, and the boss knew it, but Jack didn't want to be the one to tell Scout.

"No, we don't know that," she insisted. "We won't know until I make my report to him. Once I tell him everything I know, he might want to talk to these guys. I only want what's best for him, Jack. I'm just not sure what that is yet."

He understood. It was hard to know what was best for Con, because it was damn near impossible to know what all had been done to him.

Twice he'd been hired by the broker in Taipei to pick up packages at Dr. Souk's in Bangkok. The first time, he'd seen Con and the Marine officer who'd been in such damn bad shape. The second time, there'd been nothing left of Souk's "hospital"—and for whatever harebrained reason he'd come up with and long forgotten, he'd decided to check the situation out.

Even years later, the memory of Souk's basement was enough to make him sweat, but he'd found Con and gotten him out of there alive.

"All I'm saying is that maybe we should be the ones to figure that out," Scout continued. "That maybe we should be the ones to decide what's best for him."

Geezus.

"If you want to do that, babe, then you've got more balls than I do." The two of them going behind Con's back and setting him up for these assholes?

Jack didn't think so.

Con Farrel was the toughest son of a bitch Jack had ever met in his life, and Jack had been around the block with some of the world's best.

Con was also the most incisively tactical person Jack

had ever known. Calm, articulate, intelligent, he'd taken Jack's courier and protection business and shot it into the stratosphere. He'd known how to score bigger commissions off of larger, multinational companies and wealthier private clients. He was a fixer. He knew where to lay money down and where to pick it up, how to hot-wire anything with an engine, and how to fight—definitely knew how to fight—and over the course of the first few months of their partnership, they'd built a war chest.

When Jack had asked him for what, Con had given him a succinct answer: the hunt.

They'd been hunting ever since, and it had all gone down real well, just the way they'd planned, until Con had decided it was time to hunt down Garrett Leesom's daughter. It had taken them two years to find her, and nothing had been the same for Jack ever since.

A Boy Scout, that's what he'd been, a damn Boy Scout, curious as hell, wondering what in the world two U.S. Marines had been doing in that hellhole, and wondering if he should check to see if maybe they'd been left behind when Souk had packed up his "hospital" and disappeared off the map.

One had been left behind: Con.

The other had died: Garret Leesom, Scout's father.

Hell. He'd never told her that he'd been one of the last people to see her father alive.

He shot her a quick glance—and decided that, once again, today was not the day to broach that subject.

Hell.

He reached for his prepaid cellphone.

"Alpha One, come in," he said into his radio mike, his finger jabbing a curt text message into the phone. "Alpha One, this is Alpha Two. Where the hell are you, Alpha One?"

CHAPTER FIFTEEN

"I might throw up."

"No. You won't." It was an order, not a medical opinion.

Screw him.

"Yes, I might." And Jane meant it. Her stomach was in her throat, and her heart was down in her gut. She'd hit her head, and her legs were shaking, and the thin line of terrified horror that had shot through her when Corinna had taken her dive was still thrumming through her body.

She'd thought it was the end. That he'd forgotten where he was and taken a wrong turn. No one, she'd thought, who remembered that there was no floor in a certain warehouse would drive into that warehouse at eighty miles an hour, just hitting the brakes after it was damn well too late.

"You're fine," he said calmly.

"That's what you said when we crashed."

"We didn't crash."

The hell we didn't.

God, it was dark.

What in the world had she gotten herself into? she wondered. The scraping sound of metal. The vertigo-inducing angle of their descent into this black pit. The rolling of her stomach. The awful sinking feeling of thinking she'd come to her end—the fear, stark and terrifying...*Mother of God, pray for us sinners, now and at the hour of our death.*

Three years at the Immaculate Heart School for Young Women in Phoenix hadn't left her particularly prayerful. The whole time she'd been there, a good ninety percent of her prayers had been to get out. But tonight she'd found a reason to petition the Sacred Virgin.

"If you turn on the lights, we can see where we are," she suggested.

"I know where we are."

Good. That was great—for him, king of the one-line response. For the record, *she* didn't know where they were, enough reason for her to want to shed a little light on the situation, that and the trembling she couldn't seem to control.

"We can't just sit here in the dark." Really, she couldn't, not pitch dark, not tomb dark, and if he'd remembered anything about her, he would have remembered that.

"Yes, we can."

Okay. Fine. If he wanted to play it that way, she could sit in the dark as long as he could, maybe longer... maybe not.

The last time she'd seen him, the night before he'd left and not come back, they'd ended up in a place this dark. He'd taken her out east of the city, to the Midnight Doubles, a place she'd heard about lots of times but had never seen. They'd watched the races and wagered a meal on the outcome, and as much as she'd known she was going to miss him, she was glad to have the bet: win or lose. She'd wanted to know she would see him again, and he'd promised her she would. That he'd be gone for a few months, but probably not six months, and that he'd be thinking about her while he was gone to wherever he was going, which he'd never said. She'd found out later, at his funeral, when the country of Colombia had been mentioned during the service.

Colombia—she'd thought at the time that she'd never heard of such an exotic place, and that she'd never so hated a place, because J. T. Chronopolous had gone down there and died.

But the night before he'd left hadn't been about dying—it had been about living...

Wynkoop and 18th, eight p.m.—Jane hurried along the street, excitement running through her veins, happy. She was meeting J.T. again. Two days after their breakfast at Duffy's, they'd had lunch at a great Mexican restaurant in town, Mama Guadaloupe's. The whole thing had been very cool. He was practically famous at Mama's, and everyone had made a big fuss over him and over her, and tonight they were meeting for dinner.

They weren't dating. There was nothing date-like about the meals they shared. She very much got the feeling that he was feeding her—and she had no complaints. Great food served hot was always welcome.

But he thought she was beautiful. He'd said so that first night, and they were headed out to the car races at the Midnight Doubles.

Three more blocks to go and right on time. She came around the corner onto Wynkoop from 15th and ran into a man coming out of the bookstore with a bag of books. It was nothing, just a small run-in, an accident, the sort of thing that happened hundreds of times a day on every block in the city—but she got the guy's wallet.

She ran into people all the time, at least four or five times a day when the conditions were right, and she always got the wallet.

But she was losing her touch, or getting too big to pass unnoticed, or something, because just like that night with J.T. and Christian Hawkins, this guy immediately noticed something was wrong.

"Hey!" he yelled, and the chase was on.

Jane didn't look back. She poured on the speed, wondering what in the world would have made her do something so dumb as to pick a pocket and get caught on her way to meet J.T.

Instinct, she knew, pure and simple. She was trained to make the score, to seize opportunities and keep moving.

But hell, J.T. saw her coming as she darted between the pedestrians on the sidewalk and the cars turning up 17th—and he instantly realized what was happening. She saw it all over his face—his very calm, expressionless face. She saw it in the casual glance he cast at the guy and the way he appeared not to notice her.

He was good, and he must have been damn good on the streets.

She wasn't going to involve him in her current crisis, and, still dodging people, she ran by him—and that was all she wrote. The guy chasing her got stopped cold.

"Get, get out—" The man spluttered, trying to get by J.T.

"Oh, sorry, man," J.T. said, and she was gone. All she'd needed was a chance, and he gave it to her.

She slipped into a parking garage and didn't stop running until she was on the third level, and if the guy with the books could get past J.T. and keep up, he deserved his wallet back.

A stitch in her side, the wallet in her hand, she leaned back against a Mercedes and tried to catch her breath.

J.T. wasn't too far behind.

"Come on," he said, his hand out. "Let's have it."

She knew what he wanted, and against her better judgment, she gave him the wallet.

Hell. What a waste of effort, and she still had a stitch

in her side, and he probably hadn't even noticed the beautiful shirt she was wearing, a stretchy T-shirt in a dozen shades of blue with little buttons up the front. It looked like a waterfall—and it was new, brand-new, never been worn by anyone else, and she'd bought it, paid cash.

Geez, all that work.

"You know this is no good," he said.

"It usually works out better than that," she told him.

"Yeah, well, maybe you better rethink your career."

Career, right; picking pockets wasn't her career. He sounded so old when he talked like that.

"Come on," he said. "I'm parked down on the street. With a little luck, we can get this guy's wallet home before he gets there."

Oh, hell. What a frickin' waste.

He flipped open the wallet to check the address, and, after a second, his gaze lifted and locked onto hers.

"Cop," he said. "C-O-P."

Oh, hell. Now she'd done it.

The thought barely registered before the sirens sounded.

He gave her a look that said he really did know better—and then they both broke into a run.

She was hard-pressed to keep up. Geez, he was fast. They practically slid down the stairs, one level after another, while the cop car whoop-whooped *up the ramp in hot pursuit.*

She couldn't believe it. She'd stolen a cop's wallet. No wonder the guy had been so quick to notice. And this soldier-boy she was following, he was quick, too. They hit street level, and he grabbed her, keeping her from going out on the sidewalk. She didn't know where the hell else he was planning on going. There was no place else—or so she'd thought for all the years she'd been working this part of town.

J.T. knew differently. With a move so fast, she didn't really see everything he did, he jimmied open the maintenance room door and pulled her inside.

Great, she thought. Now they were trapped in a place not much bigger than a closet.

But he kept going, all the way to the back, and slid a metal plate out from under a shelving unit.

And there was a hole in the floor, a big, dark, pitch-black hole into the bowels of the earth.

"Go, go, go," he said, waving her in.

Hell, no, no, no. She balked, and would have continued balking, except for the sound of running feet and another siren whooping *into the garage.*

Oh, hell. Down she went, like Alice into the rabbit hole. There was a ladder, and she was scrambling like mad with him coming down above her, and when he pulled the metal plate back over the hole, it was dark.

Pure dark.

No light.

None.

And she froze like a limpet on a rock.

"I can't see anything," she whispered.

"Just follow the ladder, babe. Trust me, it only goes down."

That's what she was afraid of.

"Maybe we should just hang right here."

"Maybe not. The cops know about this place, but they never follow anybody past the first level or two. If we can get that far before they catch us, the only problem we'll have is how to get back out."

Oh, God.

"I can't move." And she couldn't. She was stuck.

"Suck it up, babe."

She heard the metal plate being dragged off the hole above, and the thinnest sliver of light shone down.

"Move," he ordered.

And she moved—fast.

Oh, God. Oh, God. Every step she took down felt crazy, like there had to be a better way.

Above them, she heard the cops coming in, and she moved even faster down the ladder to only God knew where. At one point, she felt a cool breeze and she guessed they were at the first level. The next breeze she felt was warm, and that had to be level 2, and then came the big nothing, a sense of vastness with no breeze at all, and above them, only the tiniest pinprick of light and the receding sound of the cops leaving.

Then the light went out.

"Hey, good job," J.T. said.

No, she didn't think so. She thought this was insane. They were three floors down under the city in pitch darkness.

"How long do we have to stay down here?" she asked.

"As long as it takes."

"For what? Hell to freeze over?"

He laughed, which really didn't make her feel better.

And then a miracle, a small beam of light shined down from above. He had a flashlight.

"Can you see the floor?"

"Yes." Thank God. She could see the floor.

"We'll head north for about a quarter mile and then come up under St. Benedict's."

North. For a quarter of a mile. In this black tunnel. She knew the big church, but she hadn't known about this underground labyrinth—and, quite frankly, she'd have been happier not knowing about it.

"Oh, geezus, what was that?" She'd heard something, some skittery thing in the dark.

"Rats, most likely."

Oh, crap.

"How did you find this place?" She made it to the

floor and stepped off the ladder onto concrete. "Nobody knows about this place."

He laughed at that, with good reason, she guessed.

"It's old-school, babe. We were all just screwing around one night, the same way kids always find stuff, especially trouble. Hold on to the back of my pants, and let's see if we can get out of here before the rats eat us."

"Very funny." But it wasn't, and she was scared, and she held on to the back of his pants for what seemed like hours, before he found the rusted-out old ladder he was looking for and they started back up.

She was exhausted by the time they came up in the basement of St. Benedict's, which was another labyrinth of rooms full of junk and broken pews and church documents, boxes of them. Much to her dismay, they didn't head out onto the street. They only crossed the basement to get to another door, which led to another hole in the floor.

"This next stretch is just between you and me, okay?"

"Secret passageway?" A part of her thought he was kidding, but the expression on his face was dead serious.

"Yes or no?" he asked, and she gave him her honest answer.

"Yes."

And down they went again, with their path winding through old passageways with tumbledown walls and tunnels with the guts of the city running through them, and she knew her promise had been true. Even if she wanted to tell someone about this place, she could never have found her way through it without him.

After a long while, they came through a narrow corridor to a place where the walls didn't quite meet. He squeezed through, and so did she, and then they were in a real building again. They passed through one room and then another, before coming to an elevator—and she had to wonder where in the world in Denver would they turn out to be.

Home, it turned out. His home. They got off on the eleventh floor, and when he opened the door leading into his apartment, she knew exactly where they were: 738 Steele Street. A hundred feet of floor-to-ceiling windows looked out over the eastern half of the city all the way to the plains. The floors were all hardwood. The furniture was minimal, most of it grouped around a big fireplace on the southern wall.

"The bathroom's over there," he said, pointing to a door. "I'll fix us something to eat..."

She'd stayed with him until dawn, and hell, even after all these years, she wasn't sure if she'd done the right thing. Regardless, she didn't think she'd be getting anything to eat tonight. It was *really* dark in the basement. She couldn't see her hand in front of her face, and she was trying.

She took a breath and told herself to calm down, to take a cue from him.

"How long are we going to stay down here?" A fair question, she assured herself, and not just a knee-jerk reaction to being bitchy and breathless with near-death anxiety. They were under the building, in some kind of basement, an underground storage room, or a supply area, or a utility access, or maybe an old coal bin. And his whole argument about not crashing was pitifully weak. Tires had left earth. They'd been airborne, even if only for a second. Corinna had scraped her front end on the landing, and if anyone had ever used that supposed "ramp" they'd come down to get an automotive vehicle in here, Jane would eat her socks.

"As long as it takes."

Oh, for crying out loud.

"As long as it takes for what? Because if you're waiting for me to—"

"Shhh," he said softly, interrupting her.

Fine. She could *shhhh*.

She took another breath. Then she heard it, the sound of the other cars. Steele Street muscle was unmistakable. Even from a distance, she could tell Roxanne from Angelina and that was Roxy up there. Coralie sounded like Corinna, and she was coming in from the other side of the building. Angelina must have gone in another direction, probably trying to cut them off at the pass. Roxanne was little more than a brief sound signature echoing in the darkness, but Coralie was prowling the parking lot, the low rumble of her engine tracking west to east behind them. Then Jane heard sirens.

Cops.

She stiffened in her seat, the sound giving her a start. Coralie must have been startled, too. The GTO revved back to full-bore life and took off, and the police car followed her. For one long minute after another, she and J.T. sat silently in Corinna, in the dark, listening to the fading sound of the sirens and to each other breathe.

Cripes. Cops—the last thing she needed. She had a clean record now, and there were a few folks, like Lieutenant Loretta, of the Denver Police Department, whose good graces Jane worked very hard to retain.

So maybe she should have thought about that before she'd ended up sliding off the map into the basement of an abandoned factory over on the west side with a guy with God knew what kind of criminal tendencies.

As a matter of fact, sitting in the dark at the bottom of a virtual pit with a man who had no recollection of himself as one of the good guys—well, on second thought, maybe that hadn't been her best move.

"Is there a way out of here?" she asked, tossing a question into the great pool of silence between them, trying to sound nonchalant, like it was a matter of business, not of survival.

"The way we came in."

She gave him an incredulous look, not that he could see it, which in no way stopped her from flat-out staring in his direction like he was nuts.

"And Plan B?" she asked, because his Plan A sounded like a homeless kid's Christmas list: a whole lot of wishful thinking.

"We don't need Plan B," he said. "This is doable."

"With a jetpack and a winch?" She didn't mean to sound skeptical, but she was damned skeptical.

"No." He started the car, and suddenly she could see the basement in the twin-beam illumination of Corinna's headlights.

The place was a dump, literally, full of junk and garbage. It looked like bad things happened here, and that was the voice of experience. She'd been homeless. She knew about the Christmas list, and she knew what homeless looked like, and it looked like this.

"I've gotten a car up that ramp," he said. "Driven one out of here." He paused for a moment. "It was a deal for a guy named...Sparky. Yeah, Sparky...a BMW 535i, black, an '89."

Oh-kay. That definitely got her attention. He couldn't remember his own name, but he remembered a car he'd stolen. Oh, yeah, he was J. T. Chronopolous, all right. She knew Sparky Klimaszewski, remembered him from a few years back. J.T. must have dealt with old Sparky quite a bit in his younger years. Mr. Klimaszewski was a hard nut, a guy who'd been brokering half the cars stolen in Denver for the last twenty years.

"You must have scraped the hell out of the front cowling, getting a Beemer out of here."

He let out a short laugh. "Yeah. I did. It's why I never told anybody about this place. We lost money on the

535i. Sparky was . . ." His voice trailed off as he took in the basement, looking around.

She felt the hesitation in his thoughts, heard the confusion, but she didn't press him. It was obvious which guys he'd never told, or Hawkins would have driven Roxanne right down on top of Corinna in this basement, anything to hold him in place.

God, it had to be tearing them all up, to know J.T. was alive, to be wondering what had happened to him—to wonder who they'd buried in that grave in Sheffield Cemetery.

"So this is one of your old hangouts?" If it was, it was one he hadn't shared with her.

"No," he said, putting the car in reverse and backing up. "It was a rabbit hole, a one-off deal that didn't work out."

Smooth and easy, he executed a three-point Y-turn, getting the GTO lined back up in front of the opening a half a floor above them at the other end of the impossibly steep ramp.

"Maybe I'll just get out and walk it." She did *not* want to be part of any more drop-of-death roller-coaster insanity. Maybe he was right. Maybe they weren't trapped down here. Inconvenienced, sure, but not trapped. Frazzled and frayed, but not falling apart. Anxious, sure, but not out-and-out panicked.

She didn't care. She didn't want to get out of here in a reverse play of how they'd gotten in. She reached for the door.

"Stay put," he said, shifting gears and backing up. "You're fine."

Oh, right, she'd heard that before.

She felt Corinna's rear bumper come softly up against the wall behind them, and he stopped and shifted gears again.

Technically, at that point, she had a couple of seconds to get out, but she missed it, and then it was too late.

With all the mind-numbing, bone-shaking roar and rumble of a Ram Air 400 going balls-out in neutral with a heavy foot on the gas pedal, she braced herself. He didn't drive a car. He *launched* a car, and Corinna was being prepped for another rocket ride.

When he released the clutch, she was already pressed back into her seat, holding her breath, reciting Hail Marys.

Power. That's what he needed, and that's what he got, all the power Corinna could deliver in one screaming, smoking blast. Slingshot, all the way. He pushed the car as hard and fast as the beast could go in an impossibly short distance, and even then, Jane wasn't sure they were going to clear the top of the ramp. When they did, it was with air to spare and a subsequent body-slamming descent of the front end onto the asphalt of the parking lot.

Things crunched.

She winced.

And he drove.

CHAPTER SIXTEEN

"Rick Karola at ten o'clock," Scout said, seeing Lancaster's errand boy driving by where she and Jack were still parked close to Coors Field, not far from Steele Street. "In the blue Lexus ES350."

"Got him," Jack said. "Do we follow the bastard, or do I go back into Steele Street? What do you think?"

What did she think?

Well, she spent a helluva lot of her time trying *not* to think about that blond bimbo in Key Largo four months ago. That's what she thought. She'd hated him for that, truly hated him. And she knew the blonde had just been one in a long, long line of women in his bed.

"I think we follow Karola," she said, all business. "See what he's up to. He's alone, and from the way he's craning his head around, I say he's looking for something, or somebody, like maybe Sam Walls. And if we can, we need to get a fix on Lancaster. If Con hasn't checked in with us by the time we do that, then we consider going back into the building."

She was always all business with Jack. It was the only way for her to function without her heart breaking all over the place.

"I've got a notebook in my pack," he said. "Draw me a layout of the building."

"Check." She reached into the backseat for his pack.

Sure, he'd rescued her, but that's what he did, Jack's Big Thing: Save the girl, dazzle and amaze, damn the torpedoes, full speed ahead. He was a pirate, pure and simple, six feet of swash, buckle, and balls.

Jack started the Buick and put it in gear, and she began drawing what she knew about 738 Steele Street, every room, every hall, not that they'd let her see too much—except when it came to Kid. They'd made damn sure she'd had plenty of time to see him, and there wasn't a doubt in her mind that he was Con's younger brother.

She looked up when Jack pulled into the street. Two sets of eyes were better than one on a tail, and she sure didn't need to be staring at him. He had one of those faces that for reasons she did her damnedest to ignore had imprinted itself on her brain the first time she'd seen him: lost boy, all the way, pure trouble, high cheekbones, firm mouth, a slight cleft in his chin, beautiful. His nose was a swoop of Irish mischief, his hair a rich, deep shade of auburn and usually wildly tousled on his head, never completely under control, like Jack himself. His eyes were nearly the same color as his hair, a rich, warm brown beneath auburn eyebrows, totally incongruous with the reality of Jack Traeger. There was very little warmth to be had in the ex-Ranger. To the core of his being, and despite his Fair Isle looks, he could be the coldest bastard on the face of the earth. She'd seen him in action, and as far as his operational skills, all she had to say was that he was the best, which was why he worked for Con. It was his personal life where he fell far, far short of the mark.

"Sonuvabitch," he muttered under his breath, and oh, hell, she saw it, too, a beer truck pulling onto the road between them and Karola and taking up both lanes to make a wide turn.

"Well, hell."

"Dammit."

"We'll go three blocks—"

"Take a right and—"

"Check the cross street," she finished the drill, and he flashed her a grin. That's the way it used to be between them: fast and fluid, the two of them on the same wavelength.

Ten minutes later, Jack pulled over and parked a block over from their first parking spot. If Karola was looking for something around Steele Street, chances were, he'd come back around.

Scout went back to sketching a plan of the building and ignoring Jack Traeger.

Hell, he'd probably imprinted himself on her soul and done it on purpose, just so he could torture her.

But she was done with that. She'd been done since Key Largo. She had no more emotion left to give to the lost cause that was Jack Traeger. None. Zero. *Nada.* It was time for her to grow up and move on. If he hadn't noticed her by now, he probably wasn't going to notice her.

God, it was times like this when she really missed her mother. Girls with mothers didn't end up in strange cities in rented Buicks with pirates who'd broken their heart more times than she could count. At least that's what she always told herself any time she was sad or in trouble—that if her mother were alive, things would be better, life different, her troubles a thing of the past.

But there was never a mother—only Con and the pirate, Black Jack Traeger.

"Hey, there's Karola, going around the block again," he said, putting the Buick back in gear.

She peeked up from her drawing. "He still looks lost."

"Yeah," Jack agreed. "Let's go see what he's up to."

"Roger, that." She sat up a little straighter in her seat. The sooner they found Con and tied this mess up, the sooner she could get herself somewhere halfway around the world from wherever Black Jack ended up. "Let's follow this bastard and see where he lights."

Half an hour of wandering around later, Karola finally found a place to call home.

"The Kashmir Club," Scout said, and gave a low whistle.

Jack concurred. The hotel was anything but discreet. Indian in design, it had shades of the Taj Mahal in its architecture, an exotic addition to the Denver skyline, and, from the looks of it, a recent one. The grand entrance to the downtown hotel was elegantly wrapped in pillared arches. The large, mullioned windows revealed a lobby lush with exotic chandeliers and sumptuous furnishings in rich shades of ruby red, gold, and deep sage green.

"What do you think?" Scout asked. "Five stars?"

"At least four."

"It looks like a place Lancaster would stay," she said, and he agreed. The man was used to high living. It disgusted him, the way Lancaster had made his money, selling the best of America's war-fighters to the highest bidder.

"And there goes Karola," he said, watching the man pull into the hotel's underground parking lot. At the barrier, Karola handed the attendant a card, and after a moment, the barrier was raised, and Karola drove in and disappeared from view.

"We've got him." Scout's voice was edged in excitement.

Jack understood. He felt the same way. The bastard was in there.

"What do you want to do?" she asked.

"Go in and take him out," he said flatly.

"I'll need a weapon." She was succinct. If they were going in, she needed to be armed.

And if they had been going in, Jack couldn't have agreed more, but her statement cleared his head like a cold north wind. He wasn't taking her into the line of fire—ever.

"We can't do it without Con." It was a flat-out lie. He could do it, clean and fast. That was the best way. Drop her off at the Star Motel first. Come back and get the lay of the land at the Kashmir Club. Find out how many men were with Lancaster and plan accordingly, including a foolproof escape—good to go.

But not with Scout.

Never with Scout.

"Yes, we can."

He shook his head. "Con has questions. He deserves answers. If we kill Lancaster before Con can talk with him, he may never get those answers." He shook his head again. "It's too much to risk." All true, but he still liked the idea of dumping Scout at the motel and just taking care of business.

Liking it and doing it were two different things, though. Tactically, killing a guy was pretty damn easy. Abducting a guy wasn't, and Con did have a lot of questions for Lancaster. He wanted to know names, dates, missions. He wanted to know if there was anybody else out there who needed help, some guy like him who hadn't survived as well as he had.

Scout seemed to mull his explanation over for a moment. Then she agreed.

"So we go for the long shot."

The perfect solution, of course, and he agreed with it one hundred percent. There was only one hitch.

"What's the long shot?"

"Give me your phone," she said, and he complied, taking it out of his pocket and handing it over, curious as to what she thought she could do that he hadn't tried.

They finished cruising by the parking garage entrance,

and he picked up some speed. By the time she'd keyed a number into his phone and gotten an answer, they'd traveled a couple more blocks. He turned the corner and pulled over into the first available parking space.

"Miller," he heard her say. "It's Scout. I need a favor. Hold on." She looked over at him. "What's the number on the phone Con's using?"

He gave her the number, and she repeated it to Miller. Jack liked the U.S. Army vet. Miller had been in Special Forces before he'd been wounded. Now he lived in Nevada with a girlfriend named Carlotta Aragon, a buxom, dark-haired beauty, and between them, they had five kids, a passel, a posse, a bunch, all of them cuter than bugs on a milkweed pod. Scout loved them.

She'd make a good mother. Jack knew it in his heart, but it was the last damn thing he wanted to think about, except when he'd been drinking too much and got all maudlin. Then he thought about it plenty. The girls would be gorgeous, mixed-race beauties with brains like their momma, and the boys would have his and Garrett Leesom's blood running through their veins—warriors all, cunning and skilled. He'd make damn sure of it.

"I need you to ping that number off a cell tower if he makes a call, and don't tell me you can't do it. We're in Denver," she said, still talking to Miller.

Great plan, Jack thought, except for one obvious fact. He made the time-out gesture.

"The only person Con is going to call is me," he said, when he had her attention. "And if he does, I'll be sure and ask him where in the hell he is."

To his credit, he managed the news flash without so much as a hint of sarcasm—for all the good it did him.

"I'm fully operational, Traeger," she said, giving him a look that said he was an idiot for thinking otherwise. "I'm just covering bases. If anybody uses that phone for any reason, we're going to know where it is. With luck,

Con will be in the same place. If we need to go back into Steele Street to get him, at least you'll have a better idea of the layout than you probably had going in the first time."

Damn good point. There was a reason he loved her, and it was the same reason he made a point of taking up with more intellectually challenged women. No one could compare, not in beauty or brains, so he saved himself the trouble of even attempting to find someone who could hold his interest beyond the bedroom.

He was a jerk. He knew it. But he was a heartbroken jerk, a condition he didn't see a solution for, so he cut himself a lot of slack in the romance, such as it was, department.

Karl the college professor—hell. Just when he'd decided to try to move their relationship to the next level, to take a chance and put himself out there, she'd had to go get a boyfriend who had a damn good chance of being a real step up in life, somebody a helluva lot classier than an ex–Army Ranger, somebody who probably never got shot at.

"We should go back to the motel and wait for him there. That was the original plan," he said.

"Motel?" She slanted her gaze at him from across the interior of the Buick, both of her eyebrows raised.

"The Star Motel, a dump on the north end of Denver, up in the suburbs." He knew she was used to much nicer digs. When they were on a job, he and Con holed up in whatever place was least likely to get them noticed. But on missions he did with Scout, Con usually managed damn nice accommodations. Of course, he let Scout in on only the most benign operations, doing things no one even half as skilled could get hurt executing, like low-risk surveillance, document preparation, money shuffling, and the occasional security analysis for people who had more money than actual trouble. She was a good courier, too, a world-class traveler who slid through airport security, overworked customs agents, and foreign cities with ease. She always delivered.

Con would skin him alive if he took Scout into the Kashmir Club after Lancaster. The best thing he could do, for her and for himself, was take her back to the motel and lie low. Jack knew Con would rather miss his chance at Lancaster a hundred times over than put Scout in danger again.

"A dump?" She sounded appropriately skeptical.

"The sheets are clean, the water's hot, and I'm on the couch, so you've got a bed. Not that you'll need it for long. We're booked on a jet out of here at seven a.m."

"Headed to?"

"Paraguay."

"How's the river house?" she asked. It had been her home, on and off, for the last four years.

"There's not much left, but Con thought you might want to go through it before we move on."

"Move on where?"

He shrugged. "Paris, I think, the apartment."

The words were no sooner out of his mouth than she smiled, a grin that lit up her face and broke his heart all over again for about the millionth fucking time. She loved Paris. He knew it. Con knew it. And if she loved a place, they were both hoping it meant she would stay put.

After this job, it was downhill for everybody, especially Con, and one of them, either he or Con, really needed to step up and tell her. If for no other reason on the face of the earth, that was why he needed to find the boss: so Con could do the dirty work.

There had been a time when he and Scout had been easier with each other, when she'd been younger, and they'd been friends. Not that he'd ever wanted to be just her friend, but as badly as he'd wanted to kiss her, he'd never gotten the job done, not even when he might have had a chance, and now he wished he had—before she'd gone and gotten herself a damn boyfriend named Karl.

God, he was such a sap.

Turning on his blinker, he eased the Buick back into traffic and headed toward the motel.

Such an idiotic, star-crossed, ridiculous, romantic sap.

CHAPTER SEVENTEEN

Randolph Lancaster was good at his job, all of his jobs, and he had a good half a dozen on any given day of the week. In all of his various high-ranking endeavors, he was always the smartest guy in the room, no matter who else was present, and he'd played some of the toughest rooms in the world, from the Oval Office to Number 10 Downing Street.

The room he was in at Denver's newest luxury hotel, the Kashmir Club, was no different. His assistant, Tyler Crutchfield, a young Harvard-trained lawyer, was a particularly brilliant protégé destined to work himself into a cabinet position someday.

But today was not that day.

Today, Crutchfield still worked for Randolph, still had a lot to learn, and still had a job to do.

"Skeeter Bang has a reputation for being tough and smart," Randolph said. "But she's got a soft spot when it comes to her husband, Dylan Hart. We threaten him, and she'll come around, guaranteed."

"Yes, sir." Tyler Crutchfield was East Coast born and bred but had the blue-eyed blond good looks of a California surfer, if California surfers ever wore handmade Italian suits.

"You cut her from the herd, get her to meet you, and we'll have this game on our turf. But watch yourself, and I mean physically. She's an operator, an independent thinker, as tough as the rest of that crowd, a wild card. That's why we're here to rein them in."

"Yes, sir," Crutchfield said. "What about Traeger and the girl, Scout Leesom?"

"Traeger's a mercenary, plain and simple. If he'd stayed in the Army longer, he might have become a contender for LeedTech's export program, but as a civilian, he doesn't pose a threat, and the girl matters only if she gets in the way. Karola and Walls will make sure she doesn't. All we need is Conroy Farrel, and if we can do a hostage trade, Skeeter Bang for Farrel, then Ms. Bang can go to bed at night dreaming of her happily-ever-after."

For all the good that was going to do her in the end. She was his leverage in the deal, nothing more. If his guys could capture Farrel without him getting his hands dirty with the woman, all the better. If not, she was his backup plan. Either way, her fate was sealed, but she wouldn't know it, until it was far too late.

"Don't worry," Crutchfield said, his smile and his gaze filled with all the confidence conferred by inherited wealth and an Ivy League degree. "We're offering her a good deal. She either meets with me, or her husband ends up in Leavenworth for life, and she probably right along with him. I'll convince her we can make the case for treason, because we can."

Randolph almost returned the smile—almost, but not quite. The boy was like a bulldog with the prime directive, pumped up with self-righteous conviction, focused on the goal of shutting down a rogue team of black ops warriors, dark shadow warriors who had tapped into American taxpayer dollars to fund their own skewed vision of the nation's defense. Assassins, Randolph had told him, operating outside the bounds of the military and intelligence communities that had spawned them.

Special Defense Force, SDF, needed to be wiped off the face of the earth as if it had never existed.

That last part was true. Randolph had started SDF, and he was going to end it tonight, right here in Denver. LeedTech was turning into a disaster for him. His house of cards was slipping out from under him. He needed distance, and he couldn't get it from LeedTech with Conroy Farrel breathing down his neck, and he couldn't get distance from Conroy Farrel with SDF breathing down Farrel's neck. So they all had to go. Their total annihilation was the only victory that offered him any protection.

"Where's Walls?" he asked. "I want him backing you up. She might not go with you willingly."

"I can handle a woman, Randolph," Crutchfield said, not bothering to hide his irritation. "I was the captain of my water polo team for two years running."

Clueless, Lancaster thought. Crutchfield was absolutely clueless about what it meant to be an operator of SDF's caliber.

"She'll be armed."

"So am I." The lawyer opened the jacket on his Italian suit to reveal a semiautomatic pistol in a shoulder holster. "Don't worry. Once I have the meet set up, I'll contact Walls and pull him off Steele Street. He'll be there to make sure she cooperates."

"Are King and Rock locked on a target yet? Or are they still chasing their tails?" he asked.

He'd brought four operators with him, and he damn well expected them to do their jobs. He had especially high expectations for King Banner and Rock Howe, the last two LeedTech soldiers to come out of Souk's lab. They were the pinnacle of the good doctor's twisted art.

Rick Karola and Sam Walls were the flotsam and jetsam of Souk's lab—not quite whole, a couple of mistakes, but skilled and exceptionally loyal. Basic, true loyalty went a long way with Lancaster. It made up for any number of other deficiencies.

And then there was MNK-1.

He pulled a handkerchief out of his coat pocket and dabbed at his upper lip.

Monk, the doctor had called it. Monk the mistake is what Lancaster had called it, the Bangkok disaster. Dr. Souk hadn't been the only doctor experimenting with creating the ultimate soldier, and after Souk's untimely death, a man named Greg Patterson had risen to the top of the heap. If the MNK-1 thing had functioned, it would have gone a long way toward redeeming Patterson, the Bangkok bungler, a half-American, quarter-German, quarter–mad genius Irishman. Lancaster hesitated even to call the man a doctor or scientist, not after what he'd come up with. Certainly Patterson wasn't getting any more contracts or money out of him. He needed distance and plenty of it between him and...and the abomination Patterson had tried to foist off on him as the world's ultimate warrior.

The very thought of the thing made his skin crawl, made him feel unclean.

God, he'd been there when Patterson had woken the creature up, and he hoped never to have such a shock again. Those weird albino eyes snapping open and locking onto his with such painful intensity, that mouth gaping wide, then wider, words choking in its throat. Its hair had been long and streaked, platinum blond and pale gray, almost silver, and crazily matted in twists and knots. The creature had looked human, remarkably still like the young man Lancaster had recruited in San Diego, but along with adding strength and speed and cunning and fifty more pounds of sheer muscle mass, Patterson had turned something inside out in the man, and it showed. What Patterson had been left with was not a soldier of any kind Lancaster could bear to have on board his LeedTech juggernaut, which made MNK-1 useless except as combat fodder, like a rabid wolf to be carted around in a cage and let loose to kill and feed.

He'd walked out on the deal and gone back to the basics, to the tried and true, good guys like Rock and King. They'd been following the Mercedes in an SUV, and when four cars had exited Steele Street like bats out of hell, Lancaster had sicced his good guys on them. But they'd lost the one car they'd almost caught, and now they were cruising the city, checking out the chop shop boys' old haunts.

His two knuckle draggers sure as hell had better have caught something by now. Failure was not an option.

Crutchfield pulled a cellphone out of his pocket and punched in a speed-dial.

"Status report," he said. After a moment, he met Randolph's gaze. "King says they picked up another one of the cars, a GTO. They think it's Farrel, and they're closing in."

"Good." He wasn't impressed. He expected results. "Remind them of their rules of engagement. No lethal force. I want him alive, and I want him here. I have questions. When they're answered, Rock and King can have him back and take him apart." He meant it literally, and knew that's exactly what he'd get, Conroy Farrel, his most dangerous mistake, utterly destroyed to the point where no amount of drugs and pills and elixirs could bring him back to life.

He refused to take the blame for MNK-1. That was Patterson's mistake, not his. He'd divorced himself from the Thai lab and its line of products. No one could tie him to Dr. Patterson's creation, and now it was dead. There were no records of the transaction anywhere. He'd made certain of it. To the world's knowledge, MNK-1 had not and did not exist. Only Lancaster and the Bangkok bunglers knew what they'd done—and perhaps Crutchfield had a slight supposition.

Genetic imprinting, Patterson had called his great breakthrough, a loyalty gene, a small chromosomal reconstruction way down in the double helix, a way to assure absolute obedience.

Lancaster hadn't seen obedience or obeisance, or whatever the hell Patterson had wanted to call it. What he'd seen was far more disturbing.

He'd seen love—passionate, absolute, sickening. The creature had longed for him. Not sexually, but with such intensity that Lancaster had still felt dirty and threatened, as if the last little push into unnaturalness could happen at any time.

Patterson had assured him it would not. He'd engineered all sexual motivation out of MNK-1. In essence, while scientists and engineers all over the world were trying to make robots more human, Patterson had made a human into a very cunning robot, literally programmable, and MNK-1 had been programmed to brutalize anyone Lancaster chose, better than a whole army of slaves. The buyer's will alone ruled the creature.

Fucking nuts, that's all Lancaster had thought. Souk had been demented, but Patterson was nuts.

He had arrived back at the hotel in a state of disorientation, his mind reeling from the sight and the smell and especially the sound the creature had made.

Lan-castaaa, it had cried out after him, the eerie sound of its voice chasing him down the hall. *Lan-castaaa*—he still heard it in his sleep sometimes. So he'd stopped sleeping. Mix that with a few drinks, and he might have blubbered more than he'd meant to, though God only knew what. He'd woken up the next morning with the hangover from hell and headed back to the States with Crutchfield by his side—his hands clean, his conscience clear, and his course set.

And so help him God, he still could not believe Patterson had told that bastardish thing his name. Kill it, he'd told the doctor. Destroy it and dispose of any and all evidence that it had ever existed. *Christ.* MNK-1 had been a Navy SEAL, and Patterson had utterly ruined him.

"There's a woman with Farrel," Crutchfield said, still on the phone. "Neither of them recognize her. She's not one of the SDF women."

"Bring her in. Rock and King can have her, too." There would be no loose ends on this mission, not a black heart left beating.

He looked down at the chessboard set up in front of the windows overlooking the city's lower downtown. He'd done a lot of good work in Washington, D.C., over the last forty-five years. At seventy years old, he'd spent his whole life in service to his country. If at one point he'd seen a way to further the interests and better protect the United States of America, by God, he'd taken it, and if he'd benefited financially from his vision and his efforts, by God, he'd earned his money the hard way.

But he could feel the noose tightening around his neck. Too many things weren't going his way, too much unfinished business from too many missions was starting to accumulate in all the wrong places, and here and there around Washington, people were starting to notice that it was all sliding in his direction.

It shouldn't have turned out that way. Expanding LeedTech's business to include a few dozen transactions with Atlas Exports shouldn't have gotten away from them. There shouldn't have been any mistakes, and there hadn't been—until J. T. Chronopolous. He'd gone rogue almost from the get-go, losing his memory and taking the name Conroy Farrel and setting out on his grand quest to destroy everything Randolph had worked for all his life.

He wasn't going to let that happen.

Randolph looked down at the chessboard again, and picked up one of the heavy pieces, his favorite, for good luck. It was a rook, the white rook. He slipped it in his pocket and lifted his gaze back to Crutchfield.

"It's time," he said. "You've got Skeeter Bang's number. Go ahead and make your call."

CHAPTER EIGHTEEN

Keeping Corinna to a low rumble, Con turned onto the street fronting the Tatsunaka Produce buildings and headed back into the neighborhoods of the west side. He knew what he was looking for—a restaurant, or some other public place where Jane could either call a taxi or make a phone call to get picked up, a place where he could dump her. Without the Steele Street guys on his ass, he could take the time to get the job done, to just get out of the car and physically pry her out of the passenger seat.

The sooner the better. This deal was done, the escape over. He needed to check in with Jack and Scout, see where they were, what their ETA was for the Star Motel, and then head there himself.

Or he could drive all night long... just drive, on and on and on.

He reached up and rubbed the side of his arm where the Halox dart had gotten him through his coat. His skin was hot at the injection point, and *fuck,* there was swelling, tenderness, just like with the damn ketamine.

Well, hell.

He could fire Corinna up and try to outrun the drug. Jack knew as much as he did about maybe saving his ass one more time, if he could get to the motel and his med kit. But *geezus,* he was tired of running.

Fucking Halox. He didn't know if he had it in him to get through another stretch of the kind of hell ahead of him—physical collapse, the endless twisting pain, the anguish, the fucking doubts of whether he'd make it and what kind of condition he'd be in even if he did survive, if he'd be too physically destroyed to function, or if his mind would finally break.

He'd seen all that and worse happen to stronger men than he at Souk's.

A wave of heat pulsed to sudden life across his upper chest, raising his body temperature a dangerous number of degrees for the space of a heartbeat. Sweat broke out on his brow. Then as quickly as it had come, the heat was gone, but probably not for long.

Fuck. Stronger men than he.

He shoved his hand in his pocket, pulled it out full of pills, bet the house on one of the blues, and shoved the rest back—and he kept driving, taking the turns slow, looking over the city and wondering about every damn thing in his life. At least the greenies had finished off the headache the reds hadn't quite killed. Time alone would tell if all that and a blue were going to do him a damn bit of good.

Yeah, time would tell, but he was running out of time. He felt it with each passing day.

A small beep coming from his jacket had him reaching for his cellphone. He pulled it out of the jacket's inside pocket and quickly read the text message: *Mission accomplished. Report.*

A smile almost curved his mouth. He'd report in as soon as he dropped off his passenger, but his boy had done good, damn good. Scout was safe, and she was going to be a treasure trove of intel. She'd been with these Steele Street guys for eight weeks, and he knew her. She wouldn't have forgotten a word, not a fact, not a breath any of them had taken.

But *hell*. He had to let that girl go, too.

He'd done plenty of private bitching over the last four years about Jack Traeger, plenty and then some, but Jack was who she'd need in the months ahead, and Paris was where she'd go. He had an apartment there she loved, and he'd put her name on the lease.

Jack knew where most of the money was, and Con had encrypted the data on the accounts Jack didn't know about and put it all on a flash drive he'd left with a tech stringer they used out of Nevada, a U.S. Army vet named Miller. He'd get it to Scout.

Garrett Leesom's girl was smart. She'd figure out the account codes, and when she looked at the numbers, she would know she was set for life. No more hanging on the edge, no more skirting the dark side. No more missions.

Reaching up, he wiped the back of his hand across his mouth and then turned on the car's windshield wipers. While they'd been underground, night had fallen, bringing a drop in the temperature and a late spring rain. The cool drizzle ran down Corinna's glass and was swept away in long, curving arcs by the wiper blades. Water pooled in the gutters. Steam rose from the streets.

He'd known he was an American citizen. Jack had told him. But he hadn't known Denver, Colorado, was his hometown—not until today.

Maybe he wouldn't leave the city.

Maybe he shouldn't.

Christ. He had a brother.

A brother he didn't really remember, so what did it really mean?

Not much, he decided. Not enough. No matter how much he wished it could be otherwise. It was too late. Whatever life he'd lived in this place, it was gone. Denver was an interlude, not a change in direction. The mission was still Randolph Lancaster, destroying the man and his company, LeedTech.

He pulled to a stop at a red light and checked the cross traffic going by, looking for big-block monsters, any trouble headed his way, and a place to say good-bye to Wild Thing. There were a few businesses at the intersection, but none of them met his criteria. The junk and stuff store was closed for the night. The bar was a hole-in-the-wall dive. The gas station looked like it was just waiting to get knocked off, and the other corner was an empty field.

He could play this game all night long, trying to find the perfect place to let her go, when what he needed was to just do it and move on.

"Where are we going?" she asked him from the other side of the car.

Good question, he thought, turning and looking at her, giving in to an impulse he'd been trying to resist. He let his gaze drift over the shadowed delicacy of her face, the curves highlighted by the golden sheath of her dress, and down the long silky length of her legs.

His gaze narrowed.

"What happened to your knee?" It was skinned, and it hadn't been when he'd first seen her in LoDo.

"Well," she said slowly, "a couple of lifetimes ago, when I was in the Steele Street garage just minding my own business, somebody threw a grenade at me, and I fell to the floor and scraped the hell out of it."

As the somebody in question, he didn't have much to offer. He'd have thrown the flash bang even knowing she was going to get her knee scraped, but he'd rather she hadn't gotten injured. There weren't many perfect things in the world, but she was one, the way she'd looked walking down Wazee, owning the street.

"Don't worry," she said. "It doesn't hurt . . . much."

Hell. He let out a long breath.

"Okay, it hurts a lot, but it's just a scrape, and I'm getting a bruise from where I hit my head."

"At Tatsunaka's." He remembered her mentioning it—and him dismissing the complaint. She'd been scared and shook up, but for someone who looked like a catwalk queen, she was pretty tough. He'd figured that out the instant he'd seen her hot-wiring the car.

"Yes. See?" She turned in her seat and pulled her hair back from the right side of her face, and, yes, he could see a little swelling on her forehead near her hairline, and maybe a little bruising, too.

He was so tempted to reach out and touch her face, smooth her hair back from the bruise and tell her she was going to be fine. But of course she *was* going to be fine, and she didn't need him telling her anything, and it was damn near suicidal for him to touch her.

Hell. He usually had more sense. The blue pills were always a crapshoot and always messed with his head a little.

She messed with his head, too, all by herself, just sitting there, with or without a scraped knee and a bruised forehead. Within the confines of the car, her scent surrounded him, seeped into his senses and made him long for something he didn't know if he'd ever had—a woman like her, a refuge, someone he could count on to watch his back. Someone to love.

"So where *are* we going?"

"I'm looking for a restaurant," he said, choosing the truth, always a good plan.

"Oh." She sounded a little surprised. "What are you...uh, hungry for? Mexican, Chinese, sushi, cheeseburger and fries?"

You, he thought. Somebody so gorgeous it hurt. A smart, tough, unafraid girl with the tactical sense to draw down on him. Up against anyone else, she'd have had a better-than-average chance of coming out on top, way better.

"A nice place, that's all. Something you would like."

It didn't matter to him. He wasn't planning on eating. He put Corinna back into gear, his gaze automatically checking the rearview mirror while they waited for the light to change.

"Jane," he said her name again, thinking it over. "Jane what?"

"Linden," she answered with barely a moment's hesitation, which told him way more than she probably knew. Nobody in his business gave their name away that easily. She was pure civilian, all right. "I manage an art gallery over on 17th."

Well, this was getting damned interesting, right down to employment addresses, and she was a manager, no less. He was impressed.

"What were you doing at Steele Street?" he asked, thinking why the hell not? He seemed to have a willing conversation partner.

"What were *you* doing at Steele Street?" she shot back. "Besides practically blowing the place up?"

Taking a cue from her, he kept his thoughts on that one to himself. She didn't need to know anything about Randolph Lancaster.

"All righty, fine," she said, not bothering to hide her frustration. "I was headed home from work to get ready for—*oh, cripes.*"

"Ready for what?" He had an idea, and there was no reason on earth for it to bother him, but it did.

"A date," she said, checking her watch, her brow furrowing. "*Damn.*"

Well, hell.

"I live just a couple of blocks from Steele Street," she said, opening her purse and rummaging around inside.

"So it wasn't really out of my way, and when I saw you, I knew I had to . . . well, I had to, uh, go tell Superman."

"Superman," he repeated, hearing her whisper another *damn* under her breath while she continued digging through the contents of the zebra bag. "You mean the Hawkins guy in the green Challenger?"

She nodded, starting to pull stuff out of the purse—a makeup bag, a wallet, what looked like a day's worth of mail—and piling it all in her lap, which reminded him that he had a few of her things himself. "He's the best friend you ever had, right next to Creed, and that's the God's truth."

So she'd said.

"Creed. The guy in the Chevelle Super Sport."

She nodded. "You were all a bunch of car thieves in the old days, when you were teenagers, and then everybody got busted, but Dylan, the boss, made it all okay, and now I don't really know what you guys do, but I'd lay money down on you doing it for the government, and the only reason I know anybody at Steele Street is because . . . well, you and uh . . . Superman ran into me, sort of, one night outside the Blue Iguana Lounge." She was still piling things up in her lap, a small brush, sunglass case, coin purse, keys on an elaborate key chain with all kinds of charms and baubles on it. "And then a few years later, Hawkins married Kat, and a few years after that, when I moved up here from Phoenix, Kat hired me to work in her gallery—end of story."

Geezus.

Nobody in his world blabbered on, not without a load of Sodium Pentothal jacked into their system. But more than likely, she was dead-on about the Steele Street boys working for the government if they were involved with Lancaster, and he knew for damn sure she was dead-on about the carjacking crew. He'd done it. He'd known it the instant the guy named Hawkins had called her name. The juice, the smell, the sound of ratchets and wrenches, of burning rubber and grinding gears, it had all suddenly been there in his mind.

"Didn't anybody ever tell you not to talk to strangers?" Really, she was so far out of the box, it was a little unnerving.

"You're not a stranger," she said, letting out an exasperated sigh and jamming everything in her lap back into the striped purse. For a moment, she just sat still, her eyes closed. Then, after voicing a weary, muttered "What the hell," she turned and faced him, meeting his gaze straight on. "You're John Thomas Chronopolous. That's your real name."

John Thomas.

He sat back in his seat

All right, sure, whatever she thought. Like he'd said, he must have been somebody before he'd become Conroy Farrel, and he guessed there was a ring of truth in the name somewhere... somewhere just outside his ability to verify.

John Thomas Chronopolous.

It beat the hell out of a lot of names he'd been called, but it didn't quite give him the same memory jolt as when he'd seen Peter, Kid Chaos, standing in the garage. That guy's name sure as hell had come to him in a crackling flash of light and truth, which was great, just what he needed, more crackling, flashing, lightning bolts of long-lost truth firing up the dead brain cells in his memory banks. Enough of those and maybe he'd figure out who he used to be and what in the world had happened to him between *Then* and *Now,* or he'd get the mother of all headaches and the pain would break him, crack his head straight open, from skull to gullet.

In the six years of life he remembered, there had been no shortage of physical suffering. For the most part, he'd been able to manage it with the dwindling stash of rainbow-colored gelcaps he'd taken from Souk's lab in Bangkok. But time was running out on him, time and pills, and when his little rainbow beauties were gone, he'd be right behind them: *gone*. Before that happened, he wanted Lancaster dead.

John Thomas.

Geezus, he thought, reaching for his jacket and taking her gun out of the pocket. Very methodically, he released the magazine, let it drop into his hand, and then slid the cartridges out one by one.

He believed her, whether he had a clear memory of the name or not—and that was a definite "or not."

"Here," he said, dropping her empty gun, the empty magazine, and the handful of cartridges into the open top of her purse. "When we get to the restaurant, you might want to start putting that all back together."

She gave him a look that said he could eat worms and die and immediately starting fishing the cartridges out of her purse.

"What about my knife?" she said, very genteelly leaving off the implied "you jerk."

He pulled the pearl-handled beauty out of his front jeans pocket and handed it over. She knew how fast he was. He figured she wasn't going to try to shank him or shoot him. No, they'd had some kind of personal relationship. She was on his side.

The light changed, and he pressed on the gas, letting the GTO rumble and crawl down the road, keeping just under the speed limit.

Despite her babbling on, Jane was a smart girl, too. Once he drove off, it wouldn't take her too long to put her weapons in order and figure things out, and then she'd go home. Tonight would just be an odd entry in her Dear Jane diary. By the time she woke up in the morning, he'd be halfway to South America or on his way to Bangkok.

Either way, it didn't matter to him. He just needed to stay on the move, working his mission, and getting Wild Thing out of the car was the next step.

Three streets down, he found what he'd been looking for and pulled to a stop in front of a stucco building. A bright blue neon sign of a howling wolf graced the building. The place was about halfway down the block, midway between a stretch of bars and clubs, and it looked busy, with lots of people inside.

"Mama Guadaloupe's?" she asked, giving him an incredulous look he didn't quite understand, like maybe it was a strip joint in disguise.

Glancing up through the windshield, he read the words flowing in pink neon script above the blue wolf, then checked the clientele through the window. It was family night in there, all the way, not a strip club.

"Yeah," he said. "This looks good."

"It is good," she said, her tone very sure. "The best Santa Fe gourmet in the city."

Well, great. Maybe she could get dinner while she was waiting for her ride—and that was that, time for goodbye, the big *adios,* time to exfiltrate her out of the front seat. He'd take her inside, get her settled in Mama's, and she'd be fine, a whole helluva lot better off than she was with him—and he hated having to admit that.

CHAPTER NINETEEN

"Slow down. I see the car up ahead, in the next block, parked on the right," King said. A blond bruiser, he weighed in at one ninety-eight, all muscle, with a "recon" high-and-tight haircut. Dressed in civvies, a pair of jeans with a gray T-shirt and a double-X brown hoodie, he looked like the biggest and cleanest-cut hoodlum ever to hit the streets of the west side. His face was hard and chiseled, lantern-jawed, and devoid of expression. His boots were pure military issue, flat black and lace-up, and he had a reputation for getting the job done, whatever the job.

"The woman is still with him," his partner said. Rock was driving the Jeep SUV Lancaster had rented for them at the airport. Rock's head was completely shaved, and he was far more comfortable in a combat zone, any combat zone, than he ever felt in a city not under fire. At two hundred fifteen pounds, he was the bigger of the two, a muscled, flat-faced, square-headed war-fighter wearing desert tan cargo pants and a long-sleeved Corps T-shirt with an unbuttoned gray shirt over the top.

Both men carried .45-caliber pistols in paddle holsters concealed on their right sides and sheath knives on their left, with razor-edged folding knifes in their pockets.

"You take the woman," King said. He didn't care if they were after the damn-near-mythical Conroy Farrel or not, it wouldn't take the two of them to take the man down. Farrel was a Bangkok boy, just like them, but they'd had better juice, the Gen X soup. If Lancaster had sent them in the first place, instead of all those now-dead CIA agents, Farrel would be ancient history by now.

"*Shit*," Rock whispered, and King knew it wasn't because of being stuck with taking the woman. Farrel had gotten out of the car and was going around to the passenger side. "This just got messy."

He was right. Farrel and the woman were going inside the restaurant, a place called Mama Guadaloupe's. Extracting two people from a car on the street was one thing. Getting them out of a crowded restaurant, when at least one of them had the potential of putting up a helluva fight, was another.

"I'll take a black syringe with me," he said. Doping the bastard was the best bet. The trick would be getting him out of the restaurant before he collapsed. He and Rock could always bring Farrel around once they got him to Lancaster's suite at the Kashmir Club.

Rock pulled to a stop two cars behind the GTO, and they both got out of the Jeep. As they passed the Pontiac, Rock bent down and slashed the tires—standard operating procedure.

Inside the restaurant, he and Rock found a place at the end of the bar, ordered a couple of beers, and started looking around. It didn't take long to spot their targets, even in the crowd. The pair was getting settled into a table, the woman sliding out of her coat and hanging it on the chair, the hostess still chatting them up and handing them their menus. For dining purposes, their location sucked. For what King had in mind, it was perfect. The table was back by the kitchen, where everybody and their dog was swinging by, toting food out and dirty dishes in.

"*Hot damn,*" Rock said.

King concurred. The woman was a stunner, like a fashion model, the way she was dressed, all sexed up in a short-short gold dress and hot little black boots, her hair so long and dark, so silky shiny. And her face. *Christ.* He'd laid a woman like her once in Dallas, a girl too rich and beautiful for her own good who'd just wanted a walk on the wild side.

He'd given it to her.

"I think we'll just mosey over there, Rock, and let Farrel see that you've got a gun on the woman. My guess is that he'll want to go real peaceful-like. Come on."

He stood up, and he and Rock started across the room. It didn't take Farrel long to spot them, either, and as soon as he did, King lifted the right side of his hoodie, just enough to give Farrel a glimpse of his .45. Next to him, Rock let his hand graze the outside of his shirt, letting his pistol print for a brief second, with the added gesture of pointing at the woman.

Farrel would get the picture real quick—any sign of a fight, and the girl was a goner. Rock's first shot was for her.

Cretins, Monk thought, watching King and Rock weave their way across the restaurant dining room, flashing weapons and telegraphing threats against the woman with Conroy Farrel. He could see it all through the front window, feel it all, and he'd have expected better of men working for Randolph Lancaster.

They had what he wanted more than anything, and they didn't deserve it. They didn't deserve their position in Lancaster's life.

It made him sick in his heart.

Threats were for weaklings. If he'd wanted the woman dead, he'd have killed her. One good backhand would take her head off, damn near literally. There'd be none of this mincing around with guns.

Mama Guadaloupe's—he glanced up at the sign, squinting even behind his sunglasses. It was no accident that he'd found Farrel here. Monk knew everything about Farrel and his former life in Denver as J. T. Chronopolous, all the places he'd liked to hang out, the houses and apartments where he'd lived before moving into 738 Steele Street. Monk knew where he'd gone to school and what recruiting office he'd gone to when he'd enlisted in the Marines. He knew some of the women he'd been with and where they were now. He knew what cars J.T. had owned and a few that he'd stolen, and he knew Mama Guadaloupe's had been his favorite restaurant, a home away from home. J.T. had been a legend here, and Monk had mapped out a route of J.T.'s most important places, putting his reconnaissance plan together while he'd still been in Bangkok, spreading his maps and schedules and data across Dr. Patterson's desk while chewing on the good doctor's bones.

He'd tasted like chicken.

Monk wasn't a cannibal. He was a survivor, an animal in every vicious, feral sense of the word, an animal with a human's brain. He was exactly what Lancaster had promised him he'd be, the ultimate warrior, with no boundaries, no barriers, no conscience. When he succeeded in his task, Lancaster would welcome him into the fold, into the inner sanctum of his most loyal and fearsome soldiers.

And there, in the light of Lancaster's rising sun, Monk would shine like the unholy terror he was.

CHAPTER TWENTY

"We'll take them out the back, through the kitchen," King said, crossing the dining room, heading for Conroy Farrel and the woman.

Going through the kitchen might cause a bit of ruckus with the staff, but it was the quickest way out and beat the hell out of maneuvering two hostages at gunpoint back through the crowded dance floor.

"Con," he said like they were old friends, coming to a stop in front of the table where Farrel sat with the woman. He smiled warmly, cocked his head a little to one side, and relaxed his shoulders. "I remember you from school. East High, right?"

Actually, he knew everything about Conroy Farrel, from his blood type to his shoe size. He knew the day he'd been born, where he'd been baptized and where he'd been busted, where he'd graduated, when he'd enlisted, and King knew the day he'd "died." In truth, he knew more about Conroy Farrel and where he'd come from than Conroy Farrel did. King knew he'd started out life as John Thomas Chronopolous. He knew why the SDF boys had snatched Scout Leesom, why they wanted Farrel back, and he knew, whatever he was called, exactly when the man would die for the last time—finished, smoked, ain't no never coming back.

King gave it six more hours tops, definitely before

sunrise. He and Rock would kill Farrel first, then the woman, dispose of the bodies, and they could all get back to the twisted ways of a corrupt world and doing what they were really good at: making money by helping people.

That's the way King thought of LeedTech, the most humanitarian assholes on the planet. Humanitarian, that was, if you were the folks with the money, the firepower, and the political desire to straighten your world out, maybe have a few of your problems smoothed away.

If you needed a war, LeedTech could deliver one to your door. If you just needed some personnel shifted, LeedTech could shift them straight out of your life and into their next one. Got some enemies strutting around, threatening your ass and your assets? LeedTech would bury the limp-dicked bastards—for a price.

Needless to say, business was good. It was always good, recession proof.

"King Banner," Farrel said, something settling in his eyes, something more than just recognition, something hard, and King figured he knew what Farrel had recalled.

He and Rock had a reputation, signed, sealed, and delivered on a deal in Paris four years ago. Some guys balked at killing a woman, but King and Rock hadn't hesitated for a second to take the job of wringing the life out of a Liberian minister's ex-mistress in her five-star hotel room.

"Yeah," King said. "An old friend of yours sent us. He's going to be damn glad to see you again. It's been a while."

Farrel didn't say anything, just continued to hold his gaze, cool and calm, until Rock came to a stop close behind the woman. She'd taken off her black leather jacket and draped it over the back of her chair, and King really had to wonder if he'd ever seen a prettier pair of shoulders. Her skin looked flawless, silky creamy.

He and Rock were going to have a lot of fun with her.

"She's not part of this," Farrel said, his voice as calm as his gaze.

The hell she wasn't, King thought.

"Leave her out of it, and we won't have any problems."

"Oh, we're not going to have any problems," King assured him, still smiling. "We're just going for a ride, that's all."

Next to him, Rock put his hands on the woman's shoulders, up real close to her neck, like he was giving her a friendly little massage, which King could guarantee he wasn't. The woman's face paled, and he saw Farrel's gaze narrow ever so slightly.

Tsk, tsk, tsk, he thought. Weakness, pure and simple, and the reason he never got involved with a woman. They were weakness for a man, a soft spot where he could get gutted, and Farrel was looking right at it. The fashion queen was absolutely frozen in place, no doubt understanding that she was only a thought and a twist away from having her neck snapped by one of the world's truly great neck snappers.

"This will go a lot smoother if you boys leave the woman out of it," Farrel said, still so calm.

Oh, this guy was a riot, King thought.

"Smoother for who?" he asked with a short laugh. "She'll be fine, Con old buddy, as long as you hold up your end. Nobody's out to hurt the woman, so let's just get going."

It was a lie, but so what? Once he got Farrel outside, he'd hit him with the black syringe. Rock could bring the Jeep around into the alley, and they could load the guy up with the woman and head out.

Or if there was a problem, he'd hit Farrel up the instant he sensed it and not an instant later.

King was nobody's fool. He hadn't really expected the snatch to be easy, and he wasn't convinced it was, but Farrel had made a couple of mistakes he'd never made before, and both of those mistakes were female: Scout Leesom and the long-legged fashionista.

"Jane," Farrel said, ignoring King and looking at the woman. "These guys are two of the worst bastards on the face of the earth."

King let out a laugh and had to stop himself from thanking Farrel for the compliment.

"Don't worry, Jane, honey. Things really aren't as bad as Con here thinks," he said. They were, but fuck Farrel, and fuck the girl. He and Rock were in charge.

Farrel didn't seem to get the message.

"I want you to get up and leave," the man said, still looking at the girl. "Now."

"No." Rock tightened his grip on her, and she gasped, probably with damn good reason. Rock had a hundred holds he put on people, none of them less than punishing. "The woman is part of the deal."

"What deal?" Farrel asked.

King smiled and let out another small laugh, like they were all having a friendly conversation. "I don't ask questions, buddy. I deliver results. You know how it goes, and this time, the woman goes with us."

Her face had grown pale under Rock's not-so-gentle touch, and King liked it. She started to tremble in her seat, her purse in her lap, clutched in close like she just needed some damn thing to hold on to, and he liked that, too. Having her scared, her fear all ramped up, was very helpful. Frightened people were easy to push around. It was the cold bastards like Conroy Farrel that a guy had to guard against.

"We'll go through the swinging door with you in the

lead," King said, giving the cold bastard precise directions. "Once you're through the door, keep walking. The door to the alley will be in front of you. Fifteen seconds, that's the amount of time I'm giving you to walk through the kitchen and get out the alley door."

He gave Rock a quick glance, and his partner gave the slightest nod. Rock would follow with the woman.

Good. King didn't want any mistakes. If Farrel so much as twitched, Rock needed to be ready to back him up. Fuck the woman. They could pick her up before she got too far. But nobody would be going anywhere if Conroy Farrel got the drop on them.

Smooth and easy, Farrel stood up from the table.

"Hold on, Con." King grinned and moved in close to the guy. "It's just so damn good to see you."

He put one arm around Farrel's shoulders and frisked him with the other, coming up with the inevitable automatic pistol. With Rock blocking everyone else from viewing the transaction, King slid Farrel's gun inside one of his hoodie pockets and zipped it closed. He also took Con's folding knife and stuck it next to his in his pants pocket.

"One thing I want to make perfectly clear, Con, is that Rock would just as soon shoot the woman as not. Personally, I'd keep her alive for obvious reasons. She's a real looker, that's clear, and I'm sure she's a lot of fun. But Rock's kinda twitchy. He'll be covering her with his .45 all the way, and he's only got about two and a half pounds on that trigger of his. Hell, if he sneezes, she's dead, and if you do anything, she's dead. So don't do anything. Don't even think it, because if you think it, I'll feel it, and Rock will bag the girl." He was only being straight with the guy, and he hoped Con appreciated his candor. He could tell by the flat, frightened look on the girl's face that she'd understood every word he'd said.

"Smile, honey. We don't want people thinking we're not having a good time—and I mean it. Smile."

She did her best, which was pretty damn good. Hell, she was so beautiful, he liked looking at her whether she was smiling or not.

Stepping away from the table, he slipped his left hand into his hoodie pocket and, after flipping off the safety cover, palmed the black syringe. He kept his right hand carefully in front of him, close to his waist, his thumb and fingertips lightly resting on his belt buckle. From that position, he could push the hoodie back and pull his .45 clear of its holster in a lightning-fast draw. Despite Lancaster's rules of engagement, he wasn't going to let Conroy Farrel get ahold of him. He'd see the bastard dead first.

"Fifteen seconds," he repeated, stepping aside and pushing open the kitchen door. "Don't fuck with me."

CHAPTER TWENTY-ONE

Fifteen seconds.

They would never make it.

Jane kept putting one foot in front of the other, following King, with Rock following her, and all of them following J.T.

She'd been in the kitchen at Mama Guadaloupe's before, picking up dinner one night with Skeeter, and the place had not changed. It was still orchestrated chaos, pans rattling, a dozen people talking, half in Spanish, half in English, constant movement, nobody standing still, and everybody getting in their way.

People were crowded up against the pickup line, stacking plates up their arms, putting finishing touches on meals, expediting orders, and the four of them were going the wrong way, trying to jostle their way through, moving against the flow.

Ten seconds.

She was counting it in her head, and they would never make it.

The kitchen was hot, about ninety-five degrees, the air rich with the spicy smells of food. It had hit her like a blast furnace when they'd come through the door. Between the heat and the fear, she didn't know what was making her sweat more—but she was betting on fear.

"Hey, hey, you there, *ustedes ahí, los gringos, deberían*

estar de vuelta aquí," somebody called out to them—*you shouldn't be back here*—and as quickly as that, their bubble of momentary invisibility popped. Everyone saw them, which only added to the chaos.

"*Los baños* are the other way, through the dining room," one of the busboys said. And how anybody could mistake their phalanx of fear and intimidation for four people who'd gotten lost looking for the bathroom was beyond Jane. She was just your average Josephine, but all three men looked like serious contenders for some kind of Death Fighters of Doom videogame.

"No, no, it's okay," somebody called out. "It's J.T. *Oye, Juanio... oye..."* The voice trailed off in confusion.

Oh, God, a cook had recognized J.T., one of the old men standing next to the grill. King Banner couldn't have expected that. She could only pray that the cook would take the bull by the horns and call the police or, better yet, call Steele Street.

Of course, whatever bad thing happened was going to happen faster than any of the good guys could get there. And it was definitely going to be a bad thing. She knew why J.T. had held her gaze and told her to get out any way she could, and so help her God, she was going to do her best. She needed to be ready.

"Oye... chico?" the old man continued softly, standing stock-still, watching J.T. go by, a look of shock on his face.

Jane understood completely. She'd had the same reaction to seeing J. T. Chronopolous back from the dead.

Five seconds.

The four of them were starting to bunch up, getting closer to the door, and she felt Rock shove his gun against the small of her back—*the bastard.*

Two and a half pounds of pressure and she was a dead girl in a gold dress.

No.

The one word was very clear in her mind. She wasn't dying in an alley on the west side, shot in the back by some behemoth bastard. And she didn't care if King Banner and his buddy drove around all night long, she was most definitely not getting in their car and going for a ride—no way. She was going to make her stand right here. She'd rather die fighting in the alley, where she still had a chance, than be kidnapped, tortured, raped, abused, and end up dead anyway.

Oh, hell, yeah, she was going to fight for her life—with everything she had, right here, in about three more seconds.

She'd been quiet at the table, but she sure as hell had been thinking, and she had a plan—a plan far better to execute in the alley than in Mama Guadaloupe's packed-to-the-rafters dining room.

Her mind was clear, her choices limited, her decision made.

There were only a thousand things that could go wrong.

Con reached the door to the alley and gave it a hard push, sending it back on its hinges. There was only one thing that could go wrong with his plan. If he failed in any way, Jane died.

So he would not fail.

He knew precisely where everyone was behind him, to the millimeter. He had a damn good guess about the amount of time it would take a soldier with King Banner's training and skills to draw his pistol and knew he was dealing with a second or less. There would be a few more tenths of a second available while Rock comprehended what was happening. Con planned on using every single hundredth of a second to his advantage.

He'd heard about these guys, King Banner and Rock

Howe, and they were the worst of what happened when elite soldiers, men who had been trained to the point of ultimate superiority, crossed over into the underworld. Add Souk's chemical fortification, and the die for destruction was cast in stone. These men were brutal, without conscience or humanity.

The door hit the outside wall of the restaurant and bounced back, a tremor running through it from the impact. He crossed the threshold, walking through to the alley, which left the door heading straight for King, moving fast enough that the man's instincts overcame his diligence. The bastard lifted his arm to keep the metal slab from hitting him, his attention shifting for an instant, and in that instant, Con moved, pivoting on his right foot, bypassing King, and reaching past Jane. Both of them were swept aside as he locked onto his target: Rock Howe's gun hand.

His fingers closed on the bigger man's wrist, pushing it up and away from Jane even as he slammed the palm of his right hand straight up under Rock's chin. He felt bone give way, and he was betting he'd broken old Rock's jaw. The gun fired—too late to do the man any good. From the angle, Con knew the bullet had gone up into the air.

He kicked backward at King, connecting with the man's torso, and nearly simultaneously he heard another shot go off and King hitting the ground with a grunt.

Fuck. A second shot. Where the hell had it come from? Not from Rock's pistol. And even more important, where in the hell had it gone?

He smelled blood. Somebody had been hit.

Next to him, Rock dropped like a stone, his body hitting the pavement, half in and half out of the door, blocking it open, his gun falling from his hand and skittering behind him across the floor of the kitchen.

Con instantly turned to meet his other threat. King was back on his feet, knocking Jane out of the way, lunging into the fight, ready to grapple.

Con blocked his first strike and, at the apex of King's next swing, saw what the man was holding: a syringe, its needle glinting sharp and wicked in the light, its contents black. He instinctively went for control, grabbing the man's wrist and using his leverage to swing King around and slam him into the wall. In the kitchen, all hell had broken out, people screaming, plates crashing, the sound of running footsteps. Somebody was bound to be pulling out a cellphone and punching in 911. It was inevitable, but he sure as hell didn't want to be here when the cops showed up, especially if King prevailed with that damn needle.

A black syringe.

Fuck.

Black was no good. He never used the black gelcaps. They were a guaranteed pain stopper but sported a couple of bad side effects, like turning a guy's body into rubber, or throwing him into cardiac arrest. Use them or not, though, a badass dose of the toxic pharmaceutical was headed his way—unless he stopped it.

A gun would have been damned handy, but he'd caught sight of King's pistol lying on the ground where the man had first fallen, Rock's was in Mexican food territory, and his own Wilson Combat .45 was zipped inside a damn pocket on King's hoodie. Any second, though, and he was going to get a chance to get his knife back, and as soon as he did, he was gutting this bastard.

Backed up against the wall, King was bearing down with the syringe, his muscles bulging, sweat breaking out on his brow. He pressed his arm closer, bringing his hand nearer and nearer Con's neck, pushing hard, forcing the needle toward Con's skin. The guy was bulldozer strong, like a freaking machine.

Fuck.

Con kneed him, threw an elbow strike, blocked an incoming uppercut . . . and kept holding the syringe at bay, twisting King's wrist and forcing the needle in another direction.

He took a blow to the body, and then another. Mustering his strength, he slammed King even harder into the wall, but King Banner wasn't one of those CIA spooks he'd been outrunning and outfighting all these years. The man was a warrior, and his blows came fast and hard, one after the other, each one a pile driver. The bastard caught him up the side of his head, and pain shot through Con like a whip crack. Then another strike came at him, sharp and fast and deep.

Fuck.

He knocked King's next blow away and twisted under the man's other arm, bringing it over his shoulder and jerking it down hard, leveraging it against King's elbow and having the satisfaction of feeling the joint give way.

King let out a deep, surprised groan.

Yeah, Con understood. The guy was built like a steel brick. Nobody was supposed to be able to break him.

The syringe fell to the ground from King's suddenly nerveless fingers.

Pendejo, Con swore to himself. *Asshole.*

But he wasn't out of it yet.

As King slumped against the wall, his good arm snaked around Con's torso, holding on tight, squeezing him hard and dragging him down into the open doorway where Rock was struggling back to a sitting position, pulling himself up against the door, his eyes glazed with pain.

Shit.

That was the bad thing about Bangkok boys. They didn't know when they were down.

Rock lunged forward, one hand reaching out and grabbing hold of the black syringe.

This was going to get messy.

King was rolling over the top of him, and Rock was coming down on top of King, the black syringe in his hand. For a moment, their combined weight was going to be an insurmountable advantage, and a moment was all it was going to take for Rock to stick him.

Sonuvabitch.

He tried to twist clear, heaving his body up and out from under, but he was bucking over four hundred pounds of scrap and grapple, and wherever the goddamn needle was, he could smell it locking in on him like a tractor beam, and so it would have...

Except there was another shot.

From where he was, scrunched up tight and scrambling for a hold and trying to protect his flank, he heard a gun go off, loud and cracking, an explosion of sound. He felt Rock's body jerk hard and then slump on top of him, felt the fierce kinetic energy of King's whole being still reaching for him, still in the fight despite his broken elbow joint, and then he felt King collapse, all the fight and energy draining out of him in an instant.

He dragged himself out from under the two limp bodies and immediately saw King's problem—the syringe hanging out of his arm. Rock must have gotten him when he fell. Poor bastard.

Rock's problem was just as obvious, but standing five feet away—Jane, her Bersa Thunder .380 smoking in her hand.

Good girl.

Behind him, he heard Rock come back from the initial shock of getting shot, gasping in agony. The bastard cursed and groaned, his breath harsh and raspy, and when Con looked, it was easy to see why. Jane had shot him in the left knee he no longer had. That thing had been shattered.

"Good shot," he said, glancing back at her. Her dress had been torn straight up the seam from the hem, probably by King, during the brief intense scuffle they'd all had at the door, and she had a lot of leg showing. Her hair was wild from the fall she'd taken, her knee was bleeding again, and her face was deathly pale, but she was still on target, ready to shoot again if necessary.

He was impressed, with her steadiness and her shot placement. Rock had stretched his leg out behind him, using it for leverage. It was about the only place she could have shot him without possibly shooting Con, too. He was damned grateful she'd figured that all out at light speed, and he wondered for just a second what the odds were that a guy would see a drop-dead-gorgeous woman on the street at sunset and, a couple of hours or so later, wind up having her turn out to be one helluva shot and save his ass.

Slim, he decided, damn slim, and yet there she was, a keeper, if he'd been in the business of keeping anything.

He wasn't. For six years, his life, everything he had of it, had been operating on a hit-and-run system. There were no keepers.

Leaning down, he made short work of frisking the men, emptying their pockets and retrieving his own knife. He'd have slit their throats without batting an eye, if they'd needed killing. But King wasn't going anywhere for a very long time, and Rock wasn't, either, not with what was left of his knee. So he let them live, and planned on them telling Lancaster everything they knew: that Conroy Farrel was alive and well, and on the hunt. That he was close and getting closer, and, above all, that he was still winning the fight, even with Lancaster sending his best boys.

A beast—he knew what his reputation was, across the

board and around the world. He'd killed too many of Lancaster's assassins to be underestimated, and now he and the Wild Thing had taken down Banner and Howe.

He thumbed his knife open and sliced King's hoodie pocket with the razor-sharp tip to get at his gun. The guy was damn near comatose, lying inert in a pile, his pupils dilated, his breathing shallow, his brain somewhere off in never-never land. As a bonus, Con found where the second bullet had gone—into King. There was blood seeping out of a wound just under his rib cage on the right side. Not a lethal shot, but it had bought them some time.

He was going to let Rock buy a little time, too, for what it was worth. Unless Souk had worked the kinks out of his drugs that last year he'd been alive, all these boys were on their way out.

Just like him.

Fuck.

He knelt down in front of the guy, bringing them face-to-face, and pressed the tip of his blade into the side of Rock's neck. The guy knew the drill. He knew what happened next.

"You can bleed out here in this alley, Rock," Con said. "Or you can tell me what I want to know." He was very matter-of-fact, very calm, and he knew Rock had been around the block enough times to believe him. It was in the guy's fierce black gaze and in the strength he was using to keep from screaming his guts out.

Yeah, Con figured Rock was taking the option of a deal under very serious consideration.

Smart move.

"Nothing that's happened here can't be undone," he continued, giving Rock an honest assessment of his injuries. "I bet you know somebody who can fix your knee up like new." Literally. "But if I cut you it's over. So tell me where my old friend is, and I'll walk away."

Rock was thinking, staring at him and thinking and struggling with the pain that had to be exploding through him like incendiary fireworks. He was drenched in sweat. A long streak of it dampened the front of his shirt. His breath was blowing in and out of him like he was hooked to a pair of bellows.

"I'm running out of time, sweetheart." Con pressed the blade in a little deeper.

"*K-kash . . .*" Rock muttered, the effort to speak making his eyes roll back.

"Cash?" What the fuck? The knife went in another eighth of an inch. "Come again, Rock old buddy?"

"*K-kashmir . . . you . . . you asshole.*" And that was all she wrote. Rock collapsed, his eyes rolling up into his head until only the whites were showing, his body jerking like he was having a seizure, which was totally possible, but he wasn't dead yet.

The Bangkok dope worked great for making a guy bigger and badder, but when the shit hit the fan, nine times out of ten, Souk's soup went fucking haywire—like what had happened to him with the ketamine.

Con looked over the mess of bad boys in the doorway and rose to his feet, shaking his head. Despite his restraint, King and Rock might not make it.

Well, hell. He guessed Lancaster would get the message either way.

"Come on," he said, stepping back and taking Jane by the arm to move her along. "We need to get out of here." Before she got all focused on how much carnage she'd wrought with her last shot. Light from the door was spilling out in a long rectangle into the alley, but King and Rock were slumped off to the side, more in the shadows.

Just as well.

She nodded, rotated the Bersa's decocker down, and slipped the gun back into her purse. That's when he noticed the hole between a pair of the zebra stripes on her bag. He also noticed her hand was trembling. She'd been rock solid in her gunfighting stance, but she was losing it fast.

"You shot King with your pistol still inside your purse?" One-handed, he folded his knife back up and stuck it in his pocket. They were almost to the corner of the building, and Corinna was parked in front of the restaurant.

"Y-yes," she said. "I slipped my hand in and grabbed my gun as soon as you told me to get up and leave, while we were still at the table. I was waiting for a chance to use it. I figured I'd get one as soon as we got outside." She gave a quick glance around. "And I guess I was right."

Very good girl, indeed. He was impressed as hell, and no wonder she'd been clutching her purse like her life depended on it.

"It was real stupid of them not to think that a girl might have a gun," she continued, her voice trembling but still managing to sound tough.

He had to agree, but he also had to cut the guys a break.

"They're not used to girls like you."

A stricken expression crossed her face but passed almost as quickly as it had come.

"What do you mean, girls like me?" she asked, keeping her gaze straight ahead, the hesitancy of her tone telling him more than the question.

What could he possibly mean? he wondered, curious as hell. What could possibly have given her such a wounded look of uncertainty?

"Drop-dead gorgeous, pure hothouse, like you're from another planet," he said, not having any trouble coming up with the truth, or any trouble recognizing the relief on her face when he said it. "You look like you should be on the cover of a magazine, not like you're strapped."

She gave a small smile, shaky but there.

"I've been 'strapped' since Superman taught me how to shoot on the firing range at Steele Street—about four years ago."

This Superman guy again. Con was beginning to think he should make a point of meeting the man, but according to Jane, he already knew him—and he hadn't seen a damn thing to tell him she was wrong.

No, his old life was here. It was here with Kid Chaos and this guy called Superman, if he wanted it.

But wanting it wasn't going to be enough for him to get it.

"Well, that's all I meant," he said. "That when a guy looks at you, the last thing he's thinking is that he's going to get shot with anything you could drag out of a zebra-striped purse." Or any other kind of purse, for that matter. Oh, hell, no. Every guy who saw her was definitely thinking something else—the same damn, impossible thing he was thinking.

He increased their speed, hustling her up the alley toward the street, passing the backs of a whatnot shop and the hardware store on the corner, moving faster, ignoring the burning pain in his side, his hand still on her arm.

She stumbled on the edge of a pothole, but he kept her from falling and tightened his hold on her. Off in the distance, he heard the first siren headed their way, but when they reached the corner of the building, he realized it wouldn't matter even if they did make it to Corinna before the cops arrived. The GTO was sitting right where he'd left her, and her tires had been slashed.

Hell.

Two dead bodies, plenty of witnesses, and a damn good description of him and Jane weren't exactly going to make the crime scene a cakewalk, but pretty damn close—except the cops wouldn't find him in their database, not in any database. Every piece of identification he owned he'd either made himself or tagged an underworld expert to create. He was a clean slate in both hemispheres and on any continent.

He hesitated a second longer, looking in every direction. Like the elevator at Steele Street, and the garage, there was something familiar here, right here on this corner.

The first siren was joined by a second, both of them drawing closer. He looked around again. This was not the time to dawdle, but...

But his instincts were telling him to back up, go the other way. There was another way out of the alley about halfway down, where an opening in the tall fence led to a rough track that ran straight into the parking lots, loading docks, and service entrances for the businesses on the next street over, a concrete and corrugated steel wasteland.

The track is there. Everybody uses it.

The thought was clear and true, and he didn't second-guess his plan any more than that. On his own, they'd never catch him.

Jane, who was now shaking like a leaf in her little high-heeled boots, was another story—but this wasn't her fight, no matter what she'd done.

He pulled her back into the alley, up close to the wall where they couldn't be seen.

"Give me your gun," he said.

She gave one short shake of her head and clutched her zebra bag closer. "We already played this game."

"No game," he said. "I'm leaving, you're staying, and

I want to put my prints on the grip. Tell them I did all the shooting."

"No." She shook her head again. "I'm going with you."

Which made no damn sense at all. He didn't get it.

Jane Linden—who was she that she wouldn't let him go? He could only think of one thing.

A third siren sounded off in the distance, drawing his attention to the street. Yeah, this was big for Denver, a fair amount of gunplay and, despite Rock's previous yowling, what must look like a double homicide in the alley to whoever had called it in to the cops. In Ciudad del Este, it wouldn't have made the morning news.

He turned back to her, his one idea pressing hard on him.

"Were we lovers?" he asked, a part of him wishing it was so, that the Wild Thing had once been his—and the hotness of her blush, the sudden startled starkness of her gaze told him it was true.

Geezus.

"I was a fool to leave you." And it was time to leave her again. The cops were on the block. They'd be screeching to a halt any second now, and that was perfect timing. They wouldn't catch him, but he wanted them to catch her, to take her in, get her off the streets for a while. By the time they let her go, he and Scout and Jack would be long gone, and this would all be over—at least in Denver.

"I want you to go with the cops," he said. "Tell them anything you want about me, everything you know. There's no reason to lie, and the more you can give them, the easier it'll go on you. Now open your purse."

After another moment's hesitation, she did, and he reached in and quickly but firmly pressed his hand around the Bersa's grip. Pulling his hand back out, he thought there should be something else, something he could say, but there wasn't. No matter what they'd been, he didn't know her now, and whatever happened, he was going to have to get out of the country and stay out. There really wasn't anyplace for this to go and nothing for him to do except walk away.

And to give her a kiss.

One kiss for a wild thing on a wild night.

A bad idea, he silently admitted.

But irresistible.

Light from the police cars pulling up flashed into the alley, bright strobes of red and blue bathing the two of them in quick bursts of color. He raised his hand to her face, his thumb brushing across the softness of her cheek. If she wanted to run or turn away, that was her cue, her only chance.

But she didn't turn away. She lifted her face, her eyes meeting his, her expression one of nerves and flat-out curiosity—and excitement. He could smell it on her, felt it in the sudden rise of warmth of her skin, heard it in the shallowness of her breath—and so he lowered his mouth and met her lips with his own.

Bad idea.

She melted into him, and it felt too good, tasted too good, of softness and sex, things he'd been too long without. The sigh of her breath into his mouth was sweet and unexpected and went all the way to his groin. Caught for a moment, he lingered, letting himself fall deeper into the pleasure of her kiss, the wonder of her mouth, its silkiness, and the intimacy of tracing her teeth with his tongue. Then it was time to break away, and he almost made it—but not quite.

She opened her mouth wider, and he slid in even deeper, and so it would have gone, down, down, down into the sweet darkness of desire, down to the sharp, bare edge of need cutting through him. He wanted her.

He pressed against her, pulled her closer, felt the

pressure of her body up against his—and then came the sounds of stopping cars, doors opening, and guns coming out of holsters.

He dragged his mouth away from hers, then kissed her once more, hard and fast.

"Don't forget me." The words came out of nowhere, unexpected, just like her, but the instant they did, he knew he meant them. He'd forgotten everything and everyone—but he didn't want her to forget him.

"Police!" The shout came from the street, and he turned and ran, a lightning-quick slip into the shadows, more speed than any local cop could understand, and he was gone.

But he could still smell her, even halfway down the alley, where he found the dirt track leading off between two lines of fencing. Even there in the darkness, two hundred feet away, her scent was with him.

CHAPTER TWENTY-TWO

J. T. Chronopolous had kissed her.

Jane was stunned, frozen in place up against the back-alley wall of the building two doors down from Mama Guadaloupe's.

True, he didn't know who he was, and he didn't know who she was, but the kiss had been real, as real as the first time he'd kissed her, when things had gotten so out of hand. She'd been eighteen, not the twenty-two she'd told him, and he'd been a Special Ops soldier on the eve of his last mission.

It had been a wild night—steal a wallet, outrun the cops, get about half lost in the tunnels beneath the city, and make love with J. T. Chronopolous on his living room floor.

Yep. That was about right. That's the way she remembered it, a wild, wild night...

The fire crackled and snapped in his big old fireplace, and Jane figured that's what had awakened her. They'd eaten dinner sitting on the floor in his living room area with the city lights sparkling in the darkness through the windows on one side of them and the fire keeping them warm on another. The food had been good, the company better, and they'd both been thrumming with the night's adventure—not much of one for him, she'd learned as he'd talked about his work, sharing parts of some of the missions he'd been on and telling her about the places he'd been all over the world.

Over the course of hours, the conversation had grown more and more intermittent, and now she realized she must have drifted off.

He had fallen asleep, too. He'd told her he was a Special Ops soldier, combat trained, combat ready, which had done nothing to make her feel better.

It must pay good, she figured, looking around at the wonderful place he lived in—and then she looked at him, sleeping on his side with a couch pillow under his head.

She was hurting like crazy already, knowing he was leaving to go off soldiering somewhere in the morning. It was terrible, really it was. She'd gone and fallen in love with a guy who was supposed to have been an unattainable crush.

So stupid to have done that.

And he was too old for her. He'd made that clear.

"You're not twenty-two," he'd said while they'd eaten, and he'd said it in a way that had told her she wasn't going to convince him otherwise.

One kiss, she decided. That wouldn't be such a bad thing, and if she was careful, and kissed him very carefully on the cheek while he was asleep, he might not even know she'd done it. He was snoring softly and looked to her like he was long gone, down for the count.

Yes, she decided. She was going to do this. Another minute passed while she figured out her best approach.

Situating herself closer to him, she leaned down and lightly pressed her lips to his cheek, and his arm came around her waist, slowly, easily, dragging her closer.

"Hey, babe," he murmured, and then drifted off again, except this time she was wrapped in his arms.

Not such a bad place to be.

She wasn't stupid, but she was safer than she'd ever

been in her whole life, lying there with him in this beautiful place with a warm fire and clean furniture and all the other hundreds of things she didn't have in her life. She wanted more of it, who wouldn't? But mostly she wanted more of him. *She spent her life taking care of her crew, always, every day, the scrapes, the troubles, the feeding them—and here was this amazing man who didn't need anybody to take care of him. He was the strongest person she'd ever met, and he'd been her crush, and she'd fallen in love.*

"Hey, babe," she whispered back, and kissed his lips, so lightly, but it made him smile, and then he was really kissing her, his arms coming around her more tightly, one of his hands sliding up between her legs.

Making out, that's what they were doing, with him still half asleep and her loving the taste and feel of him, the incredible strength of his arms, the way he was exploring her body with his hands. She got lost in it, and in the low light of the flickering flames, their clothes came off, piece by piece, a zipper here, a button there, every move meant to reveal more skin, make their bodies more accessible.

The more naked they got, the more awake he became, his mouth moving all over her, getting her hot, then hotter, until his name was all she was thinking, and that she wanted more.

Pressing her down onto the rug, he came up between her legs, his shaft hard and searching, his kiss consuming her, his hands so hot on her body, molding her to him.

"Jane," he sighed her name and pushed into her, and he held himself there for a long moment, kissing her mouth, his body gently rocking.

It was her first time, and it was wonderful, no pain, only need. She shifted her hips and he sank home, and she never wanted it to end—the sweet hard rhythm of his lovemaking. When he found his release, she wrapped her legs around him and held him close, wanting everything he had to give.

"God, you are so beautiful... so beautiful," he murmured. "We shouldn't have done that, but I'm glad we did, so glad. I'll take you with me." And he'd fallen back asleep, still holding her close.

The next time she'd woken up had been when he'd carried her into his bed. It had been early morning, and he'd been dressed all in camouflage, and there had been a couple of huge packs stacked by the door.

"I've got to go, babe," he'd said. "Remember where we had lunch the other day, Mama Guadaloupe's?"

She'd nodded.

"Mama and a crew will be here later to clean the apartment. Stay here until then, and they'll take you home. If you need any help at all while I'm gone, any kind of help at all, call this number and ask for Christian Hawkins. He'll take care of anything while I'm gone. Anything. God, I'm sorry, Jane. That shouldn't have happened last night—and yet I can't regret it."

And then he'd left, and then she'd cried, and when Mama had showed up with her crew, she'd left Steele Street for the first time.

He'd been right about Christian Hawkins. Superman had come straight to her rescue the night she and Sandman had hit the wall.

She'd spent years wondering what might have been, if J. T. Chronopolous hadn't died in Colombia—but she'd moved on, only to end up here, smack-dab in the middle of trouble.

For as far as she'd come from her beginnings, and all the changes she'd made, at heart she was still a street rat, and street rats had only one reaction to a bunch of cops bearing down on them.

Run.

It was instinct, and she did it like a gazelle. Fear burned all the shakiness out of her and put wings on her feet. The alley was dark, and the farther she ran, the darker it got, until a pair of headlights and flashers beamed down its length behind her. She didn't turn and look. She didn't need to—the weight and momentum of the police car coming down the alley after her felt like a force field, tires rolling, engine running, lights flashing, and somebody squawking on the radio. Seconds, that's all she had before they caught up to her.

Nearing the restaurant, she told herself not to look at the men collapsed in the doorway. She'd done a lot of damage there, and it made her feel a little sick. Her survival instincts prevailed, though, and she did look, to make sure neither of them lunged for her as she darted past—but what she saw made no sense.

They'd been moved.

It hit her in a flash, the whole scene.

King had been sitting back against the wall, anesthetized into oblivion by that needle full of something, and Rock had been sprawled across King's legs, bleeding and twitching and very much alive.

But neither one of them was alive now. The slumped look of death was unmistakable, as unmistakable as the oddly contorted angles of their bodies.

Someone had snapped their necks, twisted their heads sideways, and broken their limbs, all of them. Arms and legs were sticking out all over, and one of King's arms had been ripped clean off his body and was just lying there on the asphalt, a couple of feet away from the rest of him. She saw bone jutting through skin and blood pouring out everywhere. It was more than she could comprehend. Nothing about what she saw made sense.

Jesus, sweet Jesus. She kept running, faster and faster,

a scream lodged in her throat, choking her. *Oh, my God.*

Away, away, away... every instinct she had told her to get away. *My God.* She was going to be sick.

She raced past the kitchen door, arms pumping, heart pounding, and ran even faster. Where was J.T.? Where had he gone? God, what had happened? Could he have done that to those two men? Stopped as he'd run by and mutilated them?

It didn't make sense. If he'd wanted them dead, he could have done it before they'd left the doorway. He'd already had his knife at Rock's throat.

Jesus, sweet Jesus. The cops were going to lock her up and throw away the key. This wasn't the first time she'd been in an alley with a dead man, and the Denver police were going to find that out in about two seconds flat once they ran her name.

But this was crazy... and she... she was doomed. She needed away faster, to get away faster.

A new burst of light hit her in the face, and she skidded to a stop, her heart in her throat. *Oh, damn, damn, damn.* Another cop car had turned into the other end of the alley and was picking up speed, coming at her full bore, flashing, rolling, and wailing.

Even if there was a way to the street, she wouldn't take it. That's where the other cops were piling in. And she couldn't go back. The alley behind her was full of cops, and gore, and mind-numbing horror.

She squeezed her eyes shut for an instant and shook her head, as if she could rid herself of what she'd seen, and she stumbled.

My God. Scrambling now, she looked for a way out. The other side of the alley was blocked by a high chain-link fence with strips of vinyl woven through the links. She couldn't see past it, except to know that it was dark on the other side. A few trees poked above the top.

Maybe she could find some cover over there, but there was no way through it, and she knew she couldn't climb over the fence fast enough to get away.

But she had to move, and she had to move now, before she was completely trapped between the two cars. They'd both hit their sirens, just to scare the crap out of her. It was overload. She was already terrorized. The noise and flashing lights and the undeniable impending doom racing straight at her from both directions rattled her down to her bones.

She gulped in a breath, her sides aching from her run. Panic was consuming her, getting ready to drag her under, when she saw it: a dark slash in the fence.

Without a thought, she ran like hell and dashed through the opening. The cop cars came screeching to a halt behind her. She could smell them, the burning rubber and exhaust. When the car doors opened, she put on another burst of speed, her feet pounding on a dirt track—running straight into the dark and gloom.

"What do you want first, Dylan, the good news, the bad news, or the worst news?"

"Good news," Dylan said, manning the communication console in the Steele Street office and listening to Zach Prade come in over their secure radio frequency.

"The fifth-floor maid at the Kashmir Club hotel downtown would sell her own mother for fifty bucks," Zach said.

"Sam Walls mentioned the Kashmir Club when we picked him up tonight."

A short laugh came over the phone. "Yeah, I bet he did."

"The bad news?" Dylan asked.

"A guy named Tyler Crutchfield arrived late this afternoon. He checked into their India Gate suite, which takes up about a fourth of the fifth floor and has a master bedroom and three smaller bedrooms—smaller only in the sense that each bedroom comes in at just under three hundred square feet with two queen-size beds and a private bath. Crutchfield's party filled the India Gate suite with only one bed left empty. Do you want me to do the math for you?"

"A six-man team."

"Actually, Crutchfield's a lawyer, so he's useless for any mano a mano, and the guy in the master bedroom is older than dirt and has a reputation for hiring all his muscle."

"Randolph Lancaster."

"*Bueno*," Zach said, nice work. "Must have been a helluva party you had with Sam Walls. Sorry I missed it."

"It was pretty low-key, no food, no booze, though I did serve a couple of cocktails."

Zach laughed again. "Sodium Pentothal?"

"Walls's luck wasn't running that good," Dylan said. "Give me the worst news."

"Lancaster isn't CIA. We tracked him from the agency a few times, but he's a lot bigger than spookville. He comes up all over the place, one of those guys in the shadows of places like the State Department and the Pentagon who wield way more power than the folks making the headlines. He's slick, very smooth, nobody can lay a hand on him, but a few people here and there are starting to think somebody should, like the Justice Department and a few of the guys and girls over at my old stomping grounds."

"I'm not sure he can be touched through the Justice Department."

"Yeah, that seems to be a real concern down on the Farm, too. The guy makes Teflon look like Velcro. He's a real slippery bastard."

Zach sure as hell had that right, Dylan thought.

"Where are you now?"

"Well, just to be on the safe side, and given what we're dealing with here tonight, I'm five floors up in the building directly across the street from the India Gate suite in a not-nearly-as-nice hotel called the Mission Inn, room 514. I've got some glass but could use better, maybe something in a Schmidt and Bender 4-16 × 50mm PMIIK attached to something with a .308 bore."

"I'll send Kid."

"Have him bring a pizza."

"Anything else?"

"Yeah. Tell me what you aren't telling me, Dylan," Zach said. "You just authorized a Level One SOTIC sniper to come over here and set up on a guy who eats lunch with the president of the United States."

"You made the request. What are you thinking?"

"That maybe I know something I'm not sure I really know."

"Like?"

"I know Walls was in Coveñas when Creed and J.T. were there, and I know he and his team were blacker than black, running so far under the radar I can guarantee they didn't know who they were working for and didn't care. And other than Walls, I'm not sure any of them made it out of South America alive. What I am sure of is that they had a contact who had a contact who had a contact—you know the routine."

Yes, he'd been there and done that more times than he could remember. They all had.

"And?"

"Well, when I looked, the Coveñas deal dead-ended at a guy with a code name that slid around the outside of Lancaster's world. We could never pin anything on him. All we could do was guess at the connection between Lancaster and this code name."

"White Rook." That's what Skeeter had pulled out of

the decrypted LeedTech files, that all of them, the whole SDF crew, had been made, especially Dylan.

"Yeah, that's it," Zach said after a brief pause. "So are you just a better guesser than me, or is this why you're the boss?"

"A better guesser with a gigabyte of data taken off of a computer owned by a company called LeedTech, which is a subsidiary to World Resources—"

"Otherwise known as Wars R Us," Zach interrupted. "The go-to guys in a dozen sub-Saharan countries whose idea of government begins and ends with armed conflict."

"What did you hear about LeedTech?"

"Not much," Zach said. "Years ago, there was some strange stuff in Bangkok with their name attached, but I was working heroin, straight Golden Triangle, not synthetics, and whatever they were up to, nobody was really talking. What do you have?"

"Hamzah Negara, Erich Warner, Dr. Souk, Tony Royce, Randolph Lancaster, and John Thomas Chronopolous, not to mention myself, and, probably by tomorrow morning, you and everybody else who works here."

"*Qué carajo.*" Zach breathed the words out in a harsh whisper. "You can tie Lancaster to LeedTech to J.T.?"

"Yes," he said. "Along with dozens of other soldiers from U.S. services."

"That's treason."

"Abso-fucking-lutely."

"Who's on J.T.?"

"Nobody," Dylan admitted. "We lost him over on the west side."

"We better find him before Lancaster does."

"Yes," he agreed. "I have a feeling he's the guest of honor at this get-together in Denver. We invited him, and I'm damn sure Lancaster invited us."

"Uh, we live here, boss. This is our town."

"Yeah, but White Rook is the guy who put me in charge of SDF fourteen years ago."

There was a much longer pause on the other end of the radio this time. Dylan could almost hear Prade churning through that boatload of "we're so fucking screwed."

"Does Buck Grant know?" Zach finally asked.

"He knows the name White Rook, but I don't know if he knows it's Randolph Lancaster. I just found out this afternoon, after Skeeter decrypted the files I got from LeedTech."

"And you were going to share this intel when?"

"I hit the office about the same time J.T. hit our garage. Regardless of how we disseminate the intelligence, we need to protect him first. I don't think we can do that on the street."

"How good is your data?" Zach asked.

"Pristine."

"Send me Kid, and I guarantee nothing will get by us on this end."

"He's on his way." And if Lancaster had any gut instincts at all, the hair should already be rising on the back of his neck.

CHAPTER TWENTY-THREE

No action.

Not a sign of life.

The Star Motel looked dead to the world, like it had gone out of business and forgotten to turn off the lights.

Skeeter took a sip of the chai latte she'd brought with her from Steele Street. She'd been sitting in the garage's current "Sheila," a gray, late-model Buick so nondescript nobody ever noticed it. The car was like part of the pavement. She'd been parked up the street from the motel for damn near an hour and hadn't seen one thing worth reporting. There were two cars in the motel's off-street parking area, both of them clearly visible from her vantage point, and neither of them could possibly be J.T.'s getaway car. A ten-year-old Jeep Wrangler four-banger was not anybody's idea of a getaway car, and neither was a Yugo.

Unbelievable.

A Yugo. Just the thought of an underpowered shoebox on wheels was enough to make her stomach churn, which was the last thing she needed.

She took another sip of latte and stretched back into the seat. A lot was going on out there on the streets tonight, but not on this street out in the middle of BFE, Bum Fuck Egypt.

Dylan wanted her out of the way? Well, he'd gotten

her out of the way. The only thing that could rock this place was J.T. showing up out of the blue. That was the score. Maybe she'd get lucky, but just because J.T. and crew had staged from the Star Motel didn't mean they were coming back. They could go anywhere, drive all night and fly out of Cheyenne, or Colorado Springs, Grand Junction, or even Salt Lake City.

She needed to check the room, and there'd been a time when she would have done that alone, but not now. Dylan had promised her backup, and when it got here, they'd check the room together.

She'd sure like to rescue Jane. A few years ago, she'd been pretty skeptical about a street thief of Jane Linden's renown being brought into the Steele Street fold, even if it was mostly through the Toussi Gallery, but the girl had proven out, and Skeeter was worried. The former most famous pickpocket in Denver was now a good friend—and J.T. was something else. She didn't know what.

Juiced. That was for damn sure. God, he'd moved through Steele Street like a storm.

A small green line tracking across the screen of the small computer she'd installed in the Sheila, a Bazo 700 series PC, drew her attention to the dashboard and told her she had a call coming in.

It was about time.

She pressed a button on the unit.

"This is Skeet," she said.

"Red Dog here, ready to relieve you," a female voice said.

Red Dog, she thought, wondering if that meant they'd lost J.T. She'd been thinking Dylan would send Quinn or Kid, or both, after the interrogation of Sam Walls.

"Your location?" she asked.

"We're two blocks behind you and one block over. Come on up and park again on Meldrum, where you can still see the motel, and we'll switch cars. You'll drive Coralie home, and we'll take the Sheila."

"We should check the room." She had the key. It was a no-brainer.

"Got that covered. We're on it. You're expected back at home base, and I'm not bucking the boss just so you can tromp around in some dingy old motel in your combat boots."

She grinned. She'd been wearing heels earlier, but Gillian would know she'd changed before she'd headed out on the street. Good footgear was just good sense, and there was nothing like a pair of combat boots to let people know you were a girl who could do whatever, whenever, to whoever—and she could.

So why let Travis and Gillian have all the fun? Skeeter was beginning to feel like a bookmark in this mission, instead of the operator she was trained to be.

"That's—"

"Uh, Skeet," Gillian interrupted her. "Whatever you're thinking, stop. I noticed the boss is a little tense right now, and I actually think we can all do our jobs just a bit better if you're safe at Steele Street, and he's not breathing fire down the back of our necks."

What a crock.

"I was kicking ass—"

"When I was still shuffling papers," Gillian interrupted her again. "And since then we've taken a lot of names together, but—"

"We had this conversation two months ago, Red." Skeeter had been the one who'd given Gillian the code name Red Dog, and over the last few years, the two of them had kicked butt from Kandahar to Caracas. They had a reputation, the highest, among a small, intensely skilled group of people, the people who did the same job they did, top-rung, elite military forces. They were the

SDF girls, the Ghost and the Darkness, Hell and Fury, Skeet and the Dog.

"And this time we're both being overruled. The leader of this pack says you go home, and this is not the time for any of us to step outside the lines. We've got a lot at stake."

Coming from Red Dog, that was quite a statement. That girl had been reborn outside the lines.

"Copy that," she said, sucking it up. She knew Gillian and Travis wouldn't miss anything in the room, and if the girl, Scout, and the guy who had rescued her showed back up at the Star Motel, she knew Gillian and Travis would bring them in.

J.T. was another ball game altogether. Even after having witnessed most of it firsthand, she was still set back on her heels by how quickly he'd eluded them at Steele Street. They'd had everybody on him.

"Skeet, I don't see you moving." Gillian's voice came through the Bazo.

Geez.

"Moving. Roger and out." She turned the key in the ignition and pulled out onto Meldrum Street.

"*Whoa*... oh, whoa, whoa, whoa. Don't turn into the motel," Scout said, ducking down in the seat next to Jack in the Buick Regal. "Just keep moving. Keep driving and take the next left. We need to circle around again, but don't come back by the motel."

Jack didn't question her orders. She'd obviously seen something.

But he looked, and *yowza*. Whoa, whoa, whoa was right, a gorgeous, bodaciously built blonde in a slinky dress and combat boots was getting out of a car on Meldrum, a couple of blocks up the street from the motel. *Geezus*. He'd died and gone to heaven.

"The blonde?"

"How in the hell?" she answered, which was no answer at all. She peeked up and looked over the seat through the back windshield. "You didn't happen to drop a motel receipt when you came through that door on the tenth floor, did you?"

"You're kidding me," he said, not quite believing it. "She's from Steele Street?" Scout knew he wouldn't have left so much as a fingerprint in that building, let alone a forwarding address.

"Oh, yeah," she said. "Her name is Skeeter Bang-Hart, a real serious piece of work, and she's heading up the street. They must have somebody else up there, backing her up."

Jack didn't have to work too hard to detect the awe and admiration in Scout's voice, and he was surprised. They didn't run into too many women who had what it took to impress Scout.

He made the next two left-hand turns, went up the hill for another two blocks, and started to slow down.

"Keep going," Scout said. "I see another car that looks like trouble. We need to come in behind it."

He glanced down the cross street and saw it, too, the tail end of something that looked vintage, well cared for, and muscled under the hood—a gold GTO, undoubtedly Steele Street iron. He kept cruising and took the next cross street over to Meldrum, where he pulled to a stop, far enough away to be discreet but where they could see the gold Goat off on a side street, the blonde walking toward it, and, at the bottom of the hill, the rattrap Star Motel.

This was all just getting too damned interesting for him. How in the hell had they found the Star? He had only one answer, and it didn't compute.

"They got Con." *Sonuvabitch.* Now what?

"No way."

"You got a better explanation?"

"Even if they'd gotten him, he wouldn't have given us up. You know that."

And he did.

Torture wouldn't have worked on Con, and the only two people he cared about were sitting in this Buick Regal on Meldrum. SDF couldn't have leveraged the information out of him.

"Something sure as hell happened, because they are sure as hell all sitting there waiting for us to show up."

"Ah, hell," she whispered.

Yeah, he saw it, too, the woman from the tenth floor, the redhead, got out from the GTO's passenger side, and a blond man got out from behind the steering wheel.

They'd just tripled their trouble.

Make that doubled.

After a few moments of conversation, Skeeter Bang-Hart slid into the Goat's driver's seat and drove off.

Funny how that didn't make Jack feel any better.

"Her name is Red Dog," Scout said. "And that's Travis with her. She calls him the Angel Boy. They're married."

How wonderful for them. Married. Hell. The only girl he was interested in marrying was hooking up with a college professor.

"And they're headed down to the motel," he said, watching the two operators pass the gray car the blonde had left on Meldrum and keep walking down the hill.

"Did you guys travel clean?" Scout asked.

"We always travel clean." Red Dog and the Angel Boy wouldn't find anything in the room that could identify him or Con, but they'd find a few items of interest to folks with an operational turn of mind.

"I could call her," Scout said.

Ohh-kay.

He slanted her a curious, disbelieving glance. "And ask her to please not break into our motel room?"

"She gave me a phone," Scout said, pulling said item out of a pocket in her pants. "It only calls one number. Hers."

"So you can turn Con in whenever it seems convenient." It wasn't a question.

"She says she can help him."

"Help him what?" He couldn't believe they were still having this conversation.

"Survive."

Well, that sent a chill down his spine, striking a little too close to home.

"Survive Lancaster's goons?" More than likely, Lancaster had brought someone besides his B team to Denver. Karola and Walls were both flawed examples of Souk's twisted art. Lancaster had plenty of the good stuff to choose from and a couple of soldiers he seldom traveled without, in particular two men named King and Rock.

Jack wouldn't have minded meeting them in a dark alley, but he didn't want Scout anywhere around when he did.

"No." She shook her head, looking at the phone in her hand. "She says she can help him survive until next year, maybe the year after that. Maybe longer. It all depends."

"On *what*?" He was surprised he could even choke the words out. This was the subject he did not want to discuss with her, the one where she realized Con was dying.

Hell, he didn't want to have this conversation with himself.

"On what Souk gave him, and—"

"Everything," he said, his voice cold. "The bastard gave him everything." And your father, too—but he couldn't tell her that.

Suddenly he needed a little air. He rolled the window

down and watched Travis, the Angel Boy, who didn't look anything like a "boy" at all, cross the street into the motel parking lot, guessing that nobody went around calling somebody the Badass Angel MoFo from Hell, because *that's* what the guy looked like, more than tough enough, and his girl did, too. She circled the motel, going around back.

Yes, that's the way he would have done it, just in case someone inside the room decided to make a run for it. Put the big guy on the door, because that's where the shit really hit the fan, and put the girl who looked like she could kick everybody's ass on the back. Actually, she looked like she could handle the door.

Any door.

As a matter of fact, watching her move reminded him of something—or someone.

"Is there something I need to know about her?" he asked Scout.

"Her real name is Gillian Pentycote."

"You know what I mean." God, the woman moved so smoothly, with so much power and grace. She was lithe, and strong, and—

"Souk injected her with XT7 four and a half years ago, and needless to say, she hasn't been the same since."

Oh, hell, no.

"I thought Shoko was the only woman he ever juiced." And she'd turned out so demented as to be almost worthless. Her only value had been as a psycho-bitch pet for Erich Warner, one of the few men in the world who could have afforded to feed her. The woman had come out of Souk's lab with some very twisted appetites.

"She's not like Shoko," Scout said. "Not at all. She lost her memory completely, just like Con, but she's gotten a lot of it back, working with a Dr. Brandt at Walter Reed."

"Walter Reed Medical Center?" He couldn't believe this conversation. "Forget it. The place is part of the system," he said, dismissing the whole thing out of hand.

Con had been part of the system when he'd been sold. Randolph Lancaster had his hands in everything in Washington, D.C., from the State Department, to the CIA, to the Pentagon, and probably to Walter Reed. He was a power broker at the very highest levels of government, and most of the people whose strings he pulled never even felt the tug. He was that much a part of the status quo.

"I think we need to consider our options," she said, still with the phone in her hand.

Not that option.

"I know they didn't buy you, Scout." The girl couldn't be bought. "So what did they do to make you think that giving him up was in *any* way the best thing for him? I'm just damned curious." And he just didn't damn believe it.

"Convinced me," she said. "That they could help him. Red Dog is proof. You know the kind of headaches Con gets. She doesn't get those anymore. And the pain and the shakes? Hers are almost completely under control. You've seen Con. You know what he goes through sometimes, why he takes all those pills. I've just been guessing at it these last few months, but you've probably known. Known he's dying." She stopped to take a breath. "And you didn't tell me."

Her words fell on him like a five-hundred-pound weight.

Guilty.

He rolled the window on the Buick down a little farther, tried to get a little more air into the car.

Down at the motel, Red Dog had disappeared around the corner of the building, and the Angel from Hell had his ear to the door, listening. All he'd hear was the television they'd left on.

After a second or two, the guy moved back from the door, standing off to the side, up against the brick wall for the same reason Con and Jack had chosen the dump in the first place. It was old and built solid. The whole damn building was brick, in desperate need of a major remodel on the inside but built to last on the outside.

Travis knocked and said something, and Jack could just imagine what—something like "This is the manager. We've got a fire in the lobby, and the fire department wants us to evacuate," or "So sorry. This is the manager, and somebody just broke a window out on your car."

Jack might have fallen for either one of those, especially the car window, especially in this neighborhood.

But Travis didn't get any action off the ruse, because Con was hell and gone somewhere in this damn city, and Jack was sitting up here on this hill, doing his best to breathe in some fresh air and avoid the subject at hand. Con dying was more than he could bear, truly, let alone share with someone, even Scout—especially Scout.

Red Dog came back around the building then, no doubt signaling Travis that there was no way out the back of Room 107. In many old motels, the bathroom had a window that opened out the back, but not at the Star.

With the two of them together, the entering of the room went very smoothly. Red Dog lined up with Travis, and one of them must have electronically scrambled the lock. Jack couldn't see which one, but Travis opened the door and entered first, his gun drawn and ready to go, go, go.

It was a short trip inside. Jack and Con were a pretty tidy crew, and all the really good stuff, like the laptop and the laser microphone, was in Jack's backpack in the back of the Regal.

In less than five minutes, the two had looked their fill and come out of the room empty-handed, heading back up the hill to their stakeout car, no doubt leaving the place exactly as they'd found it. No reason to tip their hand at this stage of the game.

"What are we going to do here, Jack?" Scout asked him, watching the whole scene down at the motel as intently as he was watching it.

The woman, Red Dog, was amazing, so sleek. She moved like a cat, one of the big ones, with a supple, easy grace, radiating strength and power with every step. She and Travis got back in their car and settled in to wait.

"They don't have him, Scout," he told her. "If they did, they wouldn't be wasting their time here. You were bait, a way to get to Con, nothing more, and I'm even less. I'm just the pain in the ass who stole their bait. It's Con they want, not us."

"So what are we going to do?" she repeated her question. "I've got the phone."

Fuck the phone, he thought.

And it rang.

Except it wasn't hers. It was his.

Geezus. He whipped his phone out of his pocket.

"Go," he said.

"Location?"

It was Con. It couldn't possibly have been anyone else, but Jack was still damn relieved to hear his voice.

"Three blocks south of the motel, up on the hill. We've got a surveillance team, two people, a block north of us. They're confirmed SDF operators."

There was a brief silence.

"Do you know how they found the place?"

"No, but they broke into the room, stayed a couple of minutes, and came back out."

He heard Con swear under his breath.

"Did they take anything?"

"Not that we could see. They came out empty-handed, and neither one of them is wearing a jacket."

There was another brief silence, and Jack thought he could hear sirens in the background.

"Where are you?"

"On the west side of town."

Jack could tell Con was moving.

"We had a visual sighting of Lancaster on our way out of Steele Street." Jack gave him the news. "No possibility of a mistake, and we ran into Rick Karola and Sam Walls immediately thereafter. We tailed Karola to a downtown hotel called the Kashmir Club."

"Kashmir Club? So it's a hotel. Rock Howe confirmed it as Lancaster's location, so we're in. King Banner is here, too, but he and Rock are both out of the equation, which means Lancaster is way down on his team."

Damn. It had been a busy night all over.

"We should regroup." That was putting it mildly.

"We need something close to the Kashmir Club—"

Oh, Jack could see where this was going.

"—but not too close."

They were going in, dropping on Lancaster tonight.

He was all for it.

"There's a hotel, the Armstrong," he said. "At Champa and 14th."

"Roger. Turn on the news and lay low until I get there. King and Rock are bound to be the breaking story. I'm temporarily on foot, heading away from the circus over here. King and Rock caught us in a restaurant, very public, very messy. Some shots were fired, but they're both alive. Listen to the reports in case somebody comes up with something we can use."

"Copy." Con had stopped to eat? "Who's us?"

"Unplanned hostage," Con's voice came over the phone. "She slowed me down."

Jack just bet she had, especially if they'd stopped to

grab a bite to eat. *Geezus.* He was starting to get a little confused.

"Are you on your own now?" A legitimate question, if he'd ever heard one.

"Affirmative. I'll meet you at the Armstrong. Out."

"Roger and out."

He turned to Scout, and she looked as relieved as he felt.

"We're not turning anybody in to SDF," he said. "We'll tell Con everything you've seen and heard, and I'll confirm about Kid, and then we'll do exactly what he tells us to do."

"That'll be a first." She gave him a pointed look.

Which he ignored. So he'd been running a little wild these last few months. He'd settled down since she'd been gone, for a whole eight weeks now, and he had something else to say, something kind of new for him, but it was pressing him hard, and he needed to get it off his chest.

"I'm sorry, Scout. I'm sorry I wasn't in Paraguay when these *pendejos* dropped in on you and Con." If he'd been with them when Erich Warner and SDF had all piled in on top of the river house, chances were she wouldn't have been captured, and he'd thought long and hard about that. "I'm going to be sticking a lot closer to home for a while—for a long while." He'd thought damn hard and long about that, too. Whatever happened with Con, he really did need to be with her when it all came down. He couldn't run from the fallout, no matter how many college professors she was seeing.

"I'd like that," she said.

Okay, then—he slanted her a quick look, surprised as hell. She'd like him hanging around. For the last couple of years, she'd usually been so angry with him that he'd gotten in the habit of staying as far away from her and Con as possible.

But this was great.

Perfect.

And too damn late. She'd gone off and found somebody, but he'd take it as long as he could, hanging around while she and old Karl billed and cooed, and if things went bad with Con, he'd take it no matter what. The whole Denver thing was just too god-awful, and he'd sworn nothing bad would ever happen to her again, not on his watch.

He started up the Regal but didn't turn on the headlights, keeping the car dark. Easing away from the curb, he backed up the hill and drove onto a side street before he made the U-turn to head back to downtown.

So everything was straight between them, except for the part about the blonde, the one in Key Largo, the only woman she'd ever actually seen him with. He wasn't particularly discreet, except with Scout. For reasons he didn't completely understand, he'd never wanted her to know about any of his fly-by-night romances, not a single one. He guessed he didn't want her to think he was a jerk—for all the good that had done him. And maybe he had, in some odd way, just always wanted her to think he was available, in case she ever wanted to kick their relationship up a notch.

There had been nothing discreet about her and Con finding him shacked up in a tiki hut condo in the Florida Keys, and from the moment he'd opened the door and seen her standing there, instantly zeroing in on the little cocktail waitress cooking his breakfast in the kitchen, he'd wanted to apologize to her from the bottom of his heart. Maggie had cost him his last chance with Scout—and that was a loss that went way beyond sorry.

Now was his chance.

"I'm...uh, sorry about what happened, well, everything, actually, in, uh, Florida, with Maggie and all." He was wincing by the time he got it all spit out. It was embarrassing, really, what a crappy apology that had been.

And she must have agreed. Dead silence greeted him from the other side of the car. She'd gone so silent, he could feel the absence of sound sitting like a two-ton boulder on the seat between them.

What had happened?

One minute she'd been glad he was going to stay closer to home, and the next she was freezing him out.

So, great. He'd apologized and somehow made things worse.

CHAPTER TWENTY-FOUR

Skeeter took the exit ramp off the interstate at 20th Street and was halfway to Blake Street when her cellphone rang. She'd just gotten off the computer bolted into Coralie's dashboard, checking in with Travis and Red Dog. They'd photographed a medication chart in J.T.'s motel room and sent it to Dylan and to Dr. Brandt.

Hell, she loved Red Dog, knew what the woman had been through and what she could do, but she really didn't want a world full of juiced-up spooks and operators muddying the alphabet soup of covert ops.

She reached for her phone, thinking it might be Dylan again, but when she looked, she didn't recognize the number—which was damned odd.

Her brow furrowed. She knew every phone number Red Dog and the guys had ever used to call her on her private line—and this wasn't one of them.

"Uptown Autos," she said. "We only sell the best."

"Mrs. Hart." A voice she didn't recognize came over the phone, a man's voice, and she immediately reached over and keyed in a three-stroke code to connect her Bazo to Dylan and the comm console at Steele Street. Then she put her phone on speaker.

"Mrs. Hart isn't here," she said. "May I take a message and have her return your call?" Her voice was chipper and bright in her receptionist's mode. She glanced at the Bazo and saw Dylan's tracking and recording signal come up on her screen.

"My name is Tyler Crutchfield. I'm an aide to Randolph Lancaster at the State Department."

That got her attention.

"How can I help you, Mr. Crutchfield?" she said, dropping the enthusiasm out of her voice.

"I'm in Denver, and I'd like to meet with you."

TYLER CRUTCHFIELD CONFIRMED AIDE TO LANCASTER—the message appeared on her computer screen.

"What about?" She turned on her blinker and eased over into the right-hand lane.

"A trade. I have some information I believe you will be personally interested in, and we'd like Conroy Farrel. We at State have been informed that your team here in Denver suffered a mission failure in Paraguay but that SDF has Scout Leesom..."

Had Scout Leesom, Skeeter thought.

"And our most recent intelligence reports are telling us that Farrel is going to try to get her back."

Get. Got. Gone, Skeeter thought.

"What kind of information do you have?"

"I'd rather show you the files in person; some are state matters from your husband's time in Moscow, and I have more recent photographs of him in Washington, D.C. When you see the photos, I think you'll appreciate my discretion."

She doubted it, but he'd definitely piqued her interest. The Moscow deal was older than dirt, the threat of a treason charge that had never yet materialized. But Crutchfield's coy assertion of the personal nature of his other information and the addition of undoubtedly glossy 8x10 pics was enough to fire up any married woman's imagination.

DON'T GO THERE, BABE. Sure, easy for him to say.

"This is a very private number you've called me on,

Mr. Crutchfield. Do you want to tell me how you got it?" If he worked for Lancaster, alias White Rook, the truthful answer was obvious, but she doubted if he'd be telling her the truth. He'd save it for later, if he had any truth to sell.

"Mr. Lancaster, through his position at State, has been a champion of national security for many years and has developed a cooperative relationship with many of our country's specialized agencies," Crutchfield said. "His associates in those agencies were happy to comply with our request for a way to contact you privately."

Bull. There was no love lost between the State Department and just about everyone else.

"Laws may have been broken here, Mr. Crutchfield. Are you sure you want to continue this conversation?" Whatever he wanted, she was going to make him work for it. That was just good business, and it was good business to keep him talking.

"Laws have already been broken by your husband, Mrs. Hart, some of the most sacred laws of our country," he said solemnly, giving a damn good impression of someone who believed what he was saying. "Two diplomatic pouches entrusted to him in Moscow some years ago ended up in the possession of a former KGB officer. The man who pulled him out of those fires of treason is now willing to come forward. Randolph Lancaster is not without influence, and if Conroy Farrel can be delivered to him, he offers you his full assurance that no charges will be leveled against your husband."

"This is very old news, Mr. Crutchfield."

"Old but still relevant, Mrs. Hart. We feel the chance of him being convicted of his Moscow crimes is very high given new evidence that has come to light, and, quite frankly, some of your actions have also come under scrutiny at the State Department. I'm sure you'd both rather not be incarcerated for the rest of your lives."

Quite right, but what Crutchfield apparently didn't realize was how far she'd go to keep anything even remotely like that from happening. Probably a whole lot farther than he could imagine from his cushy office at the State Department.

Poor boy—he was in her playground now.

"There is no new evidence," she said. There'd been damn little old evidence.

"Yes, there is, Mrs. Hart, and I can assure you it will stand up in a court of law."

WELL WITHIN LANCASTER'S CAPABILITIES TO MANUFACTURE CREDIBLE EVIDENCE, IF HE'S DECIDED TO LOWER THE HAMMER. Not exactly what she wanted to hear.

WE CAN COUNTERACT. They always did counteract threats, but this was different, and it had been hanging over Dylan's head for fourteen years. It was the hold White Rook had on him, and now they knew White Rook was bad to the bone—a very dangerous situation.

"What do you want?" she asked.

"Conroy Farrel has long been a person of interest to the State Department, and Mr. Lancaster feels an opportunity has arisen for someone to drop a net on him and bring him in. He believes the people to do that are the operators of SDF."

"We sure would like another shot at Farrel," she said.

"And we're sure that's why you picked up Scout Leesom, to lure him here," Crutchfield agreed, sounding a little smug, like he'd just launched a major salvo in her direction. "Our concern is that SDF may have a different agenda than the State Department."

No shit, Sherlock. And the piece about Scout was good. Only a handful of people in the world knew where that girl had been for the last eight weeks, and most of them were right here in Denver.

"That's where you come in, Mrs. Hart."

"I'm listening," she said.

"I'd rather you listened in person," Crutchfield said. "I'm hoping the information I have will convince you to make our interests your highest personal priority, should SDF take Farrel into custody."

AGREE TO MEET NOW. O'SHAUNESSY'S. Another message from Dylan appeared on her computer screen.

"Then we need to meet now, Mr. Crutchfield. Our team is already moving in on him."

There was a slight pause.

"You know where he is?"

"We've been tracking him all day. If you can meet me at O'Shaunessy's Bar, just off 16th at Blake, I'll take a look at what you've got, but I doubt if it'll be worth what you're asking." Asking her to put her own interests above the team's—not very damn likely, no matter what he had.

"Agreed. I need you to come alone. If I see another SDF operator, the deal is off. I'll head back to D.C. tonight and have charges filed against your husband by noon tomorrow. The more personal information will be available online before I even get to the airport—so tread carefully, Mrs. Hart."

REDIRECTING KID FROM THE KASHMIR CLUB TO O'SHAUNESSY'S. And that pretty much sealed Mr. Crutchfield's fate. He wouldn't see Kid. The boy was a sniper. He had a way of disappearing just by standing still.

"The deal I'm offering is only for you," the doomed Crutchfield continued. "Come alone. I guarantee it will be worth your time."

And she could guarantee he was right about that. It was well worth her time to get her hands on Randolph Lancaster's personal aide.

CHAPTER TWENTY-FIVE

Jane could barely breathe, but she kept running, spurred on by the fear clutching at her chest. Branches slapped at her face and scratched her arms. The stitch in her side threatened to stop her cold—but she didn't dare stop. Not here in this no-man's land.

It was dark beyond the fence, the only light coming in flashes from the police cars in the alley behind her and from the streetlamps on the next street over. In between those two places was a rough, paved area backing up to a block of buildings. It was full of dumpsters and junked cars, different kinds of fencing, and lengths of chain marking off parking areas and loading docks, and there was trash—boxes stacked behind the stores, old tires from an automotive shop, and fast-food wrappers trapped in the weeds.

Big mistake—that's all she could think. She shouldn't have run into this place just because she'd seen something horrifying. She'd seen a lot of bad stuff on the streets growing up.

Nothing as bad as torn-off body parts, sure, but she still shouldn't have let shock take over. It was the one clear thought she had, now when it was too late and she'd already jumped out of the damn frying pan and into the fire—*I shouldn't be back here*—along with a strong dose of *So help me God, Banner's arm is lying in the alley.*

That her first instinct had been to run away from the cops instead of toward them told her exactly how far she'd come from her homeless child roots: not very. Not nearly as far as she'd thought. Not as far as she'd been convincing herself these last few years.

Once a street rat, always a street rat. If she hadn't been so damned scared, it would have been damned depressing.

And look where it had gotten her.

Breathe, she told herself, feeling the ache in her chest and her side. She slowed to a fast walk, half running when she could, her arms tight around her torso, and she kept moving.

Something rustled in the bushes next to the path, and she whirled in an instant, jerking her Bersa Thunder out of her purse and leveling it at a brambly patch of weeds. She still had five shots left in the .380, and she was most definitely in the mood to use them.

A feral cat skittered across the path, but Jane didn't feel any relief. She was still in the wrong place, but running back to the restaurant and getting hauled downtown by the police didn't seem like a wise move.

Keep going. That was the better plan. She'd been lucky to get through the straggly, unlit stretch of cottonwoods, wild lilacs, old tires, and junked trash cans the first time.

God. It was the perfect hiding place for a maniac. If whoever had done that to Banner was back here, running fast and hard might have been the only thing that had kept her safe from him—or from it. Anything that could rip a man's arm right out of its socket most definitely qualified as an "it."

She clutched her side more tightly and forged ahead, her goal clear: the street on the other side of the buildings ahead. She'd dropped her phone when the first grenade had hit in the garage—*good God, what a strange, bad night*—but there was a bar or two on the other side where she could make a call, get a cab, and get the hell out of there.

And head straight to Steele Street. J.T. needed help, and she needed help to save him.

He'd tried to give her another way out, but there was no way out of this without him. Wherever he'd been these last six years, she wasn't letting him disappear back there without some answers. She wanted them, and the guys at Steele Street deserved them.

She made it the last bit of way through the scrubby grass and was partway across the paved area, coming abreast a junked pickup truck, when a cry ripped through the night air and stopped her cold.

Fear, stark and utter and pure, nearly dropped her to her knees.

She wasn't alone back here.

Oh, geezus.

She blasted into a run—and landed smack-dab in a pile of trash.

The cry came again, low and keening and agonized, and she was trapped, trying to dance her way out of a loose tangle of wire and cardboard.

Ohgeezus, ohgeezus, ohgeezus—terror was lodged so tightly in her throat, she could hardly drag a breath into her lungs.

Con slipped his phone in his pocket and gingerly lifted the edge of his T-shirt.

Fuck.

He had a bloody gash an inch long in the meaty part of his waist, no vitals hit, but hell. He'd known King had cut him, but in the heat of the fight, it hadn't felt like more than a nick.

It was more than a nick. He'd been stabbed clean through, and it was definitely starting to burn.

Dammit.

He lowered the edge of his T-shirt and slipped out of his jacket. With his knife, he cut a long strip out of the sleeves and back and wrapped the material around his waist, good and tight, then tied the rest of the jacket over the top of the makeshift bandage to stanch the bleeding. Jack could fix him up better at the Armstrong.

Behind him, he could hear the police sirens still going, and they were starting to spread out. They would have gotten Jane by now, which was good, and would be looking for him, which was not good.

They weren't going to find him, though, not in this back-alley labyrinth of dumpsters, loading docks, and parking spots. There were a dozen businesses fronting the street, and they each had their own area in the back. There were fences delineating property lines, a few cinder-block walls had been put up, some chains closing off a few parking spaces here and there. Overstock from the tire store had been stacked up inside a chain cage next to a garage door. Piles of empty boxes littered the alley behind a grocery store. A couple of homeless guys were bivouacked about fifty yards away from a junked car and a pickup truck parked under a couple of straggly trees.

Up ahead, he could see where the area opened out onto a street with an old but nice neighborhood of small houses on the other side. There'd be a car on one of those streets, something he could hot-wire.

The place was damned familiar, just like a lot of things in this city were familiar, including Jane.

He shouldn't have kissed her. He had no business wanting things he couldn't have, especially when what he really wanted had been delivered on a silver platter; Randolph Lancaster. Here in Denver.

The bastard was never going to know what hit him. Con wanted the LeedTech files, and there was damn little he wouldn't do to Lancaster to get them. Considering what had been done to him six years ago, he figured he could come up with something that would get the bastard's attention and get the job done. He'd love to share a few of his and Garrett's experiences in Souk's lab with old Randolph.

The spymaster had to be seventy, if he was a day. He'd had a lot of years to do a lot of damage. More years than Con was likely to get, and that made him think of Jane, of the loss. He'd left her, and he needed to know why.

The image came back to him, of how he'd first seen her on the street tonight—her hair lifting in the breeze, her long legs and big sunglasses, her urban girl attitude in every step she'd taken, and then the surprise, the way she'd stopped and stared.

Geezus. He couldn't have been such a fool as to walk away from her—and the heat was back, another wave of it rolling through his body and leaving a metallic taste in his mouth.

Shit. The blue pill wasn't working. He reached up and felt his arm. The tenderness and swelling were gone, but his skin was even hotter to the touch—very hot. He reached into his pocket, then turned to check behind him, the handful of pills only halfway out.

Something had caught his attention, a scuffling noise. He quartered the area with his gaze, listening, and heard it again. Glancing back, he saw the homeless men exactly where they'd been, resting in their makeshift shanty of boxes and tarps, but they were looking in the same direction he'd been looking—due east.

Two sounds came next and had him breaking into a run, the first a cry of pain, guttural and beastly, an anguished howl of distress, the second a cry of fear, utter and absolute and undeniably female.

Undeniably Jane.

* * *

He wanted her.

Scrabbling in his pocket, Monk pulled out three silver gelcaps and popped them in his mouth

He wanted her with every breath he took. He could smell her, almost taste her, the woman from the restaurant, and she was running loose, an easy catch—except for the pain breaking him on every breath.

Strobelike flashes of light were tearing into him, streaking off the police cars with their raucous sirens and cutting straight into his brain. They'd already forced him off his prey, the two easy kills he'd had in the alley.

Two righteous kills.

He knew who the bastards had been, and they had not been worthy of Lancaster's patronage. They would not be missed. Monk could single-handedly do both their jobs. He certainly wouldn't have let Farrel and the woman get the drop on him. Banner and Howe had gotten no better or worse than they'd deserved.

Their deaths were another gift from him to Lancaster.

Lancaster.

Lancassstaaa. He cried out the name in his mind, and the bile of hatred rose in his throat, filling him with wretchedness and confusion. He loved Lancaster. It was his mission, the reason he'd been reborn, and yet, in his heart, he hated the man with a passion as profound and full of pain as his longing to be with him. He opened his mouth and released a cry, putting voice to his agony and his shame.

Abandoned.

They'd tried to kill him, the doctors and the lab techs in Bangkok. *MNK-1 is a mistake... twisted, wrong, a monster.*

Not the soldier he'd been promised he would be, better than the one he'd already been, and he'd been one of the very best.

They could have fixed him, the sodding bastards, but

had decided to kill him instead. It was their fault, all of it. They'd brought him to this craven state. They were twisted, not him.

He let out another cry and curled in tighter on himself where he was crouched in the boxes behind Bagger's Market, hiding from the painful police lights.

Then he heard it, a struggling sound and the edge of a whimper—fear—and the sound was not moving. It was staying in one place, on one pinpoint of space out there in the darkness.

Trapped! The woman was trapped.

He lifted his head, and across fifty yards of flashing light and night shadows, he could see her: a golden waif, her dress shimmering in the starlight, her face contorted with panic. She'd gotten caught in a tangle of wire and trash and couldn't get out.

Rising to his feet, he felt himself thrill to the chase. Farrel would be easy to track. The man's wretched scent was everywhere, and Monk would hunt his enemy down and kill him tonight—right after he took care of the woman.

CHAPTER TWENTY-SIX

Between the radio and the phones in the office, and the Bazo 700s bolted into the cars, Dylan was in touch with everybody except the man he most wanted to find: J.T.

He'd lost track of Scout Leesom the minute she'd dropped over the side of the building with a guy Red Dog could only describe as a cross between Luke Skywalker pulling the "Save the Princess" moves from both *Star Wars* and *Return of the Jedi* and the cop from *Demolition Man.* But Scout was not Dylan's problem, and neither was the man who'd rescued her.

Jane was his problem. Though truth be told, his gut was telling him J.T. was in far more danger than the gallery girl. Hawkins had reported that the GTO had pulled over to the curb and stopped in front of the Quick Mart for a few seconds, and at 30th and Vallejo for longer than that, both times long enough for her to have gotten out, if she'd wanted to—and she hadn't.

Of course, J.T. could have been holding a weapon on her . . . but maybe not.

Dylan wasn't exactly the social butterfly of Special Defense Force—that honor was a toss-up between Hawkins and Skeeter—but even he remembered the young woman who'd hung around the Steele Street alley way back when, trying to get a look or two at J.T. Quinn and Creed had teased him about her mercilessly. She'd been a real hard case, a survivor, all skinny arms and skinny legs and lanky hair hanging in her pretty green eyes, about half fed most of the time.

No one would tease J.T. about her now. The urchin had turned into a heartbreaker with all the gloss and sophistication Katya Hawkins and Suzi Toussi could infuse in and slather on a young woman.

It was difficult to believe she might still be nursing a crush on J.T., but women were hardly his area of expertise. Again, that honor went to Christian Hawkins, Superman.

He leaned forward and keyed the mike on the radio. "Hey, Superman."

"Copy," Hawkins said.

"Give me the sitrep." The "situation report"—Dylan was hoping for better than he'd gotten five minutes ago.

"*Nada,*" his second in command said. "We've got nothing. We're getting a little spread out. It might be time to come in and regroup."

Not a bad idea.

"What did Travis and Red Dog find at the motel?" Hawkins asked.

"Meds," Dylan told him. "Lots of meds, and a chart book he keeps, tallying what he's taking for different symptoms. Gillian looked it all over and didn't like what she saw. She thinks he may be going down faster than she feared."

He heard Hawkins swear under his breath.

"She and Travis are still staking out the motel," Dylan continued. "They're hoping he comes in to get something, especially since we hit him with the Halox."

"We need a break," Hawkins said, and Dylan could only agree. Denver wasn't a big city by international standards, but it was big enough to get lost in. "Do Zach and Kid still have Lancaster in their sights?"

"Zach is locked onto him like a tractor beam," he

said. "Kid's got a date with Crutchfield at O'Shaunessy's. The lawyer called Skeeter about ten minutes ago, wanting to buy her a drink, or maybe just flat-out buy her, but we all know how much fun Kid can be, so I sent him, too, to keep the party going. That leaves Lancaster all on his own at the Kashmir Club."

"And Sam gave up six all total?"

"The management duo and two teams, Karola and Walls on one team, and two other guys named King and Rock working together."

"Hell," Hawkins swore.

Dylan agreed.

"Why didn't Jane get out of Corinna?" he asked. "She had two chances to get out, and she didn't."

"Man of her dreams comes back to life after six long years? The girl is sticking." Christian didn't hesitate to answer. "Out of curiosity, if nothing else, and she's enough of a team player to know we want him."

"You don't think he's threatening her, holding her against her will? That he might hurt her?"

"Hell, Dylan. If he wanted to hurt people, he would have been throwing fragmentation grenades, not flash bangs." Again Hawkins didn't hesitate. "And Red Dog said he had her dead to rights on the tenth floor, and he obviously didn't pull the trigger. And he didn't hurt Suzi Toussi in Paraguay, either. Jane's a burden, an accident that happened in his getaway car. She's not an asset. He came for the girl, and you saw Scout. You can't beat that kind of loyalty into somebody. She's a straight-up girl, fully self-actualized. She's been well cared for and well loved. Whatever J.T. remembers of himself, he hasn't lost his intrinsic guardian tendencies. How many times did he save you?"

More times than Dylan was going to admit to at this late date. He'd been a real prick when he'd landed in Denver at age fifteen—too god-awful rich, too class-conscious, and too self-indulgently angry to be anything other than a royal pain in the ass.

He'd had a natural inclination for leadership, or totalitarianism, to hear Hawkins and Quinn tell it, and he'd had an innate talent for getting people so pissed off they wanted to cut his gizzard out.

Exactly that. His gizzard. Cut right out of him. He hadn't even known what a gizzard was until some wino down on Wazee had flashed a blade and threatened to show him.

"He bailed me out a few times." Twice with the gizzard guy alone. It had taken Dylan a few weeks to understand that someone could have squatting rights to a stretch of sidewalk, or a heat grate, or a parking meter—whatever the hell they wanted—and anyone who trod on that piece of turf did it at their own risk. "Why don't you and Creed come in? Skeeter's on her way. Maybe we can shake something loose . . . hold on. I've got a call. Uptown Autos." He answered the phone and could hear the faint *whoop-whoop* of sirens in the background.

"Liam Dylan Magnuson Hart, I need you *now.*" He recognized the voice. What he didn't recognize was the panic in the voice. Lieutenant Loretta did not panic, ever, but the edge of it was there, causing her to almost hyperventilate.

"Where are you?" He was already rising from his chair, pulling his keys out of his pocket.

"Mama Guadaloupe's. *Geezus.*" He heard her stop to take a breath. "*Geezus,* Dylan, get down here, and call Grant, and . . . and Cristo. We need him and Creed. Yes, call Creed. Don't call Kid. No. Not until you get down here and see this. It's . . . brutal. Folks are running around down here like crazy."

Dylan keyed the radio mike and leaned in close. "Hawkins, Creed, go to Mama G's, *inmediatamente.*"

Don't call Kid.

It's brutal.

With those words, a vise had clamped itself around his chest.

"Copy," he heard Hawkins reply. "Three minutes."

"Four minutes." Creed came in over the radio.

"Make it less."

"Copy."

"Hey!" He heard Loretta through his phone. "Get these people back. Do your job, Sergeant, or I'll get someone who can!"

"Tell me what's going on, Lieutenant." Dylan used her rank on purpose and kept his own voice very calm, despite the fear flooding his veins.

This was about J.T. There was no other reason for her to contact him. Something bad had happened. He signaled Cherie to take over the console. He was leaving as soon as he got the facts.

"So I'm called down here to Mama's," Loretta said, slightly breathless, as if she'd been running, or was scared, "and four of my cruisers are already here, going balls-out with lights and whistles—"

She stopped and took another breath.

"Hey!" she hollered again. "Where are the EMTs? Why isn't there a fire truck in here yet? Let's move, people! And one of the first things I see out front is Corinna with two of her tires slashed."

It took him half a second to figure out she'd switched and was talking to him again, and another half a second to realize what she'd said.

"And Geronimo latches on to me like a leech, babbling about a ghost monster."

He knew Geronimo, one of the old cooks.

"J.T. was driving Corinna when he left here two hours ago," Dylan said, and yes, he knew why the old man might think he'd seen a ghost.

He hoped he didn't know why Geronimo thought he'd seen a monster.

"How, Dylan? Tell me how in the hell a man who's been dead for six years is driving a car that got its tires slashed in front of Mama Guadaloupe's?"

"He wasn't dead two hours ago, Loretta." He said the obvious, and heard her swear, one very succinct word, under her breath.

"And he's not one of the vics lying out here behind Mama's now."

Dylan felt a flood of relief wash through him. *Geezus.*

"But if he's alive, then who did we bury at Sheffield Cemetery?" she demanded, still talking to him. "Who is in that grave?"

"General Grant is finding out. Tell me about Corinna."

"She's parked, no damage except to the tires, and if it was J.T. driving her, well, he isn't anywhere to be had now. But Geronimo swears he walked through Mama's kitchen less than ten minutes ago with a dark-haired woman—"

"Jane Linden," Dylan said, sitting back down. This was still a hunting party, not the end of the line, and he needed to stay in charge of it all—and he needed to find his wife *now*.

"You see why I need you down here, Dylan? This is your boat taking on water, and I need you down here. Have you called Grant yet?"

He looked up and signaled Cherie again. "Grant," he said, before returning his attention to Loretta. "Cherie's getting him on the horn, and Hawkins and Creed will be there in less than three minutes."

"Good—and Geronimo is telling me that J.T. and Jane went out the back door with two men, and I'm standing out here right now, and I'm telling you it is fucking brutal in this alley, Dylan."

"What *exactly* are you looking at, Lieutenant?"

"Two dead men, each at two hundred pounds, their necks snapped, their heads damn near twisted clean off, all their legs broken. They've both been shot, and one of them has been shot up, the syringe still hanging out of his arm—the arm still attached to his body, that is—and his other arm, the left one, has been ripped right off him, right at the shoulder joint. Not sawed off, not shot off, not blown off, but twisted off like it was a damn chicken leg. It's lying in the alley about two feet away from the rest of him."

Geezus.

"Dylan?"

"Yes, Lieutenant?"

"If J.T. really is alive, and he did this, then he's insane."

CHAPTER TWENTY-SEVEN

Squinting against the pain of the lights, Monk pushed himself to his feet. He deserved the woman. For all the pain he'd been through and for all the pain ahead, he deserved the few moments of pleasure to be had with this golden creature—the soft tenderness of her skin, the sweet smell of her taking the stench of his own sweat out of his nostrils.

He picked up speed, lured by her struggles. He couldn't have devised a more perfect trap himself. She was easy prey.

So close, so fragile, so very afraid—and rightly so. He was the unexpected death. The one no one had ever imagined—because no one had ever imagined him before Dr. Gregory Patterson.

Thirty yards and closing, and he felt saliva forming on his tongue. She had no chance, no chance at all.

The police were spreading out, circling around the neighborhood, the sirens coming closer. He could hear them on two sides now, but he had the seconds he needed to snatch her out of her world and into his, where he was the only thing she would smell, and feel, and hear, and see. He would consume her senses. If she bit him, and he'd been bitten by women before, she would taste him, as well, but he would allow only so much of that and then he'd break her jaw. After that, there would be no more biting.

Women. They were such a solace in a lonely world. He'd had women, lots of them, and they were all so endearingly helpless. Even the rare ones who fought him endeared themselves to him with the feebleness of their attacks.

Twenty yards.

Fifteen yards.

And a shot rang out.

Then another.

And another.

Con didn't have any trouble finding the source of his quickly ratcheting fear—Jane, standing next to the junked truck, blasting away with her .380, shooting into the dark.

With two shots left, she stopped pulling the trigger but kept her pistol aimed straight ahead. Her chest was heaving, her body trembling.

"Jane!" He called her name and hoped to hell she didn't have a knee-jerk reaction and just swing around and shoot before she knew it was him.

To the girl's credit, she did not budge off target.

"J.T.?" she cried out, her voice tremulous.

"Yes," he said, going along with the name. His gun was drawn, and he was monitoring his approach, coming in behind her, looking for whomever or whatever she was shooting at, and not seeing anything—but he sensed there was something out there. His hackles were up, his internal warning system on full alert. There were enough cops running around to give anyone a wake-up call, but he didn't think any of them were lurking in the dark behind the dumpsters, waiting for another chance to get shot at by a beautiful girl in a slinky gold dress.

No, whatever was out there wasn't a cop. A trace of

unusual stench ran through the rank scents of garbage, gas, and rotting produce, a chemical smell of sweat and metal. It had been in the air when he'd first come through the alleys. He didn't know what in the hell it was, but the police were starting to spread out all over the neighborhood. Squad car lights were spilling into the alley area from the east. He had to get Jane and head west as quickly as possible. He was running out of time, his body temperature rising, his gun hand starting to shake.

"J.T., be careful." She kicked a loop of wire away from her, sounding frightened out of her wits. "It's . . . it's back there, something."

Something they didn't have time to deal with, not with the police closing in and him falling apart.

Coming up next to her, he kept the area in front of him covered with his pistol, wondering if what had scared her could have been something as simple as a stray dog, or another homeless guy setting up house, or just some trash skittering across the pavement—but he didn't think so.

"Come on," he said when he reached her side. "Let's get out of here, before the cops show up." And they were less than a minute away—way less.

She didn't hesitate to move out with him but kept her gun drawn. A police cruiser turned into the patchwork area of parking lots and junk, its light bar going full-out, and when he broke into a run, she did, too.

"You heard me, babe. Stand down and get your butt home," Dylan repeated, and he didn't like repeating himself. When he gave an order, he wanted to hear only one thing in reply: Yes, sir.

"Crutchfield is expecting me. If we want him, and we do, it's better to play the hand the way we dealt it."

His wife had a point, but so did he.

"The game has changed. We've either got a player we don't know about, or J.T. is a certifiable psychopath."

"What's happened?"

Cherie signaled him that she had Grant on the line, and he gave her a short nod.

"Loretta called me. J.T. and Jane were spotted at Mama Guadaloupe's, and shortly after the sighting, King Banner and Rock Howe were massacred in the alley, and I mean massacred, not just killed. They were overkilled, literally torn to pieces. Hawkins and Creed are there now, and I need you here."

He heard her swear softly under her breath, the shock hitting home, but it took her less than a moment to rally, her voice growing hard.

"All the more reason to pick up Crutchfield, Dylan, and you know it."

"And Kid is on it. He's already at O'Shaunessy's, but I need you here." About another ten seconds and she was going to have him on his knees.

"Dylan, my job is going up against bad guys. It's what I do, and I—"

He heard the insistence building in her voice, and he cut her off.

"This isn't about you, Skeeter," he said. "It's about me, and I *need* you here. If we lose Crutchfield, we'll get him another day. If I lose you . . ." He couldn't even say it.

Thank God, she didn't make him.

"I'm turning around now."

"Good." That was good. Very good. Now he could breathe.

CHAPTER TWENTY-EIGHT

She'd shot him, the bitch. Shot him clean through the meaty part of his upper arm, in one side and out the other. Her next shot had grazed him, and the last had gone wide of its mark, but the bitch had hit him solid with her first bullet.

It was a new dynamic, a woman with a gun, unexpected, most unwelcome. Worse, it had been one helluva shot, at fifteen yards, with him on the run and moving in on her fast and low. She wouldn't be an easy catch, but he would catch her, and her helluva shot was going to cost her. She could have died fast and clean, but now she'd added to his pain, and he was vengefully angry.

She would pay for his blood with her blood.

It was justice.

They both would pay, her and Farrel. The Bangkok beast had taken her from Monk, interfered in the kill, and sealed his doom. His death would not be a simple one, either.

Monk cowered deeper into the trash and boxes behind the grocery store and tore off one of his sleeves to bind his wounds and stanch the flow of blood. Million-dollar blood is what Dr. Patterson had called it, and Monk couldn't afford to lose it. MNK-1 had been worth a million dollars on the open market, all because of the chemically enhanced brew pumping through his veins and transforming him.

Four months, that's how long he'd been with Patterson in Bangkok, four months of being on and off a gurney while they'd injected him and transfused him and genetically cut away at little parts of him and added other parts for their experiments and their controls.

And then Lancaster had come and gone, all in less than a single afternoon. Monk hadn't had a chance to prove himself—until now.

Farrel had the woman, and if Farrel was anything like Monk, there'd be damn little of her left by morning, nothing left for him.

He felt a howl rising in his throat, raging to be released, but he held it in, tamped it down, and swallowed his pain, subsuming it with another need. More cops had arrived. They were cruising the streets and heading into the alleyway and parking lots, looking for him.

They wouldn't find him.

With the sleeve tight around his arm, he worked his way to the edge of the grocery store's loading dock and levered himself up onto the platform. From there, he climbed to the roof. A giant cottonwood tree overhung the gable behind the neon sign proclaiming Bagger's Market to the world, and, grabbing hold of the biggest limb, he swung himself out and upward into the branches. It was easy from there to make it to the next tree, and, high up in the heart of that cottonwood, he settled in to wait. The ground was crawling with cops and cars now. They were killing him with their lights and sirens.

They'd come in from both ends, east and west, and were everywhere, like the bits and pieces of trash littering the area. If she hadn't shot him, he might have made it out of the cordon. He'd lost precious seconds taking the hit and tying up his wound—the bitch.

He dug in his pocket for more silver gelcaps. Dr. Patterson had given them to him along with the glasses to help mitigate his searing sensitivity, and they worked—to a point. Huddled in the treetops, he breathed into the pain, his eyes squeezed shut, his hands over the glasses. Patterson had promised him new eyes, and if Monk had let him live, he might have gotten them. Except by then the die had been cast. Patterson would have as soon destroyed him as helped him.

No. There had been no other choice. He'd had to kill Patterson, and he had to suffer now, but soon he would slay the bastard Farrel and take his remains to Lancaster—lay them at his master's feet, and thus he would be welcomed home. Lancaster had the resources and the men to fix Patterson's mistakes. Monk would be the whole, pure soldier he was meant to be.

It wouldn't be long now.

Geezus. Con jerked Jane to a halt at the edge of the alleyway and pulled her back into the shadows with him. His heart was pounding, his pulse racing, and it pissed him off. If he was going down, he couldn't afford to go down tonight, not in this damn alley.

He reached in his pocket and pulled out a handful of pills. *La vida loca,* crazy, crazy frickin' life, living on gelcaps and justice, or at least his version of it.

He popped another blue gelcap in his mouth, hoped it damn well worked this time, and shoved the rest of the pills back in his pocket.

Out on the street, a cop car roared up and came to a screeching halt. Then another did the same, with both sets of policemen quickly getting out of their vehicles—and he had to wonder what in the hell was going on. These guys were on the hunt, with more police coming in from every direction. Why?

Two thugs on the losing end of a fight in an alley did

not warrant this kind of law enforcement reaction. Even with gunfire involved, it seemed excessive. Or maybe he'd just been living in the Third World for too long.

He and Jane were in a narrow walkway between an Italian restaurant and a club bar, and people were starting to come out of both buildings, wanting to see what all the excitement was about.

He turned toward her and refrained from a weary curse. He wasn't doing a very good job of taking care of her—or of getting rid of her. It had stopped raining, but the air was still damp, and she was shaking like a leaf.

"Put your pistol back in your purse," he said. "Are you cold?"

"N-no." Which only left option B—her being damned scared, and more than a little roughed up.

Scraped knee, scratches on her arms and face, torn dress, and her jacket long gone back at Mama's, and she was still exquisite, still looking like a woodland sprite, if Gucci had taken to designing woodland sprites this year.

"Here," he said, taking her arm and pulling her closer. "Lift your face, let me look at you." He knew what he looked like. He was a rough-and-tumble, ready-to-wear type of guy with a knife wound in his side and blood running down his leg. Luckily, he was wearing dark jeans.

She, on the other hand, needed some straightening up and some calming down if they were going to stroll into the crowd on the sidewalk without every cop on the block noticing that the beautiful girl in the gold dress looked like she'd been dragged through the alley backward.

All they had to do was get across the street, into the neighborhood of old houses, and they could disappear.

She tilted her chin up, and he combed through her hair

with his fingers, getting a couple of the tangles and a few twigs and leaves out.

Lovers.

They'd been lovers, and he'd let her go. It didn't make sense.

He smoothed his thumb over the satiny skin of her cheek. "Why did I leave you?" He really needed to know.

"W-work," she said. "You had a job to do."

"What kind of work?"

"With the Army. You told me once that your boss was a general."

In the big picture, that made perfect sense. Even without his memories, he'd known he was a soldier. All his skills, all his technical knowledge was tactical and weapons-based.

Pulling up the edge of his T-shirt, he gently wiped the scratches on her face. She was a mess, her teeth chattering, the look in her eyes a distressed clash of confusion and fear.

"I-I sh-shot it," she said, her voice trembling right along with the rest of her.

"Shot what?" He went ahead and straightened her dress, but it had gotten torn again, and there was only so much he could do with it. So he rearranged the buckle on her belt to front and center and hoped no one would notice her clothes were a little topsy-turvy. She still had all her jungle bangles on her wrist, so that was good, and throughout it all, she'd kept a death grip on her zebra-striped purse.

"I-I sh-shot that... that—that thing back there," she said, her breath still not quite caught.

He looked down at her for an instant more, then looked over her head to where they'd just come from.

"What kind of thing?" He searched the shadows again for any movement other than the cops, who were moving everywhere. *Geezus.* They needed to get out of here.

He checked the sidewalk to see if there was enough cover yet.

"A-a ghost..."

No.

He didn't think so.

He didn't know what she'd been shooting at, but he was pretty darn sure it hadn't been a ghost.

"...and I h-hit it...h-hit it hard," she said. "My last shot might have missed, but I'm dead-on about my first one...d-dead-on, and it hit."

"Good," he said, and gave her arm a quick, supportive squeeze, bucking her up, letting her know he was with her, proud of her. Hitting what you were shooting at was always good.

Always. Though technically, he didn't think nailing a ghost with a .380 did much actual damage. *Geezus.*

"I-I shouldn't have run. I sh-shouldn't have left Mama's."

No. She shouldn't have run.

"You would have been safer with the police," he agreed, which was exactly what he'd told her, which he wasn't going to mention, but if she'd done as he'd suggested—okay, *ordered* her to do—she wouldn't have ended up blasting away at something in the alley—probably a rat, or a muskrat, or a raccoon, and he hoped to hell not a homeless person. Any one of those was enough to spook somebody.

Not really.

They were enough to spook a high-end girl who looked like she'd spent half her life getting a pedicure and the other half getting a shiatsu massage, no matter how good a shot she'd turned out to be at Mama's.

And hell, if it had been a homeless person, at least

there were enough cops congregating back there to find him and give aid.

"You d-didn't do that, did you? To King and Rock. You d-didn't tear them up like... like that, right?" she asked, dragging her hand back through her hair, tangling it all up again, her gaze locked onto him like she was trying to think and figure things out and wasn't having much luck doing either.

Yeah, they made a helluva pair. He was spiking at about a hundred and three degrees now, and she looked like she'd been hit by a Mack truck.

"It was self-defense, Jane. You saw the whole thing," he said, trying again with her hair, lowering her hand away and sifting through the new tangle. "There were witnesses. Everyone in the kitchen saw what went down. You wouldn't have been charged with anything if you'd stayed." He didn't know much, but he knew that.

"No." She shook her head. "N-no, no, it's worse, the two of them all broken up, so broken it's awful, and the cops know me, from way back."

Well, yes, he'd busted those boys pretty hard, and so had she, but it was the "way back" part of her statement that got his attention.

"I-I couldn't stay," she kept on. "I c-couldn't take the chance... and... and—" She gulped in a breath and brought her hand up to cover her eyes—and she stood there and trembled.

He was headed there himself, out-and-out trembling territory, headed toward the shakes, and if things didn't go his way with that second blue pill, maybe there was a seizure of some god-awful sort in his near future—very near future.

Hell. He looked back to the sidewalk and the people coming out of the bar and the Italian place. About another thirty seconds or so and there'd be enough folks outside for him and Jane to step into the crowd and make their getaway.

Shifting his attention back to her, it took a lot of what he had not to just pull her close, lift her up into his arms, and carry her away from this mess—but *that* would definitely get the cops' attention.

"Did you do time?"

He wasn't going to ask himself why that was the first question that came to mind, except for some odd little inflection in her voice telling him it wasn't nearly as incomprehensible as he was going to wish it was, and when she just stood there, silent and trembling, with her hand still over her face, he knew it was true.

Perfect. He'd entered the country under a name he'd made up himself six years ago, and so far he'd illegally accessed a building and set off a few explosive devices. He'd stolen a car, easily committed a hundred or more traffic violations, kidnapped a woman, trespassed on all kinds of private property and damaged most of it, was knee-deep in assault and battery—and out of half a million people in Denver, he'd hooked up with a felon.

Somehow, somewhere, he couldn't help but think that there had been a time when he'd spent most of his life on the right side of the law—just one more thing he'd lost, his legal bearings.

Hell.

"Cañon City?" he asked, flat-out curious and figuring if she'd been sent up to Super Max in Florence, she'd still be behind bars.

"N-no." She shook her head. "The Immaculate Heart School for Young Women . . . in Phoenix."

He looked down at her, more than a little nonplussed. The Immaculate Heart School for Young Women? That wasn't exactly his idea of a lockup.

"What did you do? Steal the Communion wine?"

She shook her head again. "I . . . I killed a man," she

said, her voice barely audible. "Back when I was a kid. A gangbanger junkie over on Blake, me and Sandman. The cops haven't forgotten. They never forget."

Yeah, well, so now it was official. She'd shocked the hell out of him.

And geezus. She was right, cops didn't forget murder.

And yes, he was damn sorry he'd busted King and Rock so hard that she seemed to have gone into damn near instant posttraumatic stress disorder. And for the record, who in the hell was Sandman?

He had about a hundred questions, and not a one of them relevant to the mission at hand. She wasn't his problem. Scout was the reason he'd come to Denver, and Lancaster was the reason he was going to stay until the job was done. Everything always came back to Lancaster—not to waiflike beauties with sketchy pasts who had somehow fallen into the middle of his deal and locked on to him like a heat-seeking missile.

"The junkie grabbed one of my kids, thinking we had drugs on us," she said, going on, explaining something that didn't need an explanation. In his book, gangs and junkies and trouble went together like peanut butter and jelly—and, yeah, sometimes he wondered what that made him, with his stash of Souk's magic elixirs.

Hell.

"It all went bad so fast," she said. "There was a fight. He had his hands around my throat, shaking me hard, and I sh-shot him. Hawkins is the only reason I didn't get tossed into the state pen."

He could see it, some damn junkie trying to literally shake down a teenage girl for cash, or drugs, or whatever, and he wished to hell he'd been there. At least this Hawkins guy had saved her from going to jail. One more thing Con owed him for—and then the craziness of the thought hit him.

Christ. He was in trouble here.

"I... I thought he was going to kill me, the junkie, and he probably would have, but the cops still wanted to lock me up, because I was a street kid," she said. "You know how it is with street kids. They're always in the wrong place, because they've got no place else to go."

Yeah. He knew that much. He'd seen them all over the world, but he'd never in all his life seen one even half as beautiful as her.

"T-tell me," she said. "Tell me you didn't d-do it." She lifted her head, and her gaze met his straight on, unflinching, and in that instant, something changed.

He didn't know what "it" he hadn't done, but with a sudden clarity of awareness unlike anything he'd felt in the last six years, he saw beyond the moment. He saw beyond her past, beyond the pale green allure of her eyes and the smoky smudge of her makeup, beyond her intelligence and her dead-on marksmanship. Here in the darkened alleyway, with her so close, he saw something else in her eyes and in her face, and it changed everything.

He knew her.

Really knew her.

In the shadows, scraped and roughed up with her hair in tangles and her clothes askew, with the scar on her cheek and the freckles across her nose, he recognized her, the waif, the renegade, the street runner. He didn't remember being her lover, but he remembered her hanging around the place on Steele Street, waiting and watching for him, and remembered fantasizing about her, the street kid with the intense green eyes, the stringy hair, and the wildly beautiful face. He remembered he'd been a soldier, and she'd been eighteen, too damn young and too damn skittish, a fascinating, feral creature of the streets, living off her wits and her skills.

A pickpocket. The best Denver had ever seen.

The thought no sooner hit than he swore: *Sonuvabitch.*

He reached back for his wallet and felt the empty pocket, and he didn't know whether to curse again or grin.

She was good. Always had been.

Oh, yeah. She was damn good, and he'd been completely spun up, mesmerized, staring into her incredible green eyes and not even noticing that when she'd stopped on the street and reached for him, she'd been stealing his wallet. She'd had about three seconds to recognize him, come up with a plan, and execute the lift.

And she'd pulled it off.

"Can I have my wallet back?" he asked, and after a slight hesitation, she shook her head.

"Why not?" he asked.

"I lost it in the garage."

Well, she hadn't denied it, and at least now he had a pretty good idea of how SDF had found the Star Motel, but he was still a little confused on one point.

"Why did you take it?"

"I-I thought you were dead, and then there you were on the street, and I had to know if it was really you, if you were really J. T. Chronopolous . . . and . . . and I need to know whether or not you did that to King and Rock. Whether you ripped King's arm off and left it lying in the alley. You're strong enough. I swear you are."

And just like that, the whole night took another deep dive into the twilight zone. *Geezus.* King Banner's arm had been ripped off?

Ripped off?

No wonder there were so damn many cops swarming this block. He looked over her shoulder, down the alley. This was bad. Explosions tore people into pieces, but there hadn't been an explosion. So what in the ever-loving world could have—

It came to him then, just an idea, but a damned awful idea, that the Bangkok rumors he and Jack had heard were true. That Lancaster, dealing with a subpar Thai lab, had commissioned a monster—and possibly, for whatever reason, had brought the beast with him to Denver.

Either that, or there was a pack of wolves running loose on the west side, but even a pack of wolves couldn't have worked that fast—and they wouldn't have left the arm in the alley.

So what the hell else could it be, if it wasn't a guy like him juiced to the next plane, where humanity took a backseat to violence? He'd seen it in Souk's lab, when the good doctor's mistakes stretched the bounds of the imagination—twisted experiments gone wrong, like Shoko.

"No," he said clearly, meeting Jane's gaze again. "When I went back, both men were exactly as we'd left them. One of the cooks had come out into the alley, but he was small and old, not big enough to do that kind of damage."

"Something was."

She had that right.

"Your ghost," he said. "How good of a look did you get at it?"

"Not very," she admitted. "What I saw was a pale blur in the darkness—something big, moving fast, maybe with long white hair, or maybe that was just a trick of the light."

Big and fast he understood. A lot of the LeedTech warriors were big, and they were all fast. The long white hair—he didn't know about that. He'd never come up against a LeedTech assassin with long hair, white or otherwise, and he didn't want to tonight, not when he was heading toward his own personal Three Mile Island, a meltdown at his core, and not when Jane was within a hundred miles of him.

"Come on," he said. There were enough people on the street now, enough chaos to cover their escape, and they needed to move out. Somewhere up there on the hill, in that old neighborhood of winding roads, was a place where they would be safe. He could almost hear it calling to him, like a siren's song.

CHAPTER TWENTY-NINE

Creed had seen some pretty wild things in his life, some real bad stuff, but nothing quite like this.

Standing in the alley behind Mama Guadaloupe's, a few things were immediately obvious. First, a lot of people back here in the alley hadn't seen much bad stuff. Two of the cops and a fireman had upchucked their suppers, and it looked like one of the EMTs was going to be next. Second, typically, there were at least four versions of the truth in two languages being tossed around. Last, but far from least, there was one bad motherfucker out there somewhere. King Banner's arm had been twisted clean off at the shoulder and been tossed aside.

Amazing.

Shades of Beowulf came to mind, and the monster Grendel. He was also thinking about Red Dog, and what a man juiced like her would be capable of doing—a man like J.T.

It was a lot to think about.

"You got enough light?" he asked Hawkins, who was photographing everything with his cellphone. The detectives were going to be there any second, and they were traditionally territorial about their crime scenes. But Loretta had given Superman the go-ahead, and they were running with it under her firm command not to touch anything.

He was good with that—except for one thing. He sure would like to take the syringe hanging out of the arm still attached to King. He'd seen others like it. He knew what it was, and so did everybody else on SDF: a Thai syringe, strange stuff that the forensics lab here in Denver was going to have a helluva time deciphering.

"This place is lit up like the inside of a klieg light," Hawkins answered.

Yeah, it was.

"You might want to get close-ups of their faces," he said. "In case there's family somewhere. If we can come up with a match in the LeedTech files Dylan snagged, somebody might get called down to a cop shop someplace to identify them."

"Thank you, Mother Teresa."

Yeah, yeah. Whatever. It was damn nice of Loretta to let them in on this, but he doubted if Dylan was going to be sharing the LeedTech files with her. That was going to be their piece of the puzzle.

He lifted his face into the night air and closed his eyes.

"There's a lot of blood," Hawkins said.

Yeah, he could smell it. Carnage.

He turned his head a few degrees to the south. Three more shots had been heard coming from that direction, and according to Geronimo, Jane had run into the parking lot on the other side of the fence.

He looked back at the two corpses and let his gaze trail over them and to the loose arm lying two feet from King Banner's body.

Sonuvabitch.

"Hey, Superman, better get a shot of this." He gestured at the arm.

Hawkins stepped over and, after looking at the arm for a couple of seconds, let out a long, low whistle.

"Do you want to call the boss, or do you want me to do it?" he asked.

"I'm on it." Creed already had his phone out, and while Hawkins angled his camera toward the arm and clicked off a series of photos, he waited for somebody to answer at Steele Street.

"Uptown Autos—"

"Skeet," he cut her off. "Are you getting all these pictures?"

"Yes," she said. "With a new set coming in now."

Tough girl. She didn't sound at all freaked out, but she'd been in combat.

"Zoom in on the upper part of the biceps on that loose arm."

"Looking now, Jungle Boy," she said, and he knew she was seeing the odd wound just below where the arm had been separated from the shoulder.

"What are you thinking?"

"I'm thinking something took a bite out of Mr. Banner, maybe took some shirt with it."

"That's what I was thinking, too."

"Wild dogs?" she asked after a moment, and he understood the brief delay. She was hoping for the best.

"I don't think so, Skeet. Let Dylan know, and we'll get back to you when we find something." He hung up and turned back to Hawkins. "This is getting weird."

"Copy that," Hawkins said, pocketing his phone. "You ready?"

"Yeah, we need to get moving," he said. There were at least three other cop cars whooping and flashing in the parking lot alley on the other side of the fence, but Creed knew it was going to take more than that to find anybody back there. It was a great place to hide. He'd done it hundreds of times as a kid.

So had J.T.

CHAPTER THIRTY

Lancaster stood at the window of his suite, looking down at the city streets. Denver was starting to unnerve him. The whole mission was starting to unnerve him. He was too exposed, the situation had become too uncontrolled.

He checked his watch. Crutchfield had been gone for half an hour and hadn't checked in. Lancaster was going to give him ten more minutes, and then he was jerking the lawyer's chain. That damn gimp Walls had never checked in. Neither had King and Rock after their call from Crutchfield.

If King and Rock had failed and SDF had snatched Farrel right out from under their noses, he could understand why they hadn't called him. They'd be executing their contingency plans, still working the mission, going for the win—and if they weren't, he would replace them in a heartbeat. He had a hundred names in his files of men who had been through Souk's lab and could do the jobs he needed done.

What he needed now was the woman, and Crutchfield had better damn well deliver her. Dylan Hart would go to the ends of the earth for her. He would certainly give up a man who didn't even remember him. Conroy Farrel was a stranger, not a friend, not a brother in blood and arms the way J. T. Chronopolous had been.

A mistake—that's what Conroy Farrel really was, a mistake Lancaster needed to fix, the same way he'd fixed the mistake called MNK-1. Death was the only possible solution, and, by God, he wanted it done, and then he was getting out of this town.

Karola was checking in like clockwork, for what little that was worth. He'd spotted Scout Leesom once and then quickly proceeded to lose her. Karola hadn't seen Walls since the gimp had taken off out of the ally in the opposite direction, intending to intercept the girl. The Leesom brat couldn't have given them much trouble, if they'd caught her, and neither could that bastard Jack Traeger. Traeger did not have a chemically enhanced edge. He wasn't a LeedTech warrior.

Lancaster picked up a glass of Scotch off a side table and took a long swallow. He'd bought an island off the coast of Venezuela, and that's where he was going when he was finished here in Denver, a much-needed vacation from all the prying minds in Washington. He'd already resigned his board positions on two financial corporations and his advisory position at the Schumaker Institute. The old man was pulling in his horns, making way for the new bucks.

He took another swallow of Scotch and checked his watch again.

Nothing felt right anymore. All his sure footing had turned to sand, and he wanted out, before he got buried. He didn't want Washington, D.C., to turn out to be his grave—and he didn't want this damn town to turn out to be his grave, either.

God, it was hell getting old. Maybe he'd stayed in the game too long.

Eight minutes, that was it, and then he was calling Crutchfield and finding out where in the hell he was and what in the hell he was doing, farting around out there in Denver, when their asses were on the line.

* * *

From where he was sitting, Tyler Crutchfield could see his suit jacket dragging in the water of a low-lit swimming pool in a subterranean, granite-encased room.

After Peter Chronopolous had literally kidnapped him and wrestled him down here, the guy had stripped him out of his jacket and all too casually let it drop on the pool deck, the cretin. One of the sleeves had fallen into the water, and now the whole jacket was ruined, half of a four-thousand-dollar suit. Tyler had become fixated on it—the way the sleeve had started out floating on the surface of the pool, how it had slowly lost its buoyancy and drifted underwater, the stain creeping up the material. The suit was new, his sartorial pride and joy, and he'd have given it and every other handmade Italian suit in his closet to anyone who could have gotten him out of this basement.

It wasn't going to be Sam Walls. Lancaster's bullyboy was across the room, lying in a crumpled heap, wet and, from the looks of him, dead. Tortured, Tyler was certain, with the bleak rig of ropes and pulleys hanging from the ceiling over the edge of the pool. As a two-year captain of his university's water polo team, Tyler had spent half his life in a swimming pool. He had an affinity for pools, an affection for them, but not this one. The wet, dead lump of Walls terrified him, and so did the other two men in the basement, one of whom was behind him somewhere in the dark, silent and waiting, a man he'd recognized as Quinn Younger. The other man was standing in full light, right in front of him—calm, in control, soft-spoken, harder than iron, and the most ruthless SDF operator of them all.

Tyler had memorized the team's bios. He knew who he was dealing with, and it made his gut churn. For Liam Dylan Magnuson Hart, there was no past too far removed, no future too distant, and no intellectual path or strategic configuration too complicated to bring to bear on current circumstances.

Tyler was a current circumstance, and he felt the weight of that truth with every breath he took. Even if he lived, which he sorely doubted, he'd be run to ground and ruined in a thousand unforeseen ways, ad infinitum, unless Lancaster destroyed SDF.

Tonight was none too soon, before something truly terrible happened to him, but Tyler wasn't putting his money on a rescue.

Trapped in this fucking basement, in the bowels of Steele Street, face-to-face with Dylan Hart, he finally understood why Lancaster had failed to kill this team off long before now.

A clean snatch and grab, that's what Dylan liked, and he was looking right at one: Tyler Crutchfield. The man had all but given himself up when Kid had approached him in O'Shaunessy's Bar, but not until after he'd first made the mistake of flashing a weapon at the Boy Wonder. Dylan was sure the guy was still hurting from the half-dozen ways Kid had hit him, ways no one else in the bar would even have noticed. Up until that point, Kid had said the guy hadn't looked like he'd ever gotten dirty in his life.

Things had changed for Tyler Crutchfield. He was sweating like a pig and as white as a sheet. Kid swore that he'd barely touched him after relieving him of his pistol, but the guy still looked like he'd been messed with, and things had gone downhill for him from there. He'd already given up everyone except his mother, and Dylan had barely gotten started.

"Tyler, you've been real cooperative so far, and I appreciate all the information you've given me about Lancaster and his plans for the teams he created," Dylan said, and truly, the man had given him everything he'd asked for, one question after another. "But you're in the wrong game for a guy with no balls. Just an FYI."

Dylan had known some tough lawyers, but Crutchfield wasn't one of them. Skeeter could have taken him down with one arm tied behind her back, literally, but Dylan was damn glad to say that she hadn't. His girl was back up on the comm console where she belonged—at least for now.

"That's Sam Walls over there," Tyler said with a lift of his head. He couldn't lift anything else. After Kid had dropped him off and headed back to the Kashmir Club, Dylan and Quinn had given Crutchfield the deluxe duct tape restraint workup. The guy was practically married to his chair.

"Yep, that's Walls." Who was no longer married to his chair.

"Is he dead?"

"Not yet" was the honest reply. Walls wasn't dead, and there wasn't a mark on him, except where Quinn had pulled off the duct tape, but he was more or less comatose over on the pool deck, sleeping off his Thai syringe.

With King and Rock massacred at Mama's, and Walls and Crutchfield secure in Steele Street's pool room, that left only Rick Karola and Lancaster on the loose—and Dylan didn't think either of them had killed King and Rock. And so help him God, deep in his heart, he didn't think J.T. had torn the two men apart, either, and that only left him with one other choice.

There was somebody else running wild on Lieutenant Loretta's streets tonight, but who?

"I've only got one more question for you, Tyler. I know you and Walls and Karola came to Denver with Lancaster, and I know King Banner and Rock Howe are here, so to speak, but did you bring someone else?

Somebody who maybe had some kind of beef with King and Rock?"

Crutchfield's gaze narrowed. "No," he said hesitantly. "No one else. What do you mean, King and Rock are here 'so to speak'? What does that mean?"

It was a pure lawyer question, and Dylan was happy to explain.

He whipped out his cellphone and brought up the photos Hawkins had sent. They were damn grim by anybody's standards.

Stepping closer to Tyler's chair, he showed the first photo to him and then clicked through the next four. At number five, the lawyer threw up on himself.

Geezus.

Dylan carefully stepped away from the guy.

"Do you know anybody who had it in for those boys?" Everybody had enemies. What Dylan wanted was names.

"You're . . . you're smarter than this, Hart."

Yeah, maybe he was.

"I'm not saying Conroy Farrel didn't kill them," he said. "He certainly had every reason in the world, including self-defense, if it came down to that. But this is vicious, unlike him—"

"You don't know what he's like," Crutchfield snapped, his nerves obviously fried, frazzled, and frayed.

"No," Dylan agreed. "But I know what he used to be like, and nothing I saw here today, when he came and rescued the girl, told me anything different than what I used to know. I don't think he did this."

"Then you're a fool. The man is a beast."

"Then he's a beast of Lancaster's making. You might want to think about that while you contemplate the pool." He signaled Quinn, then turned and headed for the door.

Quinn walked over to where the pulleys hung from a

boom on the ceiling. Taking hold of one of the ropes, he started swinging the whole rig around to Tyler's side of the pool deck.

"No!" Crutchfield cried out, squirming in his chair, his voice sharp with panic. "You...you can't...can't do this. Can't let him...can't. You can't."

Oh, yes, I can, Dylan thought, still walking.

"I know all about Moscow." The man's voice rose along with his panic. "About the deal you had with the KGB. How you sold them state secrets you...you *bastard!*"

Tyler Crutchfield didn't know anything other than what Randolph Lancaster had told him, and it was all lies. Dylan had delivered the diplomatic pouch exactly to where White Rook had told him to deliver it. The deal had gone south and had been hanging over Dylan's head for the last fourteen years.

But that was over tonight.

It would die with Randolph Lancaster.

Dylan wasn't planning on killing Lancaster, but the faster this night wound down, the less sure he was that he could do anything to keep him alive.

"*Wait!*" Crutchfield called out. "Wait...please wait."

Dylan stopped and, after a moment, turned back to the lawyer.

Crutchfield just sat there and stared at him, panting for breath with puke on his shirt and eyes full of fear and distress.

"Don't waste my time," he warned the guy.

"There...there might be someone, an operator besides Farrel who's...*enhanced*, or whatever all these guys are. We were in Bangkok, and—"

"We?"

"Lancaster and I, two weeks ago," Crutchfield said. "He had an appointment somewhere in the city. I didn't go with him. I don't know where it was, or why he went there, but he came back to the hotel very disturbed, distraught. He . . . I don't know, he . . ." His voice trailed off.

"Continue," Dylan ordered.

The lawyer squeezed his eyes shut for a moment. "Randolph looked really shook up, panicked, and he had a few drinks. Maybe more than a few, and he started talking, mumbling, about some Navy SEAL who'd become an abomination. That's what he called it, an abomination, a twisted mistake, a creature that had been crying out for him, calling his name over and over—and he blamed himself, said some crazy things about experiments going wrong in a lab somewhere. He's been spooked ever since, like I've never seen him."

Not good, Dylan thought. Not good at all. Navy SEALs were pirates to begin with, the real wild cards in the elite warrior deck, and with Souk dead, he could only imagine who might be out there trying to continue the demented doctor's work.

"Tell me everything you know about the SEAL."

"That's it," Crutchfield said. "That's everything. I don't know what kind of lab makes guys like Farrel and Banner, but this one scared him. It scared him badly."

"You know more." People always did. "Think back to the hotel that night and tell me what else he said."

Crutchfield just stared at him, his face blank, and then his expression suddenly changed.

"Monk," he said. "That's what he called the SEAL, Monk."

Perfect.

Dylan keyed the mike on his radio and contacted Skeeter.

"We're looking for a guy named Monk," he said. "He was a Navy SEAL. It'll be a recent entry in the LeedTech files."

Quinn dropped the rope and walked over to retrieve Crutchfield's phone from the pile of stuff they'd taken off the guy. Dylan watched him scroll down the contact list and press the send key. Randolph Lancaster was about to get a call.

Coming up behind Crutchfield, Quinn held the phone to the lawyer's ear and a gun to the back of his head. From the sudden look of blank, unadulterated terror on the man's face, Dylan figured he could count on Mr. Crutchfield's full cooperation.

Walking back over to the pool edge, he pulled a piece of paper with a carefully scripted statement typed on it out of his pocket. He waited until he heard Lancaster answer, then held the paper in front of Tyler's face at eye level—and the guy did great, just great.

"It's me," Crutchfield said, reading the lines. "I've got her. I'm bringing her up. Let me in."

As soon as Crutchfield was finished reading, Quinn cut off the call, and Dylan hit a number on his own phone. When the Boy Wonder answered, he said only one word. "Go."

The party had started.

CHAPTER THIRTY-ONE

"Are you sure this is okay?" Jane asked.

"Yes."

Well, he was wrong, she thought, shifting uneasily on her feet. No way in the world was it okay to be breaking into this bungalow tucked into the last lot on a dead-end street, especially when he was taking way too damn long to do it. Baby-blue clapboard and green trim made the house the most colorful home on the block. The multi-layer gardens surrounding the place turned it into a gem hidden in a jungle of trees, budding bushes, and flowers coming into bloom. The place smelled wonderful, and she could hear a fountain bubbling and splashing from somewhere around back.

It was an unexpected and oddly disconcerting oasis in a night of violence and fear. They'd been on the run for hours and had suddenly washed up in a quiet, pastoral corner of the suburbs.

She looked back to the east, and the neighborhood instantly went to hell. A police cruiser was rolling into view. It stopped at an intersection two blocks away, its lights flashing, its siren silent, then slowly turned in their direction and began easing its way up the block.

Oh, cripes.

"Here," she said, stepping closer to him and taking the lockpicks out of his hands. "Let me do this."

He didn't resist, and she wasn't surprised. He'd started trembling right about the time she'd stopped, about halfway up the street. He could hardly hold the picks, and his skin was hot—too hot to be anything but bad.

"What's wrong?" she asked, sliding the second pick into the lock alongside the first one. "You're shaking all over."

"Fever," he said, taking a match out of a small container affixed to the house and dragging it across the striker. The match flared to life.

"Are you sick?"

He shook his head no and touched the flame to an incense brazier set on a small iron table next to the door.

"What are you doing?" She was feeling for the pins in the lock but was watching him.

"Something I've done before." The coals ignited, and he sniffed the air. "Copal, sweetgrass, and sage, to purify and protect. This house has a lot of ritual associated with it."

The brazier started to smoke in earnest, infusing the air with an aromatic scent, earthy and feminine. In a couple of more seconds, she had the door open, and they were slipping inside with the police cruiser still a full block away. Not until after he'd closed the door behind them did it occur to her that they might not be alone. The house was dark, with only one small light turned on in the back, in the kitchen, a "welcome home" light.

"So you know the person who lives here." That was a comfort.

"I'm not sure."

O-kay, she thought, so maybe not so much of a comfort. From the entryway, the house looked as well kept and brightly decorated as the outside. Colorful rugs covered a wood floor. The couch and chairs were all upholstered in cream-colored canvas with an abundance of striped serapes and a dozen or so pillows piled on them.

The coffee table had a blue slate top, and a fire had been laid in the fireplace, ready to go. She didn't sense another person in the house.

What she did sense was the sanctity of the place. It threatened to be her undoing, the quiet warmth and security of this small home on the west side. She'd been running on ragged energy shot through with bolts of terror all night. It was what had kept her going. If they really were safe, if she didn't need a boatload of adrenaline jacking her up to stay alive, then she needed to stop where she stood, before exhaustion dropped her like a stone.

"Maybe . . . m-maybe we should sit down." It seemed a reasonable idea. Her knees were weakening, whether it was time to give in to exhaustion or not.

"Go ahead," he said, lifting the curtains at the living room window and peering out.

She headed toward the chair nearest the fireplace but stopped short when cop car lights flashed through the curtains.

"Tell me they're not stopping," she said, hoping against hope.

"Can't," he said. "They pulled up in front. Come on." Turning away from the window, he took her by the hand and pulled her along with him, across the living room and deeper into the house.

"Can we even get out the back without them seeing us?" *Damn*—she stumbled trying to keep up.

Without missing a beat, he turned partway around and swung her up into his embrace. She landed in his arms with a small *oomph*. *Cripes*, he was strong.

"We're not going out the back," he said. "We're done running."

In theory, maybe, she thought, plastered up against his rock-hard chest, clinging to him, but her reality check was still saying "run like hell."

In three more steps they were through an archway and in a wide hallway with doors opening off into bedrooms and a bath, with another arch leading into the kitchen. It was the center of the house, a small space with a bookcase against one wall and a bench against another.

A couple of car doors slammed shut outside, and what little was left of her adrenal gland crackled and snapped back to life—and there she was again, in fight-or-flight mode, and if it wasn't going to be the back door, it was going to be fight. But, man, if this was showdown time, they needed Superman and Dylan. They needed Creed and Skeeter, with a side order of Travis and Kid. There was no one else she trusted.

Except for him, she realized. From the minute he'd first grabbed her and put her in Corinna, he'd done nothing but try to get her out of this rolling disaster.

"We—" she started, but he caught her gaze and touched his finger to his lips.

"Shhh..." he said so softly she could barely hear him. *Shhh*... of course, *shhh,* but—

"We can't blast our way through a bunch of cops," she whispered. Honest to God, they couldn't, and the hall wasn't exactly the hiding place of the century.

"They won't come inside." He carried her to the farthest corner and sat down with his back against the wall, effortlessly lowering himself to the floor as if she weighed nothing in his arms. God, he was strong, superhuman strong, but he was wrong about the cops.

Nobody knew cops like a street rat, and in her experience, if the cops wanted in, they came in—done deal, no questions or permission asked. Hell, she'd been chased by cops into some of the sketchiest hidey-holes in the city. They were like weasels, unstoppable by any barrier known to man when they wanted something. She'd been dragged out of places by her feet and dragged out by her hair. It had always been damned discouraging, not to mention painful.

But the cops were only one of their problems.

Sitting in the shadows, cradled in his lap, she got the full up-close-and-personal lowdown on his physical condition, and it was not good. He was burning up, and his muscles were twitching under his skin, like something really bad could happen any second. Considering the way the whole damn night had gone down, there wasn't a doubt in her mind that it would—something bad, any frickin' second.

A flashlight beam angled into the hallway from one of the bedroom windows, and she leaned in closer to him.

"I have aspirin in my purse," she whispered in his ear. "A whole bottle, if you need it. Or do you have another pill you can take?" Or more like half a dozen or so.

He shook his head no, and a wave of frustration washed through her. What in the world was she going to do if he collapsed? She'd be damned if she'd let the cops have him, and she sure as hell wasn't going back out into the dark without him. She didn't want to get caught, either, not and spend the rest of her days in the slammer—not for a crime she hadn't committed, and not for the one she had. Sure, she'd shot King and Rock, but she hadn't been the one who'd killed them—and neither had he. She knew that down to her bones.

Another beam of light danced across the bathroom window, and she drew herself in closer to him, all but laminating herself to his chest, and the closer she got, the tighter he held on to her, but whether that was for her sake or his, she didn't know. He felt like he was falling apart, and she wasn't in much better shape.

God, that...that *thing* in the alley. It had torn King's arm off and snapped those men's necks, and it was still out there somewhere. A tremor of fear snaked through her, and she buried her face against his chest, wishing everything out there in the night trying to get them would just go away.

Well, hell, Con thought. He heard the police walk back around to the porch and rattle the front door. When that didn't get them anywhere, they shined a flashlight through the window again. He reached down and gently took hold of Jane's ankle, pulling her foot back a few inches, out of the cops' line of sight. He'd been in tough places before, and this most definitely wasn't one of them—except for her being there.

The flashlight beam danced partway down the hall again, and she leaned closer into him, clinging to his side, curling into his lap. He could smell her, the soft fragrance of her skin and the edge of her surrender to all the wrong things, like fear and exhaustion.

He wasn't in much better shape, shaking like a damn leaf.

Geezus. They made a pair.

The flashlight moved away, and he stretched one of his legs out, lifting his hip a slight bit and shoving his hand into his front pocket, searching for the small plastic case he'd taken off King Banner when he'd frisked the man.

He hadn't lied to her. He didn't have another pill he could take, but maybe King did.

He found the case, pulled it out, and flipped open the lid, being careful not to spill the contents.

"You didn't always look the way you do now," he said, keeping his voice low and tipping the case this way and that into the flashing light coming through the curtains from the squad car. "The way you're dressed. The way you wear your hair."

She lifted her head from his shoulder, and he glanced up, catching the curious look she gave him. Yeah, he was pretty damn curious about his memories of her, too, why they were there in his mind, so clear, so undeniable.

He shifted his attention back to the case. It was full of gelcaps, all the colors, including the ones he'd run out of a few days ago. That sorry bastard King Banner hadn't been any better off than he. No matter how Souk had sold his research to Lancaster, every soldier who'd been through Atlas Exports was playing a losing game.

"Jane," he said her name. Jane Linden. But that wasn't the whole truth. "You have another name." A name he'd heard many times. And the mere fact that he recalled it made something shift deep inside him, like a widening crack in a fault line. "They called you Robin Rulz."

And he knew why. It was a shout-out to Robin Hood, with the wild girl ruling the streets instead of the forest, stealing from the rich to feed all those grimy little brats who had always been underfoot everyplace she'd gone. He picked a white pill out of King's case and put it under his tongue.

Geezus.

He tilted his head back and closed his eyes, and he breathed—deep and slow, soft and easy. With luck, and King's meds, he just might make it through the night.

The cops continued to rustle around outside, shining their lights everywhere and talking on the radio, and through it all, the white pill slowly dissolved until it was nothing more than a citrus taste in his mouth.

"That was your street name, Robin Rulz," he said, waiting for the first wave of relief to wash over him.

He didn't have to wait long.

"I thought you'd lost your memory."

"So did I. For forever, I'd figured, but since I got to Denver, things have been changing for me, especially since I saw you on the street."

"Me?" She sounded disbelieving, then let out a short

laugh. "Do us both a favor, and don't remember too much about me."

Yeah, he understood. She'd had a helluva life.

"Too late," he said. "I think I've just about got it all: the kids, your street-rat days running a crew for that bastard who got sent up for importing heroin through his rug business. That must be how you got in trouble with that junkie, you and Sandman."

She stiffened in his arms, swearing under her breath, and tried to push away from him.

"Hey, hey, don't go anywhere, not yet," he whispered, pulling her back.

He kept his hold on her gentle but firm, and after a moment, she relented. She wrapped her arms around herself, keeping her distance, but stayed within the protective shelter of his lap.

"You got a rough start," he said. "There's no shame in that, and as soon as you saw another way, you took it. That's the best any of us can do." And she'd done it in spades. No one looking at her would ever see the grimy kid she used to be. He'd been looking at her all night and hadn't seen anything but—

Trouble.

Hell. He let out a sigh and relaxed more deeply into the corner, feeling the shakes slowly fading away. The white pill worked fast, and he was starting to feel pretty good, like he was going to make it through the next few hours.

She felt good, too, all soft curves, silky dress, and even silkier hair, long and loose and sliding down his T-shirt, catching on his arm. He wanted her, but he sure didn't see that going anywhere.

Outside, he heard a pair of car doors slam shut, and then the flashing lights faded from the windows. The cops were leaving. It was time to move.

"Come on," he said, gathering her close and standing

up. He let her feet slide to the floor, and as soon as he knew she was stable, he released her and headed into the bathroom. "Can you make us some coffee, maybe see if there's something in the fridge to eat?"

There would be. The kitchen in this house was always stocked, the woman who lived here always generous in a thousand ways that had kept him coming back year after year.

This place... this place... He stopped and looked around. He'd come here for a reason. He just wasn't sure what it was, or who the woman was who owned it.

Nothing was as clear to him as the Wild Thing. Every time he looked at her, another image from the past slid across his mind. Some of them not so great, like one night when he'd caught her on the street, literally, he'd had his hands on her, holding her, and she'd been a mess, coughing, her nose running, wearing a jacket two sizes too big, and yet under her straggly hair and dirty face, he'd seen a kindred spirit, a survivor, a fighter.

She'd been up to no good. He knew that but nothing more about what she'd been doing that night.

From out of nowhere, another memory flashed across the corner of his mind, of a powerful hand, a man's hand, and a strong wrist, and the tattoo that snaked up both of them and disappeared under the cuff of a pale gray shirt. A sudden pain had him lifting his hand to his heart, and for a split second, it was hard to breathe. Then the moment passed, but not the memory.

Yeah, he knew people here. He'd had a life in this city, one at least as rich and rough as hers, and maybe it was still there for him, if he wanted it.

"Sure," she said, turning toward the kitchen, going to make the coffee.

He watched her leave, fighting a sense of futility. Even if he wanted his old life back, he didn't want it as much as he wanted Lancaster, and that truth still begged the question he was facing tonight.

How much did he want her?

Too much.

Fuck. He stepped into the bathroom and stripped off his makeshift bandage and his T-shirt in order to give his knife wound a good look-see. He'd gotten off easy this time. Despite King's ultimate warrior skill set, he'd gotten only one good strike in, right in Con's side meat, missing all his vitals and his ribs.

Without giving it a thought, he opened the door to the linen closet and found exactly what he was looking for, a plastic tub full of first aid supplies, including a suture kit. In the other room, he could hear Jane opening cupboard doors, and he went to work.

About halfway through his fourth stitch, he realized he wasn't alone.

He glanced up and found her standing stock-still in the doorway, staring at him.

"Why don't you wait for me in the kitchen," he said. "I'll be out in a minute."

"S-sure." She choked out the word, but she didn't move, not one inch.

Hell. He didn't blame her for staring. He knew what he looked like, and he was a mess. More mess than she would want to deal with, and he didn't blame her.

"Was it King who cut you?" she asked.

"Yes, and if you're going to faint, you're on your own until I'm done," he warned her, finishing off the stitch and reaching for the povidone-iodine.

She didn't budge.

"Who did *that* to you?"

He had a lot of scars, but he knew which one she meant, the epic track running down the center of his chest.

"Maybe a guy named Dr. Souk, maybe not," he said,

disinfecting the stitches. "I try not to spend a lot of time wondering about the things I don't remember. In this case"—he shrugged—"I think it's best that particular memory is gone."

He pressed a thick gauze bandage over the sutures and started wrapping more gauze around his waist to hold the bandage in place.

"How's the coffee coming?" he asked, glancing up.

She was really looking him over now, cataloging every wound he'd ever suffered, every cut of the knife.

Good.

She needed to see it all.

Some of the butchery he remembered, being strapped to a gurney, going under with Souk's face looming over him, and waking to a new set of bloody bandages—and, without fail, a new level of strength and power and speed that in the end wasn't worth the price to be paid.

He was glad someone, somewhere, had blown that bastard's brains out.

"The coffee?" she said. "It's, uh, coming along fine." Moving another step into the bathroom, she reached into the tub for the first aid tape.

He ran out of gauze, held the end, and waited while she tore off a piece of tape and smoothed it into place. Her fingers were cool to the touch, sweetly feminine, gentle—and enough to make him want all the trouble she could deliver.

"Thanks," he said, deliberately moving away. "We should—" He stopped in the same instant that her gaze flew up to meet his. The stark look on her face told him she'd heard it, too, the creaking sound of someone stepping up onto the front porch.

CHAPTER THIRTY-TWO

He wanted in.

Beneath the oddly rotten stench of this end of the block, Monk could smell the woman from the alley, the one in the golden dress with the bangles on her wrist. He'd followed her trail up the hill, and it had led him to exactly where he'd known she would be: 1822 Secaro Street, Alazne Morello's house, an address and a name he'd found in J. T. Chronopolous's files. The golden woman's scent seeped through the walls of the house, and he wanted her.

The other strong scent, the one reeking of testosterone, had enraged him every step of the way. It would be good to have Conroy Farrel dead.

But first the woman.

Monk walked through the gardens surrounding the small house at the end of the block and stepped up onto the front porch. The rotten smell immediately became even more disgustingly intense, like overripe fruit left in the hot sun for far too long.

He spied the smoldering brazier, the apparent cause of the reeking stench infusing the whole street, and reached for the door, intending to make quick work of his prey—but the smoke thickened and caused him to pause.

Odd.

Unexpected.

Maddening.

In less than a second, he ran through the series of thoughts, all of them inadequate until he reached the last one: *maddening*. He understood maddening. He felt it often, the bone-deep anger that pushed him beyond his ability to reason.

But this wasn't reasonable.

This place...this place... he looked to either end of the porch, still trying to ignore the smoking brazier. There was something about this place, something impenetrable, something disturbing, something besides the smoke threatening to gag him.

He brought his arm up and buried his nose in the crook of his elbow, reaching for the door with his other hand.

Sickening.

More than sickening, the smoke burned his nostrils and made his eyes water. The smell of it made his skin crawl and curled around inside his stomach, tightening it into knots.

He kicked the brazier off the porch, but even in the wet loam of the gardens, the coals smoldered, and now the smell was at his back as well as lingering around the door in wisps of the nauseating, gut-churning smoke.

He coughed and gagged, and backed down off the porch, stumbling away from the assault on his senses.

The woman who lived here, the one from J. T. Chronopolous's past, was a *bruja*, a self-proclaimed witch. Alazne Morello called herself a sorceress. Monk had dismissed the claim out of hand, but he sensed a woman's presence in this place, a fierce, disturbing presence.

There was power beyond the merely human in the world, and he had it in spades, hard-won and paid for in blood and pain. This Latina in Denver did not have that kind of power. No one did, except the men who had come out of Souk's and Patterson's laboratories. Men who had paid a price no woman could have borne.

And yet he barely made it to the sidewalk before the churning, cramping agony in his gut had him retching out the contents of his stomach.

The pain was brutal, like a beast clawing at him from the inside, something he thought he'd left behind in Bangkok. *The bitch,* to have done this to him. He would come back for her someday and make her pay.

Rising from his crouched position, he wiped the back of his hand across his mouth and started back toward the house. But the smell hit him again, cloying and rich, and so thick he could barely breathe.

He tried another route to get inside, skirting the property from a distance and coming around from the back. But the smoke, the insidious smoke curled around the whole damn place. He didn't know how. He'd dumped the brazier, but the smell and the smoke were everywhere, wisps of it winding through the gardens and hanging from the eaves of the house.

He tried approaching the back door off a small stone patio but was turned back once more by the nauseous cramping induced by the smoke. Standing at the edge of the garden, he used the tail of his shirt to wipe the sweat from his face, mindless of the viscera and blood splattered on it.

There was another way.

He turned his face into the wind, felt it rising from the west and bringing rain in its wake. Soon it would be upon them, and the smoke and smell would dissipate. He would have them then, Farrel for slaughter and the woman...perhaps the woman for something else, something he hadn't experienced since before Bangkok. She was Farrel's, reason enough to want to take her like a man, but even more, this woman, unlike the ones he'd killed, teased his lust to life.

He would capture her and use her, and when he was done, not even a beast like Farrel would want what was left.

Turning away from the house, he broke into a run, heading downwind to higher ground where he would watch the house and wait.

Con reached over Jane's shoulder and hit the bathroom light switch, plunging them into darkness.

Whoever the hell was out there, he wasn't going to give them any kind of advantage. Far from it, he was going to break them in half.

Holding tight to Jane's arm, he escorted her back out into the hallway, the most protected place in the house.

"Stay here," he said, and got all of half a step before she grabbed him.

"*No,*" she said, pulling him back into the corner. "You're staying here with me."

No, he wasn't.

"This won't take long." And it wouldn't. He'd caught a scent, the same rancid sweat and oddly metallic smell from the darkened alleys behind Mama Guadaloupe's, and whoever that sonuvabitch was, he'd made his last mistake. "I'm only going outside for a minute." If it even took that much time to bust this guy.

"The *hell* you are," she whispered harshly. "So help me God, you're not going *anywhere.*"

"Jane—" he began, only to get cut off by a clattering sound coming from the porch.

She swore and shifted her hold to his waist, grabbing onto his jeans.

Dammit. He needed to get out there.

"I need—"

"You're *not* leaving me here alone." Her hand curled around his waistband.

"I'm going to be right outside the front door." She

wouldn't be alone. He reached down and took hold of her hand, intending to pry her loose, but she just held on tighter.

"*No,*" she insisted, whispering fast. "It never works that way. The guy always leaves, and then something terrible happens to the woman. You're not leaving me in this house, where . . . where *anything* could get in here and . . . and . . . you're *not* leaving." She moved in closer, making it all that much harder to get away.

But honest to God, he could have put up more of a fight.

She was scared, really scared, which was all the more reason for him to get out there and take care of business. He heard the guy move off the steps, and then there was silence for a moment, before he picked up the sound of someone walking around the outside edge of the garden.

The bastard was trying to flank them.

He could slip out the bedroom window and come up behind the guy, or be waiting for him when he came in the back door, but either option entailed somehow extricating himself from her grip.

"Where's your purse?" he asked. "I'll get your gun for you."

"It's in the kitchen. I'll go with you."

"No." He didn't want her exposed through the windows.

"Yes, I'll—"

"*Shhhh . . .*" he said, touching his finger to her lips. Something had changed outside.

He turned his head toward the back door and listened, waiting, but there was nothing, not a sound, and the rancid, chemical smell of sweat and metal was quickly fading.

If he didn't move fast, he was going to lose the bastard. He turned to tell her as much and then realized with a dawning sense of inevitability that it didn't matter. If he chased the guy down the street, then he really would be abandoning her—and he'd already done enough damage in that quarter for one night.

"Hell," he muttered, dragging his hand back through his hair.

"What?" she asked, still with that death grip on his jeans. It was crazy, the way she was holding on to him. "What?"

Damn, he thought. This was never going to work.

"He's gone," he said. "Whoever was out on the porch is gone."

"That's good?"

He shook his head. "Not really. I wanted to talk to him." To put it nicely. Not so nicely, things probably would have gone down a completely different way.

"So you think it was the ghost guy?" Her face paled a little more at the thought.

"No," he lied. "Could have just been a neighbor, wondering why the cops were here."

She nodded, like she was working that idea around and maybe not quite buying his story.

"I...I don't think he's much of a talker, the ghost guy," she said.

"Probably not," he agreed, refraining from a weary sigh. She was so damn beautiful. "How's your head? Still hurting?"

"A little."

"And your knee?" He'd never seen it coming, that he would end up in a house tucked into the middle of nowhere, hell and gone in the Denver suburbs with a woman who broke his heart just by standing there. It made him feel uncomfortably exposed, vulnerable.

Edgy.

"It smarts...a little." She shrugged her oh-so-elegant shoulders, a gesture of such profound, unfolding grace he felt an echoing ache in his chest.

He was so screwed.

"But I'm okay," she said.

Yeah, sure, him, too.

"Good." It took a lot to get the word out, and in the ensuing silence of his failure to voice another one, she cast her gaze downward—which pretty much fascinated the hell out of him. Like she needed any more help in that department.

They were probably both in over their heads.

"Look at me," he said, and, after a slight hesitation, she complied, tilting her chin up.

This was the time to tell her he needed to go after that guy, whoever he was. To tell her the ghostly tracker wouldn't get by him—and the bastard wouldn't, no matter what kind of laboratory had made him. To tell her she was safe in this house, and that he'd be back.

But, God, she was exquisite.

Abso-fucking-lutely irresistible.

He knew better, but "better" didn't seem to matter, not in the heated shadows of this hallway with her hands practically in his pants, still holding on to him so tightly.

Geezus, baby, do you know? He lifted his hand and slid the tips of his fingers across her cheek, feeling the softness of her skin, watching her eyes darken to an even more verdant shade of green. *Do you know what you're doing to me?*

He'd be crazy to get involved with her. With half a chance, he could still make a break for it.

But she didn't give him half a chance. Without another move, without so much as the blink of an eye or a twitch of a smile, between one breath and the next, she captured him completely.

There was no help for it and no escape.

None.

She was the Wild Thing, everything he remembered and something he hadn't known for a long time. The lush, alluring scent of her awareness filled his senses, all of it female. Every fiber of her being was alert to their closeness. She fairly vibrated with it, and it was turning him inside out with longing.

"I'm not the man you knew." No matter what happened here tonight, he couldn't afford to be anything less than honest with her.

"No," she said. "No, you're not." Her voice was soft, barely audible, but her gaze was direct, and the temperature of her skin subtly rose with a blush, a more telling confession than the words themselves.

"I don't know how much time I have, maybe only weeks, maybe months." More brutal honesty. He really didn't think he would live out the year, not the way things had been going for him lately.

Distress flattened her expression, but her gaze stayed locked onto him.

"Okay," she said slowly. "I understand."

He doubted it. Hell, he didn't understand it himself, how he could be so strong one minute and crash the next. Souk had been such a sick bastard. In the hands of a humanitarian, of a doctor who cared, Souk's research could have changed the world. He could have helped people and saved lives.

Instead, along had come another crazy sick bastard working somewhere out of Thailand, jacking warriors up for profit and unleashing a monster on the earth.

Lancaster had a lot to answer for.

"Six years in the wasteland," he said, gently rubbing his thumb across the soft fullness of her lower lip. "And then there you are, walking down Wazee Street, turning my world inside out, and things start coming back to me."

Maybe this was it, he thought, maybe he was dying and this thing with her was his whole-life-flashing-before-his-eyes setup, except his "flash" was going in slow motion, one memory at a time, starting with Corinna and Hawkins, and Kid, and Denver, memories of 738 Steele Street and this house on the west side, and especially of her, Jane Linden, Robin Rulz.

His recollections of her were so clear, but sex had a way of focusing a guy's mind like a laser beam—and his feelings for her were very sexual.

"So," he said, "this guy you had the date with tonight..."

"Wouldn't have gotten me into half the trouble you did."

Sweet thing, she said it with a straight face, as if there might actually be somebody out there who could have gotten her into even more trouble.

He doubted it.

"An accountant?" he guessed.

"Cop."

Geezus. He couldn't help himself, he grinned.

"Yeah," she said, a small grin lifting a corner of her mouth, as well. "I know."

"Steady boyfriend?" He needed to know, not that he thought her answer was going to make too damn much of a difference—not when she was still holding on to him like she was never going to let him go.

"No," she said, shaking her head. "Blind date."

Good, he thought, feeling the last of his safeguards slide out from under him like so much shifting sand. The poor cop was never going to know what he'd missed.

CHAPTER THIRTY-THREE

Crazy, crazy night.

J. T. Chronopolous back from the dead, and he was getting ready to kiss her all over again. Jane saw it in his eyes, felt it in her own response and the heated tension filling the hall—and for no known reason on the face of the earth, she found herself tightening her grip on his waistband.

Wrong. The smart money told her to back off, to be the good girl, to play things safe. She really didn't know him, which didn't begin to explain why she had hold of his pants. He wasn't who he used to be, not even close, this stranger with the scars and the missing finger, the one who didn't know his own name or his own brother.

And yet he knew her—and that knowledge held her where she stood, her heart racing and breaking at the same time.

Maybe only weeks, maybe months—he was telling the truth, and the truth hurt. She could see it all now, the worst of it running down the middle of his chest.

Lord, she didn't want him to die. With every beat of her heart she wanted him to have a chance. Whatever life had done to him, she wanted him to have better. Six years in the wasteland, he'd said, and she understood exactly what he'd meant.

She let her gaze slide down the length of him, past his

bandage. Scars or not, he was a work of art, every muscle delineated, the veins in his arms running like rivers into his palms, each a confluence of strength and testosterone, of conviction and the iron will to survive.

A war-fighter, that's what he'd been, and what he still was, a soldier to the core, and he wanted her. She felt it with every breath he took, the rising tide of his desire—and she knew there'd be no playing it safe tonight.

Wild night. Wild girl, Con thought. She'd kicked some major ass for him in the alley, taking on those two *pendejos* at Mama's, the poor bastards—and she'd called him a liar.

She had it right. He remembered more than he wanted to admit, especially to her, of nights so dark he'd thought they'd never end, of fear and the pain that had broken him again and again, of grief so deep he'd prayed for death. But he'd been too strong to die, literally, every part of him honed and enhanced for indestructibility—except for the expiration date Dr. Souk had carved into his genes.

Yeah, she'd seen right through him.

He liked smart women. He could have walked away, gotten her gun back in her hand, and gone to find that damned ghost tracker. Or he could stay here and play Beauty and the Beast in the hallway with her.

It was no contest in his mind, no contest in his heart, and she wasn't running away, either.

Done deal.

He slid his hand around the back of her neck, and she slowly tilted her chin up and captured him with her long, green-eyed gaze. Yeah, she wanted this.

Combing his fingers up through her hair, he closed his fist around a handful of silken strands and brought them to his face, and he breathed her in, the rich mélange of all she was: the girl of his forgotten dreams.

She intrigued him like no other, enchanted him, everything about her. She worked in an art gallery, of all things, looked like she'd stepped off a catwalk, was fiercely street smart right down to her bones, and she was soft and smelled so damn good.

God, he'd been without this for too long, always on the move, always on the hunt for the spymaster, and somewhere, deep down inside him, always on the hunt for her, the rarest thing on earth, a woman who knew him and cared.

He'd had sex and, a few times, maybe even traces of love, since he'd broken free from Souk's lab—but he hadn't been known, and he'd felt the lack with every lover.

Hell, he hadn't known himself. There'd been no way for a woman to know him—but this one did. Even more amazing, he knew her. His longing for her had a past, and his need to be with her had taken on a life of its own.

Lowering his mouth to hers, he kissed her, gently sliding his tongue inside when she opened for him. A small groan escaped her, and he deepened the kiss, feeling her body soften against him in a thousand lush and lovely ways.

This was what he'd needed.

Her.

He'd needed to sink himself into the sweet mystery of a woman's sensuality—this woman's, the urban jungle girl with the backbone of steel and the .380 to back it up.

Cupping her face in his other hand, he pressed her back against the wall and kissed her like there was no tomorrow—because who knew if there would be?

Who in the hell ever knew?

Not him, that was for damn sure.

Opening his mouth wider, he kissed her deeper, longer, exploring her mouth and letting the taste of her slip into his veins like a drug. She sighed in his mouth, all the while with that compelling, fascinating grip on the waistband of his jeans, the backs of her fingers brushing against his skin. *Geezus.*

The wind picked up outside, bringing with it a faint smattering of rain and a drumroll of far-off thunder—and he kissed her, endlessly, the taste of her infusing his senses, on and on and on. Through it all, through every moment of mouths and tongues, of need and heat, she moved with him, her body all curves and desire, the sheer eroticism of her running like wildfire from his heart to his groin.

Geezus, she smelled like an angel, so female, so profoundly rich, a thousand scents layering and melding together to form a picture of her in his mind. She was golden light with a rose-colored center pulsing brightly at her core.

"*J.T.*" she murmured, and for the first time, the name felt right, the way she felt right.

"*Hey, baby,*" he whispered against her lips. *I'm here for you.* And he was, whatever she wanted, whatever she needed, he was the man who could bring it.

"You . . . me, this is . . ." Her voice trailed off as she tunneled her hands up into his hair and held him for the sweet kisses she was pressing to the side of his face, along the length of his jaw, to his lips.

"Real," he murmured. So real.

Four years ago, on a night when he'd been high in the mountains of Honduras, on a wild and lonely stretch of the Cordillera Isabella, he'd fallen asleep and woken to a sky full of stars, millions upon millions of them strewn across the darkness. In all of them, there had been one brighter than all the rest, one that had held his attention and drawn him in, until he'd felt the scent and essence of it reaching across the eons of endless time, felt it tease him with an incomprehensible nearness from light-years away—and he'd wondered, *oh, God*, he'd wondered what Souk had really wrought within him, what the possibilities were, how far he could go, if he dared.

She was the same, the star here on earth, incomprehensibly alluring, beyond the erotic lushness of her body, beyond the compelling enticement of her kiss—farther, deeper, to the taste of her sinking into his cells and freeing him from the bondage of loneliness, of always and forever being alone.

This was his need, not hers. Out of the millions of people who'd passed him on thousands of street corners in hundreds of cities across the world, only one had ever stopped him in his tracks, only one had triggered the most primal parts of his brain with remembrance.

Her.

"I missed you," she murmured. "Even if you weren't ever my boyfriend, I missed you."

So sweet, so welcome. He'd missed everybody in the world, including himself. It had been a strange, mind-bending dilemma, wondering why he was so goddamned alone. Knowing there had to be someone somewhere who knew him. Hoping there was someone who missed him.

And all along, there had been her.

She shifted her hips, and with his hand sliding up her leg and under her dress, pulling her in close, they found their rhythm—up against the wall and going down fast.

Yeah, he needed this. Precious woman, he wanted to get lost in her, and there wasn't a doubt in his mind that she could do it for him.

He cupped her bottom, and her fingers went to the top button on his jeans.

"John Thomas," she whispered. *"John Thomas Chronopolous."*

Yeah, that was him, the guy she was undressing one button at a time.

Helping her out and helping himself, he took off her belt, then found the zipper tab on her dress and eased it down her back. When he reached the end, she gave another graceful shrug of her shoulders, and the golden sheath slipped off her and pooled in a pile at her feet.

Geezus. He followed the slide of material down her body with his gaze, and every part of him that was hard got harder—the curvaceous mounds of her breasts filling out the lacy cups of a black bra, a waist he could span with his hands, black lace panties slung around a pair of silky hips, and she was standing there in front of him in a pair of spike-heeled ankle boots.

All was right with the world—and it only got better when she shoved his jeans and boxers over his hips.

"*Oh*," she said, staring down at him. "Oh, my."

Oh, my, my, my was right, he thought. Just having her look at him sent a surge of pleasure through him, made him ache with wanting her, with wanting to see her beautifully, wonderfully naked. The panties were nice, real heartbreakers, but they had to go, along with the bra.

He quickly untied his boots and toed out of them, then pushed his jeans the rest of the way off his body and kicked them aside.

"Don't worry, Jane. I won't hurt you," he promised, leaning down, kissing her cheek, and pushing her undies down her legs. He'd had a plan for what happened next, a real simple plan that began and ended with removing her bra—but he got sidetracked with the panty business.

He wanted to be careful with her. He wanted to take things slow, to really savor the taste and feel of her—next time.

This time slid past "careful" the moment he slid his hand between her legs, into the soft, secret warmth of her, into intimacy. It was surrender to the heat of the moment, the strung-out sweetness. It was hot and getting hotter with every soft kiss she pressed to his mouth, with every slide of her hands over his body, with every time he teased her with his fingers. She read him like a page of Braille, her fingers tracing every curve of muscle, every line of scar tissue. He was a beast, no doubt about it, but there was only tenderness and need in her touch—and only reverence in his. She was silky hot and wet, and softly whispering in his mouth of her needs and desire.

Oh, yeah, sweetheart. It had been a real big night, lots of speed and screamin' tires, lots of danger and some bad, rough stuff—and what they needed, what he was going to give her was release from all that tension, a chance to escape the harshness of the night, if only for a while.

He reached for her leg and drew it up around his waist, making room for himself in the cradle of her hips, and he rocked against her.

"*Mmmm...*" She moved with him, pressing herself against him, and he pushed up inside her—so slowly, so mind-bendingly slowly.

When he was only partway in, she caught her breath on a small gasp, and he kissed her mouth.

"I won't hurt you, baby," he whispered against her lips. And he wouldn't. He was going to give her pleasure, as much as she could take.

With his hands holding on to her hips, pressing her back against the wall, he dropped to his knees and kissed her belly.

"J.T.?"

He answered her question with the soft slide of his tongue up through the center of her desire—and so it went, with her melting into his mouth and him loving every minute of it while the rain came down and the thunder rolled.

When she came, it was so intensely erotic, an electrifying turn-on for him, the way her body went rigid in his arms with her hands tangled in his hair, holding him close. He let her ride the sweetness for as long as it lasted, his tongue teasing her, until she went limp against the wall. With the taste of her still warm and wondrous in his mouth, he rose to his feet and fitted himself to her. He was so ready, and this time when he slid in, so was she, soft and still pulsing with the contractions of her pleasure.

She sighed, and the deeper he went, the softer she groaned.

"*Mmmm...J.T.*" She spread her legs a little wider, taking him in, taking all of him, her hands linked behind his neck, her hips moving with him on every thrust.

The girl was a rock star, the rhythm of her lovemaking running through her, matching his own, her hands still in his hair. The temperature in the hall rose by degrees, and he felt every one of them on his skin and in the sheen of sweat limning them both.

"I cried for you," she whispered against his mouth, then dragged her tongue across his lower lip and bit him so very softly—and he didn't know what tore him up more, the gentle bite or her confession. Both went straight through him on a wave of desperate need to fuck her so sweetly, to dry her long-gone tears, and somehow to love her until she was his.

Wild Thing. He'd known the first time he'd seen her, known there was something between them, some connection making her impossible to ignore. He'd seen her so many times, and every time, she'd made an indelible impression on his heart.

Now they were here, wrapped around each other, drenched in desire and need, and all he wanted to do was thrust into her harder and faster, more and more and more, to find his pleasure in her body, to let the sweet, slick heat of her consume him and take everything he had.

One deep slide after another, he pumped himself into her, again and again, reaching and striving for the moment of inevitable release. When it came, it came on him slow and hard, pulsing through him and damn near dragging him to his knees.

Geezus.

He pushed deeper, burying himself to the hilt inside her, and she tightened around him. He groaned with the pleasure and pushed into her again, loving the hot, wet feel of her around his cock. This was life. Her breath was warm on his neck, coming in short gasps. Her breasts were pressed against his chest, and one of her legs was half wrapped around him with the heel of her black suede ankle boot pressing into his ass. He could feel her heart racing, feel the heat of her satisfaction. Whatever else he was, he was safely, surely, wildly, intensely alive deep inside her.

She turned her head and opened her mouth on his shoulder, her teeth closing on him not so gently this time, and he felt half a smile curve the corner of his mouth.

Sweet woman. For this moment in time, she was all his.

He carried her into the closest bedroom and followed her down onto the bed, onto the luxury of a soft cotton patchwork quilt, still inside her. With their arms around each other and her leg coming around him again, her head still nestled into the crook of his shoulder, they were cocooned, one entity—and so they breathed, warm and safe, so very safe.

Off in the distance, he could see the lightning flash, the rain moving west, toward the heart of the city.

He held her close and felt her relax in his arms, her body softening against his, her hand coming up between them. Slowly she ran her fingers down the long, torturous path of the scar tracking the length of his chest.

A sigh escaped her, and he tightened his hold on her. He should have died from such a wound. Sometimes he wondered if he had and then been the recipient of a miracle—like tonight. She felt like a miracle to him.

He could protect her. He could protect her without fail, no matter what she'd seen, no matter what or who came after her. He was the rock against which all others were broken. Until his last breath, he was the Guardian down to the marrow of his bones, and, somehow, she was tied up in all of it.

CHAPTER THIRTY-FOUR

"Scott Church, went by the call sign Monk, yeah, I got it," Hawkins said into his radio. "A Navy SEAL?" Un-fucking-believable. "It took more than a Navy SEAL to do what we saw at Mama's back door."

"Skeeter's searching the LeedTech files at light speed," Dylan's voice came back at him. "Three years ago, Lancaster started selling our boys to a doc named Greg Patterson. He took up where Souk left off and tweaked the whole system... hold on..."

The line went silent. After a moment, Dylan came back on the radio.

"This mission just hit the fan again."

Hawkins swore under his breath.

"Skeeter ran a search," Dylan continued, "and came across a news story out of Bangkok dated two weeks ago. Greg Patterson is dead. So she and Cherie hacked their way into the police report, and it looks like he was... *fuck*..."

Hawkins waited through a moment of silence, then jumped in. "Fuck what?"

"Eaten."

"Eaten?" *Geezus*. He flashed back on the bite taken out of King's arm. This was starting to piss him off.

"Yeah," Dylan said, "a real gruesome crime scene.

The report also had a list of the files on Dr. Patterson's desk at the time of his demise."

"LeedTech?" It had to be.

"Specifically, the file on J. T. Chronopolous, a.k.a. Conroy Farrel. The Thai cops matched the bloody fingerprints on it to Scott Church, but they can't find the Frogman."

"Because they're not looking in Denver." He swore again. "Maybe we should give them a call."

"No," Dylan said. "The bastard is ours. If you so much as get a glimpse of this asshole, you take him out. No introductions, no warning, no questions. There's a damn good chance he's after our boy. Any questions we've got, we'll ask Randolph Lancaster. No one on my team gets torn apart like King and Rock, or goddamn eaten. Nobody. Got it?" Dylan's voice was hard, uncompromising.

"Loretta ain't gonna like it," Hawkins felt obliged to point out, no matter how much he agreed with Dylan. "She's going to want to cuff him, read him his rights, print him, and lock him up, all legal-like and prosecutable."

"Nobody's going to get this guy in front of a judge," Dylan said. "Think Red Dog with another hundred pounds of muscle and less than half the usable brain space, flood it with testosterone and a freaking boatload of psychopharmacueticals. Scott Church is the first soldier Patterson didn't kill. All the other men Lancaster sold to him died under the knife. From what we've seen, this Monk guy is barely human, and I mean that genetically. I want him dead."

"Copy." Hawkins glanced over at Creed, who wasn't any happier in this damn urban jungle behind Bagger's Market than he was right now. Dropping a .45 into the guy wasn't the problem. He and Creed would both happily take the shot and let the boss go mano a mano with

Lieutenant Loretta over the fallout, but finding the inhuman bastard was proving to be one helluva problem.

"I want you and Creed to quit dicking around out there and get the damn job done," Dylan said. "Make it so, Superman."

Dicking around?

"Yes, sir."

The radio went silent, and Creed gave him a questioning look. "What's up?"

"We're supposed to quit dicking around."

Creed nodded. "Good idea."

Yeah, a damn good idea.

"Navy SEAL, huh?" Creed said.

"Scott Church," Hawkins told him. "The guy was called Monk, so the doctor who fixed him up in Bangkok gave him the ID of MNK-1. But all that anybody has seen of the doctor lately is a bunch of gnawed-on bones in his lab."

Even the Jungle Boy blanched at that. "Kill on sight, I hope?"

"You got it," Hawkins said, looking around at the dumpsters and the trash and the loading docks and the dozen or so police cruisers and all the cops. "This trail is cold."

"Maybe we should call in Red Dog," Creed said. "She could track the bastard."

Hawkins looked over at him. "Or we could track the guy he's tracking."

"J.T.?" Creed asked.

He nodded. "Looks like Con Farrel is the reason Monk is in town. King and Rock just got in the way."

"So it's back to the restaurant . . . or not . . ." Creed's voice trailed off, and he turned and looked to the west.

Yeah, they were both on the same wavelength here.

"I know where I'd go if I was in trouble on this side of town," Creed continued.

Hawkins knew where he'd go, too.

"Alazne's." The witch had some definite *mojo* she'd worked for the chop shop boys over the years. He didn't claim to understand it, but he'd sure as hell benefited from it. They all had. "Do you think J.T. remembers Alazne?"

Creed looked at him like he had to be kidding.

"It was a long time ago," he said in his own defense.

"It was sex," Creed said. "Wild, witchy-woman sex. No guy forgets that."

Hawkins wasn't so sure. "He doesn't remember anything, total amnesia."

"Bull," Creed said. "We've been chasing him all over Denver, and he hasn't made a wrong turn yet. He knows this town inside out and backward, the same way he always did. He was here at Mama's and got into one helluva fight. He's in trouble. He's still got Jane. He's lost his transportation, and Alazne's is just up the hill. This is a no-brainer, Christian. We've at least got to check it out."

Yeah, maybe Creed was right. It was a long shot, but long shot or not, they were running out of time.

CHAPTER THIRTY-FIVE

Jane slowly wound herself up from a drowsy sleep, waking to a familiar sound: the deep-throated growl and chassis-shaking roar of Steele Street iron pulling to a stop in front of the house. Her money said Roxanne and Angelina had arrived, and wherever the two Detroit girls were, Christian Hawkins and Creed Rivera were bound to be with them.

I'm saved. The thought went through her on a wave of relief.

Or maybe she'd already been saved.

She looked over at the man sleeping by her side. He was so beautiful, the lines of his features so perfectly formed. Not even the scars running from his temple down to his jaw could take away from the cleanly chiseled artistry of his face. His nose was straight, his mouth firm, his dark hair cut short and tousled. His cheekbones were high, adding a hint of elegance to his bad-boy edge and reminding her of Kid. There was a reason she'd fallen so hard for him at first sight all those years ago, and nothing in him had changed enough to change her feelings. He was still the Guardian.

She let out a soft breath. *Damn.* She was usually more careful, always more careful than she'd been with him, but oh, God, what he'd done to her—made love to her, cherished her, and held her like he was never going to let her go.

She was such a fool.

She was so tempted to wake him and keep running, to the ends of the earth if that's what it took to keep him by her side—but that was no good. He belonged to Steele Street, and whatever she could do to get him back there was the best for him. With the chop shop boys close outside, she only needed to hold on to him for a few more minutes. Wherever he'd been, whatever he'd done, whatever had been done to him, they were his best chance.

Which left her to wonder if he was her best chance.

Salvation and acceptance, that's what she'd been looking for all these years, a few times in some pretty unlikely places, like with the art crowd in Los Angeles during the years she'd worked in Katya Hawkins's gallery there. She'd met her share of movie stars, politicians, newsroom anchors, and artists, and been charmed by more of them than she could recall.

But it was men like the Steele Street crew who had always grabbed her the hardest, captured her attention the surest, and held it year after year. The first night she'd seen J.T. on the street, she'd recognized him for what he was: a kindred spirit, a warrior, a fighter like her.

And that hadn't changed. It would never change.

She heard the muted *thunk* of car doors being shut and turned deeper into his arms, smoothing her fingers across his cheek and up into his hair. She could think of only one thing that could last as long as her fascination with him had: love, and it demoralized the hell out of her.

A smile curved his mouth in his sleep, and she melted even more inside. This was so impossible. J. T. Chronopolous barely existed. There was only this man, Con, and yet he was everything she remembered.

"Jane," he murmured, his eyes slowly opening, his voice soothingly low and deep. His arm came tighter around her, pulling her in even closer, until her breasts were up against his chest and his hand could slide down over her hip. "Do they still call you Robin Rulz?"

She let out a short laugh. "Not to my face."

"So no more princess of the underground?"

"No." She shook her head. "I'm completely legit now, have been for years." *Where were Christian and Creed?* she wondered. She should have heard them coming up the walk by now.

He nodded thoughtfully and reached up to smooth a few stray strands of her hair behind her ear. "You're thinking awfully hard about something."

She gave a little shrug. "It's been a big night."

"Yeah, it has." His smile broadened. "So you run an art gallery and sell paintings for a living." His gaze was steady on her, with the smile lingering about his lips.

"Yes," she said, then decided to take another chance. "All kinds of paintings. We even had one of you for a while."

At that, his smile faded. "Of me?"

She nodded. "The artist, Nikki McKinney, used a drawing of you made by a friend you had back then, Skeeter Bang."

He seemed to think that over for a moment or two, before speaking. "Skeeter?"

"Mmm-hmm."

"No." He gave his head a slight shake. "I don't remember anybody named Skeeter. I remember *you.*" He bent his head and kissed her, running his tongue across her lips and, when she opened for him, plundering her mouth.

And she melted again. No woman in her right mind would try to resist him. He tasted like heaven, was built like a god, and had the heart of a warrior. Memories, whatever he had or didn't have, would have to wait—but her chance to turn him over to Steele Street wouldn't wait. A few more seconds, she promised herself, just a few more of sinking into his magic, then she'd break off the kiss, grab her dress, and race for the door.

Oh, right, she thought, doubting herself when second after second passed and she did nothing to implement her plan. He felt too good, and then he felt even better. He pressed against her, and desire rose between them like a flood tide.

Oh, hell. She was going down in flames, without putting up even the smallest fight.

But the fight wasn't hers to lose.

Between one breath and the next, he stiffened in her arms.

"Get dressed," he said suddenly, and was moving away from her, out of the bed.

He stepped into the hall and brought back her clothes.

"What's your address?" he asked, tossing the clothes and her boots on the bed and reaching for his jeans.

"My . . . ?" Things were moving too fast. He quickly buttoned his jeans and grabbed his T-shirt, slipping it over his head while he headed back toward the hall.

Cripes. She'd never seen anyone move so fluidly, with so much speed and surety.

"Address," he repeated, stopping at the bedroom door to listen.

She heard it then, too, men talking outside. It was definitely Creed. She would recognize the Jungle Boy's voice anywhere.

Con looked back at her and held her gaze. "I want to see you later, if that's all right with you."

"Yes," she said, clutching her dress to her chest. "Yes." Absolutely. "Twenty-one eleven Blake Street, number five-oh-eight. I have the loft condo on the top floor."

"I'll find it," he said, the words rock-solid, like a promise, like the man.

"Where are you going? Why... what, I..." She didn't know what to think. He had knelt down and was putting on his boots.

Trying to catch up, she started scrambling into her dress, dragging it over her head, reaching for her panties, getting off the bed.

"I have a job to do," he said, quickly tying his laces. "A guy named Randolph Lancaster. You can tell that to your friends, if they don't already know he's been jerking their chains. When I'm done meeting with Lancaster, I'll come to you."

"But I—"

He came back around the bed and cupped her face in his palms—and he kissed her, his mouth hard, the kiss hot and wet and deep. Even when he pulled back, he continued to cup her face in his hands.

"Those are your friends out there, the guys from Steele Street. I need you to go with them. You'll be safe, and—"

"No," she said, grabbing on to his arms. "No, you're not going anywhere without me."

"Jane—"

"*No.*" Her pulse was suddenly racing with the realization that he was leaving her. "Whatever you need to do... meet with this... this guy Lancaster, I can help you. I can—"

"You can help me by going with your friends," he interrupted her. "I'm leaving. *Do not* stay in this house alone once I'm gone. You know what's out there, and it knows you're here. You won't be safe."

Oh, God.

"Jane." He kissed her again, his breath soft against her lips, his hands gentle on her face. "You're important to me, very important. I'll come to you tonight."

And then he was gone. With more speed than she could comprehend, he was out of the bedroom, out of the kitchen, and out of the house—damn near silently—and she was left holding her shoes in one hand, her underwear in the other, and wondering what in the hell to do next.

"Oh, *whoa,*" Creed said. "Oh, fuck."

"Okay, let's not *dwell* on this."

"I'm not fucking *dwelling,* but *geezus.*"

Geezus was right. Hawkins switched off his flashlight. They'd seen enough.

"I think we should bag it," Creed said, still looking down at what could only be somebody's upchucked dinner, which just happened to be a chunk of King Banner's arm and a piece of blue shirt.

It was the shirt that had given it all away.

And yes, they should bag it up as evidence. They might have walked right by it on their way up the sidewalk, but the stench had been overwhelming, demanding further investigation. The only good thing in the night air was the smoky remnants of Alazne's smudge pot.

"We'll call Loretta," he said. "Tell her to get somebody up here. We may be close to having this bastard cornered. Do you want the front or the back?"

"The back," Creed said, checking the load on his .45-caliber semiautomatic H&K man-eater.

It was damn dark in the back of the house, but Creed was good in the dark, always had been.

Hawkins was reaching for his own pistol when Dylan's voice came at him from over the radio. He drew the weapon and press-checked the chamber as he listened.

"Roger and out," he said when Dylan signed off.

"What?" Creed asked.

"Kid and Zach have Lancaster. They're taking him to Steele Street, and Dylan wants us back at the homestead."

"So let's do this."

They started up the walk to the front door when the man they'd been chasing half the night and halfway around the world stepped out from the side of the house.

They instantly had Conroy Farrel in their sights.

Geezus. J.T.

"Let me see your hands!" Hawkins shouted. *Geezus. J.T.*

Farrel obeyed, lifting his hands shoulder height, showing Hawkins his open, empty palms.

"She's inside. Jane. Take her with you," Farrel said. His voice was calm, his presence commanding every ounce of Hawkins's attention.

And then he was gone, moving so fast, it was almost as if he'd simply disappeared.

Creed started out after him but stopped in his tracks when the front door slammed open.

"Christian!" Jane called out. "Creed! Don't shoot! It's me. Jane!"

"Are you alone?" He kept moving quickly forward with his gun returned to a low-ready angle. Creed peeled off, heading down the side yard.

"J.T. just went out the back door!" she yelled, and out of the corner of his eye, he saw Creed break into a run, but that wasn't going to help. The Jungle Boy was fast but nothing like what they'd just seen.

Jane stepped onto the porch, looking like hell, her hair wild, her dress torn. There was blood on her knee and a bruise on her forehead.

"You can catch him," she said breathlessly, her face pale. "He's after someone, J.T. is, but there's this ... this *monster,* and he, and he *killed* these men at Mama's, and he *chased* me, and J.T.—and, Christian, you *have* to help him. I think he's sick, and—"

In two more steps he had his arm around her. She was trembling.

"Are you hurt?"

"N-no, not hurt, just scared. You have to help him."

"That's exactly what we're—" A shot rang out from the back of the house, a .45, and he put her aside with a barked order. "*Get down, stay put.*" Then he was on the run.

Get down, stay put. Get down, stay put.

Too late.

Monk had seen it all, heard it all, and the moment Farrel had taken off, he'd moved from his downwind hiding place to the witch's stinking roof. It had cost him, and now he was bleeding, but the night still belonged to him. Christian Hawkins turned on his heels and headed for the back door, following the shot, and Monk dropped silently from the roof to the porch and grabbed the girl.

It's me. Jane!

He was not gentle with Jane. But the asshole in the backyard had not been gentle with him, skinning him with a .45-caliber slug across his cheekbone.

Too fast. Too fast for them all. From one split second to the next, he was never where someone thought he would be. When he was on the run, no part of him was static.

Keep moving. Keep moving.

Wrenching Jane up from her crouched position, he cuffed her up the side of the head, hard. She went instantly limp.

Just what he needed.

Throwing her over his shoulder, he ran into the night, staying in backyards, leaping fences. A man shouted behind him, and he heard the sound of running feet. Lightning flashed on the eastern plains, followed by a long roll of thunder, and then came the roar of an engine firing up.

Fools.

They would never catch him. He was headed straight into the heart of their fortress, 738 Steele Street, but they would never catch him.

They had Lancaster, the bastards. He'd heard them talking. Conroy Farrel would figure it out soon enough and head to Steele Street, too, and as soon as he killed Farrel, he would lay his enemy's body at his master's feet.

And then he would kill his master, the heartless bastard who had made him and left him alone in the world to suffer his pain.

CHAPTER THIRTY-SIX

Maggie.

The name had frozen Scout solid. *Maggie.*

Hell, she'd actually seen the girl, so why was it so awful knowing her name?

Because Jack should have forgotten it.

Screw having him stick around. She needed him gone, the farther away the better.

Maggie.

Geez, that ticked her off—a blond bimbo in Key Largo? That was the kind of girl he liked?

For four years, she'd been running around with her heart on her sleeve for Jack Traeger. A girl really needed to be smarter than that.

And where was Con?

All sorts of warning bells were going off inside her, and if it had been up to her, they'd have been long gone. This town was no good for them. Something was wrong here, terribly wrong.

"We need to get the hell out of here, Jack. This place..." She couldn't even find the right word for the kind of dread she felt. "It's a... a bad place."

Right, Jack silently agreed, watching Scout pace their room at the Armstrong. This was a terrible place, one of the classiest old hotels he'd ever been in, but he was stuck here with the woman of his dreams, and she'd been getting busy with some other guy.

He should have seen that coming. He should have headed that off at the pass a long time ago.

Dammit. He was such a coward. He could face guys with Uzis all day long, but every time he'd thought about coming home and facing her, he'd tripped over himself and gone the other way.

They had the television on and turned to the local news, just like Con had ordered, but they hadn't seen anything about Rock Howe and King Banner.

"Where is Con?" she asked, still pacing.

That was the real problem here, not the hotel, and if Jack had known where Con was, trust him, he'd have been there by now, and they'd be making their getaway.

"Are you hungry?" he asked. He could use a meal, that was for damn sure.

"You're going to eat? Now?" She looked dumbfounded by the concept. She also looked stressed out, out of sorts, and like she could sizzle and fuss herself into going ballistic any second. "You could eat with all this going on?"

"Yes"—he tried to use his calmest tone of voice—"I've eaten hanging upside down off a bridge in a snowstorm. I've eaten in the dark, jammed sideways in a ventilation shaft for six hours. Hell, I've eaten street food in Bangladesh and rattlesnake in the Sonoran Desert. Trust me, I can eat room service in a four-star hotel."

"Very funny, Jack. You make me so . . . so damn . . ."

Words seemed to fail her, but Jack had a few, starting with furious, as in "you make me so damn furious." It seemed to be his specialty. And for him, he would have picked horny, as in "you make me so damn horny." Because she did, flat out.

Or maybe it was this damn room. It was made for

decadence. *Geezus.* The ceiling was twelve feet high, and all the walls were covered in baby blue wallpaper with a lot of ornate stuff everywhere. The bed was huge and piled high with brocade pillows, and the whole thing looked about as silky, sexy, and soft as she did.

Who had skin like hers, he wondered, besides her? Not most girls, he knew that much. Scout's skin was so smooth and creamy. He figured she must taste delicious—like he was ever going to find out.

"Steak," he said, heading past her for the phone. "I'm ordering one." And under any other circumstances, he would have added a bottle of Patrón. "If you want to stay mission-ready, Pansy, I suggest you order—"

"What did you call me?" she cut him off in midsentence, her voice sharp.

"Pansy," he said, daring all and damn the torpedoes. "Pansy Louise Leesom, baby, that's you."

"*Nobody* calls me Pansy."

"Well, I'm starting," he said, on the move again, heading toward the phone and his steak. It was time to set a few things straight between them, and Pansy was one of those things.

But the girl was quick. She grabbed hold of his arm as he passed and held him where he stood—and he let her.

She opened her mouth to say something smart-ass and probably mean, then changed her mind and came out with the truth. "Nobody's called me Pansy since my mom died. It was my dad who always called me Scout. He said he needed me to be strong."

And that just tore him up.

Jack could just imagine her as a little girl, with her hair all wildly curly. She'd have been the cutest little Pansy Louise ever.

"The people at Steele Street," she said. "They knew about my mom, and they knew a lot about my dad being a Marine, but they don't know what happened to him in the end. They didn't know that, Jack. Con does, I'm sure, but it's one of those things he won't talk about ever, so I think the worst, and I look at Con, at how he's scarred, and I wonder what happened to my dad."

Oh, man, he couldn't go there. She was tough, but she wasn't that tough.

Hell, he wasn't that tough, and he'd seen it.

"Do you want me to go back in there and see what I can find out?" He would, and she knew it, and maybe he would find something he could tell her, something bearable that would fill in the empty places for her. No matter how much they fought, she knew she could count on him, that he would go straight into the fires of hell for her. That was how they rolled, together, a team.

"No," she said, shaking her head and looking away, releasing him. "I don't want you going back into Steele Street, but God, I wish Con was here."

Yeah, he did, too.

"So what about this Dutch guy you met in London?" He didn't really want to know, but he could be polite. What he wanted was to pretend she would always just be with Con, taking care of the boss, while Jack ran around the world taking care of business. "Con said his name was Karl."

"Karl is—"

"Wait a minute," he cut her off, and was damned grateful for the excuse. "Look at this." He directed her attention to the television.

Geezus. Two guys had been torn apart over on the west side of Denver. The news stations weren't identifying them, but from what Con had told him, Jack figured it was King Banner and Rock Howe—but they were dead. Con had left them alive.

Fuck.

Now, who in the hell had dropped them? he wondered.

King and Rock had been two of the most skilled scumbags on the face of the earth.

And the hostage Con had talked about was a woman named Jane Linden. The station kept her picture up in the corner of the screen, asking people to call in if they saw her. The rest of the screen was full of cop cars and an ambulance, lights flashing, and lots of uniformed people running around.

"Cripes, Jack. There's a manhunt going on out there," Scout said. "These people think Con killed King and Rock and that he kidnapped that woman, and they're out for blood."

It didn't look good, and then the night really went to hell.

His phone rang.

He took it out of his pocket and keyed the receive button. "Go."

"Are you at the hotel?" Con asked.

"Yes." Jack still had his eyes on the television. "We're watching the news, and your party over on the west side is all over it. Everybody out there covering the story is pretty wound up. I hope you're watching your ass."

"I am. Stay put at the hotel. I'll be there in an hour, maybe two."

An hour? Two? What the hell was the boss going to be doing for an hour or two?

"Why so long? What's up?"

"Complications."

"The girl?" Jack was looking right at Ms. Jane Linden, and, yeah, she looked plenty complicated to him.

There was a brief pause before Con spoke again.

"We got what we came for. You keep Scout safe. That's the job, your only job. I'll contact you, if I need you." And he signed off.

Well, hell. Jack looked over at Scout, who was looking

at him like she wanted to know what was going on—and all he could think was that so the hell did he.

Standing inside the India Gate suite at the Kashmir Club, Con hung up the phone. There had been no forced entry here, not by him or anybody else, but there had been a struggle.

A streak of blood on the wall looked like somebody had been slammed into it with a fair amount of force. The painting above the smear was hanging crookedly. One lamp had been knocked over in the suite, and a chair had been pulled off center, as if someone had grabbed on to it or been knocked into it.

Con had a good idea of who that someone had been—Randolph Lancaster—and he didn't need Jack or Scout for what happened next. Where he was going, their presence was a complication, not a help. He knew who had taken Lancaster, and he knew where they'd taken him: 738 Steele Street.

CHAPTER THIRTY-SEVEN

Cool and smooth in the gusting rain, hard and hollow like his heart, Monk climbed hand over hand up the old freight elevator at 738 Steele Street, an old-style contraption of iron and steel, of I-beams and bolts, a beast from the machine age. He'd seen the cameras trained on the alley below and had crawled the wall to avoid them. The building was old brick with lots of handholds for the strong.

The girl was out cold.

Balancing on a strut, he wiped the rain from his face and looked up to see lightning crackling across the sky. He'd taken a sheet off a clothesline on Secaro Street and wrapped it around Jane, securing her in a cotton cocoon. Slung over his shoulder, sodden wet and limp as a rag, she wasn't giving him any trouble.

Somewhere inside the building there would be a safe place to stash her, a hidey-hole no one would ever find, a private place where he could come back to her when he finished with Farrel and Lancaster. She would be his prize then, his gift to himself, his warrior's tribute.

Thunder rolled in after the lightning, and he kept climbing. At the seventh floor, the old elevator ended, and light shone from every window. With one blow, he could break the glass and enter, but when he swung over and looked inside, his breath caught for a suspended moment, and he stayed his fist.

Three—he counted the people in the high-tech office. Two for killing, the men, both dark-haired and heavily armed, and one for stealing and keeping, the one on the communications console—Skeeter Bang-Hart.

She was more beautiful in real life than in her photographs, unexpected, like the woman over his shoulder, a fantasy vision of long-ago nights, of rough city streets and the men who ruled them, and of the women who ruled those men. She was one of those women, pale of skin with a scar on her face and a Glock tucked under her arm in a shoulder holster. Her hair was long and silvery, her body lithe and strong. He could see the supple movement of her muscles beneath the thin material of her dress, and he was riveted by the sight.

He wanted her, the same way he wanted the girl in the golden dress, viscerally, like a heated need in his blood, and in an instant, he made his decision. If nothing else this night, she, too, would be his tribute, his by right of victory and plunder.

Tonight, he ruled the world.

The truth welled up inside him and filled his heart with desire and his throat with a howl he dared not give voice to—not if he was to fulfill his mission.

She would be his, though. He promised himself.

Grasping the sill and leaning back, he looked up the side of the building. The floors directly above him were dark and had balconies. He would enter from up there, secure both of the women, and go hunting for Farrel and Lancaster.

He took one more look into the office, at the woman, then swung himself over to the next handhold and began climbing higher up the side of the building, moving toward the balcony a few yards above him.

* * *

Skeeter stood in front of the comm console in the main office at Steele Street, frozen in place, listening to Hawkins on the radio. Zach and Quinn were with her, hearing the same damn bad news, and she'd routed it to Dylan down in the basement. Kid was scheduled to return to the office any minute to relieve Quinn—but Skeeter doubted if anyone was going to get relieved tonight.

"It was Monk. We're sure of it." Hawkins's voice was calm and steady, but Skeeter's pulse was racing. "Creed saw him cut through the neighbor's yard. MNK-1 is fast, faster than Red Dog."

Lancaster's beast, the one who had twisted King Banner's arm off and taken a bite out of it—*geezus,* it made her blood run cold, and the bastard had snatched Jane and taken off with her just seconds after J.T. had disappeared from Alazne Morello's. SDF was losing on every front.

Jane. Skeeter had to fight a desperate urge to hit the streets and find her friend.

"Have you called Gillian?" Dylan asked, his voice terse. No one else could track like Gillian, not even Creed.

"Yes, and the Jungle Boy is with her at Alazne's," Hawkins said.

"How far out are you?" Dylan asked.

"Five minutes."

"Call me when you get here," Dylan said. "We need to be ready to deploy the instant we get word on Jane."

Hawkins no sooner signed off than the hairs along the back of Skeeter's neck suddenly rose straight up.

She whirled toward the window at her back and saw a pale flash of something slip off to the side. *Geezus.* A bolt of lightning crashed in the night sky, and for an instant, she wondered if that's what she'd seen, a precursor of the lightning strike.

Bull, she decided. She'd never been afraid of lightning in her life, and no matter how bad the night had become, she wasn't a girl who jumped at shadows.

Striding over to the window, she drew her Glock .45 out of her shoulder holster.

"Do we have a problem, Skeeter?" Zach asked, drawing his own semiautomatic pistol.

"I've got a bad feeling, that's all." And she knew that was enough for him. It was enough for everybody at Steele Street.

At the window, she threw open the sash and started to look out, but Zach stepped in front of her.

"Let me do this," he said, then carefully checked out the edges of the opening before venturing a bit farther out to see all around.

Skeeter held her tongue, knowing nothing was going to keep these boys from trying to rein her in.

Quinn had taken up a position on the east wall, where he could see out his side.

A loud roll of thunder bellowed and rumbled above the city, and when Zach ducked his head back inside, he was wiping rain off his face.

"I'm heading upstairs, going to check things out."

"Did you see anything?" she asked.

"No," he said. "But that doesn't mean you didn't. Is Kid on his way up here?"

"Should arrive any minute," she said, checking the time on her computer screen.

"Good. When he gets here, we'll—"

The sound of breaking glass and a scuffling thump came from the floor above them, and the three were off like shots, weapons drawn, heading for the stairs. They cleared the single flight in seconds and came out onto Steele Street's state-of-the-art shooting range, a large open area that took up half the eighth floor. The other half housed the armory workshops and weapons rooms.

Quickly, one by one, they cleared the range and the rooms, working their way back to the workshop directly above the office, only to find it empty save for the wet footprints leading out of it and the broken glass on the floor below the window.

Skeeter reached the glass and bent down to pick up a blood-smeared piece. When she brought it to her nose, every "Spidey" sense she had red-lined with the smell and weight of the intruder. *Sweet geezus.* Dread coursed through her veins. Then came the cry, a muffled sound of panic and fear coming from the floor above them.

Jane. She knew it down to her bones.

"Get back to the comm. Call Creed and get him here," Zach said, running for the stairs that led to the ninth floor. Quinn was already hitting the first step.

Skeeter dropped the bloody shard and ran back through the firing range, heading toward the stairs leading down to the office. She didn't question Zach's orders—and she didn't see MNK-1 drop out of the rafters and land silently in a crouch behind her, ready to spring.

CHAPTER THIRTY-EIGHT

"I'm scared, Jack."

Yeah, so was he.

"Are you going to order a steak?"

It wasn't at the top of his list anymore, not after talking to Con.

What he wanted to do was get over to the Kashmir Club. He had a feeling that's where Con had gone—but that meant leaving Scout alone at the Armstrong, and that was not going to happen, and he sure as hell was not going to take her anyplace he might run into trouble, like the Kashmir Club.

Con had tied his hands, and the boss damn well knew it.

"Yeah," he said. "I think it's a good idea to get some food. If you can, Scout, it would be good for you to eat something, too."

"Sure, I guess I—" She stopped abruptly when the phone in her pocket rang.

It could be only one person, Red Dog, and he quickly reached out and took her hand before she could pull the phone out.

"Not yet, Scout," he said. "It may get to that before the night is over, but not yet... please."

And there they stood, the two of them in the middle of the room, holding hands while the phone rang and rang.

She didn't try to answer it, and he didn't let go of her, and when it finally quit ringing, he was still holding her hand.

Unable to resist, he smoothed his thumb across her skin—and he reveled at the softness. She wasn't like other girls, not like any other girl he'd ever met.

"Pansy," he said, and let out a short laugh. "I couldn't believe it when Con told me. You, of all girls, named Pansy."

"Pansy Louise." She was holding his hand, too, and Jack was very aware of the fact.

"So what does this Karl guy call you?" He was giving himself away. He knew it, but he wanted to hear it from her.

"Ms. Leesom."

"Ms. Leesom?" He looked at her, not quite sure what she meant.

"Dr. Karl Reynder is the man teaching me to speak Dutch."

"He's your teacher, not your boyfriend?" Oh, man, was Con going to get it—if they all got out of here.

"Teacher, sixty-four years old if he's a day," she confirmed.

He'd be damned.

"So why did Con—" He cut himself off. So why did Con make it sound like she was in love with the guy—that's what he'd been about to ask.

But he knew the answer.

Con was tying up loose ends, getting ready for the endgame. Jack had been played.

And rightly so.

He was going to need Scout as much as she needed him by the time this was all over.

He smoothed his thumb across the back of her hand again. He was paler than she, his skin rougher, his hands a lot bigger. Hell, the veins in his arms were bigger than her fingers—okay, not quite, but he was a big guy, and Pansy Louise "Scout" Leesom was everything he'd ever dreamed of, everything he'd ever wanted but had just been too damned chicken to try to get. Rejection from her would have thrown him for a loop. The only thing worse would have been her falling for another guy—and Con had known it.

He'd never known the boss to meddle in anybody's personal life—except for raising Scout. He'd taken that job on because of her father, but he'd stayed on the job because of Scout. Con loved her, and the boss wasn't alone in those heartfelt feelings.

"I love you, Scout." The words slipped out so easily, words he'd never dreamed he would dare to say—words he'd never said to another woman. "I love everything about you, even the way you get mad at me."

He kept smoothing his thumb over her hand and marveling at the softness of her skin. She was so beautiful, so much more than he deserved, but she was meant to be his. He knew that for certain, but he also knew things didn't always work out the way they should.

Looking up, he met her gaze. "I love you, Scout. I've loved you since forever."

She was gorgeous, her hair still all tied up with the scarf, dark curls tumbling down every which way, her eyes so green and so focused on him with a look that said she didn't quite believe him. "You've done a darn good job of hiding the fact, Jack."

He was a jerk. He knew it. But the truth was out now, and he was going to run with it.

"You're the only thing on the face of the earth that scares me, Scout. I figured if I never told you how I felt, then I could keep cruising on, thinking there might be a chance. But if I stepped up and you turned away, then it was over, no coming back."

"So you're stepping up now?"

How she could doubt him was beyond him. He'd never been more serious in his life, at least not without a weapon shouldered and his finger squeezing off rounds. He was damned serious then.

"Yes, I am." But about ten more seconds of her looking at him like she wasn't sure what to think, and he was stepping out the door and doing a damage evaluation.

"You're starting to sweat, Jack."

Yes, he was.

"I love you, Scout, and I'm not backing off from that statement." Whether he had to make a run for the door or not.

"You're nothing but trouble, always have been," she said.

Oh, hell, if they were going to do a rundown of his faults, they needed to order in supplies.

"We're good together. You know we are, and there isn't a doubt in my mind that I am the best man for you, or I wouldn't be laying myself out here like this." And that was the God's truth.

"I don't know, Jack, it's been—"

He silenced her with a kiss, sliding his free hand around the back of her neck and lowering his mouth to hers, bending her into him—and at the first taste, he knew he should have done this years ago.

She melted against him, rising up on her toes, her arms coming around his neck, her body pressing up against his, every luscious curve. He slid his hand up under her shirt and held her close, kissing her wildly, and when she did the same, slipped her hands up under his shirt, instant need became his driving force, replacing every other thought in his body.

He wanted her. He loved her. And he needed her to be his, wholly and completely, on the bed with him inside her.

One of her hands went to the waistband of his pants,

and just the thought of her touching him made him hard.

"Scout," he whispered her name and undid his pants, asking her to please, please, please...

And she did, sliding her hand into his pants and stroking his cock—and the clothes started coming off.

"I need you, Jack," she said between hot kisses. Pants hit the floor, shirts went flying, shoes disappeared, underwear melted away, and he scooped her up in his arms, both of them naked, and her so beautiful, she took his breath away.

Laying her on the bed, he came down on top of her, and he kissed her and teased her, rubbing himself against her, until she was moving beneath him.

"God, Scout, you're so beautiful, so damned beautiful." He kissed her breasts and cupped them in his hands, and he slid down her body to tease her with his mouth.

This was Scout, his love, his lover, and everything about her excited him: the taste and softness of her, the way she responded to every lick of his tongue. It was going to take days, weeks, years to get enough of her, if he ever could.

Oh, my God. Oh, my God... Jack.

Scout was melting from the inside out. She'd imagined making love with Black Jack Traeger hundreds of times, if not thousands—but nothing in her imagination had prepared her for Jack in love and in her bed.

Jack loved her—it was all she needed. He loved her, and he was giving her pleasure unlike anything she'd ever known. Forever, he'd said, and oh, God, she believed him. She'd wanted him forever—and the more he aroused her, the more she never wanted him to stop, not ever, not when he felt so amazingly good, not until he took her straight over the edge.

"Jack..." His name sighed out of her on a groan of

pleasure more intense than anything she'd ever known. *"Oh, Jack . . . Jack."*

When she'd gone limp beneath him, he came up her body and fitted himself to her—and she was so ready for him to thrust inside, to fill her up. He was hot, and hard, and heavy, and he held her so strongly, giving her even more pleasure. He was a big man, every inch of him solid muscle, and when his release came, she felt every last pulsing thrust, her body alive and in tune with his.

He didn't withdraw for a long time, just held her there, keeping her close in his arms, breathing softly against the side of her face.

"That was crazy," he finally said.

"Yeah." It sure had been, sweetly intense, wildly out of control.

"Crazy wonderful."

"Yeah." She'd go there with him. It had been wonderful.

"We should do it again."

A smile curved her mouth. Now, that was the Jack she knew.

"Yeah," she said, sliding her hand up to cup his face. "We should do it again."

He looked down at her and grinned—and they did it again.

CHAPTER THIRTY-NINE

Dylan Hart had a well-earned and well-deserved reputation for coolness under pressure. He owned the words "cold bastard." He was the iceman, his emotions always tempered by reason. *Always.*

Except for tonight.

With the terrifying abduction of Jane, and faced with the crimes committed by the man Kid and Zach had hauled down into Steele Street's basement, he was struggling inside, in a fierce conflict with himself. Under other circumstances, he would have gone to Skeeter to talk things through. The kick-ass blond bombshell was his mate, his sounding board, the balm to his soul, but the bad girl had nothing to offer him here. She wanted Lancaster dead, and she was counting on him to give the order that would make it so.

The problem, the temptation burning through him, was to do it himself, long and slow and brutal and final—starting now. Right now. He had four syringes left, and any combination thereof would do the deed, give Lancaster a taste of the crazy, fucking hell he'd sold over a hundred American soldiers into for money and his own twisted reasons.

The bastard needed to suffer and wail, to be undone, to lose his mind and be brought back only to lose it again.

Pain beyond bearing—that's what Lancaster needed. He needed it like Dylan needed his next breath.

Standing in the shadows, he silently waited and watched as Kid tied Lancaster to the rope and pulley rig hanging from a boom secured to the ceiling. A hundred years ago, the rig had been used to move crates of goods into storage for Errol Steele's Mercantile, the building's first incarnation.

Tonight it had a far grimmer purpose.

General Richard "Buck" Grant, Special Defense Force's commanding officer, was on his way to Denver to deal with Randolph Lancaster, but until Buck arrived, the man known as White Rook was under Dylan's tender care.

He saw the old man wince as Kid tightened the ropes tying him to the pulleys.

"I want him chained," he said, and Lancaster jerked his head around to peer into the darkness, looking for him.

Kid didn't miss a beat. He quickly secured the ropes, then walked over to the corner and picked up a heavy length of chain.

"Hart?" Lancaster gasped, his voice feeble, his face gray beneath the shock of white hair he wore so proudly. "Is that you?"

Kid had not been gentle with the man who had taken his brother from him. One of Lancaster's eyes was swollen shut. A trickle of blood seeped out of the corner of his mouth and dripped on his pale blue dress shirt. His tie was askew, his black suit coat scuffed and tossed aside. The old man's left hand was limp, likely broken at the wrist. Regardless, Kid had gone ahead and cuffed him before tying him to the pulley rig.

Things happened.

Especially to evil men unlucky enough to end up here, Dylan thought.

Tyler Crutchfield was still taped to his chair, perched on the edge of the pool deck, hardly daring to breathe. Dylan understood. The lawyer did not want to draw Kid's attention, not when every hard line in the Boy Wonder's face said his restraint was hanging by the same thin thread holding Dylan back.

"White Rook," he said, walking into the light. "It's been a while."

"Hart." Lancaster slumped against his restraints. He was hanging at an odd angle that kept him from being able to stand upright or kneel. "Re-release me. There's been a mistake."

"A terrible mistake," Dylan agreed. "One of hundreds, starting with the sale of J. T. Chronopolous to Atlas Exports and ending tonight with the abduction of Jane Linden.

"I-I don't know any Jane Linden."

Not only possible but probable.

"How about Scott Church?"

The old man went perfectly still, except for the fresh sheen of sweat suddenly beading on his forehead and his upper lip. "No, n-no. I don't know him."

"Liar." Dylan referred to the sheaf of papers he held in his hand and read off a long series of letters and numbers. "Your international bank account number. I've got your balance here, Rook: forty-nine million plus change, including the last deposit you took in for the sale of Scott Church. You've done well for a government employee."

The old man was shaking his head vigorously. "No," he said. "No, no, it's not what you think."

"What do I think, Rook? You tell me."

When Lancaster didn't reply other than to keep shaking his head, Dylan continued. "I'm thinking I didn't know you were on the board of World Resources."

"N-no," Lancaster said. "You-you don't understand

what you're dealing with here. Release me. I... I can't—" A gasp of pain escaped him.

Good.

"Actually, Rook, I think it's you who doesn't understand what you're dealing with here—or who."

"SDF," Lancaster ground out with effort. Spittle came with the words, and more blood, and Dylan decided that maybe Kid had hit him harder than he'd thought. "Special Defense Force. I m-made you, created you out of *nothing*."

"The same way you created LeedTech out of nothing?"

"No. No. That's a CIA operation, LeedTech, not mine."

Dylan referred to his papers again. "And yet, over the years, you've deposited funds in excess of ten million dollars straight out of LeedTech into your personal Swiss bank account. Tax free, too, and all those unreported assets you've got stashed in half a dozen shell corporations in the Caribbean, that's going to bite you in the ass, Rook. You should have known better than that."

"Y-you're wrong, Dylan." The old man wheezed and let out a cough, before he could continue. "The money is for black ops, a slush fund, duly authorized by the agency's director. You're digging your own grave here, not mine. You need to... to release me *now*."

Not very damn likely.

"No, Rook. That's not the way it's going to work tonight," he said, watching Kid leave through the main door to go up and relieve Quinn. "Buck Grant is on his way, and if he doesn't bury you, I will. But first I want Jane Linden and J. T. Chronoplous back. If you can help me, good. If you can't, I've got no use for you."

"Use for me?" The old man let out a short, strained laugh. "You're insane, Hart. It's why the team has to be destroyed. *Crutchfield!*" He turned his head to face the lawyer and shouted again. "*Crutchfield*, tell him. He can't prove anything. Nothing, not . . . not *anything*."

Dylan glanced at the lawyer, but Tyler Crutchfield wasn't having any of it. If any man could have ever disappeared while taped to a chair, Crutchfield was going to be that guy. Lancaster was on his own.

"Actually, I can prove everything. The trail leading to you and Atlas Exports is starting to look like the Beltway at rush hour," he said. "I only beat the Department of Justice to the LeedTech files by an hour, and I left them a copy, so you might want to be thinking about that." He paused for a moment, but just a moment, before giving in to his darker side and pulling the small stainless steel case of syringes out of his pocket.

White Rook had been his friend, his savior, he'd thought, but now . . . now things had proven different.

Walking slowly forward, he opened the box. Four syringes left.

He stopped a couple of feet in front of where Lancaster hung from his ropes and chains, the open box in his hand.

"And you might want to start thinking about these," he continued. "You know what they can do to you, old man. If you help me, they'll stay in the box. You can start by telling me everything you know about Scott Church, MNK-1."

Lancaster's face was deathly pale. "MNK-1?" The question was a bare, harsh whisper of a lie. The bastard knew exactly who he was talking about.

"Your boy Monk is here, in Denver. He kidnapped my friend, and I want her back. I want her back badly enough to break you in ways from which you will never recover."

"N-no-no, n-no no," Lancaster murmured, his body starting to shake. "No. No."

"He's a long way from home," Dylan said. "And somebody left King and Rock dead in an alley over on the west side. They were broken up bad, Rook, and somebody cannibalized King, took a bite right out of him."

Trembling, Lancaster stared at him in silent terror, his mouth agape.

"Do you think J.T. could have done a thing like that?" He had to ask, it didn't matter how tough the questions were, or how bad the answers might get.

"N-no," the old man said. "Souk's men . . . the soldiers he helped—"

"Helped?" Dylan should kill him for that alone.

"Enhanced," Lancaster clarified. "Th-they were never like . . . like MNK-1. Patterson went too far . . . too fucking far. Monk shouldn't exist."

But he did, thanks to Lancaster's greed.

"Can you call him off?" Dylan asked, his voice stone-cold serious. "Can you get my girl back?"

He wasn't in the mood to ask twice, and when the seconds passed one after another without any answers coming from the old man, he took a red syringe out of the box.

He was done with the bastard.

A faint whimper escaped the man, and Dylan swore in disgust. He had no tolerance for traitors or cowards—and Lancaster was both.

Out of patience and out of time, he stepped forward and pushed Lancaster's sleeve up. Buck wasn't going to like it—getting here and finding a mumbling, babbling mess of a high-end State Department diplomat chained in the basement—but that wasn't going to be enough to stop Dylan.

He thumbed the protective cap off the syringe, and Lancaster started to twist and struggle in his ropes.

"*N-no,*" he cried out. "No. No. I can't, can't call him

off, but I can... I can get your girl back, this Jane. I know what Monk wants. D-don't, don't, Dylan, don't stick me with that shit. I'll tell you... tell you what he wants."

The needle rested above a blue vein pulsing on the inside curve of the old man's elbow.

"Now or never, Rook." If he had something to say, he'd better say it, or Dylan was sliding the needle home. Proving the fact, he pressed it harder, letting the sharp tip bite into Lancaster's skin.

"*M-me,*" the old man finally said, his voice anguished, desperate. "Monk wants *me.*"

And Monk could have him.

Against his better judgment, Dylan put the syringe back in the box and reached up to key his mike. Before he could say a word, Zach's voice came over the radio.

"Dylan. The building is compromised. We've got someone on the loose up here, someone capable of climbing up the outside of the building, hand over fricking hand. Best guess is that it's MNK-1. We think he's got Jane with him... and..." There was a long, dreadful pause. "And I can't find Skeeter."

CHAPTER FORTY

Where in the hell am I? Skeeter wondered, opening her eyes to pitch darkness. *And what is that smell?*

Rank and metallic, it assaulted her senses.

Packed sideways into some kind of space with odd edges, her arms bound to her torso, she was wrapped up tighter than a miser's money.

But she could breathe, and her head was clearing. It hurt like hell, though, and she knew she'd been cold-cocked, ambushed on her own freakin' turf.

She swore under her breath and tried to wiggle out of whatever was binding her. The sonuvabitch who had done this to her was going down—just as soon as she got herself out of her current fix.

Take a breath, she told herself, *ignore the smell.* It was gagging.

She wiggled again and the hard surface underneath her creaked and groaned, like metal straining under weight. It didn't sound good. Twisting around, she tried to see above her and felt a breath of fresh air blow across her cheek. A drop of water fell on her face, then another, and another. Faintly, she could make out a lighter shade of darkness far above her, a ragged-edge square of the night sky. The wind gusted, and more rain blew into the space, cool and wet on her skin. Something fluttered across the opening from the outside, and as Skeeter watched, she slowly realized what it was: a piece of striped webbing off her favorite cheap-ass lawn chair. There were only two such chairs at Steele Street, both of them bolted to the roof on the square of Astroturf called "the Beach." Then she remembered. Someone had blown the Beach and the rooftop stairwell to hell. Whoever had snatched her had stuffed her into the wreckage.

She swore, and felt the remains of the stairwell creak and shudder around her.

She swore again, but more softly, much, much more softly.

Moving slowly and carefully, she turned her head to look down, hoping she was on a solid metal surface.

No such luck.

Peering through the jumbled, exploded remains of the stairwell, she could see her own damn living room.

Well, hell, she thought. Nothing had improved down there since they'd checked it earlier when they'd cleared the building. The furniture was still wet and covered with debris, chunks of metal and pipe, and about half the rafters, and . . . *oh, oh, oh, damn.*

While she'd been out cold, the guys had gone to DEFCON 4, the highest level of alert. The bright yellow M spray-painted on her living room wall above the elevator meant they'd cleared this floor again and missed her up here in the wreckage—and then they'd set up a little welcoming committee in the elevator for whoever had done this to her, a welcoming committee named "Claymore." They'd mined the elevator shaft.

Cripes, she needed out of here.

She tried another careful wiggle, and then wished she hadn't. With a yawning squeal of strained metal, another part of the wreckage broke away from underneath her and fell, and fell, and fell, until it crashed into her slate coffee table. The stone shattered under the impact, she saw $999 of "on sale" go up in a spray of shards and splinters, and now her ass was really hanging out over the abyss.

If she rolled six inches either way, she was toast—impaled toast.

Fuck.

She had to get the hell—

O geezus!

A short, muffled cough came from out of nowhere and almost sent her over the edge. *Cripes.* She wasn't alone up here in this hole.

The cough came again, real close from behind her in the wreckage, a small, muffled sound of distress—and suddenly she knew.

"Jane?" she whispered. "Is that you?"

Tyler Crutchfield sat perfectly still in his poolside chair for only one reason: He had no choice.

These SDF assholes had the damn concession on duct tape, and they'd used plenty to keep him from being able to move in any direction. Hell, he'd been trapped for so long, he was probably paralyzed by now. Otherwise he would have risen up and beaten Lancaster to a pulp with his bare hands, just finished the bastard off. He had dried vomit down the front of his shirt and was sitting in a pool of his own urine, and it was all because of Randolph Lancaster.

Tyler's last great hope, his *only* hope, had been the man bound to the pulley rig. Lancaster was slumped over, hanging limply from his restraints, having worn himself out trying to get free from the tangle of chains and cuffs and hardware tying him up. Or maybe he'd had a seizure and died.

Nope. Tyler saw him twitch, the old bastard.

"We're going to die in this damn basement," Tyler muttered, then raised his voice a few decibels to make sure Lancaster heard him. "We're going to die here, you son of a bitch."

Damn it all to hell! Tyler Thomas Crutchfield was not supposed to die like a filth-wallowing rat in a cage. It was incomprehensible—and yet he felt the doom of death bearing down on him. He wasn't a psychic, but it didn't take a crystal ball to know what happened to people tied up in basements, especially ones who'd already had a gun held to their head.

An involuntary shudder wracked his body. Never in a million years would he have believed a trip to Denver would get him killed.

Lancaster ignored him, the same way the old bastard had been ignoring him since Peter "Kid Chaos" Chronopolous had dragged him down here and chained him to the pulley rig.

Not one word. Tyler seethed with the thought. Lancaster had said nothing in Tyler's defense, made not one plea to Hart for his release, knowing he was blameless for the LeedTech sales to Atlas Exports.

Tyler had never even heard of Atlas Exports until Hart had methodically outlined Lancaster's acts of treason.

Acts his boss had not denied.

Lies.

That's all he'd ever gotten from Randolph Lancaster.

Tyler had been such a fool, but he wasn't the only one. The extent of Lancaster's treason shook the very foundations of the U.S. government, but no one would ever know. The crime would pass unnoted if he and Lancaster perished in this damn basement.

The bastard.

A muffled groan from the far end of the pool deck brought Tyler's head around. Sam Walls was reviving, for all the good that was going to do them. They were all going to die down here.

"Walls!" Tyler shouted at him. "Walls! Come on,

man, get up! Get up and get over here!" If Walls could get just one of Tyler's arms free of this damn chair, maybe they could make a break for it.

Except for Lancaster.

That sonuvabitch was doomed, imprisoned in his tangle of chains and handcuffs.

Too fucking bad, Tyler thought. *Let the treasonous bastard rot.*

"Walls!" Tyler called again. "Come on, man. Shake it off." *And get your sorry ass over here.*

Walls groaned again and rolled over onto his back. *Geezus.* The guy's leg. It was a mess, and Tyler had to wonder what had been going on with all these Atlas Exports "supersoldiers" Lancaster surrounded himself with. Nothing good, that was for damn sure. No wonder Dylan Hart was playing this game for keeps.

But it shouldn't include him. He didn't belong here. He was blameless. *Blameless.*

"I'll give you fifty grand if you can get over here, Walls. Come on. Just crawl, man. Just *crawl.*" He had to get out of here. He really did, or Hart was going to kill him. "Fifty grand, Walls! Can you hear me?"

Money was a great motivator. Not that Tyler had any damn intention of parting with fifty thousand of his hard-earned dollars, or a fifty-thousand-dollar chunk of his trust fund. Hell, no. But honest to God, Walls didn't look like he was going to last long enough to give a damn.

He broke them up and cannibalized King, took a bite out of him. Dylan Hart's words slid through Tyler's mind for about the hundred millionth time. He'd heard them, but he didn't believe them, not for a minute. Hart was just trying to scare them all senseless.

Touché. He'd succeeded. Lancaster had gone catatonic since Hart had raced out of there. It was that

Monk guy business, just like in Bangkok, when Randolph had gotten so buggy with the booze.

Cannibalized, as in *eaten*.

No fucking way. Tyler shook his head. No way. No one Tyler had ever known had been as brutish as the dynamic duo of King Banner and Rock Howe, and they'd never eaten anybody. If they had, he would have heard about it forty-eight times by now. Bragging about their badass exploits was those boys' favorite pastime.

Or it had been, Tyler thought with a slow shake of his head. Dead. It was hard to believe . . . and if Walls moved any slower, they were all—

Wait. Tyler froze in his chair, absolutely froze solid, listening with every fiber of his being, listening for . . .

"*Lancastaaaaa* . . ." The cry came from somewhere above them, unlike anything he'd ever heard.

Twenty feet away, Lancaster whimpered and started to cry.

Cry? The bastard was crying?

An unholy terror of death and destruction was descending upon them, and all the old man could do was cry?

A vacant sound of rapidly running footsteps echoed on the ceiling, and, for a moment, Tyler wished with all his might that Quinn Younger had just blown his brains out. Aything would be better than what he was facing now.

Oh, so help him God. So help him, he did *not* want to be eaten alive.

An unbearable trembling took hold of his body, and all he could do was sit there, trapped, and shake.

"*Lancassstaa* . . ." The eerie voice grew nearer and nearer, the sound of it making Tyler's blood curdle in his veins.

"W-walls," he moaned. "*Walls!* Good God, man, *get up!*"

Oh, geezus, geezus, geezus.

Over in a darkened corner, Tyler heard the sound of someone moving a heavy metal grate in the ceiling.

No, no, no, no, no... this couldn't be happening, not to Tyler Thomas Crutchfield.

"No," he said out loud, then again, more vehemently. *"No!"*

He didn't deserve this, to be butchered in a basement.

Not to be butch... butch... bu— His mind stuttered to a dead stop, his eyes growing so wide they hurt.

Whatever was coming was coming now. A huge hand reached through the hole in the ceiling and finished moving the grate aside. Then a man dropped through to the pool deck. Monk.

Ungodly big, ripped to the point of distortion, every muscle so hard, so delineated, he looked like a caricature, like a comic-book hero in the flesh.

Albino flesh. Long white hair, disheveled.

Bare-chested and bloody.

The blood was dried in streaks down his arm but still fresh and running down his face from a wound across his cheekbone.

Eyes so silvery pale they seemed to have no color at all met his across the basement, and all the energy went out of Tyler in one rushing wave of despair, every last ounce of it. The only thing holding him up was the duct tape.

Monk quickly dismissed the gutless weasel taped to the chair. That one was no warrior and none of Monk's concern. Neither was the man wallowing and struggling half naked on the pool deck, Sam Walls, one of Lancaster's idiot lackeys.

But the third man meant the world to him, the new world he'd awoken to in pain and confusion. Monk had detected his scent the minute he'd entered the building.

Lancaster himself—roped and chained and cuffed.

An emotion he couldn't describe welled up and filled Monk's chest, made him ache with longing and disgust, with love and despair.

Lancaster's last moments of life had come to him.

Monk walked across the pool deck and slowly dropped to his knees in front of the old man, bringing them face-to-face.

Lancaster was such a mess, hanging so heavily from his chains. He had blood on his shirt and tears on his old, wrinkled cheeks and no hope in his tired, weary eyes.

"Scott," Monk said, speaking the name that had once been his. He wasn't Scott anymore. He was MNK-1, a beast of strength and cunning who would never have made the mistake Scott Church had of putting his life in this man's hands.

"*Y-y-yes.*" The harsh, whispered word fell from Lancaster's mouth.

Paper-pushers, Monk thought with disgust, the money-mongers—they had no real balls. He wanted a battle. He wanted his destroyer to go out in a blaze of rage and fury, fighting for his life. But there was no getting a fight out of Lancaster any more than there'd been getting a fight out of Dr. Patterson.

It made him long for Farrel. J. T. Chronopolous had been a Marine before he'd joined SDF, and a Marine never went down without a fight.

It would be a fight to the death—especially after he used J.T.'s woman. Then he would have the other girl, the blonde, Skeeter Bang-Hart. Then he would kill them both. Break them in half and leave them for their men to find.

But first, Lancaster.

He reached out and fitted his hand around Lancaster's neck and pulled him closer. He wanted to see the fear in the old man's eyes, wanted to watch death darken them forever. It wouldn't take long.

"N-no," Lancaster pleaded. "*Please!* I have—"

He had nothing, *nothing,* and Monk slowly tightened his hand, squeezing the old man's throat, crushing it and pulling him closer and closer, until he felt Lancaster's last gasping breath leave him. Nothing else would get through his fierce grip, nothing except the tsunami wave of the old man's fear.

"Monk," he said at the last possible instant, before death claimed the bastard, wanting Lancaster to take the name with him into eternity.

When it was over, he let the old man's head fall to his chest and rose to his feet, thoroughly unsatisfied. Limb by limb, he freed Lancaster from the pulley rig, ripping off and breaking the restraints. Then he slung the old man's body over his shoulder, his burden. All his. Only his.

Lancaster. Held close at last, dead but held close.

Above him, he could hear the men of Special Defense Force scrambling, securing the building, and he had a damn good idea of what that entailed. They were warriors like him.

It didn't matter. It wouldn't save their women, and when he was finished with his prizes, he'd take on the men and vanquish every one of them.

Tilting his head back, he gave in to all the pain and longing and strength that was him, MNK-1—*Monk!*—and he roared his rage.

He roared until the sweat poured down his face. He roared until the room shook with the fierce power of his agony—and then he roared again.

CHAPTER FORTY-ONE

Fuck. Creed's eyebrows went sky high at the eerie cry reverberating through Steele Street's subbasement. He slanted a look over at Travis and Red Dog where they stood next to him in the subterranean tunnels leading up through the bowels of the building.

Unperturbed, the Angel Boy was checking the load on the Para-Ordnance P14 handgun he'd had customized by the chop shop boys' favorite gunsmith, a guy named Cullen over at Colorado Gun Works. Travis carried the full-auto-capable pistol in a shoulder rig with six eighteen-round extended, hi-cap magazines tucked under his other arm. The whole bitchin'-cool, deadly rig was easily concealable beneath a tac vest.

The hair-raising howl echoed through the tunnel again, the message crystal clear to Creed. The guy was calling them out, every last man jack of them, and Creed had to wonder, really, just how badass this Monk bastard was going to turn out to be—and he hoped to hell he and his team were the ones to find out.

Before the three of them had reached Steele Street, Dylan had called and ordered them to come through the 19th Street tunnels, their mission threefold: to look for Skeeter and Jane, to cut off any escape in that direction, and to clear the building from the bottom up, forcing the mad cannibal Monk into Dylan's trap. But it sounded like they'd landed in the gravy. That raging roar was coming from close by. While the rest of the SDF team was busy setting claymores with optic trip switches in the elevator shaft, marking and mining it, creating a tunnel of death, Creed and his crew were going to be kicking butt and taking names.

Major butt, he thought, watching Red Dog check a thirty-three-round magazine of KTW 9mm armor-piercing rounds and slam it home into another of Cullen's custom full-auto jobs on her H&K PDW. Between Red Dog and the Angel Boy, they could put fifty precision pistol rounds downrange in under five seconds—which just made Creed wonder what in the hell the two of them had been up to on all those missions General Grant sent them on that didn't originate with SDF.

Maybe it was time to find out. Given the look of their weapons, they were getting some really big scores, and he wouldn't mind a piece of the action.

When Red Dog looked up, Creed gave the signal to move out, and the three of them slipped into the darkness.

Con stood in the pouring rain in the alley, looking up at 738 Steele Street. He saw the cameras tracking him and didn't make a move to avoid them. They were no threat to J. T. Chronopolous, no threat to him, unless the men watching them tried to keep him from his mission: killing Randolph Lancaster.

It was a chance he couldn't take.

He followed the cameras through one more loop, and the next time they came to the place where he'd been, he was gone. From his calculations, there was only one possible way of getting into the building unobserved, and that was to climb it from the outside. He started with the old freight elevator, whose shadows and struts and cables hid his movements, and when the elevator ran out, he took to the wall, one finger jamb after another.

Partway up, two unexpected scents came to him off the bricks and stone-cold riveted his attention: *Jane and the beast.* The rancid, metallic smell of Lancaster's newest abomination was unmistakable, and so was the warm, wild woman smell of Jane.

Dread and confusion collided in his mind. She was here, the Wild Thing, and Lancaster's beast had her. Whatever had happened at the house on the west side, somehow the beast had gotten the better of the SDF boys.

Fuck.

Fear had been burned out of him a long time ago, but with love, he realized, it had only been lying in wait. It came back to him hard and fast now.

Doubling his speed, he scrambled higher and found the broken window on the eighth floor. When he dropped inside, he felt another punch of *home*, but it was the trail he was following that held him—and the trail led up.

Zach looked up from one of the comm console's video-feed computer screens. "Looks like we had the wrong bait for the last eight weeks. Are you going, or do you want me to do the honors?"

"This one's mine," Dylan said, reaching for the rifle he'd set on the desk earlier. He slipped the sling over his shoulder, then checked his Springfield, making sure he had a full magazine in the .45 and four extra magazines on his belt.

Behind him, Zach was already on the radio, letting everyone know J.T. had breached the building—like every other damn person on the planet tonight—and that the boss was going after him.

The boss—Dylan started up the stairs. He didn't feel like the boss of anything, not with Skeeter missing. His brain was frying on the edges with fear.

No one could see it, but it was taking everything he had to run this operation like a mission and not just go on the rampage, looking for his bad girl. The only thread of reason he had was knowing there wasn't a better way to get a whole lot of people killed.

So he was cool.

Cool, cool Dylan Hart—so torn up inside, so full of fear, so wanting to take Steele Street apart at the seams, brick by fucking brick, and howl his rage.

"The smell—"

"—is disgusting." Jane finished Skeeter's thought and wiped the rain off her face, before going back to tugging at the knot of material at Skeet's back. The man, if he could be called that, Jane's "ghost," had tied his shirt around Skeeter, and tied it so tightly, she was losing circulation in her arms.

A crackling web of chain lightning sizzled across the sky and gave her a moment's light to work by—and made her pray she and Skeeter didn't get fried.

Her head was pounding with pain, her muscles ached, and she was shivering with the cold rain beating down on her. She felt like she'd been in a dogfight, and lost. Every part of her hurt.

It had taken what had seemed like *forever* for her to work her arms out of the sheet she'd been wrapped in, and every move had cost the two women, with pieces of the stairwell dropping away underneath them like clockwork. Skeeter was hanging by a thread, almost literally, precariously perched on their diminishing island of metal trash and building guts, and the only thing holding Jane in place was Skeeter.

But they had a plan, to get them both free of their bindings and climb to the roof, which was still ninety percent intact and only five feet above them. And as long as Skeeter didn't fall to her death and drag Jane in her wake, it just might work.

"Done," she said finally, releasing the last of the knot. "Wiggle your fingers."

Steele Street's original bad girl kept herself in amazing shape, and, in seconds, she had movement back in her hands and arms.

Thank God, Jane thought, wiping at her face again.

She and Skeeter had gone hoarse calling out to the guys, hoping the team would find them—but the chances that their voices had risen above the sounds of the storm were slim to none.

They were on their own, and they needed to get the hell out of—*oh, damn, oh, damn, oh, damn.*

Skeeter had gone mannequin in front of her, and over the blonde's shoulder, Jane saw why.

The "ghost" had returned, silent and stealthy, and was watching them with a preternatural intensity from where he stood in the shadows at the other end of Skeeter and Dylan's loft. God only knew how long he'd been down there—and he was ever so much more horrible than she had imagined from her fleeting glimpse of him behind Mama Guadaloupe's, his hair crazy white and raggedly long, his muscles bulging under his pale white skin, his neck thick, his hands huge and deadly.

He'd torn King Banner's arm off, clean off—oh, geezus, oh, geezus.

And he was staring straight at them with a dead body lying at his feet, a broken, old man.

"*Go, go, go,*" Skeeter said, lifting herself up and reaching for a handhold above her.

Jane was more than ready to go, go, go, but the metal pipe Skeeter grabbed broke away, and their open-sided box of twisted metal shifted and yawed with a squealing screech of metal.

Oh, hell. Jane lunged for Skeet, grabbing her hard around the waist and pulling her back. The stairwell shuddered into a new resting spot at an angle that threatened to spill them out, and Jane held on to Skeeter even tighter.

Oh, damn, oh, damn. She braced her feet and gritted her teeth, and prayed.

Below them, the albino walked over to one of the fallen rafters.

Her arms straining, her heart racing, Jane watched in growing dread as he lifted the huge wooden beam up and braced it against the loft's outside wall. When it was solidly in place, he lodged the top end of the rafter up into the exploded stairwell, crashing and slamming it into position. The stairwell bucked and tilted under the assault but ended up throwing them back against the rear wall of their perch, giving them a reprieve from falling to the floor below.

Jane relaxed her hold and tried to slow her breathing, tried to slow the pounding of her heart and prepare herself for the coming onslaught.

Because it was coming, and it was coming fast.

The albino beast's intentions were clear, and made even clearer when he started climbing—*so fast, so freaking fast.*

"Are you ready to fight?" Skeeter asked, her voice breathless from the bone-rattling they'd just been given. They were out of time, out of choices.

"Yes, ma'am, I am," Jane said, sliding her hand down her leg and taking hold of the sheath knife she kept in her boot.

Hawkins jerked his head up at the horrendous crashing and banging coming from above them. It wasn't the storm raging outside. The sound was man-made.

He and Quinn and Kid had been working the building from the top down, clearing floors and marking and mining the elevator shaft, Plan A in the Steele Street Survival Handbook for any bastard-in-the-building scenario, a plan they'd come up with after the last time a bunch of bastards had breached their home turf. They hadn't seen a damn thing, not hide nor hair of the bastard Monk, or Jane, or Skeeter. Zach and Dylan were coordinating the SDF attack from the comm console, and Hawkins had *thought* they were holding the eighth floor, that nothing would get by Zach or the boss either way, from the top down or from the bottom up.

"I thought we cleared the upper floors," he said, his mood so far south he had nothing but cold, frigid, arctic anger running through him.

Those were *his* girls Monk had taken.

Kid had already broken into a run, heading toward the commotion.

"We don't have enough men to cover the whole damn place, Christian, not inside and out," Quinn said, lying flat on his stomach, stretched out over the shaft through the open elevator doors on the sixth floor. He was setting the last claymore—very, very carefully. "The way Monk climbed in here, he could have gotten by us by going up the outside." He set the trip switch, signaled, and Hawkins pulled him back.

"Let's go," Hawkins said, and got on the radio. "Dylan, we're headed back up."

"It's Zach, copy that. Dylan is already on the move."

Good, he thought. From what they'd seen tonight, it was going to take everything Steele Street had to prevail—and prevail they must.

CHAPTER FORTY-TWO

Sweet, so sweet. Monk could see them up there, peeking out of the wreckage, the resolve on their faces revealed with every lightning flash.

Here, he decided, was the fight he'd been wanting, in the last place he would have ever expected to find it—with a couple of women.

The one bitch had already shot him, but she was weaponless now. He'd disarmed Skeeter Bang-Hart, too.

This was going to be short and sweet—very sweet.

He never saw it coming.

Near the top of the rafter, he lunged for Skeeter, ready to jerk her out of the wreckage and shake her until her neck snapped—but it wasn't to be.

She caught him in the throat with the heel of her boot in a strike so fast, so pure, he was amazed even as it sent him staggering. He was even more amazed when he lost his balance and fell backward down the rafter into a crashing heap on the floor.

Bitch.

He rose to all fours and took stock of himself, struggling to breathe, to swallow. She could have killed him with that strike, crushed his larynx. A lesser soldier would have already been dead.

He started to his feet, when the sound of someone coming drew his attention to the far end of the loft.

From behind the rafter, he watched and waited as a shadow warrior slid into the darkness of the room.

Conroy Farrel—well armed, superbly skilled, and hunting.

Unexpectedly, Monk felt the first stirrings of redemption move within his blighted soul. This was the fight he'd come from Bangkok to get. To test himself against this man.

He let his gaze drift to the body at his feet. Kneeling, he smoothed the white lion's mane of hair back off the death-flattened face. Lancaster would soon have what he had so wanted: Conroy Farrel dead, his body broken, his life bled out of him.

Con slipped silently into the room.

This was the place. Dust still drifted down from the ceiling, shaken loose by the room-jarring pounding he'd heard on the way up. Rain was coming down through a hole in the roof, gusting in with the wind, backlit by the lightning racing across the sky. It ran down a broken pipe off to his left and was pooling around a rat's nest of exposed wires hanging uselessly off a smashed stereo system.

There was so damn little justice in the world—but he would take what he could here. Take it in his fist and make it be what he needed it to be: Jane safe. His enemies vanquished. His life . . . his life—*fuck!* He couldn't see his life, not if she died here because of him.

He closed his eyes on a harsh breath and focused on the moment at hand. Jane Linden was a street rat, he reminded himself. She was tough, a fighter, and she was here, so close, within his grasp.

Lancaster's beast was here, too, in this broken room open to the night sky and the rain. The smell of him filled the loft, overpowering everything else, the metallic stench of him assaulting Con's senses.

"*Monk!*" A woman's voice rang out from high above him, not Jane's. "Scott Church! I know you, MNK-1. I can help you. I know what went wrong!"

The slightest scuff of a footfall sounded twenty yards to the north of Con, at the other end of the loft, and he moved out, continuing around the perimeter of the room, always keeping a wall at his back.

The loft had been destroyed, the ceiling caved in, the furniture broken and getting soaked, and somewhere in the mess was the beast she called Monk.

He could smell the guy, but he couldn't see him—yet. All he needed was one good shot, and he had his Wilson Combat .45 cocked and unlocked, ready to deliver it.

"Randolph Lancaster lied to you, Monk." The woman kept talking, her voice cool and clear. "But I have Dr. Patterson's files, his records."

Con kept moving, one silent step at a time. He'd heard the name Patterson before, attached to the rumors of the subpar Thai lab that had tried to take up where Dr. Souk had left off.

"I know what Patterson did to you," the woman said, "and I know how to fix the mistakes he made."

"Not a mistake!"

The voice stopped Con cold. It was harsh and twisted, deep and menacing, thick with anger. It was madness, a howl beaten into words.

"No mistake!" the beast shouted again.

Oh, yeah, baby, you're a mistake, all right, Con thought, tightening his grip on the Wilson, even more of a mistake than I am.

Head shot, straight into the kill zone—that's what he was looking for, one second's worth of a sight picture and that bastard was dead.

Another bolt of lightning cracked and sizzled across the sky, and for one endlessly long moment of time, the loft was lit.

There was no missing Monk. The bastard was huge, easily six feet four with a tangled mass of long white hair. He was built like a Mack Truck, a carved slab of granite, an extrapolation of Souk's science taken into the bizarre zone. He barely looked human—and for that long endless moment of lightning-lit luminosity, when Con squeezed the Wilson's trigger, all the beast's attention was focused on the woman's voice.

The report of the .45 sounded. The smell of cordite followed, bitter and sharp. Then again, the whole process: trigger squeeze, the gun's report, the smell of burned powder.

In the split second of the two shots, the creature named Monk was looking up toward the ceiling. After confirming the two hits, Con's gaze shifted, following Monk's, and he saw what had been holding his attention: a long-haired blonde in a skin-tight gray dress and combat boots, and Jane, bruised and beautiful, and in mortal danger of electrocution.

He was moving before the thought even hit him, moving to haul his ass up the rafter and get them down from the tangle of steel and roof and exploded stairwell, before the lightning found them—but between the thought and the deed, in mid-flying stride, he got hit by Monk.

The beast slammed into him, knocking him into next week, moving him back ten feet, the concussion of the hit blacking him out. It was an explosion of light and pain, and then it was nothing.

Nothing for a heartbeat.

Nothing for two.

The sound of battle, a woman's scream, a cry of pain—they all brought him back.

Flat on his back, dazed, he waited for his breath to return, waited to feel his body kick back into gear. He waited, and he heard the screams—screams of rage and fear.

Monk had grabbed both of the women and was dragging them off the stairwell, fighting and cussing. Good girls. They had nothing left to lose.

But he had something to win: this damn fight.

Forcing a breath into his lungs, he got back to his feet and went after the bastard. He'd lost his gun in the fall, but he had a knife, and he had the will.

There was only win, *only* win, no other option, and he would cut the bastard's head off, inch by inch, if that was what it took to drop him.

Partway down the rafter, Monk leapt off and landed next to someone on the floor. Con barely looked, but even a glance was enough to tell him his mission had ended without him.

Randolph Lancaster was dead, a limp pile of old man in a crumpled heap on the floor. There was no mistaking the identity of the body, that thick mane of snow-white hair, and Monk seemed transfixed by it, momentarily distracted.

Con moved in fast, holding the knife in a reverse edge grip, ready to carve the bastard a new face—but Monk was fast, faster than him, faster than the two slugs of .45 Con had leveled at him. The bullets had only left grazing wounds on his head when they should have exploded inside his skull. Somehow the bastard had outmaneuvered a pair of jacketed hollowpoints rocketing at 1,100 feet per second. Con barely caught him with his knife strike, a slash up the left side of his face, but it was enough to get the beast to relinquish the blonde. With a flick of his wrist, Monk tossed her hard against the window. She hit with a sickening thud and dropped like a stone—but in a move of supreme athletic grace, she landed on the balls of her feet, conscious and ready to go, except one arm wasn't working now. Crashing into the window had dislocated her shoulder and put her out of the fight—or so he thought.

He'd thought wrong. She wasn't giving up, not for a second.

She needed to. There was no place for her in this, no safe place.

Con stepped in front of her and blocked the strike Monk had meant for her. It was a cracking blow to his forearm, but the arm held, and Con went in under the strike with the knife, burying it deep in Monk's gut.

Fuck. The blade went in, but the ripping-upward jerk he'd planned on using to eviscerate the bastard was a dismal failure. The guy's skin was like rhino hide.

So Con pulled the blade out and stuck him again, and again, and, for his efforts, Monk grabbed him by the scruff of his neck and lofted him into space, all without losing his grip on Jane.

Fucking airborne. *Geezus*. He hit the floor again and had his breath knocked out of him—again.

He did a quick calculation: him, the blonde, Jane, and dead Lancaster versus the subpar Souk knockoff who was cleaning his clock.

He needed help. He couldn't do this alone. It was like going up against an Abrams tank.

"J.T.!" Jane screamed, struggling inside Monk's heavy-handed hold.

Yeah. J.T. That was him.

He levered himself back to his feet, ready to wade back in and force Monk to release her, but to be smart about it this time, "smart" meaning not to let the bastard get a hold of him.

Unbelievably, to him, the blonde had the same idea, to get back in there and do some damage. She gave him a signal, a subtle movement with her hand—and he understood exactly what she meant. She was going to distract the bastard with a feint, staying out of his grasp and making an opening for Con to go in and make some contact that counted.

Great idea, and it worked. She drew Monk off, and Con came in high and landed a knife strike in the back of the beast's neck, trying with all his might to sever something, anything—but no go. He got the knife in and got it back out, and then he got walloped again—and that time, something got shook loose.

He tried to get up, but fell back down, the world starting to spin, his skin getting hot. White light streaked across his line of vision, bringing pain, the headache from hell. *Shit.* This wasn't just about Monk hitting him like a freight train. This was about his own personal fucked-up situation.

With agonizing effort, he got his hand in his pocket and pulled out some pills. A bunch of them fell onto the floor. *Fuck.* He could die here, and then what would happen to Jane?

The possibilities didn't bear thinking.

He grabbed a red pill and put it under his tongue to melt, and he lay there, watching everything unfold around him like a strobe-lit dream, his body rigid with pain... *Monk dismissing him with a sneer*—yeah, you, too, buddy. Up yours. *Jane reaching for him, screaming his name, and Monk pulling her in closer, lifting her off the ground*—sorry, baby, so damn sorry. *Monk reaching down and claiming Lancaster's body. The blonde holding her injured arm close to her side and backing away from the beast.*

Whatever the pill was going to do for him, it wasn't going to do it soon enough. Fuck! With another ungodly effort, he got to his hands and knees and willed himself to get back in the fight.

Geezus, Jane. He needed to find his gun. It was the only chance she had. There'd be no outmaneuvering a pistol barrel jammed in the bastard's ear. He could deliver that payload, by God.

The blonde was pleading with Monk now, begging

him to release Jane, making promises, offering deals, but the bastard just kept walking backward, carrying Jane and dragging Lancaster and watching the blonde, heading toward the elevator—which was oddly jammed open with no car stopped on the floor and with a bright yellow M spray-painted on the wall above it.

Everything about the elevator setup screamed danger to him, danger and death, and Jane was headed straight into it.

Geezus. Where was his pistol?

"Tell Red Dog to get her ass up here," Dylan shouted into his radio, running full out for the thirteenth floor. "Tell her I need everything she's got.

Skeeter was alive. He could hear her voice, hear her shouting, and she was shouting for Jane. He hoped to hell that meant Jane was alive, too.

His job was to keep them that way.

The door to his and Skeeter's loft was open. One look inside told him what he needed to know, and he went in with his gun drawn and leveled at the ready.

His wife had been injured, and that pissed him off, but she wasn't captive.

J.T. had gotten the shit beaten out of him by the fucking huge albino in the middle of Dylan's living room. Lancaster was dead, and Jane was headed to a very nasty end in the elevator shaft.

There was only one solution: to tattoo his fucking name across MNK-1's forehead with his .45.

Piece of fucking cake.

Bam, bam, bam. The sonuvabitch was fast, faster than Red Dog, which was ungodly fast, fast enough to keep Dylan from getting solid hits.

So he adjusted, without ever taking his finger off the trigger or pausing in his shots.

Bam, bam, bam—he landed those in the guy's chest,

which didn't slow the bastard down or get him to release Jane.

Bam, bam... Dylan released the empty magazine out of the pistol, letting it fall to the floor as he slammed a fresh mag home... *bam, bam.*

He never stopped shooting, but he did change his mind and his target. Those last four shots had gone into Lancaster. Sure he was dead, but Monk was dragging him around like a teddy bear. The old man had value beyond reason—a good guess that turned into a cold fact when Monk roared and dropped Jane to pull Lancaster in closer, protecting him.

Dylan liked tough girls, and despite looking like she'd been wrung through the wringer, Jane scrambled like a true street rat. The instant Monk released her, she dropped low, out of his line of fire, and took off like a shot.

And there were plenty of shots. Dylan never let up.

Bam, bam, bam—and Monk roared again. *Bam, bam, bam*... reload like a fucking speed demon... *bam, bam, bam.*

Then *bambambambambambam.* Red Dog had arrived. There were no "grazing" shots delivered by Red, or by Kid, who had entered the room a mere second behind her.

Two more guns came into play—Quinn and Hawkins lining up on either side of him and Red and Kid, cutting the pie, widening the kill zone.

Lancaster was a pile of mush in a bloody, shredded shirt and there was no reason on earth for Monk to still be standing. But he was.

They had him locked down in a crossfire with only one way out: the elevator shaft.

Good luck with that, *pendejo,* Dylan thought, reloading for the last time. *Bam, bam, bam.*

Monk fell to his knees at the open doorway of the

elevator shaft, and Dylan hoped the guy's little personal struggle with getting shot about a thousand fucking times wouldn't deter him from what must look like a pretty good plan.

It didn't.

With a final roar, Monk tightened his hold on Lancaster's limp body and lofted himself onto the elevator cable.

It was a short ride.

The first claymore exploded inside of a second—*Boom!*—and the rest came in quick succession—*Boom! Boom! Boom!*—all the way down to the sixth floor as the beast and his maker fell down the shaft.

Nobody holstered their weapons. They were SDF, and they never took death for granted. If Monk had a head left, Kid would put a bullet in it. The bastard had proven damned difficult to kill. They wanted to make sure they kept him that way.

True to form, Kid leaned into the open elevator shaft and squeezed the pressure plate on the tac light bolted onto his subgun.

Pop, pop—he threw a couple of rounds down the shaft, then turned and headed straight for J.T.

"Call Loretta," Dylan said to Hawkins. "Sweet-talk her into sending her best cleanup crew." It was going to be a mess in the elevator, but the bulk of the building was damn near indestructible.

Taking long strides across the loft, he made his way to Skeeter's side. He deliberately did not reach out and pull her in close, and without him saying a word, she answered his questions.

"I'm fine. It's just the shoulder. I swear."

He looked around, saw a chair, and pulled it over for her. "Sit," he said, then gave her a quick kiss on the side of the face.

The last two people to reach the scene finally made it

to the thirteenth floor—actually in damn good time, considering where they'd come from.

"Creed," he said, working his way back over the debris strewn all over the place. "Go get the Humvee and bring it up to the seventh floor. We've got injuries."

Skeeter's wasn't life threatening, but he couldn't say the same for J.T.

Jane had raced to his side and was all over him, one of her hands on his face, the other on his chest as she leaned close, talking to him with tears running down her cheeks. Kid had knelt and taken hold of his brother's arm. And there was the badass who'd given the CIA a run for their money for six long years, holding on to a girl, his hand on her waist, and listening to every word the younger man leaning over him had to say.

"Travis, get us a stretcher," he called out. "We're going to have to transport J.T. Gillian, get over here and tell me what you think is going on with him. He looks like hell. Quinn, get Dr. Brandt on the horn and tell him to get on the first flight out of D.C."

He reached J.T. and knelt down next to Kid, who didn't look like he would relinquish an inch of space by J.T.'s side. Dylan didn't blame him. "What's happening here?" he asked.

"I-I don't know," Jane said. "He's got pills. He takes pills, but I don't know which one to give him."

Dylan saw the gelcaps spilling out of J.T.'s pocket, and he knew exactly what they were. He'd seen Gillian take hundreds of the things, all of them prescribed by Dr. Brandt.

"Gillian!" he shouted out.

"Here, boss," she said, kneeling.

She reached for J.T.'s face, her palm down, like she was going to check his temperature, but the man caught her wrist faster than she could retreat.

"That's a good sign," she said, glancing up at Dylan,

then looking back to J.T. "What color pill did you take?"

"Red."

She nodded and sifted her fingers through the pills on the floor. "I had a run-in with Dr. Souk four years ago," she said. "Things didn't go well with me, but I'm good now. Very little memory loss. No shooting pains in my arm. No headaches like the one you're having now." She shifted her glance to meet his gaze. "Flashing white lights? In long streaks?"

He nodded.

"Yeah, those can get bad. I'm surprised you've lasted this long without help."

Dylan remained silent, watching the two of them, listening to Gillian and seeing J.T. slowly release her wrist. Kid looked tense as hell, overcome with emotion and maybe fear. He had his brother back, but nobody knew what that really meant.

Gillian continued what she was about, resting her palm on J.T.'s forehead, then along the side of his neck.

"You're spiking," she said, shifting her attention back to the pills. "And you're getting the shakes. That's a bad sign."

Indeed, J.T.'s body had started trembling.

"You're going to lock up here in a minute or two," she said, putting her hand back on his forehead. "A full-out seizure will hit you when you get to a hundred and four degrees. I've seen it, Con. I've been there, and it's a long way back. I can teach you a few things, though, to help you out, if you live long enough."

Picking one of the pills up, she touched it to her tongue. It was a deep, eggplant purple, and Dylan didn't know what in the hell it did.

"Klorizapat," she said, looking down at J.T. "You ready for this?"

He gave a short nod, she put it in his mouth, and that was it.

Two seconds later, he went out like a light.

Fuck.

"Travis!" Dylan yelled. "Where's that stretcher?"

CHAPTER FORTY-THREE

Con came back to consciousness in a hospital and immediately felt a jolt of fear. The lights were low in the room, the windows dark with night. Bad things happened to guys while they were out cold in hospitals—unless they had a guardian angel.

A strong hand came to rest on his shoulder. "It's all right, J.T. I've got your back."

Con glanced up. *J.T.*—he still didn't know much about that name, but he knew the man sitting next to his bed was his brother whether he remembered him or not, and that was a definite "or not."

"Kid . . . Chaos." He spoke the name slowly, surprised at how raspy his voice sounded.

The hand on his shoulder tightened.

"It's good to see you awake," the guy said, and his voice sounded a little tight, too. "Do you need anything?"

A memory of you, Con thought, but shook his head no. Kid Chaos looked like everything Con would have wanted a brother of his to be, and, faced with the younger man, he felt the loss of his old life more keenly than he could have anticipated.

"I know this is hard for you right now," Kid said. "Hard for everybody to figure out, and I want you to . . . uh, know there's no reason to push the situation any more than you're comfortable with. Not on anybody's account. Dr. Brandt is a good guy, one of the best, but the...uh, truth is, your memory will either come back, or it won't, and we'll deal with it either way. You take your time."

Con narrowed his gaze and tilted his head a little to one side. "Did you practice that?"

An instant grin flashed across the younger man's face. "A little," he admitted. "It's been six years, bro. I wanted to get the first words right."

"You did." In spades. This was hard on everybody, a six-year gulf full of grief and pain on all sides.

A moment of silence drew out between them, so many questions, so many unknowns.

"You look tired," he said, and the younger man nodded.

"I've been waiting for you, J.T.," Kid said, his voice low, his words heavy with the emotion Con could see in his face. "I've been waiting for you for a damn long time."

Without a thought, Con reached up and pulled his brother in close, his arms tightening around Kid's shoulders. *God.* He knew what it was like to wait for the dead, some part of your mind not accepting that the person you loved was gone from you forever.

Peter Chronopolous. Kid Chaos. J. T. Chronopolous. It was a lot to work through. Take your time, Kid had said, and Con knew the value of those words.

"Thanks." He tightened his hold on the younger man for a long moment before letting him go—except for taking hold of Kid's hand. He was exhausted, drifting back into sleep, but he wasn't ready for his little brother to leave him. Not yet...not yet...

The next time he woke, morning sunshine was streaming through the windows, and another angel was waiting for him. A beautiful woman with long dark hair, freckles across her nose, and a warm smile leaned over the bed.

God, he was glad to see her, to know she was still with him, that she hadn't been a dream.

"Hey, babe," he said.

"Hey, cowboy." She took his hand in hers, and he remembered something.

His brow furrowed. "There was a guy here earlier." His brother.

"There's been a lot of guys here," she said. "It's standing room only out in the hall, but you're talking about Kid. He's been here since you got here. He actually came in with you, and he hasn't left. He's just down in the cafeteria right now, getting some breakfast. How are you feeling?"

More awake now than when he'd been talking to Kid.

"Better." Way better. Bruised, roughed up in places, like a train had hit him, but better. He reached up and felt stitches in his head and another bolt of fear shot through him.

"No, no, baby," the woman murmured. "It's okay. You were hurt in the fight, and the doctors here stitched you back together. Nothing else happened. *Nothing*. I haven't left your side."

He believed her. Yeah, now that he thought about it, he didn't have that queasy, what-the-fuck-happened-to-me feeling he'd always had in Bangkok whenever he'd woken up. And he wasn't strapped into this bed, not like he'd been strapped into Souk's gurneys.

"Monk is dead, right?" he asked, remembering where he'd been and what he'd been doing when the lights had gone out. "Somebody got him?"

"Everybody got him," she said, offering him a cup of water. He lifted his head up and took a small swallow. "Everybody at Steele Street, the whole team. Hell, if I'd had a gun, *I* would have gotten him."

Good. He fell back on the pillow.

He'd needed to know that. Whatever Dr. Patterson

had done to that soldier, nobody should ever do it to anyone else ever again.

"Did he hurt you?" He needed to know what she'd gone through, all of it. Monk was dead, but that whole night had been rough on her.

"No," she said. "Nothing like what happened to you. I got a few bruises, a headache. That's all. The docs checked me out that night, when I came with you, and I'm fine."

A weight lifted off of him at her words. She hadn't been hurt, and suddenly, life was full of grace.

"And Randolph Lancaster?"

"You mean that little old dead guy Monk was dragging around?"

Geezus. That's what his life's work had come down to in the end: a little old dead guy getting dragged around?

"Yeah, that guy." The one who'd committed countless acts of treason against his country and ruined countless lives.

She shook her head, her smile fading. "A bad end, a real bad end. The chop shop boys mined the elevator shaft with claymores, and Monk tried to escape that way. He took Lancaster with him."

Ugly, but nothing more than he'd deserved.

His nemesis, the spymaster, Lancaster—dead.

"We've been waiting for you to come around," she said.

"How long?" He didn't have a clue.

"Two days."

Not so long.

"I know you," he said, because it seemed important to tell her.

"You sure?"

Yeah, he was sure.

"You're Jane Linden, Robin Rulz." Jane from the streets of Denver, a wild thing always on the run. Jane, sweet Jane, from a long-ago night when he'd turned to her for solace and been changed by what she'd given him.

Two nights ago, she'd turned to him for the same, and he had not forgotten, not like he'd forgotten so many things.

"And who are you?" she asked.

"Trick question?" He grinned.

"You tell me." Her eyes were so green, so warm and full of concern.

He let his grin fade. "Intellectually, I know I'm John Thomas Chronopolous, but in my heart, I'm still Con Farrel, and in between knowing those two things, there are a lot of empty places. It's more like I've got a bad memory rather than no memory."

"Dr. Brandt says it will take time, but since your amnesia was drug induced, it can be drug uninduced."

"Who is Dr. Brandt?"

"The miracle worker who keeps Red Dog in one piece, the man who brought her memory back."

Red Dog—that could only be one person.

"The woman who gave me the Klorizapat." She'd been a redhead.

Off on the other side of the bed, someone cleared her throat, and Jane looked up and smiled.

"Sorry," she said, then turned back to him. "Someone has been waiting for two days to see you."

He turned his head to see who was there.

"Scout," he said, his smile returning so big it almost hurt. His girl looked somehow different, and it took him a moment to realize why. "Nice dress."

And it was, real nice, real pretty, and unlike anything he'd ever seen her wear.

Scout in a dress.

He lifted his hand toward her, and his girl threw herself into his arms. *Scout.* Looking no worse the wear for having been in the clutches of the dreaded SDF crew for two months. She kissed his cheek, holding him close, and he shifted his gaze to the man standing next to her, holding her hand.

Oh, hell. Holding her hand.

"Geez, I missed you, Con," her sweet voice whispered in his ear. "You were s'posed to meet us at the damn Armstrong. We waited, until I finally had to call the damn *enemy* to find out what happened to you, and... and Red Dog told us you were here."

Red Dog again. He owed her.

"Jack," he said over the top of Scout's shoulder, not bothering to disguise the sternness in his voice.

Jack Traeger was not fazed. He just stood there, grinning like the wild boy he was, letting Con read it all in his face: that he'd won the girl, taken her for his own, and he wasn't giving her back.

Oh, hell. Con had seen this coming for years, but it was still a shock, especially with Scout showing up in a dress, a pink and green confection of silk and swirling cabbage roses, sleeveless with a V neck, a summer dress that fit her like a glove, hugging her hips and making her legs look like they went on forever.

Garrett would have been proud.

"Con," Jack said in greeting. "Or do you want to be called J.T.?"

Hell, he didn't know.

He wanted to be called "mistaken," but that wasn't going to happen. What he was seeing was the real deal—Jack and Scout.

A doctor walked into the room then and came over to introduce himself.

"Dr. Brandt," he said, taking Con's hand and giving it a solid shake as Scout disentangled herself with a final kiss and stepped away from the bed. "I thought you might be back with us about now." The doc was tall and thin, with graying hair and a studious pair of wire-rimmed glasses perched on his nose. His eyes were a lively blue, very discerning, and with a glance, he let it be known it was time for the business of patient care.

By the time he left, Con was more encouraged about his situation than he had been in the last six years, and especially in the last year, when he'd felt his time running out.

Scout and Jack stayed on for another hour before heading out for dinner with a promise to return later, and then he was alone with Jane.

"Come on up here," he said, pulling her onto the bed.

She didn't resist, and he knew why. She needed this, too, to just be close. Any woman who'd sat by a guy's bed for two days watching him breathe was probably well on her way to falling in love. At least that's what he hoped.

"The doc says I'll be out of here tomorrow. There's going to be a debriefing at Steele Street, and then he wants to see me at Walter Reed the beginning of next week." For a while, he was going to be Brandt's primary work in progress, until the doc figured out a medication plan that would slowly wean him off of Souk's drugs while allowing him to regain his memory and maintain his strength and speed.

She looked up at him expectantly, her hand resting lightly over his heart.

"That gives us a week to go somewhere..."

"Like?" she prompted.

"Like anywhere we want—Paris, Prague, Seattle, Munich, St. Croix, Saigon."

"Saigon?"

"Sure. You'd love it, and it would love you." He leaned down and kissed her mouth, and then lingered, loving the taste and feel of her, and wishing they were somewhere besides a hospital bed.

"Mmmmm," she murmured when he broke off the kiss. "Are you asking me out on a date?"

"Yes." Yes, he was. "A very long date." She enchanted him, and he wanted more, a lot more.

"Hmmmmm."

From *mmmmm* to *hmmmmm*? He wasn't sure if he was making progress or not.

"Is that a *hmmm* yes? Or a *hmmm* no?" He was gunning for the yes, but she still hedged her answer.

"We had a crazy night..."

"Yes," he agreed. "Our second crazy night together."

Her startled gaze flew up to meet his.

"So you *do* remember!" A hot flush of color flooded her cheeks.

"Not the details, but when we made love, it came to me that we'd done it before—you and me—and given how long ago it must have been, that there was a good chance you never heard from me again."

The color across her cheeks deepened.

"I'm sorry, Jane." And he was, that he could have hurt her unintentionally. Or maybe he had been a one-night-stand kind of guy back then. He really didn't know.

But he knew what he felt now. He knew what he wanted now.

"Give me a week, Jane," he said, looking down into her eyes. "No matter who I am, or who I turn out to be, I want a chance with you, to see what we can be together."

He'd never spoken truer words, and after a long moment, she seemed to believe him.

"One week," she said, and a measure of tension slipped away from him.

Everything was good. It was all good.

She was at least half in love with him. He could tell, and so help him, he needed that. It was a good place to start. He needed someone who took him for what he was more than whoever he turned out to be. He needed this beautiful girl to be his.

CHAPTER FORTY-FOUR

Two weeks later, 738 Steele Street

"Here's your bone dope," Buck Grant said, tossing a classified folder onto Dylan's desk. "As usual, we're about a light-year and a half ahead of the dweebs in the lab, but they've finally confirmed that it's not J.T. in that grave. The most the agency will give us is that the man we buried went by the code name Gator."

Dylan lifted his gaze to the man standing at the window watching the street.

"Danny Gleason," the man said without turning around. "He was part of a black ops team working for the CIA out of Coveñas."

"How much of your memory have you gotten back?" Grant asked.

"Enough to know you got that limp eight years ago in Afghanistan," J.T. said, and looked over his shoulder. "Good morning, Buck."

A flush of some emotion washed across the general's face, but Dylan would have been hard-pressed to define it. Relief, for sure, a serious measure of personal redemption for not having lost J.T., to have not "left one of his own behind," and a good dose of pride that his boy had made it back, mentally and physically, from the hairiest mission to ever consume the team: the six years of J.T.'s capture and amnesia. Dr. Brandt had brought Gillian back from that brink, and from what Dylan had seen this morning, the doc was achieving those same stellar results with J.T. in record time. J.T. had made significant progress since the grueling debriefing they'd all had in the days after his release from the hospital.

"I heard Brandt was sending you back to us this morning," Grant said. "When are you going to be ready to get back in the game?"

"I was born ready," J.T. said with a shit-eating grin curving his mouth.

Stellar results, Dylan thought.

"Good. We've got a mail drop three hundred miles north of Riyadh. I need delivery next week, Thursday."

"Interesting country up there," J.T. said.

"Yeah, Hawkins loves it, so you'll be in good company. The two of you need to be in and out in three days. We'll have our briefing at fifteen hundred hours here in Dylan's office."

"Yes, sir."

Dylan knew J.T. hadn't remembered everything about Steele Street, but he hadn't forgotten anything about being a spec ops warrior. If anything, his years on the run as Conroy Farrel had sharpened his edges and made him even better than he'd been before—and he'd been one of the very best.

Dylan was damn glad to have him back on the team, damn glad to have him home.

"How's your girl, Jane?" Grant asked, and J.T.'s grin broadened into a true smile.

"Still with me."

"Glad to hear it, son." Their eyes met for a moment, then Grant cleared his throat. "Well, I've got a lunch date down at that fish shack Loretta loves so much."

"McCormick's?" Dylan said, naming one of the city's premier restaurants.

"Yep," Grant said. "That's the one. I'll see you all back here at fifteen hundred."

J.T. watched the general leave before turning back to Dylan.

"You okay?" the boss asked—and Dylan *was* the boss. The fact had been proven to him many times over the last two weeks. Dylan was also his friend, and that fact had also been proven to him many times over the last two weeks.

"Yeah. I've got a date, too. Upstairs."

Dylan nodded. "He and Creed got in late last night. I'm sure he's waiting for you."

J.T. was sure of it, too. Everybody here was waiting for him. He'd seen it in all of their faces at the debriefing, which had been a very formal, very tough two days with very little personal interaction.

Dr. Brandt had been watching him like a hawk through the whole ordeal, even preempting General Grant a few times—but nobody had been watching him harder than the chop shop boys. Curiosity, anger, hope, distrust, love, confusion, more hope: He'd seen it in all of their faces. They knew what they'd lost. They just weren't sure what they'd gotten back.

Neither was he. Being J. T. Chronopolous was still pretty damn new.

The elevator shaft had been repaired, and in a few minutes, he was on the twelfth floor, standing in the middle of what had once been his loft.

He slowly circled around. The place was oddly amazing. He hadn't known surfboards could be made into wall art, or that snowboards could be made into chairs. One wall of the living area was loaded with racks of skis, cross-country skis, downhill skills, twin tips, a few pairs and sizes of each style. Four bicycles were taking up some of the floor space in the dining room, and four more bicycles were suspended from the ceiling in front of the floor-to-ceiling windows facing the east side of the building.

There was a kayak stuffed behind the couch, ski boots and poles piled here and there, a full-rig climbing harness and bivouac draped across one of the living room walls, and of all things, a life-size painting of a naked man hanging above a large fireplace.

He knew the man.

The guy looked a lot like him, only years younger, and he was sitting in one of the chairs flanking the fireplace, calmly waiting while J.T. looked around.

"So you like to ski," he finally said.

"You do, too," the younger man said. "You're the one who taught me."

Probably. Sure. That made sense.

"Where did we like to go?" he asked. He was getting his memory back, but there were still plenty of blank spots here and there, some of them damn big.

"A-Basin, the steep and deep, and Vasquez at Mary Jane. Between the two of us, we've launched off the gnarliest double black diamonds in the state."

Yeah, he could see it. A small grin curved the corner of his mouth.

"And lived to tell the tale," he said, looking over his shoulder at the younger man.

"Or some version thereof, usually embellished," Kid said with a slight grin of his own, his dark-eyed gaze meeting J.T.'s across the length of the living area.

J.T.'s smile faded.

"I remember you," he said. "But not the way I wished I did." So help him God, he didn't, even with his own face staring right back at him.

"Don't worry. We'll just take it slow and see what comes up," Kid said. "It's early yet. Hang around long enough, and I guarantee I'll do something to piss you off, and then it'll all come back to you, what a pain in the ass I am. By the time you remember me, I'll probably be wishing you didn't remember quite so much."

"Yeah," J.T. said, and looked away, out the huge expanse of windows fronting the loft. Over the last week, he'd spent hours going over every aspect of his life for the last six years with Dylan and Hawkins. In return, along with Zach, they'd told him his life story eight ways from Sunday, all the known facts, all the dates, everything except the missions. Those would remain classified until he could tell them what, when, and where they'd all done their jobs for the eight years before he and Creed Rivera had been ambushed in Colombia—if he ever could.

With Dr. Brandt's help, he was looking for memories of his life, doing regressions, using relaxation techniques, and taking a meticulously charted series of cutting-edge medicines, psychopharmaceuticals created by Dr. Brandt to counteract and mitigate Dr. Souk's drugs. They'd helped Red Dog get back nearly a hundred percent of her memory, and Brandt was optimistic that they could help J.T. regain his whole life, too.

But while he was looking for memories, he knew other members of the SDF team had a few they wished they didn't, especially Kid and Creed. They'd witnessed the brutality of his "death" firsthand, Creed in the rebel's camp and Kid when he'd gone down to Colombia to recover his brother's bones.

"I heard about you in Bangkok," he said, "through the grapevine, about this guy named Kid Chaos and the run he made through South America a few years back."

The young guy acknowledged the accolade with a slight nod of his head, accepting the praise with as much subtlety as J.T. had used to deliver it. Kid Chaos was a legend among the world's most elite soldiers. His mission to avenge his brother's death, and the consequent destruction of a whole cadre of narco-guerrillas from Colombia, was a story told on bases and in bars around the world.

Now J.T. knew he'd been part of that story, and that felt so damn odd.

"I'm sorry about what you went through on my account," he said, wishing like hell that he had more to offer. From everything he'd been told, starting with the firebombing of the cantina where Kid had been waiting to take his brother's body home, to the deadly deeds in South America, it had been a miracle the guy hadn't been killed himself.

"You can make it up to me," Kid said, and when J.T. looked, he was grinning again, a real shit-eating curve of nothing-but-trouble. It was amazing. Kid Chaos Chronopolous had dimples, just like J.T., and a helluva lot of sheer guts, just like J.T.

"If we both live long enough," he agreed, hoping like hell that they did.

"Whatever it takes." Kid's gaze was steady, his voice calm. "One way or another, we'll get it done."

Looking at him, J.T. could believe it. Kid wasn't like Jack Traeger, who had whisked Scout off to Paris and hadn't shown any signs of coming back anytime too soon. Kid was older, without a wild streak anywhere in him. He wasn't a loose cannon. The guy was solid, absolutely calm, absolutely assured, and J.T. was damned proud of him, whether he remembered having a reason to be or not.

The guy inspired confidence.

J.T. shifted his attention to the painting over the fireplace. "So your wife paints naked men."

What else was there to say when you were looking at a guy spread out over eight feet of canvas, wearing nothing but a pair of wings and looking like he had been personally infused by the hand of God with almighty grace?

"A lot of naked men," Kid elaborated without a trace of self-consciousness that J.T. could detect. "She even painted you."

Oh, hell, no.

J.T. turned to face him.

"You're kidding, right?" he said, then remembered Jane had told him the same thing.

Kid shook his head, his grin returning even wider than before. "Twice life size, a dark angel with a sword. She calls it *The Guardian,* and you're in wings, just like the rest of us."

"Naked?" Jane hadn't mentioned naked, but that didn't mean it wasn't so.

"Nah," Kid said. "You and Creed both got to keep your pants on."

He looked around the loft again, at all the gear and the great view.

"So where do we go from here?" he asked. He still wasn't comfortable with himself and all he was trying to absorb. It made it hard to be comfortable with anyone else—except Jane. The wild girl wasn't about memories. She was about now.

"The firing range," Kid said without missing a beat, as if where in the hell else would a couple of guys with an afternoon on their hands go. "We got some really cool guns in last week, and nobody's been up there yet to try them out."

Hoo-yah, J.T. thought, because really, where else would a couple of guys go, especially guys with cool new guns to shoot?

Hours later, after a long session of gunpowder therapy and the briefing on the operation with Dylan, Hawkins, and General Grant, J.T. headed for home, which to his ever-loving pleasure was Jane's place on Blake Street. So far, he and the Wild Thing had a damn good thing going.

The elevator door on the office floor closed, and just as he reached out to press the ground-floor button, he heard something that changed his mind. Someone else had moved onto the firing range, and he knew who.

Hell. He knew where he needed to go, and he knew it wasn't going to be easy.

The elevator stopped on the armory floor, and J.T. took a pair of ear protection muffs off a row hanging inside the car and slipped them on. When the door opened, it was onto the range and Creed blasting away with short bursts of a customized Para-Ordnance P14.

Creed emptied two more magazines and put a fresh one in before he acknowledged J.T.'s presence with a brief glance. He slipped the gun in his shoulder rig and put a light jacket on to conceal it before he looked up again.

"We're going for a walk," Creed said, picking up a small backpack. "Do you have all the meds you need for the night?"

When J.T. nodded, he headed down the stairwell.

J.T. didn't hesitate to follow him. Something about this man compelled him, more even than Kid, or Dylan, or any of the other operators of SDF. Creed Rivera was a breed apart, even in the wild bunch of Steele Street.

The sun had been down for an hour when they hit the alley, but the day's heat was everywhere, rising off the bricks and steaming off the asphalt. They fell into an easy stride together, and J.T. didn't think too much about where they might be going, until from one block to the next, they crossed from the busy, upscale section of historic Denver, into the railyards between Union Station and the South Platte River. From there on, the terrain took a decidedly uncivilized turn.

And so it went for hours, with Creed on point, a night march following the winding course of the river through concrete corridors and industrial wastelands, through low-end neighborhoods and natural areas where the trees grew thick and the bushes thicker.

By midnight, they'd reached the outskirts of the city—and still Creed kept leading him on, to what, J.T. didn't have a clue. But the guy was good, easy to follow, and sure of his direction, north.

A few times Creed signaled him, alerting him to other creatures and men moving in the night and changes in their course, and the communication was seamless, so fluid. They moved well together, with far more ease than he'd ever managed with Scout or Jack. It was like slipping back into his skin.

In a small clearing with a fire ring, Creed stopped, and J.T. could tell the Jungle Boy had been there before. That maybe these long walks through the wild side of Denver to the back of beyond happened fairly frequently, and probably at night.

Creed started a fire in the stone ring, and J.T. added sticks and dried brush to the flames—and he sat down and waited.

If this was all there was, he was fine with it. The march had been a good one on a long spring night. His muscles were warm and tired, his head clear, and he liked being outside.

"I remember the guy who cut you," Creed said, glancing up from stirring the fire with a stick. "If you want, I can tell you the story of how Kid and I tracked him to Puerto Blanco."

"Puerto Blanco," he said. "That's a tough town." *Oh, yeah*. He wanted to hear this. Sitting cross-legged at the side of the fire, he leaned forward—and Creed began.

"It started in Colombia, right after your funeral, when Hawkins and Kid lit out for South America. They'd gotten the go-ahead from the Defense Department, the Colombian government, and the Peruvian government to do whatever it took to get rid of the NRF rebels. So it was one of those no-holds-barred–type deals."

Yeah, he knew about those. He'd been running no-holds-barred for the last six years, and he had a feeling that he'd learned a lot of what he knew from this man.

"I think we did our share of those together," he said, watching Creed's face in the firelight.

The Jungle Boy smiled but the expression was fleeting.

"More than our share, brother, saving the world in spite of itself most every time."

Yeah, J.T. understood that, too. He watched Creed take something out of his pack, and he grinned when he recognized what the SDF guy had brought.

"Tobacco."

"Honduran cigars," Creed said. "From Danlí."

That set him back.

"Orlando's?" He'd smoked many Danlí cigars over the last few years. Handmade in the Honduran highlands, chanted over by Mario Sauza Orlando, the *brujo* who rolled them, they'd often been his first line of defense against the pain wrought by Dr. Souk's drugs.

"I found a box of them in your house on the Tambo River, sorting through the wreckage after you and I had our little run-in down in the boathouse." Creed handed him one of the cigars, then bit the end off another and stuck it in his mouth. "And I swore, so help me God and the Virgin Mary, that someday, somehow, someway, you and I would sit down and have a smoke together." He pulled the stick out of the fire and lit his cigar then held it over the flames for J.T. to do the same.

After they both got their cigars going and were puffing away, Creed slipped out of his coat and rolled up one of the sleeves of his shirt, exposing the three lines of scar tissue on his upper left arm.

"Alazne?" J.T. asked, surprised. The information on the scars he bore on his left arm had been part of his debriefing with the guys, but he hadn't expected to see the same scars on anyone else.

"No, not the witch," Creed said, a trail of smoke escaping with his words. "Kid and I marked each other in Peru, while we were chasing the NRF." He finished blowing out a stream of smoke. "Let me see your arm."

J.T. complied, pushing up the sleeve on his left arm, knowing Creed wanted to see the three stripes incised into his skin, the only scars on him that hadn't come from Dr. Souk.

Creed looked a them from across the fire. "I watched her the night she did that to you," he said, taking another long pull off the cigar, his face growing grim. "And I watched the night Pablo Castano took his knife to you."

Hard, hard times—what Creed had been through, what they'd all been through.

"He died for the deed," Creed continued. "I sent him to hell in the mountains of Peru, watched his blood soak into the ground, and took it as my revenge, but it wasn't enough, could never have been enough, until Paraguay, when I knew you were alive."

The Jungle Boy lowered his gaze and went back to stirring the fire.

J.T. had dozens of scars all over his body, but none compared to the thick ridge of scar tissue running the length of his chest, the one Creed had witnessed, Castano's work. Of all the horrors he didn't remember, he was most grateful for not remembering that night.

But his man remembered, and J.T. knew he wasn't alone in his nightmares, not anymore.

Hard, hard times.

Dylan and Red Dog had felt the bite of Souk's Thai syringes. They knew what he'd suffered in Bangkok. J.T. wasn't alone in knowing that pain, not anymore, not now that he'd made it home.

He blew a ring of smoke across the fire and watched it fall apart in the flames.

"Good cigar," he said.

"Damn good," Creed agreed.

"Thanks," he said. "Thanks for everything." Thanks for not forgetting. Thanks for killing my enemy. He didn't know how else to say what he felt, this utter thankfulness to be in this quiet wild place, to be finding his way back.

"Semper Fi," Creed said.

J.T. looked up and met the Jungle Boy's pale, gray-eyed gaze, and he'd never felt the meaning of the words more strongly—*Semper Fidelis.* Always faithful.

Always.

CHAPTER FORTY-FIVE

Seven months later, Kaua'i, Hawaii

"We're setting a record here," J.T. said.

"For most consecutive hours of doing absolutely nothing?" Jane asked, taking the last two weeks into account.

"You're not doing anything back there?" he asked, sounding genuinely shocked. "You mean I'm doing all the work?"

"Work, schmerk." She laughed. "You're not working. You're fishing, and I'm holding down the dock."

And a damn fine dock it was. Jane was soaking it up, lying on this short expanse of hardwood jutting out into the Hanalei River. She could hear the surf breaking out in the bay, and if she turned her head just right, she could see where the fresh waters ran into the ocean.

A woman was paddling up the river, standing on a surfboard, with a little dog sitting at her feet along for the ride.

The day was gorgeous, absolutely sun-dappled, the heat made bearable by a languid breeze and the pitcher of ginger lemonade they'd brought down to the dock along with their lunch.

"Do we have any more cupcakes left?"

"You mean the little vanilla ones filled with mango

mousse with the pineapple cream cheese frosting? Those cupcakes?" She turned her head the other way to look at him, and he glanced back over his shoulder with a grin.

"Yeah," he said. "One of those."

"Did you want one with the sprinkles on top?" He was so beautiful, his smile coming easier as the months had passed. He was wearing a pair of green and white swim shorts and a blue parrot shirt, unbuttoned and well worn, given to him by C. Smith Rydell for good luck.

Good luck for what? she'd asked him, and he'd just grinned. But she knew, in his job, every ounce of good anything helped to keep him safe.

He'd come home to Steele Street, and every day, in every way, the chop shop boys rallied around him. It did her heart good to see him back in the fold.

"With sprinkles, yes," he said, a little warily.

"Oops, sorry, all gone." She settled back onto her beach towel.

"How about one of the coconut macadamia nut cupcakes with the lime zest frosting?"

"Gone." She made a little gesture with her hand, as if to say they'd all just disappeared.

"And the raspberry-filled poppyseed cupcakes with chocolate frosting?"

She shrugged her shoulders and adjusted her sunglasses on her face, and she waited.

"How about if I eat you for dessert?"

Rolling onto her side, she faced him with a grin. "I'll race you to the house."

He looked up the dock to the path leading through a lush forest of trees and vines and flowers.

"You're on," he said, and then he leaned over and kissed her, settling his mouth on hers and wrapping his arm around her waist, pulling her close—and Jane was in heaven.

She never would have guessed life could get as perfect as it had been since the night she'd spotted him on Wazee Street. The missions he went on with the other SDF guys were full of risks. The chop shop boys operated on the cutting edge of Special Ops. She knew that, but she wouldn't have him be anything other than what he was: a soldier, a warrior, and hers.

The kiss was sweetly luxurious and led to the inevitable need they had for each other, for the intimacy they created and shared. His body was so hard to the touch, so strong. She loved being with him, making love with him, being his woman—and she was all his.

He slid down more fully beside her, and she intertwined her legs with his, feeling the heat rise between them. J. T. Chronopolous, the most dangerous man she'd ever met, made her feel safer than she'd ever been.

She snuggled in as close as she could get, loving the smell of him and the way he felt, like a slab of granite, except warm and vital. His hair was longer now, dark and starting to curl around the back of his neck. She loved the curve of his muscles and the strength in his arms and the stubble along his jaw.

After endless minutes of tasting his mouth and holding him close, she broke off the kiss and met his gaze.

"I've been thinking," she said.

"What a coincidence." J.T. grinned. "I've been thinking, too. What have you been thinking?"

"About my mom."

He lifted his eyebrow in question, and she continued. "Carpenter, Wyoming, isn't that far from Denver, a couple of hours, and it's been a while since I've seen her."

"That's a good idea, babe." To go up and see her mother, a woman named Leona.

Half a smile curved her mouth for a moment, then faded. "You might want to withhold judgment until you've been there, until you've met her. She and the guy she lives with, Wilbur, have a double-wide trailer on ten acres just outside of town. I've never actually figured out what it is Wilbur does for a living, except he used to be a rodeo cowboy about a hundred years ago."

"Is she happy?"

She shrugged. "She's a wanderer, but she's been with Wilbur for about eight years now, so maybe that means she's happy."

He thought that over for a while before answering. She looked sad, the way she always did when she spoke of her mother, and he didn't want to say the wrong thing. And truly, he was batting a little low in the mother department himself. Kid had told him the most persistent rumor he'd ever heard about their mother was that she'd gone to Hollywood to be a porn star. Kid also said he'd never bothered to verify or disprove the information.

J.T. was with his younger brother on that one. Apparently, she was heading out for a visit when he and Jane got home, and his plan was to just let her be what she wanted to be, to let her be a mom for a couple of days. He didn't have anything on the line with the woman.

But his girl had risk with her mother. She cared, and she'd been hurt by Leona's lack of care, a lifetime of it, but the ties were there, and neither Jane nor her mother ever let go—and he knew that was best, to not walk away from the people in your life. They were a precious part of a person, and in his experience, they had a way of slipping away without any help from you, without warning.

Hold on—that was always his advice.

He was holding on to Jane, with every fiber of his being, for as long as he could possibly make it last, and he was hoping for a lifetime.

"We get back to Denver tomorrow," he said. "We

could go up and see good old Leona and Wilbur by the end of the week."

"Thanks," she said, leaning over and kissing him. "I really want her to meet you, to see that I've done good."

Well, hell, he liked that.

"I love you, J.T." She kissed him again, and his heart filled with a comfort unlike anything he'd ever known.

Love. A year ago, he wouldn't have believed it would ever be true—that he would live long enough to see a day like today, or that there would ever be a woman who knew him well enough to love him.

He would have been wrong. The Wild Thing in her hot-pink bikini was all woman, and the love she professed was true. He knew, because it was the same love echoing in his heart.

"Do you want this?" he whispered against her lips, pressing himself against her. He was already hard. Just the smell of her was enough to arouse him, and he was breathing her in, remembering her, setting her solidly into his conscious mind. He didn't want to forget her, not for a moment, not ever again.

She nodded, and he kissed the side of her nose, her cheek, and her temple.

"Wrap your legs around me, then," he said, sliding his hand under her bottom and lifting her as he rose to his feet.

"How's that?" she murmured, settling around his waist.

An intense surge of pleasure coursed through him, and he released a small groan.

"That's good, real good. Can you keep it up all the way to the house?"

She laughed, and kissed his cheek, and bit his ear, and when he passed the bench at the end of the dock, he handed her the box of cupcakes, which was still almost full, as he'd well known, and he took the pitcher of lemonade.

It was fifty yards through the jungle to the house, but it could have been a hundred or a thousand, and it wouldn't have mattered. He could have carried her all day long. Never, not even in his most generous moments, did he thank Dr. Souk for the strength the bastard had given him, but it had proven to be a real asset for the team, and for that, he was glad.

His tactical skills were even more of an asset, and working with SDF used every skill he had. They were elite, their missions so black as to be undetectable—and that's the way Dylan and General Grant expected them to be.

He loved meeting that challenge.

And he loved the woman in his arms.

Her skin was so soft and warm beneath his hands, her hair so long and silky against his face. He loved her; with every beat of his heart, he loved her.

The house was a low-slung plantation-style cottage with more porch than house, all of it screened in. They'd set their bed on the east side, where the morning sun would wake them, but where it was cooler in the evenings.

In the privacy of their jungle-bound bower, he set the pitcher and her cupcake box on a table, then lay her on the four-poster bed and followed her down, stretching himself out beside her on a soft cotton, brightly colored quilt, and she wrapped herself around him.

She kissed his lips and the side of his face, and ran her fingers through his hair, and every act of tenderness made him want her all the more.

The hot-pink bikini was nothing but strings with four triangles of material stamped in a white hibiscus print. He had her naked in half a minute—and from there it was all one long, sweet slide into the sights, and sounds, and the scent of her, into oblivion.

She had little tiny tan lines, and he ran his tongue over each one. She giggled in some places and sighed in others, and he didn't stop until she groaned—and there, settled in between her legs, he pleased his woman, teasing her with his tongue, loving her with all his heart.

Stroke after lovely, intensely intimate stroke, he made her his, and with every taste, he got harder and hotter and heavier, until the need to be inside her became a craving. She sighed, and he felt her tighten and then tighten again, and he kept licking her, sucking on her so gently while she found her way, and when she came, he played her to the end and beyond, chasing her pleasure with every languid slide of his tongue.

"You're so soft." He licked her and she shuddered one last time. "So wet. So mine."

He lifted his head to look at her, at the satiny, golden curves of her hips and the sweet, mysterious territory in between. She was a need for him, not optional. She was home.

He dipped down and licked her again, just to taste her and hear her sigh. Then he shucked out of his clothes and levered himself up her body.

"Oh." Her eyes came open, and a warm smile teased her lips.

"Oh, yeah." He grinned and wrapped her leg around his waist, and he pressed more deeply into her, feeling the sweet edge of pleasure course through his cock and galvanize his body. Sometimes he made love to her so slowly, their whole world became one hazily sensual hour after another, endless until they melted into each other. Other times the game moved faster and the loving took on a fierceness that stole his breath—up against the wall, laid out on the dining room table, lovely, lovely Jane slick and soapy in the shower.

It was all good, and God, she was gorgeous, her long, silky hair trailing across her breasts, every slender curve moving in rhythm with his thrusts. She was hot, and wet, and welcoming, and he filled her up, sliding into her again and again, covering her with his body, making her his.

This was love, to feel so complete with another person, with his woman.

He pumped into her harder, burying himself to the hilt, reaching deep inside himself, deep inside her, for the raw surge of release. At the end, he thrust faster, harder—and was caught. She tightened around him, and his world coalesced into a single stream of pleasure so intense, he forgot to breathe...

Until it was over, and he collapsed on the bed and drew her into his arms.

"Oh, baby," she murmured, kissing his face, his ear, the side of his nose.

Oh, yeah. Oh, baby. He'd found heaven, and, safe within her arms, he drifted to sleep.

An hour later, when he woke, she was curled on her side, watching him, her hand slowly stroking his chest, her fingers running through the dark hair that covered him down to his groin.

He smiled and rolled over to kiss her mouth, and she tasted so good, felt so fine, he kissed her again—and some days, that's the way it went all day long, the two of them in their private world.

Today was shaping up to be that kind of day, at least that's what he was hoping.

"Do you have any big plans for this evening?" he asked.

She shook her head. "Eat, maybe, if we run out of cupcakes and you'll do the cooking."

Ah, cupcakes. He kissed the curve of her grin and reached across her to snag the box, and then he reached a little farther and grabbed his swim shorts. After handing her a mango mousse cupcake first, he unzipped the pocket on his shorts and pulled out a small, ribbon-wrapped box.

She stopped in midbite, frosting on her lips.

"This is it, babe," he said, holding the box up between them. "This is the forever ever I want with you."

She was ready, so ready, sitting perfectly still, perfectly naked in a pile of white sheets with the brightly colored quilt swirling around her, and if he hadn't been so damn nervous, he might have grinned.

He pulled the ribbon off the box and opened the lid, and offered her his heart along with an emerald to match her eyes.

"Will you marry me, Jane?" Wild Thing, he wanted her for his own.

He saw the emotion rising inside her, the flush coloring her cheeks, the tears welling up in her eyes—and then she was on him, kissing him, a kiss of mango mousse and pineapple frosting, with her arms around him, her mouth everywhere on his face.

"Yes," she sighed. "Yes, yes, yes."

A weight he hadn't even known he was bearing lifted off him at her answer.

She was his, for forever, for however long forever lasted, and he was home.